DISCARDED

Also by Jack Todd

Desertion

Sun Going Down

COME AGAIN NO MORE

A NOVEL

JACK TODD

A TOUCHSTONE BOOK
Published by Simon & Schuster
New York London Toronto Sydney

Touchstone
A Division of Simon & Schuster, Inc.
1230 Avenue of the Americas
New York, NY 10020

This book is a work of fiction. Names, characters, places, and incidents either are products of the author's imagination or are used fictitiously. Any resemblance to actual events or locales or persons, living or dead, is entirely coincidental.

First Touchstone hardcover edition September 2010

Designed by Renata Di Biase

Manufactured in the United States of America

10 9 8 7 6 5 4 3 2 1

Library of Congress Cataloging-in-Publication Data

Todd, Jack.
Come again no more / Jack Todd.
p. cm.
Sequel to: Sun going down
1. Ranchers—Fiction. 2. Families—West (U.S.)—Fiction. 3. Domestic fiction. I. Title.
PS3620.O318C66 2010
813'.6—dc22

2009041978

ISBN 978-1-4165-9849-7
ISBN 978-1-4391-0951-9 (ebook)

For my sisters,
Linda Todd Dittmar and
Eva Jeanne Dennison

In memory of our brother,
Donald "Red" Todd,
1927–1996

Tis the song, the sigh of the weary,
Hard times, hard times, come again no more
Many days you have lingered around my cabin door;
Oh hard times come again no more.

—Stephen Foster

WASHINGTON
Pacific Ocean
Columbia City
Millwood
Scappoose
Columbia River
Celilo Falls
The Dalles
Boardman
Umatilla
Bucks Corner
Pendleton
La Grande
Blue Mountains
IDAHO
OREGON
Boise
Snake River
CALIFORNIA
NEVADA
N
W
E
S

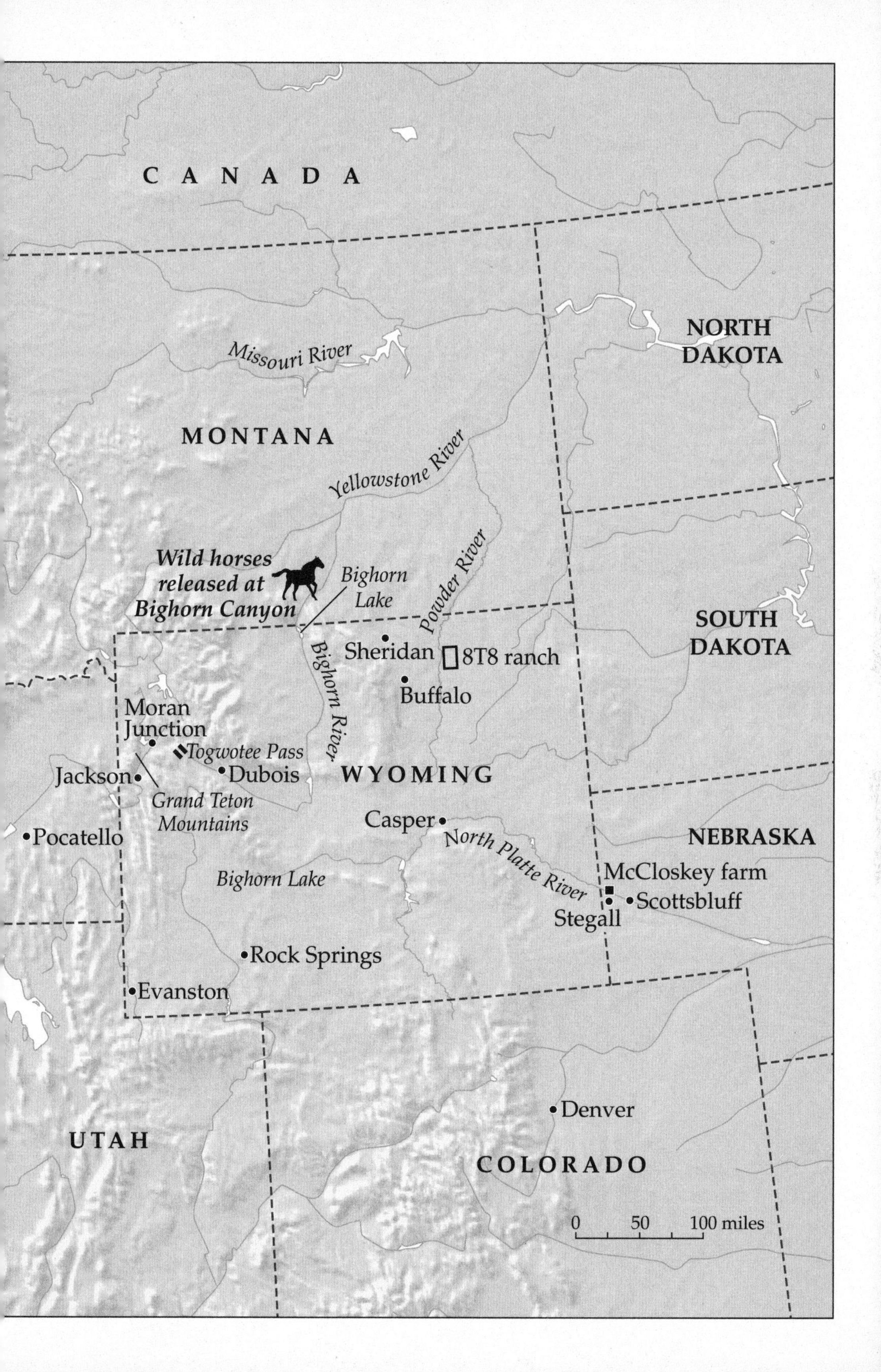

CANADA
NORTH DAKOTA
Missouri River
MONTANA
Yellowstone River
Wild horses released at Bighorn Canyon
Bighorn Lake
Powder River
SOUTH DAKOTA
Sheridan
8T8 ranch
Bighorn River
Buffalo
Moran Junction
Togwotee Pass
Jackson
Dubois
WYOMING
Grand Teton Mountains
Casper
Pocatello
North Platte River
NEBRASKA
McCloskey farm
Bighorn Lake
Scottsbluff
Stegall
Rock Springs
Evanston
Denver
UTAH
COLORADO
0 50 100 miles

PART I

The Burning Man

1933

I.

THEY WERE THREE MILES WEST OF TOWN WHEN the sun broke through. The wind tore the clouds to rags, the sun lit the rags on fire and in fiery trails they streamed across a sky that opened like a bruised and tender heart. A few pellets of snow still drifted down and where the wind scoured the asphalt there was black ice and in every dip and swale lay drifts of snow. The big Cadillac sliced through the drifts and soared over the treacherous ice. Now and again they caught up to battered jalopies tiptoeing along the road on tires that were tall and thin and bald as a buzzard, the drivers gritting their teeth as they held on to the wide steering wheels, fighting to keep an ancient Model T or a battered Studebaker from skidding into the barrow pit. Emaline knew most of these people. She hid her face in her hands when Eli swung out to pass and hoped they wouldn't see her, knowing what they would say. *Why, aint that Emaline Hughes settin in that Caddy, pretty as you please? Nothin more than a waitress at the diner, she is, ridin in a automobile like that.* The Cadillac rattled the doors of the jalopies as it passed, blinding their drivers with a plume of powdery snow.

The heater began to warm her feet and she untied her scarf, shook the snow out of it and felt her half-frozen hands burn as they thawed.

They had lingered for an hour at Velma's grave, standing too long in the snow and the raw wind, caught in a web of blood relation and antique sin. Emaline wept into the collar of Eli's sheepskin jacket, then stepped away and closed her back to him, angry with herself for letting him see how she felt inside, like a glass pitcher dropped on a marble floor. She had heard her mother's voice as plain as if she were right there beside them. *Don't stand in the corner and bawl for buttermilk.* At last Eli drew a deep breath, straightened his big gray Stetson and led the way back to the car. He held the door open for her and she stepped into the car, feeling like a sad little princess in the motion pictures. He swept the snow off the windshield with the sleeve of his jacket, started the engine and eased the big car down the hill toward town. At the junction of Route 26, he turned right and gave it the gas and the car took off like an arrow shot from a bow.

In a pasture north of the highway, a band of horses wheeled to gallop along the fence line. Their coats were heavy with winter and powdered with snow. A big roan stallion led with his mane and tail flying in the wind, his neck stretched out, his great hooves cutting a path through the drifts. Emaline wanted to straddle his broad back and ride with her cheek pressed to his arched neck and the scent of horse in her nostrils, her fingers tangled in his mane, the icy wind freezing the tears on her eyelashes so that she rode blind, trusting the great roan stallion and the snow and sky and the wild and bitter wind.

She stared out at the weathered barns, the tall silos, the barbed-wire fences. Where the powdery snow had blown away, the remnants of the sugar beet harvest lay in the frozen earth. In November, they had tramped the empty beet fields for miles around, Velma with Emaline and Bobby, dragging gunnysacks over the frozen ground, risking broken ankles to search for beets to feed the pigs. Velma had laughed about it, saying that you knew you were poor when you couldn't even afford to buy feed for the hogs. Now it was barely the end of January and Velma was dead.

⋄ ⋄ ⋄

Eli drove fifteen miles without saying a word. At Morrill he found the Stegall turnoff without needing directions and he had to slow down where the snow had drifted over the narrow gravel road. At last he spoke. "That was right kind of you to come along with me, Emaline."

"Don't mention it. She was my mother."

"Yes, she was. And quite a mother you had."

"It's nice that you finally figured that out."

"I never thought different. Not a day in my life."

"You didn't act like it."

"Well, what a man feels and what he is able to do aint always the same thing."

"They should be."

"Maybe they should. There is no way I could feel worse, honey, I know that. I wanted to get down here while she was still alive and I just never made it. You always think you're goin to have more time than you do, then it slips away and you're left holdin nothin at all."

Emaline stared out the window, not wanting to say more than she already had.

"You aren't goin to cut me any slack, are you?"

"I guess not."

"I don't blame you. I'd probably feel the same in your place, growin up the way you did."

"You mean getting bundled off to an orphanage because Mama was in the sanatorium with her consumption and you wouldn't take us in?"

Eli winced. She could see that stung him. Well, let it. Her right arm was bent and broken, crippled for life by a heavy pot of boiling soup that had fallen on her as she scrubbed a kitchen floor in the orphanage. All because Eli had turned Velma out of the house for breaking the First Commandment that he laid down for his daughters. *Thou shalt not fornicate with the hired hands.* Emaline thought she might forgive him someday, but that day was a long way off.

He tried one more time. "I came as soon as I found out she was real sick."

"It was too late."

"I know that, honey. A doggone bellhop at the hotel in Evanston mislaid the telegram. If I knew she was that sick, I would have been here a week ago."

He started to say more and thought better of it. He could see how it would look to this young woman. He had always thought he was doing the right thing, setting an example for his other children. That was not the way she would see it. He found the Lindquist farm without help, drove the quarter mile along the lane, stopped at the small white farmhouse down in a swale surrounded by tall elm and pine and cottonwood trees. He tipped his hat.

"If you don't mind, you might tell Bobby that he's more than welcome to come up to Wyoming, spend the summer on the ranch. Might do him good to be with his brother for a while."

"It would do him good. Tell him yourself. He's out back doing chores. He's old enough to make up his mind whether he wants to come or not." She reached up and touched him with her fingertips, like a blind woman trying to learn his face.

"Good-bye, Grandpa."

Eli thought she was about to say more, but she turned and opened the door, climbed out, did not look back. He watched her walk into the house, her back straight as an arrow. Closed to him, like a book in a language he couldn't read. She looked like his mother, Cora. The same black hair, the same dark, penetrating eyes, the same high cheekbones. Not much Indian blood in her, but it came through. If she was like Cora, she was stubborn as a Missouri mule. He wanted to call her back, to say something that would make her see him in a different light. *But what, you old fool? What are you going to say? Not a damned thing that is going to make a whit of difference to her.*

He felt a sudden fatigue, the all-night drive catching up to him, the shock at the hospital when he learned that the daughter he had come to visit was already dead and buried. The trip to the cemetery, standing in the snow with Emaline next to Velma's grave. It had all taken its toll. He opened the door of the Cadillac, fighting the heaviness in his limbs, followed the sound of the axe from out back of the farmhouse, beyond a barn that wasn't much bigger than a shed. He heard hogs snorting around inside and a bleat or two that might have been sheep or goats, he couldn't tell which. When he got to the edge of the barn, he saw the boy. He wasn't chopping wood. The stock tank was frozen over.

He was going at it for all he was worth, swinging a double-bladed axe that was almost as big as he was, bringing it down on the ice so hard that he jumped a little with each swing. Eli stood by the corner of the barn to watch. Bobby was maybe twelve years old, about the age of Eli's youngest boy, Leo. Only about two-thirds Leo's size. Blue eyes and a lock or two of blond hair sticking out from under his cap. A slender, small-boned kid, but he didn't lack for grit. He wasn't going to give in to that ice, no matter how thick it was. Eli didn't see a bit of himself in the boy, except maybe his determination. Bobby must have taken after his father, Ora Watson, deceased. Stepfather to Emaline and Ben, father to Bobby. Damned fool got drunk, drove himself off the side of a mountain up on Little Goose Creek, the way Eli heard it. Burned up, along with his truck. Helluva thing, when a man had children to raise.

Eli waited until the boy came up for air, then stepped up to say hello. Bobby had an easy smile. "Howdy, mister. If you're lookin for the Lindquists, Jim and Lee went to the sale barn. Ought to be back any minute now."

"Howdy yourself. No, it's you I'm lookin for. Name is Eli Paint, son. I'm your grandpa."

The boy peeled off his glove and stuck out a hand. "Bobby Watson, sir. Pleased to meet you."

Real nice manners. That would be Velma.

"I took your sister up to see your mama's grave, son. I only found out this morning that Velma had passed on. It's a terrible hard blow for you and Ben and Emaline, to lose your ma when you're so young. I'm just as sorry as I can be for all three of you, I wanted to say that."

Bobby bit his lip, looked down at his toes. "Thank you, sir. Sure was a awful shock. Seemed like she was doin fine, like she could go on and on. Then she took sick again with the tuberculosis. We thought she'd pull through, because she always had before, but then she was gone. I can't hardly get used to it, tell you the truth."

The boy looked pale. He had dark circles under his eyes, like he hadn't been sleeping much. Eli put a hand on his shoulder. "Can't nobody get used to a thing like this. Damned shame, is what it is. But you're goin at it right, doin your chores. When you come to the worst times in your life, hard work always helps. Harder the better. That way, you're too wore out at night to lay awake and stew over things."

Bobby nodded. "Yessir. Jim Lindquist told me the same thing."

"Well, your stepdad is a wise man, then. There aint no cure but time for what you feel in your gut, but there's things that can make it a little better and things that make it worse. Looks like you found yourself a heckuva job, bustin through that ice."

"Yep. I broke it out once already this mornin, but it's so darned cold it froze up again, and the livestock has to drink."

Eli took the axe, waited for Bobby to step back before he began swinging it in long steady strokes, making the ice chips fly, biting deep into the foot-thick layer of ice with each swing, putting the power of his legs and back and shoulders and wrists into it. When Eli had chopped the ice into sections, he reached into the tank barehanded, heaved a dozen heavy blocks of ice out of the frigid water. Three thirsty milk cows, a team of heavy draft horses, and an old, swaybacked saddle horse shuffled up to drink. He set the axe down, rubbed his hands dry.

"Son, I was just about your age when my twin brother Ezra and me, we lost our ma. Cora, her name was. She went out to help a neighbor, got caught in a spring blizzard and froze to death. It was me and Ezra that found her, along with the husband of the woman she went to help. Our daddy, that's your great-grandfather, was off haulin freight to the big mining outfits in the Black Hills. It was better than a week before he got the telegram sayin she had passed on. By that time she was in the ground. Pa died too, three years after Ma. He got kicked by a mule and never got over it. After that, we was on our own. It was a hard thing for us, same as this is a hard thing for you and Ben and Emaline. Aint nothin easy about it. Only way me and Ez got through it, we stuck together. You got Emaline here, she has you, you both have Ben up in Wyoming. You have your old granddad too, if you need me. When school lets out, if those big strapping Swedes can run this place by themselves, you come on up to Wyoming for the summer. Help Ben and Ezra with them Appaloosa horses. If they don't have enough work, I can find plenty more. I spoke to Emaline. She said it would be good for you, but I believe she's goin to leave it to you to decide what you want to do."

"That would be fun, to go up to Wyoming for a while, Grandpa. Jim and Lee, they're real fine fellas, but they don't hardly talk none at all except to each other, then they talk Swedish. Me and Emaline, we're goin to move into town in a week or so, cause she has to go back to work at the diner. I'm going to start at the high school in Scottsbluff next fall."

"I imagine you'll have more chances to play ball in town too. Ben says you're a heckuva ballplayer."

"I'd play ball every day if I could. I want to be like Pepper Martin."

"The St. Louis Cardinals are your team, I expect?"

"Yes, sir."

"Can you run? You got to run to play the outfield."

"I'm real quick."

"And you got to be tough to play ball."

"Me and Luke Johns, we play burnout."

"What is burnout, anyhow?"

"You stand about thirty feet apart with no gloves. Then you zing it as hard you can. The other guy has to catch every throw bare hand. First one to cry uncle, he's the loser."

"Do you ever cry uncle?"

"Never. My hands get all swole up, but it's Luke who gives up every time, and he's fifteen years old and six foot tall."

Eli grinned a little at that. He reached out and squeezed the kid's shoulder. "I got to hit the trail, son. I aim to make it home to the 8T8 tonight. It's a long drive and I didn't get a wink of sleep last night. Drove all night to get here and then found out I was too late."

"I'm sorry, Grandpa."

"Taint a bit of your fault. But thanks just the same."

Bobby trailed him back to the Cadillac. "If you mean it about this summer, I'll come up to see you."

"You do that. We'll turn you into a top hand, find a horse you can ride for the summer—long as you take care of it."

The boy smiled again. Eli felt his spirits lift a little. There was always some good a man could do somewhere. He squeezed the kid's shoulder again, hard this time, looking away so that Bobby wouldn't see him tearing up. Then he said good-bye, got behind the wheel, turned the Cadillac around, headed down the lane. He stopped at the edge of the county road, fighting the urge to try one more time with Emaline. Then he pulled out onto the gravel, bound for Wyoming.

2.

Deputy Sheriff Dexter McGuinty took off his hat, rolled down the window of his patrol car, stuck his head out as far as he could, inhaled air so cold his nostrils froze shut. There was nothing on this earth he hated more than cold, but Estelle had ladled an extra scoop of beans onto his plate when he stopped for lunch and he was tooting along like a choo-choo train, his own rising odor in the closed cabin more than he could bear. He drove a mile in second gear, his head halfway out the window, squinting against the glare of the setting sun off the snowbanks. He would give another fellow a ticket for operating an automobile this way, but Dexter was the law and he would do as he damned pleased. Bad enough that Roosevelt was set to repeal Prohibition. That would cost Dexter two-thirds of his income, until he figured out a grift to make up for the lost bribe money. Just thinking about Roosevelt made him so mad he whacked the dashboard with his knuckles as he rounded a curve and was almost decapitated by a big Cadillac speeding west on Route 26. He yelped and pulled his head in like a frightened turtle, hit the brakes too hard and sent the Model A into a skid, which turned into a full circle and left the car teetering on the edge of the barrow pit. The deputy dropped the transmission into low gear and felt the rear wheels spin and catch. He fishtailed up the road in pursuit, so mad he forgot to switch on the siren.

By the time he had his automobile in high gear, the Caddy was already a mile to the west. The driver had to be doing seventy miles an hour on this narrow blacktop, straight into the setting sun. As it topped the rise, it looked as though the big car was about to take flight. Dexter knew his cars, especially those he couldn't afford. This one was a 1925 V8 Custom Suburban, whitewall spares strapped to either side of the hood and spare gas cans fastened to the trunk. His patrol car was vibrating like a threshing machine. The Cadillac was way too much automobile for a Model A to run down.

Dexter eased back on the throttle and glanced at his wristwatch. His shift was almost over. It was around the time in the afternoon when Estelle started to get restless. It was his perpetual worry that if he wasn't there to satisfy her powerful needs she would be on the phone, offering her sugary little body to someone like his fellow deputy, Syl Whiting.

By the time he found a wide spot in the road where he could turn around and speed home to Estelle, the Caddy had vanished over a distant hill. Dexter flipped his middle finger at the rearview. *Rich sons of bitches.*

Eli didn't see the deputy. Once on the highway, he let the long spool of the unwinding road take him. U.S. Route 26 ran due west into Wyoming and beyond—follow it long enough and you'd sail through Idaho and end up in Oregon, on the shores of the Pacific Ocean. He understood why Ezra was so restless. Once you were rolling, the road pulled you along, offered movement and change, the chance to make of yourself something that you would not become if you lived your life like a big old cottonwood tree, rooted to one spot. One of his aunts from Mississippi had said the Paints were perpetually journey-bound, the way they kept moving from Wales to the New World and then from Boston through Pennsylvania and Tennessee, south as far as Mississippi, then west to South Dakota, Nebraska, Wyoming. Eli had put down permanent roots on the 8T8. He couldn't imagine moving on, but Ezra was still journey-bound. Now he was talking about Argentina, of the great estancias on the Pampas and the gauchos, the Argentine cowpokes. Ezra wanted to pull up stakes in Wyoming, take some breeding stock, raise Appaloosas in Argentina.

Eli had a stronger sense of home. He was homing now like a carrier pigeon, unable to rest until he could sleep in his own bed. He knew he ought to stop for the night, but he was feeling the kind of exhaustion that masquerades as wakefulness. He reached for the figuring rope he always kept handy and began tying knots with one hand as he drove. It was an old habit—when he had a problem he couldn't untangle, he would grab a worn-out strip of lariat and tie everything from a sheepshank to a hangman's knot while he thought it through.

He had much to ponder on this midwinter evening. How a man grows old, the way time whispers along his spine. How a fellow can set out to carve his name on the world and find, when all is said and done, that the world has carved its name on him. He was sixty-two, a big man whose power had scarcely begun to diminish, but at times he felt like an old dray horse pulling a load of bricks. Decades had passed since he had buried his wife Livvy, a woman he had loved as a man loves breathing or sunrise. Ida Mae, his second wife and the mother of the last six of his thirteen children, was lost to him and to the world—a blank, staring form in the state hospital in Evanston, her mind beyond the reach of money or medicine. When he looked at her, he could not recall what she had been like before her mind went. There was nothing more he could do for her. In his nightmares, he saw their entire brood lined up in identical wheelchairs in front of the big windows on the main floor of the hospital, all with the same blank, unseeing gaze.

Of all the sorrows that troubled him, the one that weighed most heavily was the death of his daughter Velma. Death cast regret in stone. He didn't need Emaline's rebuke to remind him of all the ways in which he had failed poor Velma. He had always thought that one day he would be able to sit down and spend time with his banished daughter, get to know her again. A dozen times he had been on the verge of paying her a visit, but something always intervened. He could stand at her graveside until doomsday, but he couldn't change a thing. She was gone and he could find no shred of forgiveness for himself.

It was impossible to keep his mind on other things when it kept circling back to Velma, but Eli was feeling of late like a man holding a pair of deuces in a high-stakes poker game. He had spent a lifetime battling heat and drought, blackleg, quicksand, rustlers, outlaws, bankers, blizzards, hail, flood. He had never faced anything like this almighty depression that had the whole country in a choke hold. Wheat was going for thirty-seven cents a bushel, a man was lucky if a field would produce eight bushels of smutty wheat to an acre. Cattle wouldn't bring the price of shipping them to market.

He couldn't see how things would get better anytime soon. The country was more than three years into this, and unless FDR had a miracle up his sleeve, it would be years before folks were back to work. He heard it was bad back east, but it couldn't come close to what farmers and ranchers were going through from Montana to Texas, heat and drought and wind and millions of acres of good earth simply blowing away. Farmers were so desperate they were grinding and salting Russian thistle to keep their stock alive. Cattle would eat it, horses wouldn't touch it. His ranch was in better shape than most, but he could ride miles on parts of his own spread and see nothing but sage, juniper, thistle, not a blade of grass in sight.

He still owed four banks for loans he had taken to buy the hundred thousand acres of the 8T8 back in 1927, when wheat and cattle were worth something. The purchase might have made sense if the rain had not ceased to fall and if the prices for cattle and wheat hadn't collapsed. He had loaned out money himself, nearly a hundred thousand dollars, most of it to neighboring ranchers who had lost their shirts in the stock market crash in '29. The loans were of the low-interest, pay-me-when-you-can variety, but he knew that he would never see a dime on the dollar. Three of the men who owed him money had already lost their ranches to foreclosure, others were teetering on the brink. The Cadillac he drove was all he would ever see for a loan made to Orie Achenbach, a rancher who had lost it all betting on General Electric and RCA. Eli would have preferred horses, but Achenbach had already sold off all his livestock.

Eli knew that most folks had it worse. Hardworking families lost their farms and ranches, piled what little they could salvage onto antique Model Ts, headed for California, where they were about as welcome as boll weevils. Men in cities stood in lines blocks long, waiting for a bowl of soup so thin they said you could read a magazine right through it. He blamed the sonsofbitches on Wall Street. The bankers and stock traders and professional liars who played with money as though it had no connection to anything real, like it was all a bunch of numbers and at the end of the day you added up your score and figured whether you won or lost. All their crazy speculation had nothing to do with putting food on the table or a roof over your head. Now the whole shebang had collapsed. Folks were scared to death, and he couldn't blame them. And yet a rich man who lost a pile of money on the stock market would go out and hang himself, while a poor man would live with his wife and five children on two filthy mattresses inside a ripped tent in a migrant camp and never give up hope.

After sundown, the cold took hold like a vise. Eli could feel it, even inside the Cadillac. As a young cowhand, he had camped out on nights so cold he could hear porcupines whimpering off in the woods. On such a night, there would be patches of black ice on the asphalt, but still he would not stop or slow down. Somewhere between Douglas and Casper, he pulled off to the side of the road, stepped out of the car, saw what a man who lived his life in cities would not see in a thousand years. The moon not yet up, a sky dark as ink, from one horizon to the other a wash of stars. It was more than forty years now since he had ridden alone most of one summer across Nebraska, looking for a likely place to homestead with Livvy. Night after night, he would lie on the open prairie, listen to the horses shuffle in their hobbles, hear the calls of the night birds, look up at the stars and think himself the luckiest man alive.

The cold revived him somewhat, but by the time he reached Casper he was driving a dozen miles at a stretch with no recollection at all of what had transpired between one point and the next. He stopped at a filling station, where a kid took his time polishing the windshield, treating the Cadillac like a prize thoroughbred.

"She's a beauty, mister."

"Thank you, son. She was payment for an old debt from a damned fool who lost most of what he had on the stock market."

The boy whistled.

"How fast will she go on the open road?"

"Too goddamned fast, truth be told."

The kid laughed and Eli tipped him a quarter. He bought a Coca-Cola and a Hershey bar, found the telephone and paid a nickel to call home. Juanita, the Mexican housekeeper, answered the phone.

"Where are you, Eli?"

"Casper. I should be home in three hours, maybe less."

"It's already past eight o'clock."

"I know. I'd sooner be home."

"Did you get to see Velma in Scottsbluff?"

"Nope. They buried her three days before I got there. I took Emaline out to visit her grave."

"Oh, I am so sorry. That is terrible for you."

"My own damned fault. I should have made it down to see her a long time ago. How are the kids?"

"They are all staying at the Ewing ranch tonight because it's Paula Ewing's birthday. They're anxious to see you, but I think you should find a place to stay and start home tomorrow."

"I've got too much on my mind to sleep anyway. I should be there by midnight."

As he climbed behind the wheel of the Cadillac again, he realized that the last time a woman's voice had offered such solace, Livvy was still alive and Velma was just a girl.

3.

ELI SPED THROUGH BUFFALO AND MADE IT TO BIG Horn, just south of Sheridan, at eleven o'clock. He turned off the main highway onto the gravel road that led northeast to the 8T8, fifty miles distant. There were no other cars on the narrow and icy road, no distant lights winking in farmhouses, nothing but the long yellow cones of the headlights sweeping over the dark prairie. A moment of illumination and then darkness again, the way a man receives a beam of intuition from the dark, pumping heart of the universe and then loses it before he can capture whatever it was. Twice he caught himself nodding off as the Cadillac slid toward the barrow pit. After it happened the second time, he stopped the car and got out and rubbed snow on his face. Within a mile or two he felt drowsy again, but he pushed on, driving too fast on a narrow road slick with packed snow. It was strange how you could know a place in daylight down to the last creek and fence post and tumbleweed, then you struck the same place on a winter night and it was like someone had moved all the furniture in the parlor and you were tripping over things in the dark.

A light snow began to fall, the flakes streaming into the headlights. He thought he might have missed the turn for the ranch until he saw the 8T8 brand on a slab of cottonwood a dozen feet above the front gate. The tires of the Cadillac rattled over the cattle guard. Fence posts, windmills, the occasional bunch of cattle wearing the same brand swam out of the headlights. The snow fell harder and the wind picked up and it was hard to see the road with the blowing snow. He slowed a bit to watch for the turn where the lane came to the big house, but he didn't see it. He drove on until he was sure he had traveled at least eight miles from the front gate. He still could not see the house. It was not until he spotted a cluster of windmills and stock tanks that he knew where he was. He had somehow overshot the last turn. He was headed down a sidetrack that was taking him due west, away from home. He found a wide spot in the road where he could turn around and gunned it back to the east.

Eli had to grin at his foolishness. It would have been impossible to get lost on the hundred and sixty acres of his original homestead in Nebraska, but on the hundred thousand acres of the 8T8 here in Powder River country, there was plenty of room for a man to lose his bearings. In the snow, everything looked strange. A rise that should have led up to Ezra's house appeared on the right side of the road rather than the left, and there were cottonwood trees where a holding corral should be. Perhaps he was mistaken and he had turned onto the old army trail that angled across his land. He rubbed his eyes and tried through a haze of fatigue to figure out where he had gone wrong. He sped up, certain that, if he could drive fast enough, the house would appear—but nothing was right. The landmarks were so unfamiliar that he began to wonder if he hadn't driven off the ranch altogether.

The road had dwindled to little more than a cattle trail, a rough one at that. He was looking for a place where he could stop and get his bearings when the Cadillac rounded a sharp curve going much too fast and hit a deep, spine-jarring rut and then another. The wheels dropped off a cutbank that was invisible in the snow and the big car was airborne, sailing like a blimp released from its moorings. The wheels came down so hard he bit his tongue, there was a thump as the car rolled over, and another bang and he was lying in the snow twenty feet from the car, broken and bleeding. The Caddy came to rest on the passenger side, its wheels still spinning.

When he came to, he was lying in the snow and he was very, very cold. He tried to crawl, felt a terrible pain somewhere between his knee and his ankle, tried to put some weight on it and almost blacked out again. His lower leg was bent out at a right angle from his knee. The leg was badly broken, there was something very wrong with his shoulder, he was bleeding from a cut on his forehead, he felt all banged up inside. He drew a long, ragged breath, felt a terrible pain in his ribs. He was in a world of trouble. He could not remain where he was. Somehow, he had to get up and walk. A half dozen times, he tried to drag himself onto his good leg, but each time he put pressure on the broken leg, a red wave of pain broke over him and he felt the world spinning. He heard a horse whinny somewhere and shouted for help, then thought how foolish that was. If there were horses out here, they were grazing. No cowpuncher would be fool enough to ride out at midnight in the dead of winter unless he had to. He sank back into the snow, fighting an overwhelming desire to sleep despite the pain.

Eli managed to turn himself partway around, far enough to spot the Cadillac lying on its side. He had peeled off his warm sheepskin coat and left it on the seat, but he was wearing his union suit under his clothing and he had on thick woolen socks, good boots, good gloves. He had kept the Stetson on his head, but that did his ears no good. They would be frostbitten in minutes in this cold. He had a long wool scarf around his neck. He wound it twice around his ears and once under his jaw and across his face to keep his nose from freezing. He pushed the Stetson down over the scarf, then drew the scarf two more turns to hold the hat over his ears. There were blankets in the car if he could reach them, but the Caddy might as well have been a hundred miles away. Even if he could get to it, with the Cadillac lying on its side, he couldn't climb up to open the door and reach the blankets. Still, the car was the only possible refuge. If nothing else, maybe he could crawl into the trunk. The trick was to get there. The only way he could move forward was to pull with his right arm and push with his left leg, putting more strain on his ribs. He began dragging himself toward the car in a steady rhythm. Pull with the hand, push with the good leg. It went well until he tried to move too fast, twisted the broken leg, blacked out again.

When he came to, he saw that he had managed to crawl a dozen feet closer to the Cadillac. The big car had rolled over completely at least once and come to rest on its side with the roof toward him. He didn't see any way to get inside, but he kept dragging himself along, a foot at a time, until he spotted his sheepskin coat in the snow. He strained to reach it, got a thumb and forefinger on one sleeve, pulled it to him. It took several attempts, but he managed to sit up enough to get an arm through one sleeve and to pull the coat up over his injured left shoulder. When he tried to get his left arm into the sleeve, he nearly blacked out again. He gave up, left the coat draped over his injured shoulder, used his good hand to button it. Lying next to the coat in the snow was his figuring rope. He stuffed it into one of the pockets of the sheepskin jacket. Then he studied the Cadillac, trying to figure out what possible use he could make of the wrecked automobile. He had heard of men slitting the abdomen of a dead horse, pulling out the intestines, crawling inside for warmth or making a fire and eating the animal, but you could not eat a car. He was pondering the sheer, utter uselessness of an automobile for any purpose other than driving on a road when he remembered the two full, five-gallon cans of gasoline lashed to the trunk. He never went anywhere without the extra gasoline and two spare tires. The spare fuel was no use with a wrecked car, but it could be used to start a helluva blaze. He had no idea whether his thoughts were lucid, but the gas cans were his only hope. If he could find a way to set the car on fire, it might save him from freezing to death. If the explosion didn't kill him, it was possible someone might see it or hear it. A forty-five-hundred-dollar bonfire.

He pulled himself up far enough to unbuckle the leather strap that held the two cans to the trunk. Both tumbled into the snow, the nearer can striking his broken leg with enough force to make him scream again. He used every curse word he knew, caught his breath, worked the lid off one of the cans, fed the entire length of his figuring rope down into it until the rope was soaked with gasoline. He left two or three feet of rope down in the can, wedged the can under the Caddy's gas tank, tugged the second gas can next to it. He stopped to rest then, taking long, deep breaths of cold air into his lungs. It took almost all he had left, but he managed to drag himself fifteen feet from the car, paying out the rope as he went. When he judged that he was far enough away to avoid being killed by the explosion, he fumbled in his pocket for matches. He smoked no more than the occasional cheroot, but it was an old habit, making sure he always had dry matches in his jeans. He mumbled a little prayer. Either the rope would burn or it would not. If it wouldn't, he would freeze to death.

Eli's hands were so cold that he had trouble lighting the wooden matches and wasted four before the flame caught and held. It took the merest touch to ignite the gasoline-soaked rope. Once it was lit, the rope became a perfect fuse. The flame raced toward the first gas can and the crippled Cadillac. He had just enough time to roll away and cover his face with his arms before the two gas cans exploded, one after the other. A few seconds later, the gas tank of the Caddy itself blew with a heavy thud. He risked a glance and saw a ball of red and blue flame rise twenty feet into the sky. He felt a rush of blistering heat before he had to cover his head as debris from the burning car fell around him. The explosion was enough to lift the car itself, and as it settled back down, it rolled a half turn toward him, so that it was once again upright on its wheels.

After the fireball from the gas tank went up, the Cadillac burned steadily. It gave off a terrible reek of burning oil and grease and body paint, but it was extremely hot. Eli crawled as close to the flames as he could bear. His feet were the coldest part of his body, so he ignored the pain and worked his way around so that his legs were toward the fire. Then he tucked his sheepskin collar behind his head and lay back to watch the spectacle. The interior burned with a bright red flame and an occasional mini-explosion. Thick, dark smoke rose from the closed windows. The flames shot twenty feet into the air, steam rose steadily from around the hood. A smaller fire, started beneath the chassis, gave off gray-brown smoke. As the heat grew more intense, the white paint on the doors blistered, then the exterior paint began to burn. All the tires, including both spare tires, gave off a heavy black smoke as they burned. Twice there was a small explosion in the front end as some part of the engine blew. The heat was so intense he could hardly bear to look at it. At last, something underneath gave way and the Cadillac settled onto its axles, first onto the rear axle and after another puff of smoke and flame from underneath, onto the front axle, so that it was a squat, dark, smoldering thing that bore little resemblance to the fine, expensive, coveted machine it had been only a few minutes before. A charred, skeletal automobile emerged slowly from the flames, like the shell of a burned house. After another fifteen or twenty minutes, the flames began to die down, but the car still gave off intense heat as the undercarriage and the tires burned on.

When Eli and Ezra were very young, their father had told them the story of a fellow named Wilmot Brookings, who had fallen through the ice of a creek in South Dakota. By the time he made it back to Sioux Falls, Wilmot's frozen feet had to be amputated. It did not keep Brookings from becoming governor of the territory, but the story made such an impression that footless wraiths staggered through Eli's nightmares for decades, leaving bloody trails in the snow. His broken leg could be set, but if his feet froze through, they would have to be amputated. Wilmot Brookings had done well for himself as a footless man, but Eli did not want to have to find out if he was old Wilmot's equal. He kept scooting closer to the car as it cooled by degrees, determined to keep his feet from freezing.

Gradually, he let himself sink into the snow, still warmed by the burning wreck. A skimpy moon was up on the horizon, swimming through thin clouds that were now spitting just a few flakes of snow, lighting the expanse of snow around him. He wiped his forehead. His hand came away smeared with congealed blood. If he died here, he would die because of his own plain damned foolishness. Juanita had begged him to find a hotel in Casper. A man with a lick of sense would have listened to her, even if she was part of the reason he was in such an all-fired hurry to get home. He could have stayed with his daughter Ruby way back on Sheep Creek, just this side of the Wyoming state line, or any number of places in between. Instead, he had pushed on like a stubborn fool and put himself in as bad a fix as he had ever known. No fool like an old fool, they said, and he was an old fool. He watched the blaze chew at the tires of the Cadillac, the black smoke pouring from inside the wheel wells and from the spares, which had rolled away from the front fenders after the leather strap that held them burned through. The burned automobile still gave off a pulsating heat that warmed his legs and his torso. It was possible he might live until dawn. Maybe someone would find him yet before it was too late.

He drifted off into a waking dream. When he opened his eyes, it was much colder and Spotted War Bonnet, the friend of his youth, crouched at his side, saying something in an Indian tongue he did not understand. He answered in Lakota, but War Bonnet went on speaking in the strange tongue. He gestured toward a pinto that was tied fifty feet away and muttered something. At last Eli understood. Spotted War Bonnet had ridden out to usher his old friend into the spirit world.

4.

THE CHOCTAW COWPOKE THEY CALLED TWO SPUDS was inside his cabin on the southwest corner of the ranch, wrapped tightly in his quilt trying to sleep, when he heard an explosion. At first he thought maybe Jenny Hoot Owl had just farted in her sleep. Jenny could let loose farts that cracked like a rifle shot, but this was more like the sound of a hand grenade dumped into an outhouse. Two Spuds had been a seventeen-year-old private in the Great War, scared shitless as he crawled through the Ardennes Forest, convinced that a shard of screaming hot shrapnel was going to tear off his balls. He'd heard plenty of grenades go off in France, along with about two hundred other kinds of ordnance, most of it meant to kill him dead. This did not sound like a grenade. He lay there shivering, wishing Jenny would get her big ass out of bed and put more coal on the fire. His nose told him how cold it was. Too damned cold to get out of bed, but the only way to get warmer was to stoke the fire again. He would have to climb out of that warm quilt into the icy air, shovel more coal into the stove, make sure it was burning good, jump back into bed, wait until the stove warmed the room. Or he could curl up tight next to Jenny, but if he did, she was apt to break his nose.

You cold, fool! You think I wanna take a bath in ice water? Don't touch me when you're froze like that. Get your skinny Indian ass back where it belongs before I cut your nuts off!

Two Spuds was inclined to stay in bed until he remembered what it was that woke him in the first place. A big damned *whooomph!* out there someplace. He tried to forget it and go back to sleep, but it gnawed at the back of his mind like mice in a sack of oats. There was nothing out on that prairie that could blow up. On a Saturday night, it might have been ranch kids, bored and drunk. Get hold of a few sticks of dynamite, blow up a steer for the pure hell of it. Such things had been known to happen, but they required the combustible combination of liquor and young cowpokes. He fretted until he could stand it no more. Finally he rose, stuffed coal into the stove and lit it, pulled on his jeans and boots, stepped outside to pee. He sniffed at the wind, which carried a faint tang of burning rubber. The wind came from the northwest, the same direction as the explosion. There was nothing out there except sagebrush and buffalo grass, all of it frozen stiff and buried under a thin layer of snow. Nothing that might burn in this weather, not even a haystack. He stepped back into the cabin, grabbed his sheepskin coat and heavy gloves and an old wool sheepherder's hat that would keep a blizzard out of a man's ears.

The pinto was fractious when he saddled it. He had to give it a brisk tug with the curb bit a time or two to remind it who was boss. Once in the saddle, he followed the smell of burning rubber. As soon as the pinto topped the rise north of his cabin, he saw it. A big automobile, burned down to a smoldering hulk. He lifted the reins, gave the pinto a little heel, rocked it into a canter, sticking to the road, taking a circular path to the burning car. Better go the long way round than cut across the prairie and have the pinto break its leg in a sinkhole in the dark.

The Cadillac still gave off a red glow and an acrid reek from the smoke of the burning tires. It was a strange beast to encounter on a night like this, in its death throes more like a living thing than it had ever been when it was just another machine. The pinto wanted no part of it. Spuds had to dig his heels hard into its flanks to get close. He found a post left from an old fence, snubbed the horse tight. He suspected the wreck might be Eli Paint's Cadillac before he got close enough to see the man himself, lying on his back on the far side of what was left of the automobile. Two Spuds went to him, his boots crunching through the frozen snow. There was just enough light from the sliver of moon so he could see that it was Eli, his face a mask of congealed blood. The Choctaw saw the broken leg, the way it made a hard right turn halfway down the shin, the tracks in the snow where Eli had dragged himself back and forth, the cinders of the burned lariat lying on the snow. Eli must have lit a fuse to the gas cans to burn the car for warmth. That was the explosion he'd heard, the gasoline going up in a ball of fire. Tough old bird, to manage that with a leg busted that bad and who knew what else. Two Spuds grabbed Eli's left wrist, held it tight to get his thumb on the pulse. He wasn't sure he felt anything, but Eli was shivering so hard he couldn't tell. Then Eli muttered something in Lakota about an Indian named War Bonnet. Two Spuds joked in Choctaw, telling Eli that he was lucky a Choctaw warrior had come to save him and not some thieving dog of a Sioux. Eli muttered something, but Two Spuds couldn't make out what he was saying. Other than the cut on his head, Eli didn't seem to be bleeding, but he moaned in pain when Two Spuds pressed on his chest.

The Choctaw stood up and walked around Eli, trying to decide what to do. He thought of lifting him over the saddle on the pinto and tying his hands and feet underneath the horse's belly, the way you would with a dead man. It would work, but it might kill him. Taking Eli back to his cabin would be worse than useless. He needed to get him to the main house, six miles away, where there was at least a telephone. The only way he could transport him safely was on the travois he had back at the cabin. It was an old-fashioned Indian pony drag, two twenty-foot lengths of crisscrossed lodgepole pine, with a willow frame stretched between them, lashed to the poles with rawhide strips.

A wagon might have been better, but he didn't have a wagon. First, he would have to leave Eli and hurry back for the travois. He took off his sheepskin hat and jacket, covered Eli's head with the hat, wrapped the jacket around his legs, jumped on the pinto wearing only his shirt and trousers, cursing the cold with every step. The way this was working out, he and Eli would both freeze to death. He had no trouble urging the pinto into a canter. The horse wanted to put distance between itself and that burning car. Two Spuds promised him a bucket of oats if they got Eli back to the ranch house alive, but he could tell the pinto didn't believe him.

Inside the cabin, he rummaged around, found an old coat of Jenny's and pulled that on, dragged out his old buffalo robe along with a couple of blankets and two ropes to tie Eli to the pony drag. The coal stove was going good. He was able to warm up a little, just being inside. Jenny was still snoring, a sound like a ripsaw in wet timber. By the time he made it back to the wreck with the travois bouncing along behind him, Eli was unconscious. It was just as well, because it took a good deal of dragging and heaving to get him onto the travois and to get the buffalo robe to fit snugly around his body with the pinto trying to shy away. Two Spuds wrapped his lariat three times around Eli's torso and the travois poles and tied it with a sheepshank knot to make sure the man didn't slip off the pony drag.

Once Eli was settled, Two Spuds mounted the pinto and set off at a walk. At this speed, the six miles to the main house was going to be a long ride in the cold. He tied his bandanna over his face, but it didn't help much. He kept looking back, checking to see if the man on the pony drag was alive or dead. There was no way to tell. He had tucked a bottle of whiskey inside his belt in case Eli wanted a jolt to keep him warm. Eli wasn't capable of drinking, so Spuds took two long pulls and felt the warmth going down. A light snow was falling, the wind was blowing, powdery snow rose like steam a hundred feet in the air. His eyes watered from the cold. He tucked his jaw into the collar of Jenny's coat and rode with plenty of slack in the reins, letting the pinto pick its way along the ruts of the road. Now and then he felt a hard tug as the travois bucked into a rut, but he had done a good job with the rope and the buffalo robe. His cargo was secure.

Juanita Barrios woke from a dream of the dead. In her dream, the spirits of the dead rose with the smoke of the kitchen fires in the little houses in her village in Chihuahua. The spirits of her father, her mother, her brothers drifted in the smoky air over the village, the restless dead refusing to lie still so that on the nights when the dreams came, she slept in snatches, trying to steal a little sleep from the spirits.

The grandfather clock in the parlor of the great house tolled once, echoing along the polished wooden floor of the hallway. One o'clock. She had fallen asleep in the rocking chair in the parlor, her index finger marking her place in the Paint family Bible. She read the Bible to improve her English, but she was often sidetracked by the pages of family history left by generations of Paint women who had recorded all the births and deaths and marriages since the Welshman Ezekiel Paint arrived in Boston before the Revolutionary War. She could imagine the women, seated as she was sitting, by the fire on a winter evening, with cups of cocoa or tea at their elbows, neatly jotting the name of a newborn or the death of a distant uncle as the wind howled outside: "John Milton Paint, b. March 1, 1903, d. March 7, 1903." Eli's baby son, followed in death a month later by the boy's mother, Livvy, her death recorded in a young girl's hand. One of the older daughters surely, Tavie or Velma or Marguerite.

Juanita envied Eli and his children. Her own past lay on the other side of the Mexican Revolution. There were no treasured photographs put away in a chest somewhere, no old letters carefully bound, no such Bible in which the births and deaths of the Barrios family had been recorded. It had all vanished in fire and massacre. She was left feeling thin and rootless, insubstantial as the spirits that haunted her sleep.

She stirred the cold cup of cocoa at her elbow, watching the brown skin of milk on the surface wind around the spoon. She sipped the cocoa and made a face. It was time to get to bed. She rose and started toward her bedroom at the back of the house but paused halfway. Something was wrong. Eli wasn't home. She tried to remember what he had said—was he supposed to arrive sometime before midnight or sometime after midnight? Before midnight, surely. A good deal before midnight, the way he drove that Cadillac. She peered outside, but she could see nothing except an expanse of white snow that seemed to go on forever and no sign of Eli or the car. She felt a chill, scooped more coal onto the stove, put a fresh pan of milk on to warm for more cocoa.

Juanita finished the cocoa and paced the floor like a worried mother, glancing at the clock every minute or two. She fluffed cushions, washed out her cup and put it away, trying to be useful. When she could stand it no more, she dressed, put on her coat, walked through the snow to the bunkhouse to wake the foreman, Willie Thaw. Willie's was the bunk closest to the stove. The bunkhouse was lit by the moon, but she could have found his bunk by the smell of Willie's whiskey. She shook him lightly. He answered with a long, ragged snore. She grabbed his shoulder and shook him until he sat up with a Colt Navy in his hand. Willie pulled the hammer back and held it to her jaw, a wild look in his eyes. He was still so drunk he had no idea who she was.

"Put that thing down, Willie. It's me."

"Who the hell are you?"

"It's Juanita, Willie. We need to look for Eli."

Willie sat up on his cot. "You lost Eli someplace?"

"He should have been here two or three hours ago."

"Naw, he's off visiting Ida Mae in the nuthouse."

"Willie! Will you pay attention? Eli called me from Casper and said he was on his way. That was hours ago. He didn't make it. I want you to help me look for him."

"Hell, he probably just stopped for a drink someplace."

The stench of alcohol from Willie was so powerful that Juanita had to take a step back. "I don't think Eli has ever stopped for a drink in his life. He hadn't slept for two days. I'm afraid he fell asleep at the wheel."

"Hell, he might a gone off the road in Casper. Or Big Horn, or any other damned place. No sense goin out after him in this weather."

Willie holstered his pistol and sank back onto the bed. She heard a deep, rattling snore. He was too drunk to ride, so she would have to saddle her horse and search for Eli herself. She dragged her saddle out of the tack shed and went to catch Ginger, a little filly Eli had given her so that she could ride with the children. The horses were pressed tightly together in the cold, their breath rising in curlicues of steam into the night air. She recognized Ginger by the lopsided diamond between her eyes and managed to get a saddle and bridle on her. She reined the horse to the south and let her pick her way along the road toward the front gate.

The filly was winter-shod and the road was icy. Her hooves rang like anvils on the ice. A light snow still fell, but the clouds were thin enough for a sliver of moon to peek through. In the moonlight Juanita could see the curving road ahead and the rise to the southwest that led to the front gate. There were no tire tracks anywhere. She wound her wool scarf tighter around her head, leaving just a slit for her eyes. She had ridden a little over a mile when Ginger lifted her head and pricked up her ears. She whinnied twice and was answered by another horse out there somewhere. Juanita rode toward the sound until she could make out Two Spuds on the pinto, dragging some strange contraption through the snow. She cantered up to meet him.

"That you, Juanita? What are you doin way out here?"

"Looking for Eli."

"Well, you found him. That's him behind my horse."

"Is he alive?"

"He was alive when I found him. His right leg is broke, maybe some ribs too. He must of got lost. He wrecked that Cadillac about a mile from my place."

Juanita was already out of the saddle, her fingertips pressed to Eli's throat. She felt a pulse, weak but steady. "We've got to get him to the house and warm him up."

"That's what I'm tryin to do."

"What is that thing?"

"Pony drag. Travois. Indian way."

She swung back into the saddle. When they started off, the travois hit a bump, and she heard Eli moan. At least he was alive enough to feel pain. It stopped snowing, the wind-blown clouds began to drift apart. She rode next to the pony drag, a little behind Two Spuds on his pinto, under a moon slender as a potato peel. In its pale light, the bare limbs of a lone cottonwood tree clawed at the sky.

5.

As they rode, Two Spuds told her what had happened, as much as he could figure out. Eli had overshot the turnoff for the house. He must have been driving too fast on the narrow track when he rolled the Cadillac. Somehow, he had dragged himself through the snow back to the car, rigged the spare gas cans to set it afire. The sound of the explosion had awakened Two Spuds in his cabin. He'd ridden out to see what it was, found Eli lying next to the wreck.

"Thank God you went to check," Juanita said. "Another hour, maybe less, and he would have frozen to death."

The first thing, she said, was to keep him from dying from the cold. Juanita knew *la hipotermia* from the years when she had worked as a nurse in clinics in the high mountains of Mexico. Her late husband, Dr. Meredith Hodgson, had trained her well in the treatment of hypothermia. In Chihuahua, the temperature could drop eighty degrees at night. People went to sleep with a thin blanket on a warm evening and froze to death before morning. She had seen patients brought in who seemed to be past saving, but if they could be warmed in the right way, they sometimes survived. It wasn't the hands and feet you had to worry about, it was the cold that penetrated to the core of a person's body. Two Spuds had done the right thing, wrapping Eli in the buffalo robe.

Now they had to warm him from the inside out. Warm the heart and lungs, the rest would follow.

When they reached the house, she checked Eli's pulse again. It was faint but steady. Two Spuds untied his rope. They used the old buffalo robe as a stretcher, carried Eli into the house and lifted him onto the long kitchen table. Juanita put a large kettle of water on the stove to boil and peeled back the buffalo robe to have a look at Eli's broken leg. It was an open fracture, but the tibia had barely broken the skin. She had seen worse.

While she waited for the water in the pot to boil, she telephoned Doc Miller. The doctor's sleepy wife answered and said that he was attending to a birth about ten miles from the 8T8. She promised to ask him to hurry over as soon as the baby was born. Juanita darted upstairs to get Dr. Hodgson's medical bag and two clean, white sheets. There was morphine in the bag, but she was afraid that morphine would slow Eli's heart rate even more. As long as he was unconscious, he didn't need anything for the pain. She took alcohol and sterile cloths from the bag and cleaned the wound around the fracture and the wound on his forehead, which had begun to bleed again.

Once the water in the kettle was boiling, Juanita had Two Spuds help her drag the heavy table closer to the stove. Then she draped an old sheet over the pot and stretched it across the chairs on either side of the table, so that he was inside a makeshift tent where the air felt hot and humid as the tropics. He would breathe the warm, moist air deep into his lungs, taking heat to where it was most needed. Again, she pressed her fingers to his neck. His pulse was still weak but steady. She got a thermometer out of the medical bag and managed to peel away enough of Eli's clothing to slip it under his armpit, waited two or three minutes, and peeked at the thermometer. His body temperature was eighty-three degrees, almost as low as it could go before he died of hypothermia. She left the steam to do its work and sat on a kitchen chair, exhausted. Two Spuds squatted on his heels, watching, not saying a word. She put a pot of coffee on to perk and slipped some day-old biscuits into the oven to warm.

Half an hour later, Eli's temperature was up to eighty-six degrees. She filled the pot on the stove again and asked Two Spuds to cut away the boot on Eli's broken leg. He produced a knife with an eight-inch blade from somewhere under his clothing and sliced the boot away with two strokes.

Two Spuds tossed what was left of the boot aside. "Shame to waste a good boot."

"He's already burned up a Cadillac. I don't think he'll care much about a boot."

Juanita removed Eli's heavy wool socks and examined his toes. He had only mild frostbite. She got the needle and sutures out of Dr. Hodgson's bag, cleaned the wound on Eli's forehead, sutured it tight with eleven stitches. He moaned and moved his head once or twice, but she got through it without waking him, then made a little breakfast on the stove in the parlor.

She had about decided to attempt to set the fractured tibia herself when the doctor called to say that he was on his way. By the time he arrived, Eli's body temperature was up to ninety degrees and he was semiconscious. Doc Miller was a tall, austere man with long, thin, spidery hands. He had been a country doctor for nearly forty years. Juanita explained what had happened, what she had been doing to bring up Eli's temperature. The doctor examined the patient quickly, checked his temperature himself, nodded.

"You two might have saved his life. Who thought of the steam?"

"I did. Dr. Hodgson used to do this in Mexico when we found people almost frozen to death."

"Yes. I had heard you were his nurse. Brightest doctor we ever had around here. Damned shame, his passing."

Juanita looked away. Grief could still ambush her now, nearly four years after Dr. Hodgson's death.

"We've got a couple of tricky operations ahead. We've got to set the leg. I suspect he's got a ruptured spleen as well. I'm going to call into Sheridan for an ambulance."

The operator at the hospital said that there would be a three-hour wait for an ambulance. Doc Miller offered to stay with Eli while Juanita got some sleep, but she refused. In that case, he said, he would catch forty winks himself if she could point him to a bed.

The doctor was still napping when Ezra turned up at the door. Not for the first time in his life, he had a sense that something had happened to Eli. He had ridden over to see, for once regretting that he refused to have a telephone installed in the cabin he shared with Ben. Juanita told him what had happened and what they had been doing for Eli.

"I shoulda known," he said. "I woke up in the middle of the night, nervous as a cat. Eli and I have always been able to tell when there was something wrong with the other one. Comes with being twins, I suppose. It's a good thing you heard the explosion, Spuds. He'd be froze to death by now."

Ezra told Two Spuds he might as well go back to his cabin and get some sleep. With Juanita and Ezra and Doc Miller around, they had plenty of help. The Choctaw nodded. He hadn't told Jenny Hoot Owl where he was going. She would be mad enough to eat his liver raw.

As Spuds was on his way out, Willie Thaw slipped through the door, looking like something that had to be scraped out of a barn with a pitchfork. He could recall a vague dream about Juanita coming to the bunkhouse, a dream he'd had many times before—except that, in this dream, she had her clothes on and she wanted him to ride out to look for Eli. When he saw the scene in the kitchen, he came to a halt as though he'd bumped into a wall. He tried a grin, exposing a picket fence of rotting teeth.

"I see you found him."

"Two Spuds found him, no thanks to you."

"I didn't see no sense ridin out in the middle of the night."

"It's a good thing Two Spuds has better sense than you do."

"I was hopin to get a little breakfast anyways."

"If you want to eat, there's cold coffee and cold biscuits. You can take some and warm it on the bunkhouse stove."

Willie rummaged around until he found a Mason jar, filled it with coffee, took a sack of cold biscuits. After he left, it was too quiet in the big house. Outside the wind picked up again, blowing powdery snow against the windows. Juanita put more coffee on to perk. Eli's children had all gone straight from the Ewing place to the schoolhouse and would not be home until late afternoon.

6.

THE AMBULANCE ARRIVED AT NOON. THE DRIVER and his assistant were big, amiable Slovenians with heavy East European accents. They had come to work in the coal mines and found an easier life hauling banged-up cowboys and roughnecks who got drunk and fell off oil rigs. Juanita went upstairs to fetch Doc Miller. He supervised while the Slovenians maneuvered Eli from the table onto a stretcher. Juanita wanted to ride to Sheridan with the ambulance, but she had already pushed herself beyond exhaustion. Ezra offered to ride along in her place and call as soon as there was any news. Juanita watched the ambulance pull away, then collapsed on her narrow bed, as weary as she had ever been in her life.

Ezra crouched next to Eli in the back of the ambulance on the long, bumpy ride. Up front, the Slovenians conversed in their language, which sounded as though it was about five vowels short of an alphabet. Now and again the wind would catch the broad side of the vehicle and the driver would have to fight to keep it on the highway. Ezra peered out through the narrow windows and saw a stretch of Wyoming that looked barren as the moon.

The whole situation felt wrong. All their lives, Eli had been the healthy one. If one of them was going to get sick, it would be Ezra. He could recall times when he had been ill, down with a fever or the flu or a terrible cold, and Eli would do the chores for both of them without complaint. When he came in from milking the cows on a frigid morning, Eli would shuck his coat and hat and boots and look in to see if Ezra needed anything. Ezra would say he was just fine, because there was always a puzzled look on Eli's face. Not angry or contemptuous or frustrated with Ezra's illness, just puzzled, like he couldn't figure out what it was to be sick. Ezra knew that, deep inside, Eli saw every illness as a sign of weakness, proof that a fellow wasn't as tough or as strong as he needed to be. He never got sick, so why should anyone else? Ezra understood why Eli had kept pushing to make it back to the ranch house. He didn't know any other way. Even when they were boys, Ezra could never beat Eli in a fight, because to beat him, you'd have to kill him. Now Eli had whipped himself, kept at it until he was shattered like window glass in a dust storm. Even so, it was just like the man to stay alive by burning up a Cadillac to keep warm when another fellow would have just curled up and died.

Ezra leaned toward the Slovenians up front. "How much farther?"

One of them turned and held up all his fingers. "Ten miles more. If we don't crash ambulance."

They both laughed. Ezra laughed with them. It was what happened if you spent a lot of time around death and dying. You laughed or you died.

When they pulled up to the back entrance of the hospital, Ezra went to help with the stretcher, but the Slovenians shouldered him out of the way, toted Eli inside almost without effort. Nurses bustled, doctors popped in and popped out again, telephones rang somewhere. Ezra waited ten long hours before Doc Miller stepped out of the operating room to give him the news. There were so many injuries that Ezra could recall only about half of them. Eli had a badly fractured tibia, a fractured collarbone and dislocated shoulder, three broken ribs, a ruptured spleen.

"He's a tough old bird," Doc Miller said, "but he's been through a lot, with the hypothermia and all, and he isn't a spring chicken anymore. We set the broken leg and removed his spleen. That will take care of the worst of it, but he's not out of danger. If he's with us tomorrow morning, he's got a better shot, but we still have to worry about infections and pneumonia."

Ezra found a telephone and got the operator to connect him to the 8T8. Juanita answered on the first ring. Ezra wondered if she had slept at all. He heard the anxiety in her voice and tried to sound as calm as he could as he told her that the surgery was done and Eli was resting.

"Listen, Juanita, I fixed it so he's got a private room. They're going to put a cot in a little room next to where he is, so somebody can stay with him. I thought it might be better if you come in to the hospital here and look after Eli. If anything was to go wrong, all I could do is holler for help. I expect the girls can take care of the house for a week or so."

"Yes, I would like that. The children are home from the Ewing place, so I have explained to them what happened. They are worried, but they know how strong their father is. They believe he will be all right."

"Well, send one of the boys over to fetch Ben and ask him to drive you into town first thing tomorrow. I'll try to get some shut-eye here tonight and see you in the morning."

Ezra didn't sleep much that night. Mostly, he listened to Eli's ragged breathing. They were giving Eli morphine for the pain and he was still unconscious, but he moaned every time he moved. At four o'clock in the morning, the hour he normally rose, Ezra got up and went down to the hospital restaurant for some breakfast and sat there looking at the newspaper and thinking about all the twists in the road that had brought them to this place. He wondered how he would handle things if Eli didn't make it. Eli always kept so much of his business to himself that even Ezra didn't know how things stood, although he knew they weren't good. Eli was a lot better at juggling all of it than he was, which was why Ezra stuck to his little Appaloosa outfit. Raise a few horses, break them, sell a few, buy now and then. It was about as much as he cared to manage, but without Eli, the 8T8 would be Ezra's by default, the whole shebang. A hundred thousand acres and six children to raise.

"You better pull through, big brother," Ezra said aloud. "I don't want no part of running that outfit."

The waitress, a plump young woman with a wad of bubble gum stuffed in her jaw, turned her head. "Was there something you needed, mister?"

Ezra shook his head, embarrassed. "No, ma'am. I'm sorry. I was just thinkin out loud."

"That's all right. We get a lot of that in here."

"I expect you do."

It was near eight o'clock when Ben arrived with Juanita. Eli was still unconscious. Ben drove Ezra back to the ranch. The nurses, run ragged with patients from a flu outbreak, were happy to have someone to look after Eli, because he would need care around the clock. Juanita talked things over with the head nurse and worked out a routine so that she could care for Eli and the regular nurses would look in only now and then. After Doc Miller visited midmorning, she kicked her shoes off, curled up on the chair next to Eli's bed, fell asleep. When she woke, Eli's eyes were open. He had been watching her sleep. She smiled.

"You're awake."

"I sure am. How'd I get here? Last I remember, I was layin in the snow watchin the Caddy burn."

His voice was so weak she could barely hear him. She checked his pulse. "That fire probably saved your life. Two Spuds found you and brought you in on that thing he calls a pony drag."

"Two Spuds? I'll be damned. I knew I'd be happy I had that Choctaw around someday. Best hand I ever seen." He winced and clutched at his midsection. "Good God. It feels like they ripped out about half my insides and a Clydesdale stomped on my leg. What did they do to me?"

"They had to remove your spleen and set your broken leg, that was the worst of it. You're lucky to be alive. I told you it would be better if you stayed in Casper."

"Might have been, at that. Although I do hate Casper worse'n I hate the blackleg. Got lost on my own land. What a damned old fool."

Something inside pained him. He winced. Juanita asked if he wanted more morphine. Eli shook his head. "I'd rather put up with some hurt than black out again. What day is it?"

She looked at the clock. "It's Saturday afternoon. I guess you crashed late Thursday night or maybe early Friday morning."

"I aint sure what happened, exactly. One minute I was tryin to find the road to the house, then I was layin in the snow. Are the kids all right?"

"Everyone is fine. I didn't tell the children about it until they came home from school Friday. I told them you had been hurt, but not to worry. I knew you would pull through. Ezra was here when they operated on you, but we traded places this morning."

"Good. I'd rather look at you than that old cuss any day."

"He's your twin brother. He looks exactly like you."

"That's what I mean."

7.

EMALINE DIDN'T LEARN ABOUT THE ACCIDENT until a week later. She saw the mailman go by on the county road, walked the quarter mile to the mailbox against a stiff wind to get the mail. She was surprised to find a letter from Ben, along with the latest issue of the *Nebraska Farmer* and a letter from Minnesota addressed to Jens Lindquist. Ben wrote no more than three or four times a year. She tucked the mail into her apron and walked back to the house, noting the high scudding clouds overhead, the leaden edges that meant snow in the wind before the day was out. She was cold, so she put on water for tea and waited for it to boil before she sat down at the kitchen table and opened his letter.

Wyoming
February 4, 1933

Dear Emaline,

I don't have much time to write, just wanted to let you know that Eli had a car accident on his way back from Scottsbluff. He hadn't slept for a couple of days. He was trying to make it home. He got all turned around once he got to the ranch and drove a ways down the wrong road and was trying to get back when he rolled that big old Cadillac.

He was throwed right out in the snow and would of froze to death, but he figured a way to set the car on fire to keep warm. A Choctaw cowboy who works here found him. Juanita, the woman who takes care of Eli's kids, was a nurse in Mexico, so she kept him alive until they got him to the hospital. He was busted up pretty bad, but Ezra says it looks like he'll pull through. If he does, he's likely to be on crutches for a while.

Eli is at the hospital in Sheridan now. Juanita is staying there with him, so she can let us know if anything happens one way or another.

love,
Ben

She read the letter over a second time, then buried her face in her hands. She had never felt so ashamed. She had known how tired Eli was. She could have asked him to stay the night, but she hadn't offered so much as a cup of coffee and a biscuit. Her mother would have been appalled. No matter what differences she had with the man, Velma would have begged him to stay or at least given him a jug of coffee and something to eat on the road. Emaline took pride in her manners and tried to be proper in all things despite her poverty, yet she had treated her own grandfather miserably. Worse, she had allowed him to leave in a state of exhaustion, which had led to an automobile accident that almost killed him.

She got out Velma's stationery and wrote to Ben, pleading with him to let her know as soon as possible if Eli's condition changed, adding that she wouldn't sleep well until she knew he was out of danger.

The house was too quiet. The Lindquist brothers had taken Bobby along on their Saturday visit to the sale barn, where they never missed a livestock auction even though they couldn't afford to buy so much as a chicken. They went to talk to other farmers, to see what prices cattle and pigs were fetching, to listen to the rapid-fire patter of the auctioneer. They had asked her to come along, but the four of them would have had to pile into the cab of their old Dodge Brothers truck.

The news of Eli's accident left her feeling even more miserable. In this house, it was impossible to escape the pain of her mother's death. Velma was in everything. Her soul was part of the fabric, the metal and wood, the tablecloth, the crocheted doilies, the hooked rugs on the floor, the neat stacks of *National Geographic* magazines on the shelf. Emaline remembered this house as it was when Jim and Velma were first married. Jim Lindquist and his brother Lee had been bachelor farmers. The house was as spare as a monk's cell, with not a rug on the hard pine floor or a picture on the wall. Between them, Jim and Lee had owned two plates, two bowls, two knives, two forks, two spoons, a coffeepot, a frying pan, two coffee cups, a rickety wooden table, two kitchen chairs, two narrow cots, a washbasin. They had possessed only one piece of furniture worth having, a hand-carved Swedish pine wardrobe with recessed side panels and a dovetailed drawer that had belonged to their mother.

After Jim married Velma, the brothers had built a two-room house for Lee a hundred feet from the first. Velma moved in, the windows grew curtains, the floors grew rugs, there were quilts on every bed and lace doilies on the tables. Every stitch of it she made herself. The narrow garden the Swedes had tended grew to an entire acre and then two and three acres as carrots, sweet corn, potatoes, turnips, peas, snap beans, strawberries all flourished under Velma's hand. Emaline wondered what would happen to the garden now, if the Swedes would be able to keep it going. Except for church Sunday mornings, they worked from dawn to dark seven days a week as it was.

Emaline boiled water for tea and sat at the kitchen table paging through an old issue of *National Geographic,* gazing at pictures of erupting volcanoes in the South Pacific and the pyramids in Egypt.

Jim had every issue going back to 1919. She loved to look through them, to travel the world from his kitchen. Sometimes she wondered if perhaps he subscribed because of the photos of half-naked women in the Congo or Tahiti that were in almost every magazine, but she pushed that to the back of her mind as a scandalous and uncharitable thought.

She listened to the wind, felt the chill of it through the cracks in the frame house, even with coal in the stove and the fire lit. There were only three rooms in the house, so she slept on a cot next to Bobby, with Jim snoring on the other side of the curtain that divided the one narrow bedroom in two. It was three miles to the nearest farm. On winter days when you couldn't be out in the garden, there was little to do but sit in the house and listen to the wind howl, the wind that never stopped blowing on the High Plains. An entire winter of this and she would go mad. They would find her in the springtime, the way they used to find pioneer women who had lived in sod houses with dirt floors, or in dugouts that were no better than caves. The poor things would listen to the wind all winter long, until they could bear it no more. Then they would go down to the root cellar, find a length of old rope, tie it to a rafter. They would stand on a pickle barrel and fashion a noose the best they knew how, put the noose around their necks, kick the barrel away. The last sound they would hear would be the howling of the prairie wind.

Velma had sat day after day exactly as Emaline was sitting now, in this chair, drinking tea and listening to the wind. But she had never complained. She would be busy at something, not idly turning the pages of a magazine, gazing at pictures of the world and wishing she could be somewhere else.

Life goes on. Velma used to say that. *Life goes on. Sometimes, that's the saddest part of all.* Emaline had talked to Charlie Naudain to tell him she needed to take a week off from her job slinging hash at the Arrowhead Diner so that she could sort Velma's things, but the truth was she just needed time to cry. Charlie told her to take all the time she needed. Business was slow in these hard times. Calla Plessman could handle things until Emaline was ready to come back to work.

After the funeral, she had packed a few of her things in a cardboard suitcase and left the little house in town that she shared with Calla to ride out to the farm with Jim. Each day since, she had put off the things she had to do. Now she had to find a way to dispose of each comb and box and costume necklace that had belonged to Velma, the accumulated effects of a gentle and often impoverished woman who had burnished her few possessions with the care that renders simple things luminous.

Emaline had expected the task to be difficult, but she couldn't find the strength to sift and sort her mother's belongings, to take the things she or Ben or Bobby might want and leave the rest to Jim or to charity. The worst of it was the wardrobe, hung with her mother's few dresses, thin from many washings. The summer dress, the winter dress, the dress for church that Velma wore in all seasons, the fancy dress she had not worn since her wedding. When Emaline opened the door to the wardrobe, she breathed her mother's scent, fell to her knees, buried her face in the winter dress, inhaling it, helpless with grief. How did people do it? How did they dispose of these tangible remnants of a life? She could not bear to give the dresses away, nor could she live with them packed away in her own narrow closet.

She left the dresses for another time. In the bottom of the wardrobe, she found her mother's old-fashioned high-button shoes, ordered from the Monkey Ward catalog and kept forever. She could see clearly the outline of Velma's toes in the leather. Velma had few vanities, but she was proud of her small, dainty feet and well-turned ankles. The shoes were too small for Emaline to wear, but she couldn't throw them away, not when farm women went through their lives with one good pair of shoes for church, wearing old brogans their sons had outgrown the rest of the week.

It was growing dark. She got up to light the kerosene lamp. Half an hour later, she saw headlights outside and heard the old Dodge Brothers truck grinding along the lane. The Lindquist brothers were back from their Saturday visit to the sale barn with Bobby. It was time to start supper.

Emaline spent the rest of the week getting ready to move back to Calla's house, this time with Bobby. Calla's husband had left her for a woman in North Platte. By renting a room to Emaline, Calla could just manage to keep up the mortgage payments on her house.

Emaline and Bobby rode into town with Lee and Jim on the next Saturday. The Swedes stared out at the fallow fields, figuring what crops their neighbors were likely to plant, noting the difference between fields plowed with tractors and those where the earth had been turned by a team pulling the plow. The tractors never ran as tight to the fence lines as a man could plow with horses. In places the fences were ripped or tilted askew by the great, churning back wheels of the noisy metal beasts, the untidy haste of man and machine. In another month, the Lindquists would hitch their team and begin the work of planting again. They could not afford a tractor, but even if they could, they would have chosen the horses Velma had named Hank and Hap, the two broad-chested, heavy-hocked bay geldings pulling in tandem, as imperfectly wedded humans so rarely did.

After a month with the cheerful crowd at the Arrowhead Diner, Emaline decided she was strong enough to face the task of sorting Velma's things. Charlie Naudain drove her out to the farm on a Saturday afternoon. Calla came along to help. The one thing Emaline particularly wanted was Velma's china, a beautiful Johann Haviland Rose pattern. The china was a wedding gift and Velma had taken enormous pride in it. The set was taken out only for Sunday dinner and then washed and dried and carefully returned to the cupboard.

Lee and Jim were away at church. The door, as always, was unlocked. Inside, the house looked as though it had been plundered. Everything was gone. Crocheted doilies. Hooked rugs. Things Watson had made, a tiny jewel box, a footstool. Vases. Souvenirs from trips up in the Bighorn Mountains. A photograph of Emaline and Ben, taken shortly before they went into the orphanage, had been left on the kitchen table, but the frame that once held it was gone. Even Velma's few dresses and her high-button shoes were missing from the pine wardrobe. The Haviland Rose china was gone. Velma's best silver was gone with it. The little farmhouse was as bare as it had been when Velma first moved in.

Charlie said it didn't look as though anyone had broken in. Whatever was missing, Jim must have given it away. Emaline sat down at the kitchen table, buried her face in her arms, wept. Calla tried to console her, but Emaline waved her away. It was as though her mother had died all over again.

When she ran out of tears, she felt again the dark bubble of anger that had risen within her the day of Velma's funeral. She had stood there in the cemetery, numb in body and soul, watching the toe of Ben's cowboy boot kicking at the dirt beside the grave, yearning for the mercy of snow to muffle the grate of the shovels striking cold earth. Bobby was off by himself, bawling in a grove of pine trees. Jim Lindquist stood next to her with his head bowed, hat in hand. That little preacher started talking, his lips flapping like turkey wattles. *Our dear Velma has gone to a far better place, she dwells in Beulah land.* Emaline had screamed, a piercing scream that echoed over the gravestones. The preacher swallowed whatever he was going to say next and stared at her. She turned on him in a fury. *How do you know she's in a better place, Preacher? How do you know? If heaven is a place where they'd allow the likes of you, it's not good enough for my mama. You kept her in your damned church past midnight on New Year's Eve, that's why she got sick, you stupid man! You stupid man! That's why she's dead!* She would have kicked him in the shins, would have kicked God in the shins if she could get at him, but Ben and Jim lifted her away from the grave and half carried her, sobbing, back to Jim's truck, where Ben sat and tried to comfort her while Jim went to watch the men pile earth on Velma's coffin.

It was all so unjust. Velma was such a good woman, such a brave woman. She was gone too soon and now Jim had given away whatever was left of her. Emaline had been angry at the preacher, angry at God, angry at Eli, but now she was angry at Jim and no one else. She marched outside and paced back and forth in front of the house while Charlie and Calla smoked cigarettes and kept their distance. She was so wrought up she finally asked for a cigarette, took one drag, bent over in a coughing fit, threw it away in disgust. At last she saw the truck coming along the county road at a steady twenty miles an hour with Jim at the wheel.

He was barely out of the truck when she was on him, beating her fists on his broad chest, screaming, crying, so angry that she could not even make him understand why she was furious with him.

"What did you do? What did you do? Where are Mother's things? Where are they? What did you do? Did you give them away?"

"Whoa, girl! Whoa! I didn't give them away, exactly. They came and just took everything."

"Who? Who came and took her things?"

"Well, it was the neighbor ladies. Some took this and some took that. There was Mrs. Albertson and the widow Nagelman and Neal Seavitts, that woman he's married to. I never saw her before, but she was right up front, stuffing things in a gunnysack she brought. Some others too I don't remember, there was eight or ten of them all at once. I was talking to them after the Sunday service last week. They asked about Velma's things, what became of them. I said you hadn't taken any of it and they could come for a look, see if there was anything they wanted. That's all I said. They came by the next day and they didn't hardly leave me and Lee enough to eat on."

"What were you thinking, Jim? How could you let them do that? They're nothing but thieves and vultures, those women. Picking over her things. The nerve of them. They were Velma's things, they belonged to us. That's all we had of her. They weren't yours to give away!"

Jim scuffed a toe in the dirt, embarrassed. Lee backed away, not wanting to put himself in the way of Emaline's wrath. Jim's blue eyes were watery. He looked as though he was feeling as bad as a man could feel.

"I would of said something if I knew you wanted all that. Didn't seem right for me and Lee to keep it all, a couple of bachelors like us. All we need is a frypan and a coffeepot and somethin to eat with, plates and forks and knives. That's about all we got left now they're through, that and the quilts on the beds. I told them not to touch those because I didn't want to freeze to death."

Jim had taken his hat off to greet her. As always when he removed his hat, his hair stuck up like a boy's. It made her unreasonably angry, as though he had acted like a boy instead of a man when he failed to protect Velma's things.

"Of *course* I wanted her things. I couldn't bear to part with any of it. That's why I didn't get it sorted out before. Charlie brought me out here this morning and Calla came to help and it's all gone."

"Gosh, I'm awful sorry, Emaline. Them ladies was so anxious to get their hands on everythin. I guess I ought to said no, but you hadn't said what you wanted to keep, so I let it go."

"My poor mother. In her whole life she never had a man who was worth a damn. Frank was a saddle tramp and Watson was a drunk and you were supposed to be the good one. And now look what you've done."

Emaline turned away and walked on shaky legs to Charlie's car. She slid into the back seat and Calla rode with Charlie up front and as they pulled out, Jim was still standing there in the driveway, holding his hat and looking positively stricken. She rode back to the city with her face buried in her hands. She thought of asking Charlie to take her around to the farmhouses of every one of those women who had taken Velma's things, but she didn't have the stomach for it. She didn't even know who they all were. It was almost worse than the day Velma died, as though she had now vanished forever. Except for the bundles of letters Velma had written over the years, there was nothing left.

The Burning Man came to her in her dreams that night, as he had so many times since she was a girl. He was an Indian warrior, tall as a lodgepole pine, with coppery skin and black hair down to his waist and hair that burned day and night with a celestial light, without harming him or causing him pain. She imagined that he was the spirit of a great Lakota warrior, perhaps Crazy Horse himself. He wore a fringed deerskin shirt with fur cuffs made from a beaver hide, a bear-tooth necklace and deerskin leggings and he carried a lance decorated with eagle feathers. Emaline followed him in a soft white antelope-skin dress decorated with porcupine quills, with wolf skins over her shoulders and deerhide leggings. She wore snowshoes as they trudged across icy rivers and frozen lakes, under bare aspen trees, poplar and pine, past rocky outcrops tall as a dozen houses, through canyons where she could hear water flowing under the ice, across snow-covered prairies where there was no other soul for a thousand miles save her and the man with his hair on fire. On and on they traveled under a splash of stars, with no sound but the crunch of the snow underfoot. When she faltered, he would pause and wait patiently, long coils of flame dancing around his face. Sometimes the fire in his hair would leap to the stars, to the edge of the universe, shimmer in all the colors of the rainbow from the mountains up to the Milky Way.

They never paused or ate, slept or rested, yet she never grew tired. Her legs felt light, her lungs clear, the trail easy even when they were climbing the steepest mountain slopes. Now and then her dream veered to panic, when she glanced away for a moment, distracted by some small animal in the snow or the flight of an owl, and lost sight of the Burning Man. Then she would see where the trail dipped down to the left or rose to the right. There he would be, turned slightly toward her, his hair in coils of flame, waiting. She would hurry to catch up. He would be close enough that she could almost touch his hand. Then he would take a single step and be far beyond her reach. No matter how hard she tried, she could never quite get close enough to touch him.

She heard a wolf howl and then another and saw the great head of the Burning Man nod to his brother the wolf. The hand holding the lance went up and pumped three times. He was pointing to the east, into the rising sun.

8.

Juanita supervised Eli's meals at the hospital, listened when he complained about the itching inside his cast, checked two or three times a day for signs of infection around the incision where his spleen had been removed, changed his bedpan, tried to prepare him for the ordeal ahead. A man as strong and fit as Eli would be able to navigate on crutches, but the separated shoulder and the broken collarbone meant that he couldn't put the weight on a crutch, so he'd be bound to a wheelchair for at least a month, edgy as a coyote in a cage.

Mercifully, he slept most of the first week. When he was awake, he tried to tend to ranch business, making notes for Ezra about things that needed to be done, worrying about the snow cover, how thin the cattle were, the spread of foot rot, whether any of the cows that should be giving birth in the spring had dropped their calves prematurely. Juanita checked out books from the library and sat reading while Eli slept. Sometimes he'd wake from a nap and reach out for her, take her hand and hold it without saying a word.

At the hospital, Juanita saw for the first time the scar around his neck. He had always worn a bandanna, summer and winter. With his neck uncovered, she could plainly see the mark of an old and vicious rope burn. Once as he slept, she traced the raised welt of the scar with her fingertips. She had heard the rumor that, in his youth, Eli had miraculously survived despite being hung as a horse thief. Ezra had been along on that caper, the way she heard it, and Teeter Spawn, the old cowhand who taught the Paint twins most of what they knew about the cattle business. Until she saw the scar around Eli's neck, Juanita had assumed that it was one of those tall tales American cowboys liked to tell. One day, she would persuade him to tell her the truth about what had happened along the Powder River back in that awful spring of 1887. It might explain why he was so stubborn and unyielding. She knew from something brittle inside herself that trauma endured at a tender age can mark a person forever.

By Valentine's Day, Eli felt stronger. Now his worst enemy was boredom. Doc Miller said he had to be kept snubbed tight to the hitching post, where he could be doctored as the need arose. The hospital was the best place to recover. The doctor would not relent, so Eli fidgeted, frustrated that he could not get back to the ranch.

They were going to need an automobile to replace the Cadillac, so Ezra bought a roomy 1928 Pontiac sedan. On the second Saturday that Eli was in the hospital, Ezra and Ben and the six youngest Paint children all piled into the car for the trip to the hospital. The children hadn't visited Eli since the accident. Their presence cheered him considerably. Juanita had never seen him as tender with anyone as he was with Leo. Eli asked them all about their schoolwork, issued instructions for work he wanted done, reminded them that he wouldn't tolerate any slugabeds sleeping past six o'clock in the morning. Then they all trooped out for hamburgers and Eli sat for an hour with Ezra. Juanita got up to leave them to talk business, but Eli asked her to stay.

"I've got no secrets from you, Juanita," he said. "Might help if you understand what we're up against."

Ezra was to meet separately with each of the four banks that held notes on the 8T8 ranch to negotiate extensions on the loans. If they needed a reason, Eli's accident would do. Ezra could remind them all that they had made a good deal of money dealing with Eli Paint in the past and would again, but not if they chose to squeeze him now. When he was up and around, he would find ways to see to it that the banks were paid, even if it meant selling part of the ranch. In the meantime, they could show a little patience.

"If they try to put the hammerlock on you, don't give 'em an inch. Bankers are like buzzards. If they think a critter is crippled and can't defend himself, they'll swoop down and start pluckin his guts while he's still alive. Snarl at 'em a little bit and they'll back off. Remember how we dealt with Bly Olp back in Brown County? We put the fear of God in that sonofabitch. Do the same with these fellas, but only if you have to. Go in easy, but if they start to push, you push back twice as hard. Tell them right off that there are four banks involved and the other three have already agreed to give us until fall to work things out. Bankers are like sheep following a goat—they don't think for themselves, they just do what the other fella does. Makes 'em feel like they're all bein smart together."

Ezra wanted to offer more help. "If they're squeezin too hard, we can always sell some of the Appaloosas. I got a fella down in Argentina will pay good money for a studhorse and five or six broodmares. Would be enough to buy you some time."

"I can't let you do that, Ez. That Appaloosa operation is yours. It has nothing to do with the rest of the ranch. That's why I signed those five thousand acres over to you. There aint no way the sonsofbitches can touch it."

All his life, Eli had been too busy for hobbies. Too busy to read, too busy to play checkers or poker, too busy to go to the picture show. Now he had time on his hands and nothing to do. Juanita tried to read to him from the books she liked, but his mind would drift. She rummaged around the hospital and found a stack of twenty-cent *Best Detective* magazines from 1930. She thought he would scoff at made-up stories, but he devoured them and sent her out in search of more. She found more detective magazines and two beat-up novels by a writer named Dashiell Hammett, *The Glass Key* and *The Maltese Falcon*. Eli read slowly, but within a week, he had finished both.

The evening he finished *The Maltese Falcon*, he put the book down and lay for a time staring at the ceiling. They could hear the wind picking up outside, another storm blowing in, more work for everyone on the 8T8. Eli took Juanita's hand. "With the wreck and all, we never got to talk. I thought about it all the way home, and then I was so buggered up I couldn't talk at all."

"It's all right. I didn't expect you to talk. I'm glad you're alive."

"I'm a lucky man, but I have to do better with my own, startin with you."

"Why me?"

"Because I don't know what I'd have done without you these past four years."

"You would have found somebody."

"No. Not somebody like you. The night I called you from Casper, it felt so good to hear your voice. When I thought I was going to die out there, I was real sorry I wouldn't get a chance to talk to you. Thing is, Juanita, I've been the same as a widower for six or seven years now. Ida Mae was lost to me a long while ago, maybe even before we left Nebraska back in 1927. She was never the easiest woman in the world to get along with. But Ida Mae was good to me until one day it was like somebody else took over her body. I'm not complaining, understand, I'm just sayin how things have been. Except for you and the kids, I've been a man alone. And I've seen how you are with the kids and how you are with me. You're a very wise woman, Juanita, and I'm plumb crazy over you."

"Plumb crazy? What is that?"

"It means I'm in love with you."

"With me?"

"Well, I aint in love with Willie Thaw."

She laughed. "Me too."

"You're not in love with Willie either?"

"No, silly. I am in love with you. *Te quiero mucho.* But you know that. You must. Sometimes I look at you when you're not watching and then you turn your head and I think you must know. It has been like this for two years. Perhaps longer."

"Two years. I'll be damned. Sometimes, a man don't see what's in front of his face. I was afraid if I told you what I was thinking, you might pack your bags and go back to Mexico."

"Never. Unless you want me to go."

"Only if you take me along. I've never been south of the border."

"Someday I will take you, then."

They fell silent for a time, Juanita lightly stroking his hand. He studied her face in the lamplight. "You never talk about Mexico, you know. You lived there until you were almost thirty, but you never mention the place."

"That is not true. I talk about things I learned from Dr. Hodgson."

"You tell me about medical things and how much you admired the doctor. You never talk about your life there. How you lived. I don't even know exactly where you're from."

"I am from Chihuahua. Do you know it?"

"I've heard the name. Is that a state?"

"Yes. It's also a town. Chihuahua, the capital of Chihuahua. We have desert and forests, but I come from the mountains, the Sierra Madre. A small village outside the town of Cuauhtémoc."

"Tell me about your life there. What it was like."

Juanita hesitated, looking at her hands. "Are you sure you want to know these things? It is not a pretty story."

"I want to know."

She listened to the wind. It was blowing hard outside. She thought of the night they found Eli, the towering plumes of snow blowing in the wind. She would tell him the story.

"I was happy when I was a girl. My father, Alberto, was a tailor. I had two brothers, Cristiano and Hernando. They were almost men, working in the tailor shop with my father. He had a good business. It was small, but there was always work. There were rich men who would not allow anyone else to clothe them.

"Then Pancho Villa came to my village, with about five hundred of his men. It was 1916. I was fifteen years old. Villa had crossed the border and killed some Yankees in New Mexico, in a town called Columbus. Your General Pershing chased Villa into Mexico, but he could not catch him. Villa hid for a few days in our village. Pershing was looking for him, so was Venustiano Carranza. My mother made me hide in the cellar. She was afraid Villa's men would take me and do terrible things. I lived for three days and three nights in the cellar with only a candle, listening to rats and cockroaches. Sometimes I would hear girls screaming. When Villa and his men left, they were a mile outside our village and someone started shooting. No one knows who fired the shots. Maybe it was the father of a girl who had been raped. One of the soldiers was killed and two others were wounded. Villa came back into the village and said that eight men would be hanged because one of his had been killed. They took the first men they found. My father's shop was right there, in the square, so they grabbed my father and my brothers and beat them so badly that we could not tell my brothers apart. Then they were hanged with the others, from lampposts in the plaza. After Villa left, my mother and I had to cut them down so that we could bury them.

"The mayor was so afraid of Villa he would not allow any of the dead to be buried in the cemetery. We had to get a wagon and take them up in the hills and dig their graves. The ground was rocky, we couldn't dig very deep. We put stones on their graves, but we knew the wolves would get them sooner or later. I made the sign of the cross, but my mother was angry with me. She said I should not bow to the church that abandoned us. The priests were too afraid of Villa to say the truth, to tell people that he was a monster."

Eli took her hand but said nothing.

"After Villa left, Venustiano Carranza's men came to the village. Carranza wanted Villa too, the same way Pershing wanted him. The Carrancistas thought the people in the village were helping Villa and the rebels. They started fires in our neighborhood as a warning. Our house burned with the rest. We lost almost everything."

"How did you survive?"

"My mother was a good seamstress. I worked with her for a time. Then Dr. Hodgson came to the village. I thought he was a wonderful man, young and hardworking. He had studied medicine at Yale, he was very brilliant. He wanted to help people, so he came to Mexico. My mother was one of his first patients. His American nurse had left after one week to go back to the United States, so he needed a nurse. He saw that I was interested in medicine and I learned quickly, so he trained me. My mother did not live long after that. After my father and brothers died, she did not want to live. Dr. Hodgson paid for her funeral. He stayed three years in the village. We were still in the village when Ezra came through, buying and selling horses. He made Wyoming sound like a wonderful place. When Dr. Hodgson got sick with the tuberculosis, he wrote to Ezra. That's how we came to the great state of Wyoming."

"I admired Doc Hodgson. I didn't know him well, but he seemed like a good man."

"He was a very great man. Very intelligent, very kind. He worked so hard to help people. He thought medicine was a gift. If you had the gift of medicine, you had to share. He never thought of money. Many patients never paid him at all, or they would give him tortillas, or a pig, or a load of bricks. He was disorganized and his hair was always a mess and he would put on the wrong clothes always, things that didn't go together. He could remember everything he read in his medical books, but he could never remember anyone's name. I learned all the names of our patients. I would say their names when they came in so the doctor would know them. He thought everyone was basically good inside. He was on the side of the revolution, which was a good revolution at first until people like Pancho Villa got too much power. It took me a long time to convince him that there are men like Villa in the world, men with no good in them at all. When Dr. Hodgson first came to Mexico, he thought Villa was like Robin Hood. Fighting the big planters and the banks, the U.S. corporations that wanted to run everything in our country. Someone had to fight for the people against all those things, but Villa did as much harm as they did. He was evil, but Dr. Hodgson never wanted to see evil, not even when it was right in front of him."

"And you married him."

"Yes, but not until I had been his nurse for a very long time. First we worked in my village, then in Chihuahua city for two years, then Mexico City. It was very exciting there, he had famous friends. The painter Frida Kahlo and her husband, Diego Rivera. He helped to care for Frida after she was terribly hurt in a bus accident. He said he never saw anyone endure so much pain. They loved him because he was an American and a doctor and he tried to help the Mexican people. After we had been together for twelve years, he asked me to marry him. We had only a few months as man and wife before he discovered he had tuberculosis."

"The same disease that killed Velma."

"Yes. Now we have both lost someone to this disease. He remembered Wyoming, the way your brother talked about it. We moved to Sheridan for the clean air, but it didn't help. He died."

"That's when Ezra brought you to us, after Doc Hodgson died and you couldn't get hired as a nurse. I'm awful sorry to hear what happened to you, Juanita. It's terrible, the things human beings will do to one another."

There was nothing more to say. They sat listening to the hospital sounds, nurses chatting, gurneys wheeled up and down the hallway, someone moaning in pain. Eli had always thought that there was forged steel in Juanita, a quality of strength not unlike his own. Now he knew why.

9.

A WEEK LATER, ELI CHECKED HIMSELF OUT OF the hospital. Juanita had returned to the ranch to look after the children, Ben Hughes happened to be in Sheridan on a Saturday to buy a new saddle after a bronc tore his old piece of leather to bits. Ben had supper with Belle Swank, a tobacco-chewing rancher's daughter he was sweet on, then went by the hospital to see if Eli needed anything. He found his grandfather sitting up, fully dressed. Eli greeted him with a smile a yard wide.

"Ben. By gosh. Just what the doctor ordered."

"What are you doin out of bed?"

"I've got to get home, Ben. I've had all I can take of this place. I was thinkin I might just head out and hitchhike back to the ranch. I managed to get myself dressed, but I'm played out. But now you're here, you can take me home."

"You can't walk. How were you going to hitchhike?"

"Is there some law against a man in a wheelchair hitchin a ride?"

"I suppose not, but what's Doc Miller say about you goin home?"

"Nothin at all. It's my busted-up old body, not his."

"You sure you're goin to get along all right at home?"

"Juanita's a nurse, whether she's got the papers for it or not. She can look after me. I can't stand this place one more night. Woman down the hall has been screamin and carryin on, a man can't get a wink of sleep. If you stay around a place where people are dyin long enough, you'll die yourself."

Ben was not in the habit of saying no to his grandfather. He carried his satchel while Eli wheeled himself down the corridor. When the night nurse asked where they were going, Eli kept right on rolling.

"Home."

"You can't go home, Mr. Paint. You haven't been released."

"The hell I can't. I just now released myself."

"I can't let you do that, Mr. Paint."

Eli spun the wheelchair to face her. "Ma'am, I have set still in this hospital long enough. You folks have taken right good care of me, but I'm through here. This is my grandson, Ben Hughes. Aint he a fine-lookin young man? He's big and strong enough to pick me up, wheelchair and all, and set me in the back of his truck. The two of us are goin out that door now. I don't expect to be back anytime soon."

"You have to sign some papers."

"No, I don't. If you need papers signed, you mail 'em out to the 8T8 ranch and I'll sign 'em and send 'em back. If it's gettin paid you're worried about, send me the bill. You know I'm good for it."

She shrugged. "Well, I guess I can't stop you unless I call the orderlies. I'm not going to do that."

The nurse had a heavy, weary face under a dark thatch of hair. She had come to work in this place as a young girl and now she was almost an old woman, too old to fret over a patient as bullheaded as Eli Paint. He was old enough to do as he pleased. She had plenty of other patients to worry about.

It was a cool, breezy evening, a whiff of snow in the air. There was a storm coming, it would be good to get home before it hit. Ben helped Eli get settled in Ezra's old Ford Model TT truck and stowed the wheelchair in the back. Eli winced now and then, but he didn't complain. They were halfway home when he asked Ben how the Appaloosas were doing.

"They're good."

"He told me he had a fella down in Argentina who might take a bunch of horses. I told him not to sell any for the sake of the ranch."

"Yep. Ezra is talking like he might send me along to Argentina to make sure them horses get there safe. He'd send them to New Orleans by train and from there by ship to Buenos Aires. Once I get down there, he wants me to take a look around, see about setting up a Appaloosa outfit."

"You don't say. Argentina. It's quite an old world, Ben."

"It is that."

"That's what a young man ought to do. Get out and see the world."

Eli thought for a time about Ben going all the way to Argentina, maybe looking to settle down there, and figured he ought to say something while he had the chance.

"Ben, you're a grown man now. You go where you please and you do what feels right to you. But it's important to stick close to your own. Young men your age, they always want to ramble. But when you settle down, settle near your people. If you get the chance to go down to Argentina, stay awhile, have a good look around. Then come back and settle down right here. I've known old Strother Swank for thirty years. His daughter is a fine gal. You can't do better than Belle, even if she does chew tobacco and she barely comes up to your belt buckle. You come back and marry her, we'll carve out of a piece of the 8T8 for the two of you. I don't like the notion of you livin your life way out at the end of the world."

Ben mumbled something about how he liked Wyoming and didn't want to stay away too long and let it go at that. It seemed like Eli was trying to reach out to him in a way he never had before. He wished he had a better answer.

✦ ✦ ✦

When Ben turned off the main track toward the house, Eli saw where he'd gone wrong the night of the wreck. There was no danger that Ben would miss the turn, crawling along in second gear in the noisy old truck. The house appeared suddenly, as it always had whether you approached it on horseback or by automobile. You topped a rise and there it was, a fourteen-room mansion built back in the 1880s by Sir Humphrey Doane as a home for his highborn English bride. The woman never saw the place. She deserted Sir Humphrey for the owner of a coffee plantation in Africa. When Eli first saw the ranch in 1886, it was known as the O-Bar and the house was inhabited by a no-account Texas gunslinger named Dermott Cull, the same Dermott Cull who had once slipped a rope around Eli's neck. Eli had waited a very long time to buy this ranch and refurbished the house at great expense. Now he could not approach it without a mingled sense of pride, regret, yearning. As long as Ida Mae lived in the house, he had always approached that porticoed facade with dread, never knowing what was in store, whether she would greet him with a smile and a bowl of soup or silent, tight-lipped rage or a screaming, dish-throwing tantrum. Now he saw the kitchen light was on and knew that Juanita was awake. It galled him that he had to wait for Ben to get his wheelchair down, ease him into it, then park it at the bottom of the steps while he went to get Juanita. The temperature was below zero and a cold wind whistled from the west, but she came to the door in a thin dress, hands on her hips, and demanded to know just exactly what it was that he thought he was doing.

"You know you should have stayed in the hospital until they said you could go home. Sometimes doctors know what they're doing."

"I got no disagreement with that. Only I was ready to be home."

"Ezra says you're the most bullheaded man alive."

"I wouldn't care to argue that. Now are you goin to leave me out here to freeze to death or help me to get indoors?"

Juanita said it was safer to let Eli rest his weight on her while Ben hoisted the wheelchair indoors. Then they both supported him while he hopped up the steps on his good leg. She got him settled on the davenport with his broken leg propped up and asked Ben if he wanted supper.

Ben shook his head. "Thanks, Juanita. I had supper in town with Belle. I'd best get home to bed. Ezra starts in early, even on a Sunday mornin."

Juanita saw him out and poured Eli two fingers of whiskey, brought her cocoa, sat next to him. She leaned her head on his shoulder.

"You should not have left the hospital, but I'm glad you're home."

"That's good to know. The way you looked at me at first, I thought you were goin to send me back."

"No. I can look after you. But we should get Doc Miller over to examine you first thing Monday, just in case."

"I've got no objection, as long as I don't have to go back to the hospital. Where are my kids? I thought I'd have a reception committee waitin out here."

"Not if you don't tell us you're coming. The girls are all back at the Ewing ranch again, where they want to go every weekend now. It's because the Ewings have a radio and they have a barn dance to the radio every Saturday night. You're going to have to buy a radio. I know you think it's a frivolous nuisance, but the age they are, they want to listen to *Amos 'n' Andy* and Jack Benny. It wouldn't do any harm."

"I expect not. I did say I was going to try to put a little more slack in my rope, didn't I?"

"You did."

"And what about the boys? They ought to be here, they got chores to do."

"They are. They've taken to sleeping down in the bunkhouse. They said they're getting an early start on roundup."

"That's two months yet."

"If I let them, they'd sleep out in the snow. There's plenty of room in the bunkhouse. We've only got Zeke and Willie down there until the extra hands start coming for roundup. I went down myself to have a little talk with Willie, told him no whiskey when the boys are around."

"Willie's been drinkin again, has he?"

"I don't know that. I just want to be sure he doesn't get drunk around the boys."

Eli caught something in her tone. "Don't protect him, Juanita. I know what Willie is. He's got the sharpest eye for livestock I ever saw, but he aint much good when he's into the sauce. All around, the best hand I've ever seen is Two Spuds. If Willie keeps drinkin, I'll give him his walkin papers and let Spuds have the job."

Juanita asked how Eli was doing with the cast on his leg. "Itches like hell. Get me a hacksaw. I'll saw the damned thing off myself."

"You know you can't do that."

"Yes, I do know. I haven't had such a heap of motherin since I was knee-high to a grasshopper, you know that?"

"I'm sorry."

"No need to be sorry. I expect I needed it. After you left the hospital, it dawned on me that I hadn't thanked you hardly at all. You and Two Spuds saved my life. I am mighty grateful to both of you."

"You don't need to say that. I was doing what I'm trained to do."

She poured him another two fingers of whiskey, offered a toast to his homecoming with her cocoa.

"We have some hard work ahead," she said. "We have to get you on crutches, then we have to start to strengthen that leg and get you more flexible at the same time. You might never be quite the same as you were, but we'll get you as close as we can, all right?"

"You're the boss."

"No, actually. You're the boss. Except when it comes to the things we have to do to get you better. Then I am the boss, for a while."

Eli drained his whiskey and she poured him another. He rarely drank, but when he did, he drank quickly.

"God, I'm just so damned grateful to you, Juanita."

She held a finger to his lips. Something had shifted between them, or perhaps it was only that they both understood how things were and what would happen next. She turned and straddled him, undid the buttons on the front of her dress, tugged it down over her shoulders, slipped her shift over her head. He brushed his cheek back and forth on her nipples. Her breasts were tiny, her skin smooth and brown. He took one breast into his mouth and then the other, nibbled in circles in a way that made her catch her breath. She bent to kiss him. Once and then again, the tender mercy of kisses.

The blizzard hit in the wee hours of the night. Eli started to reach for his boots, then sank back onto the bed. He was in no shape to be staggering around in a snowstorm. If there was one thing he had learned in forty-odd years working on the range, it was that there is not a blessed thing a man can do about a blizzard. He buried his lips in Juanita's neck, felt her push her bare flank into his groin. He hoped it would snow pretty much forever.

10.

IT WAS ELEVEN O'CLOCK IN THE MORNING IN THE Nebraska panhandle when the new president began to speak. It was a Saturday, the fourth day of March 1933. The wind rose outside, spackling the windows with grit. Emaline and Calla had taped the windows again the night before and hung wet sheets over the doors and windows to keep out the dust, but still it filtered through. Emaline wished Bobby was with her to hear it, but he had grabbed his .22 and left at dawn to go hunting down by the river. She turned the dial to get the station clearly, enchanted not only because Franklin Delano Roosevelt was speaking but because it was possible to listen to him way out here on the High Plains, two thousand miles from Washington. There were preachers who railed against the radio, calling it the instrument of the devil and the serpent of the airwaves. Emaline was sure those preachers had never sat through a winter alone in a farmhouse, with the maddening wind rattling the door. For farm women watching the dust blow in summer and the snow drift against the house in winter, a radio brought a little sweetening into their harsh days. If it was a sin to listen, then she was going to have a lot of company in hell.

She adjusted the volume and leaned closer to hear his words. His voice gave her goose bumps.

This great Nation will endure as it has endured, will revive and will prosper. So, first of all, let me assert my firm belief that the only thing we have to fear is fear itself . . .

Emaline felt a shiver of excitement. Surely this was what was needed. A leader who understood how bad things really were, a man who could chart a path out of the wilderness of debt and failure and foreclosure.

In every dark hour of our national life a leadership of frankness and vigor has met with that understanding and support of the people themselves which is essential to victory. I am convinced that you will again give that support to leadership in these critical days.

In such a spirit on my part and on yours we face our common difficulties. They concern, thank God, only material things. . . . The means of exchange are frozen in the currents of trade; the withered leaves of industrial enterprise lie on every side; farmers find no markets for their produce; the savings of many years in thousands of families are gone.

More important, a host of unemployed citizens face the grim problem of existence, and an equally great number toil with little return. Only a foolish optimist can deny the dark realities of the moment.

A foolish optimist. That would be Herbert Hoover. Hoovervilles had sprung up all over America, named for this inept and insensitive president, shantytowns for the desperate and broken. Now Hoover was gone at last and FDR was saying what millions felt but could not put into words.

Yet our distress comes from no failure of substance. We are stricken by no plague of locusts. Compared with the perils which our forefathers conquered because they believed and were not afraid,

> we have still much to be thankful for. Nature still offers her bounty. . . . Plenty is at our doorstep, but a generous use of it languishes in the very sight of the supply. . . .
>
> The money changers have fled from their high seats in the temple of our civilization. We may now restore that temple to the ancient truths. The measure of the restoration lies in the extent to which we apply social values more noble than mere monetary profit.
>
> Happiness lies not in the mere possession of money; it lies in the joy of achievement, in the thrill of creative effort. The joy and moral stimulation of work no longer must be forgotten in the mad chase of evanescent profits. These dark days will be worth all they cost us if they teach us that our true destiny is not to be ministered unto but to minister to ourselves and to our fellow men.

Would people learn? she wondered. Or would they go back to grabbing all they could grab as soon as the depression was over? Men put so much stock in money and property and possessions. Velma had always been disgusted when a wealthy banker or stockbroker killed himself because he had lost his money. She had survived two long stays in the National Jewish Hospital for Consumptives, listened through the endless nights to women coughing away their lives, watched in the morning when the cheerful, whistling orderlies gathered from the bedposts the bags stuffed with cloths soaked in blood and sputum, took the bags out past the dairy and set fire to them, warming themselves over bonfires made with the rags of the dying. The women in the sanitarium had fought so hard to live. Fought and asked for nothing except to be able to breathe freely, to have the strength to get up and walk out of that hospital on their own two legs. Some had lived, like Velma, long past their time, with so very little. You couldn't live on nothing, but you could live on a little, if you had a roof over your head and fuel for the stove, enough to eat and clothes on your back. Roosevelt seemed to understand that clearly, but Emaline wondered if folks would grasp his message and join him in the struggle to put America on a different course.

> Recognition of the falsity of material wealth as the standard of success goes hand in hand with the abandonment of the false belief that public office and high political position are to be valued only by the standards of pride of place and personal profit; and there must be an end to a conduct in banking and in business which too often has given to a sacred trust the likeness of callous and selfish wrongdoing. Small wonder that confidence languishes, for it thrives only on honesty, on honor, on the sacredness of obligations, on faithful protection, on unselfish performance; without them it cannot live.

To be unselfish. That alone would require a great change in the way people lived. Emaline had known one truth since she was a girl. The poor helped one another, the rich helped themselves. Hoboes had come knocking at Velma's door almost every day, they were never turned away. Sometimes, if things were good, they got a sit-down meal. Other times, it was only a little dry bread or whatever she could spare. The tramps passed it along as common wisdom, never knock at a rich man's door.

> Our greatest primary task is to put people to work. . . . The task can be helped by definite efforts to raise the values of agricultural products and with this the power to purchase the output of our cities. It can be helped by preventing realistically the tragedy of the growing loss through foreclosure of our small homes and our farms. . . .
>
> Finally, in our progress toward a resumption of work we require two safeguards against a return of the evils of the old order: there must be a strict supervision of all banking and credits and

> investments; so that there will be an end to speculation with other people's money; and there must be provision for an adequate but sound currency.

Emaline did not begin to understand Wall Street or the forces that had brought America to its knees, but the president seemed to understand very clearly. That was enough for her.

> If I read the temper of our people correctly, we now realize as we have never realized before our interdependence on each other; that we can not merely take but we must give as well; that if we are to go forward, we must move as a trained and loyal army willing to sacrifice for the good of a common discipline, because without such discipline no progress is made, no leadership becomes effective.

Emaline had heard people say the new president was arrogant, a rich easterner who was trying to fool common folk, but she didn't believe that for a minute. He was proof that there were still a few wealthy men who would sacrifice themselves for their country.

> We face the arduous days that lie before us in the warm courage of national unity; with the clear consciousness of seeking old and precious moral values; with the clean satisfaction that comes from the stern performance of duty by old and young alike. . . .
>
> In this dedication of a Nation we humbly ask the blessing of God. May He protect each and every one of us. May He guide me in the days to come.

When he finished speaking, she was so happy that she wept. She was fearful too, because she had seen up close how bad things really were. If there was one man who could guide the nation out of the wilderness, they had found him. He was like the Burning Man of her dreams, a beacon for the whole country to follow.

The next day, she got Charlie and Calla to take her out to the Lindquist farm again while Lee and Jim were away at church. When the Swedes came home, she had a big roast beef dinner waiting for them. She hugged Jim a good long while and apologized for getting so angry with him over Velma's things. He had been far too kind for her to stay mad at him for long. He was a good man, as good as any she had ever met. Those women had simply taken advantage of his sweet nature.

Over dinner, they got to talking about the president and the things he had to say. For the first time since the country went skidding into this depression, they were all hopeful. He couldn't fix everything at once, but he was going to make a start. Roosevelt would try to help the working man. That was more than Hoover ever did.

II.

EZRA PAINT CRAWLED OUT OF HIS BUNK WHILE IT was still darker than a stack of black cats. It was the first day of April 1933, the sixty-third birthday of the Paint twins. Juanita was baking a cake, there would be a quiet get-together at the big house. He rose cursing old age and forgotten horses, stoked the fire in the cabin, stepped outdoors in his stocking feet to pee. He peered to the east for some sign of dawn and saw nothing but streaks of pale cloud over a river of stars. He limped back inside and heard Ben still snoring on his cot. Ezra wondered how it was that, at twenty-one, Ben seemed to need about ten hours sleep a night while Ezra could make do with half as much. It ought to be the other way round. The more useless an old man became, the less sleep he needed.

He went through his usual morning ritual in front of the coal stove, edging his stiff back as close to the blaze as he could get without lighting his behind on fire and touching his toes a half dozen times. He put coffee on to perk, pulled on his flannel shirt and overalls. When the coffee was ready, he poured a tin mug black as the night outside and sat munching cold biscuits and drinking hot coffee, feeling stove up as an old banty rooster.

Most mornings, he would rouse Ben to help with the chores, but on this day, Ezra had decided to give himself a birthday present and he wanted to think it over a bit more before Ben got up. When he had finished the biscuits, Ezra drained the coffee, put on his boots, headed out to the corrals. In the dark he heard the whuff and stomp of the Appaloosas in the darkness, the whip crack of their short, stiff tails. He forked hay to them, shook buckets of oats into their troughs, checked the left front hoof of a mare he had seen limping the day before. These horses were his livelihood and passion. They were the best stock horses a man could own, in his opinion, intelligent and quick-footed and beautiful to boot. He visited the warm stall where Sourdough Biscuit, his prize studhorse, led a life of luxury. He rubbed the stallion's coat with rough fingers and promised him a good, long ride out on the prairie later.

He got around to the little Jersey milk cow after the horses were fed. He liked milking, always had, the *sssss . . . sssss . . . sssssss . . .* of the long streams of milk foaming into the bucket, the warmth of the little cow's flank against his cheek. Mabel had many virtues, including a docile disposition and the ability to produce rich, creamy milk, but her best quality was that she was a good listener.

"Aint it a fine mornin, Mabel? A little brisk, I'll grant you that, but you can just about feel spring poppin through. Before you know it the columbine will be out."

He turned a stream of milk into the mouth of a mewing cat. "Mornin, puss. You might as well hear this too, so come on over. I made up my mind. Today's the day I aim to have a little talk with the boy. There aint no way to know how it will set with him if I don't come right out and ask. What do you think, girl? You don't believe he'll turn me down, do you?"

Mabel did not voice an opinion, so Ezra gave her bag a last squeeze and used her tail to hoist himself to his feet. Back inside the cabin, he tapped Ben on the shoulder.

"Up and at 'em, son. I want you to drop your twine on that big gray and ride some of the sass out of him this morning."

Ben tugged on his britches and boots and sat at the table, trying to pry his eyes open while Ezra cracked eggs into the frying pan, two for himself and four for Ben. Ben washed down the eggs and a wedge of bacon with three big glasses of milk and a cup of coffee that was about two parts sugar and one part coffee, bolting his breakfast off an old tin plate of Ezra's that bore a layered trail of old suppers taken next to campfires and blizzard meals eaten cold as a banker's heart. Ezra liked to see Ben eat. The youngster was big enough to wrestle steers. A fellow that size had to eat.

Ezra didn't have children of his own, so he was determined to teach Ben everything a young man ought to know. Teeter Spawn had begun Ben's schooling before he died, taught him how to track a man in rough country, how to weave a rawhide lariat and deal a crooked poker hand. Now the rest was up to Ezra.

Once the breakfast dishes were scraped and stacked, they ambled down to the training corral. Walking behind Ben, Ezra could see Frank's long legs and the Paint shoulders and maybe a little of his grandmother Livvy in the way he carried himself, but when the boy got near a horse, he was all Frank Hughes, the image of his father. It was a shame Frank had been killed fighting Germans at Belleau Wood, because any man would be proud to see the way Ben and horses just slid to each other, comfortable and easy. Ben's way from the first day was Frank's. Let the horse come to you and bring your string into tune with his, like a man getting ready to play the fiddle at a square dance. It was odd how a boy could inherit that, the same way Ben had inherited the straight black Lakota hair and the strange, pale gray eyes of the Paint clan. With horses, Ezra only had to tell him a thing once. Sometimes, he seemed to know without being told at all.

It was barely daylight when Ben took the lariat from Ezra and vaulted the fence, moving easily as the horses shifted away from him. The stallion was a beauty, gray the color of cast iron, a rump mottled with white spots, arched neck, a black mane and tail. He had been shipped from Oregon, where he was named Nitro for his tendency to explode. They said he had injured a man or two, that getting him loaded on the train for the journey to Wyoming had taken eight men two hours. Ezra and Ben had no trouble getting him onto a trailer to haul him out to the ranch, but getting him saddle-broke could be a chore.

There were three horses between Ben and the gray. He waited for them to move, building his loop carefully down beside his thigh so as not to spook the horse. The others slid away and the skittish gray lifted his head just as Ben tossed the loop and caught him clean around the neck. Nitro spooked and backed hard, slinging his head and fighting the rope, but Ben hitched the rope behind his hip for leverage and held him tight. Once the gray stood still with his nostrils flared and flanks rippling, Ben made the rope fast with a double half hitch over a corral post and saddled and bridled him before he slipped the lariat off the gray's neck. Ezra perched on the rail next to the saddle, offering a steady stream of advice.

"Don't mind if he fights you a bit, he'll do that. Just don't let him get away with a solitary thing. If he beats you once and you let him, he'll keep beatin you and you'll never get the nasty out of him."

Ben nodded, feeling the strength of the animal. He knew everything Ezra was telling him, but Ezra needed to feel he still had something to teach, so Ben went along with it. Horses were big, strong, dangerous, so it didn't hurt to be reminded about things you already knew. Once he had double-checked the cinch, he swung into the saddle and the gray hopped a little to the side. He rode through it easily and held the gray and turned him to the right, toward the corral fence, then left to get him on the correct lead as he eased into a canter. The gray did three turns around the circular corral.

Neither of them saw it coming. On the fourth circuit around the corral, Nitro crow-hopped three times and then shook loose like a saddle bronc at the Cheyenne Frontier Days. Ben was so surprised that the gray almost threw him. He lost a stirrup, fumbled for it with a booted toe, found it just as the horse went into a tight, spinning turn. Ben had to grab for the saddle horn to stay on. As he did, the horse slammed into the corral fence, wedging Ben's knee between the horse's weight and an unyielding, creosote-soaked railroad tie set three feet down into the hardpan. Ezra heard Ben shout with pain and yelled at him to jump clear, but Ben was not willing to give up. The gray reared as high as he could go and came close to going over backward, but Ben's weight on his neck was enough to bring him down. Another series of crow hops jolted Ben's spine, but he hung on and managed to rein the horse away from another collision with the fence as he fishtailed across the corral and brought him to a splay-legged halt, the lathered stallion with his head down between his legs and white foam around the curb bit in his mouth.

Ben eased to the ground and winced when he put his weight on the leg that had hit the post. He got the saddle and bridle off the horse and limped over to where Ezra was perched on the rail.

"Doggone. He like to broke my leg."

"Maybe I ought to take you into the hospital."

"Naw. It'll be sore as hell for a few days, but I'll be all right. I'll have to go at him slow. I can't figure why he went off like that. What happened? He was goin along real easy and then all hell busted loose."

"Damned if I know. Maybe he had that in mind all along and he was just playin possum."

Ben grimaced. "Just when you think you're gettin to know horses. I didn't see it comin at all. Feel like a damned fool."

Ben got a halter on the horse and led him around until he cooled down, curried and brushed him, turned him loose in the corral. It hurt to put his weight on the knee, but he pressed all around it with his thumbs and it didn't feel like anything was broken. They spent the rest of the day working horses that were a whole lot easier to handle before getting cleaned up for the party at the main house.

When Ezra went to crank the truck, he went at it in too much of a hurry. The back kick of the crank handle almost broke his arm. He got it started on the second try. They bumped along the rough track in second gear. They had crawled a couple of miles when Ezra pulled over, saying that he wanted to check a windmill. Ben found it strange, because they had ridden by the windmill two days earlier and everything was fine and dandy. Maybe Ezra was getting forgetful.

Ezra killed the engine and climbed out of the truck, walked around the windmill a time or two, then perched on the edge of the stock tank. Ben got out and stood next to him. There was a good breeze blowing.

Ezra pointed to the blades of the big wheel spinning with the wind. "Aint that a beautiful sight? Currie windmill, made by a company in Topeka. Best you can buy. Don't need nothin but the wind that's been blowin out here forever. There wasn't no windmills when me and Eli first come through here in 1886."

Ben nodded, wondering why they were sitting here when the spread Juanita would put on the table was calling his name. Finally, Ezra cleared his throat. "Ben, there's a thing I've been ponderin for some time now. I thought maybe we could chew it over a little, see if you agree with me or not."

Ben assumed that Ezra was talking about Argentina. "I expect we'll be in agreement. I don't disagree with you too often, Uncle Ez."

"I know you don't, son, and I appreciate it. What I've been thinkin, it has to do with you. Now that Velma's gone, you're an orphan."

"I guess I am. I never thought of it that way."

Ezra gazed up again at the spokes of the windmill. "Anyhow, I went and talked to a lawyer fella in Sheridan. Seems that, even though you're full grown, there aint nothin to stop me from adoptin you."

"Like you adopt a kid from an orphanage?"

"Well, this is a little different, you bein older and all, but you'd be my son, all nice and legal. If you don't want this, don't let it worry you, I'll never bring it up again."

Ben kicked a booted toe into the mud next to the stock tank. "I used to hope I'd get adopted when we were in that orphanage in Alliance. Stayin with the nuns, where they'd smack us on the back of the hand with a ruler if Em and me so much as looked at each other. Some kids would get lucky and they'd get took by a family. I wanted to get adopted, but they wouldn't let us go because our parents were still alive."

"Well, I'm just as glad you didn't get took, because now we can get this thing done, if you want it. You'd be my son, same as if you was born that way. Think it over for as long as it takes. I'd be tickled pink if you was to say yes."

"Would my name be Ben Paint, then? Not Ben Hughes anymore?"

"I'd rather you was to take the Paint name, because I got nobody else to carry it on, but if you don't like that idea, you can stay Ben Hughes."

"That would be dandy with me, Ezra. Ben Paint sounds real good. I'd be proud. Heck, it aint like Frank Hughes stayed around to look after me after I was born. Only thing I got from him was long legs and a liking for horses. What about Emaline and Bobby? What does this do for them?"

"Heck, I'd adopt the two of them tomorrow," Ezra said. "But Emaline don't strike me as the kind that wants to be adopted and she treats Bobby like a son, so I don't believe she'd appreciate me stealin him away."

"You're right there. She aint a bit happy that he's comin up for the summer, but she knows it's better for him than settin around the house while she goes to work at the diner every day."

"Sure it is. Anyway, for now it will be just you and me, father and son."

"I'd like that a whole lot, Ezra."

"Then just as soon as we get a chance to get into town, we'll get this deal done."

"This don't mean I've got to call you Pa, does it?"

"I sure as hell hope not. Not when you're bigger than I am. Ezra will do just fine, or even you old sonofabitch. But I'll be your daddy, so you've got to do what I say or I'll turn you over my knee and larrup you."

"I always have, aint I?"

"You sure have, or we wouldn't be doin this. I'm too damned old to have to shake the sass out of a boy with trouble on his mind."

They shook on it. To keep Ben from seeing that his eyes were a little watery, Ezra took a serious interest in a clump of sagebrush way out on the prairie. It might not amount to much more than a piece of paper saying that Benjamin Hughes was now Benjamin Paint, but to Ezra it meant the world. Eli had eleven birth children still living and two in their graves, but Ezra would be happy with this one fine son.

It wasn't until a week later, when Ben's knee was so swollen he could barely walk, that Ezra drove him to the hospital. Doc Miller said he had a narrow fracture of the kneecap and a torn ligament. "It's what we call the anterior cruciate ligament. I can't fix it, but Doc Noulis down at the University of Wyoming can, if we can get you to Laramie. You'll walk okay after that, but I don't suppose you'll fight in any man's army. Knee won't stand up to a twenty-mile march after this."

"I can still ride?"

"You can still ride, much as you please."

12.

On a Sunday morning in mid-May, Juanita drove Eli to the little country church three miles east of the 8T8. He rarely attended church, but the long struggle to recover his health and keep the ranch in one piece had worn him down. He wasn't a religious man, but he had always found that church was a good place to think and in these times, a man could use all the help he could get. If that help came from the Lord above, so be it.

The minister was the Reverend Cletus Barnwell, a tall, bookish young man from Kansas. It was the first time in a long while that a man of the cloth had delivered a sermon that made Eli Paint sit up and take notice. The Reverend Barnwell took his theme from the twenty-fourth chapter of Job, verses 19 and 20:

> *Drought and heat consume the snow waters; so doth the grave those which have sinned. The womb shall forget him; the worm shall feed sweetly on him; he shall be no more remembered; and wickedness shall be broken as a tree.*

The Reverend Barnwell talked about things most preachers wouldn't touch, problems that mattered in this life rather than the next. He came right out and said that farmers and ranchers from Montana to

Texas had created a disaster when they allowed their cattle to overgraze the prairie or plowed up grassland and left it lying fallow for the heat and the wind to do its work. Eli agreed with every word. This was exactly the view of the agricultural experts that FDR had sent trooping across the land. They were trying to explain that folks had been going about things the wrong way for a good thirty years and that, if they didn't mend their ways, the land would be gone and the entire prairie from Montana to Texas would become a desert, a haven for rattlesnakes, buzzards, jackrabbits, rodents.

> My fellow worshipers, I say unto you today: The plow that broke the prairie has created a disaster that threatens to swallow us all. The labor that buried the tall buffalo grass that had been here for thousands of years has released the earth, and the earth has departed. We have turned tens of millions of acres of God's land wrong side up, now his wrath is upon us. The land that has been our comfort and our sustenance is in our food and in our hair and between our sheets and in the lungs of our little ones. We have sinned against the land, and the land is repaying us with dust and drought. We must pray for forgiveness for the sins we have committed, but we must also change our ways. We Americans are the most self-reliant people on this earth. Now we have to figure out a way to treat this land so we can seed it for the long haul, same as life is a long haul leading to the gates of paradise. We have to mix some common sense with our trust in ourselves. The earth belongs to the Lord, and we have mistreated that earth something awful.
>
> We have been lucky in Wyoming, because it could have been so much worse. If you take a drive down to Kansas or Oklahoma or Texas or a good bit of Nebraska, you will see places where the land is simply gone, where thousands of sections of good earth have blown away. It is not as bad here, but it's hot and dry and dusty,

and we can't expect the good Lord to fix it all without our help. We have to find a different way. Plant trees for windbreaks. Plant grass that will hold the sod. Stop plowing up fields and leaving them fallow. Men made this mess, and men are going to have to find a way to clean it up. My father has had to face that truth on our farm in Kansas, but he learned too late and the farm is gone. My folks are on their way to California right now. They hope to find another way to make a living, but they spent thirty years trying to farm that land and their hearts are broken. That is why I speak to you with such urgency today, why I beg you to listen. That is the message I have for you this morning, at a time when drought and heat consume the snow waters, when the greed of the bankers has cast us into the maw of this terrible depression, when our nation lies broken as a tree, suffering for our wickedness, for the wicked way in which we have treated one of the greatest of God's many gifts, the soil beneath our feet. God bless you all.

The Reverend Barnwell wound up his sermon and bowed his head to lead the congregation in prayer. Eli was not much for religion, but this young man had said it about as well as it could be said. *Our nation lies broken as a tree . . .* That just about summed it up.

Through the spring and into the summer of 1933, Eli worked to save the 8T8. Juanita drove him to meetings with bankers in Casper and Sheridan, where he fought for extensions, for lower interest rates, for some degree of understanding that the whole country was caught up in drought and depression and that, if people didn't help one another, they would all go under. During the meetings, Eli was as canny and unbending as ever, but each encounter with the bankers took its toll. They would step into the Pontiac for the ride back to the ranch, she would glance over and see his face, gray with fatigue. All through spring roundup, he was on horseback as much as he could stand, but it didn't amount to much more than an hour a day. He had to depend on Ezra and Two Spuds and Willie Thaw to tell him how many spring calves had survived, the shape of the grassland, the health of the cattle. He fidgeted and fussed and worried. He could deal with almost any obstacle if he could face it himself. Relying on others, even when they were trustworthy men with long experience, drove him to distraction.

Piece by piece, Eli sold off a little less than half of the 8T8's original hundred thousand acres, some of it in parcels of as little as a section. A Scottish industrialist, smitten with Wyoming, overpaid for ten thousand acres of the worst land on the 8T8, simply because he wanted a place to hunt. Each sale felt like the loss of a rib, but by June, Eli had managed to pay off in full two of the banks that held notes on the ranch and bring his payments up to date with the other two. He sold some of his breeding stock, including two prize bulls, to pay off the rest. He cut back the number of cattle he had on the range to a fraction of what he had owned before the drought. By the Fourth of July, he told Ezra and Juanita that he felt they were in a position where they could hunker down and wait it out. Wait out the drought, wait out the depression, wait for better times. He said it and he believed it, but he knew that one more calamity could be the end. Hail, prairie fire, a grasshopper plague.

No matter how hard you worked, you couldn't plan for all the disasters that could drag a rancher down. In August, Eli paid a visit to Clyde Newinger, an old-timer on Crazy Woman Creek whose ranch had been hit by a cloud of voracious grasshoppers, tens of thousands of them. Newinger had sealed himself in the house and watched in disbelief as an entire harness hanging on a corral fence dissolved under a writhing heap of bugs attracted by the smell of sweat on leather. Eli was surveying some of the damage to Newinger's pasture when Dr. Vardel Watson of the University of Wyoming came bouncing over the prairie in a 1930 Ford Woody. Watson was an entomologist, a tall, skinny gent who wore his boots on the outside of his pants. He introduced himself and bent to examine what was left of Newinger's buffalo grass.

"This is remarkable," he said as he stood up. "If you don't mind, I'd like to take some samples from your land, Mr. Newinger."

Newinger exploded. "I don't give a flyin fandango about your samples. What I want to know is, what do you sonsofbitches propose to do about these crickets?"

Watson went to polishing his glasses with a handkerchief. "Actually, that's a misconception. The bugs that hit your land weren't crickets or grasshoppers. They were shield-backed katydids."

That made Newinger so mad he threw his hat in the dust and kicked it twenty feet away. "What the goddamned hell do you know about katydids? I'll stick about a hundred of them up your ass and see if you don't holler katydid."

The entomologist shook his head. "Look, I understand you're upset. But we can't help you unless we learn more about these creatures. That's why I need to take some samples back so we can study them in the lab."

Newinger reached in the back of his pickup truck and grabbed his double-barreled shotgun. He waved the barrels at Watson and motioned for the man to get back in the Woody. "Now that's just the trouble," he said. "You bastards always got to study it up a little more before you can do a goddamned thing about a problem. If you're so smart, you'd figure out a way to stop them little peckerwoods before they eat the whole damned country. It don't matter if you call them grasshoppers or katydids or Aunt Sarah, they do more damage than I'd do to a cold bottle of beer right now—if I could afford one."

After he had run off the entomologist, Newinger was apologetic. "I expect I was too hard on that fella, but damn! He's the third or fourth one has been up here. Not one of 'em can tell me how they propose to put a stop to these damned plagues. It is a thing right out of the Bible, Eli. You see it and you want to get down on your knees and get your prayin in before Judgment Day."

That Sunday, Eli and Juanita paid another visit to the little church. This time, the Reverend Barnwell took a more optimistic theme for his sermon from Isaiah 58:11:

> *And the LORD shall guide thee continually, and satisfy thy soul in drought, and make fat thy bones: and thou shalt be like a watered garden, and like a spring of water, whose waters fail not.*

Still, the waters failed. The rain did not come and the great black dusters rolled across the plains, some of them hundreds of miles wide and ten thousand feet high. Children, old people, healthy young farmworkers died of dust pneumonia. Where waist-high buffalo grass had once stretched to every horizon, there was nothing left but grit and dust and Russian thistle and empty grain elevators tipped over by the wind. Farmers went to milk their gaunt cows and found that what was in the pail looked like chocolate milk and tasted like dust. Ceilings collapsed from the weight of the dirt in the attic. Children were lost and suffocated in dust storms. In their sod houses and shacks and dugouts, farm families shivered through icy winters and boiled through one scalding summer after another. Heat lashed the High Plains from Alberta down to Texas, from the spine of the Rocky Mountains east to the Mississippi River and beyond, a furnace of scorching drought that scalded crops, parched the land, dried up the creeks, turned sagebrush into rags of flame. Cattle and horses and old cowboys died from the heat. Bankers peered out windows on Main Street and saw thermometers stuck at temperatures they had never dreamt they would see: 115 degrees in Iowa, 118 in Nebraska.

From Montana to Texas, the earth dried and cracked. Barley stalks turned a ghostly white, drooped and died. Water tanks silted over with dust. Dying cattle leaned against the hot metal, bawling for water where there was none to be had. Tumbleweeds sailed over dusty land where no crop grew, ripgut thistle flourished and poison ivy died on the vine. Farm women squinted into the wind and dust, bit their cracked lips, wondered how a body could go on. Then they went on.

PART II

Hard Times

1931–1936

13.

THE PRIZEFIGHTER STOOD IN A CONE OF SMOKY light, punching at shadows. He was a lean man an inch over six feet, with green eyes, a shock of thick black hair, a deep cleft in a square jaw. Sinew, muscle, bone. A hard man. Born hard, raised hard, battered often, boy and man. The nose had been broken and broken again, scar tissue lay thick over both eyes, his knuckles had been broken so often that his hands looked like a bowl full of walnuts. He skipped a little on his toes to test the boards under the ring and bounced off the ropes, learning their give. He threw a flashy combination for the crowd, heard an appreciative ripple from the high rollers at ringside, felt the sheen of sweat on his body, the loose way his shoulders moved, the quick, supple strength in his legs, the deep power in his lungs.

It was 1931, two years into the Great Depression, but the fight game was bigger than ever. It might have been the worst of hard times, one worker in three without a job and no relief in sight, but folks would still pay good money to watch one man beat the hell out of another. Maybe they needed something to take their minds off the foreclosures and the soup lines. Jake McCloskey was not one to wonder why folks would spend good money to watch a prizefight. He was paid to fight, so he fought. This would be a good payday. The crowd was the biggest he had ever seen. There had to be ten thousand paying customers, easy. The arena was packed to the rafters. It stank of sweat and cheap cologne, bootleg beer, bathtub gin, piss from overflowing urinals and smoke, especially smoke. Everyone smoked. The men smoked cigars, the women smoked cigarettes. Even the trainers smoked during bouts. Smoke billowed over the ring.

Wade Wynkoop, the radio announcer, chattered into his mike like an angry squirrel.

> *Jake McCloskey is quick as a fox in a chicken house, folks. He looks ready to go against the chocolate challenger right here in Denver tonight. That's Lionel Kane, ladies and gentlemen. You know King Kane, we all know him. Kane can kill a man with a single punch, but Jake McCloskey is too slick and too quick. We are going to see a dilly of a fight tonight, folks, but when it's done, Rebel Jake will be the winner, that's the straight dope. . . .*

Wynkoop had an Adam's apple the size of a baseball. It bobbed up and down over a purple bow tie with white polka dots.

Next to Wynkoop, the sports columnist Ed Floate filled a coffee mug with hooch from a pocket flask and hoisted the mug in a silent toast to McCloskey. His lead was already written.

> *Lionel Kane's coconut was cracked last night and he was turned into one done darkie by the flying fists of Rebel Jake McCloskey. This jungle bunny found out that in the square circle there's no place to run. He was big and he was strong, but he had never seen anything like the sledgehammer left hook that sent him to cloud-cuckoo-land. So what's it going to be, Slapsie Maxie Rosenbloom? Are you world champ or world chump? Are you going to climb into the ring with Jake McCloskey and see if you can block the punches that felled the mighty King*

Kane? Or will you go on hiding from the best light-heavy west of the Mississippi?

Jake knew what Ed Floate would write, almost word for word. Friday evenings, Floate turned up at Moe Spitzer's joint on Larimer Street at eight o'clock sharp. Floate always sat at Moe's table, where Moe would treat him to a sixteen-ounce steak and a quart of good bourbon. After dinner there would be Cuban cigars a yard long. Moe would snap his fingers, a blond floozy would waltz over to their table, sit thigh to thigh with Ed Floate, let him hear the hiss of silk stockings, draw her long fingernails up his fly. Moe would blow smoke rings and watch them curl into the air over the bourbon and the broad. Then he would lean forward, explain how it was going to be.

"Listen, you dumb fuck. This is what you're gonna say. Jake McCloskey is the best light-heavy you've ever seen. Speed, power, the whole shebang. How you write it, I don't give a fuck. You're the fuckin Shakespeare. Write it backward, all I care. Write it in fuckin Swahili. Put in all them fancy words you wants. Just make sure it's loud and clear when your fuckin rag hits the streets. My man Jake McCloskey ought to be light-heavyweight champ. Tell that Hebe bastard Slapsie Maxie Rosenbloom to give my guy a shot."

"But you're a Hebe bastard yourself, Max."

"I am, you goy fuck. That's why I can say it. You say it again, I'll get a nigger to saw off your nuts with a rusty razor blade."

Jake pumped a gloved fist Floate's way. The trouble with a hack like Floate, you had to hope he was sober enough to write the story when the fight was done. Some nights, he'd be so far into the sauce that he was facedown in his typewriter before the undercard bouts were over. The snot-nosed kid who ran the pages back to the telegrapher would have to finish Ed's story and there was no telling what a kid like that would say.

Jake looked for Thelma Pearl in the crowd, found her with her friend Maggie in the third row. She smiled, offered a pretty little wave. Playing the part, the boxer's sweet little wife. It was a lot of hooey. If he lost, he'd be lucky if she didn't leave with some bird with a fat wallet and a diamond stickpin in his tie. He grinned, tapped his glove to his forehead. *Don't worry, sugar. I'll knock this bum out early and we'll head over to Boodles, drink all the champagne you want.*

Funny how the fight game drew women and gamblers. There wasn't much about this wide world that Jake understood, but he knew that three things always went together—blood, sex, and money. Fighters beat the hell out of each other for money, money drew women, the people who paid good money to watch the fights wanted blood. He had seen them snarling like junkyard dogs when a fighter was almost done. Poor bastard hanging with his arms over the top rope, crucified, might as well have had nails through his palms. His nose broke, eyes battered shut, blood from his eyes and nose and mouth pouring down his chest, two or three teeth knocked out, pink welts from dozens of punches all over his chest and shoulders, the crowd screaming, *Kill him! Kill him! Murder the punk!* Dames were the worst, squirming their little behinds on their seats, damp between the legs at the start of a fight and sopping wet if it went fifteen rounds and blood mingled with the sweat. Some women, the fights made them sick. They'd hide their eyes and leave early. The broads who were hooked on the fight game would sit through a fifteen-round bout and then take a boxer just as he was, right there on the training table. Rubbing their bare tits on his sweaty chest, snarling for sex the way they snarled for blood, carnivorous, red-lipped predators with eyes that went the color of smoke when he slipped inside them. He knew the type because he had married one, sweet little Thelma Pearl, hard as a diamond.

Joe "Little Caesar" Roma was at ringside. The biggest mobster in Denver, barely five feet tall. With a six-foot blonde beside him. Roma caught Jake's eye and nodded, cupping his mouth to shout: *Ya gotta kill that nigger, Jake. Ya gotta kill the sonofabitch. I went heavy on youse, don't let me down.* Winking, making like it was a joke. Jake raised a glove over his head. *Little bastard. I wonder how much jack he put down on me? More'n I'll ever see in my life. The man has eyes like candles that was just blowed out.*

Roma had plenty of company. The mob was out in force. Charlie Blanda was there, the Smaldone brothers. The Carlino brothers would have been in their usual spot at ringside, but some of them had been bumped off. Maybe all of them. Killed by Little Caesar, folks said. Jake couldn't keep track from one fight to the next, which mobsters were dead and which were still laying bets. Guys would come in while he was sparring, shake hands, wish him luck, strut around in their pin-striped suits with the bulges under the jackets, and before fight time rolled around they'd be all shot up, their bodies on the front pages of the papers.

Moe Spitzer took his seat near Joe Roma. Moe was so fat he wheezed sitting still. He would try to hijack half of Jake's purse for expenses before he paid up. They'd argue, Jake would lose. But he was a square shooter, Moe. Always told you what he was going to do before he did it. *You hit people, you dumb fuck. That's what you do. I take your money. It's what I do.* It was hot as hell under the lights, but Moe wore a long fur coat buttoned up to the neck. *Why the fuck wouldn't I wear it? You know what this fuckin coat cost? More'n you'll make if you fight a hundred years. I pay that much for a coat, I'm gonna wear the fuckin thing, I don't give a fuck if it's ringside in the Sahara desert.*

Jake leaned over to Bucky Betz. "What's keepin Lionel Kane, Bucky?"

"How the fuck do I know? You expect me to keep track of every jigaboo in Denver?"

The little trainer was always nettlesome and peevish before a fight. Tonight he was sour as a dill pickle, worried because King Kane was a hard case. He had killed a man in the ring, but the other fighter was colored too, so nobody paid much attention except Bucky. Bucky noticed because that was his job.

There was an ugly murmur in the back of the crowd. Kane was on his way to the ring. The boos rang from every part of the arena, except an upper gallery where the shoeshine boys and hospital orderlies and Pullman porters sat together, staying quiet, trying not to provoke the mob. Jake stood in the ring with his head down, embarrassed. He wondered what it must be like to be King Kane, to hear this crowd baying for blood, knowing they would just as soon lynch him as watch him fight.

Kane climbed through the ropes. He wore a purple robe trimmed with gold. A ring of fat hung over his belt. Jake winked at Bucky, mouthed the word. *Fat.*

The ring announcer stepped through the ropes, took the microphone. *In this corner from Louisiana, wearing the black trunks and weighing in at two hundred and twenty-nine pounds, with a record of thirty-eight wins and four losses, the man with the killer punch . . .* The boos drowned out Kane's name. Jake stood again with his head down, waiting it out, wondering if he heard right. Two hundred and twenty-nine pounds? He was fighting seven pounds over the light-heavyweight limit and he was still spotting the man almost fifty pounds.

And in this corner, from the great state of Arkansas, with a record of fifty-five wins and two losses, weighing in at one hundred and eighty-two pounds of pure speed, grace, and boxing skill. Rebel Jake McCloskey!

The roar of the crowd was like a flight of airplanes taking off. He spun, bounced, raised his gloved fists high over his head. The cheers were like a drug. He threw another flashy combination.

One of Kane's seconds peeled off his robe. The man was enormous. Shoulders like a bull buffalo. Bucky growled something in Jake's ear, one of boxing's old saws: "Don't forget what they say: Hit a nigger in the stomach and a fat man in the head."

He had to shout to be heard above the crowd: "So what am I

supposed to do with a fat nigger, Bucky?" Bucky's answer was drowned by the roar of the crowd. The bell rang. Lionel Kane rose from his stool, dark and menacing. Jake took two steps into the ring, Kane was on him. He caught a hard right on the bicep and spun away, his arm buzzing. Kane moved like a big, fat cat, heavy in the middle but quick on his feet. Jake tried to circle away from that hammer-on-anvil right, took a left hook that made his ear buzz. For the rest of the round, he was able to duck and dodge. In the second, he caught Kane flush with a four-punch combination to the head. Jake had put men on the canvas with less than that, but Kane didn't blink. He just kept boring in, down low like a submarine. Jake was taking shots to the body that made his organs move. He could hear the punches explode on his hide. Kane was bathed in sweat, which made him slippery and hard to handle in the clinches. As Kane stepped out of a clinch in the third round, he threw a left hook to the ribs. Jake felt something crack in there, like a roof timber giving way in an old barn. By the fifth round, the gamblers were hollering blue murder. There was too much money riding on this fight, most of it on Jake McCloskey.

Somewhere out there, Thelma Pearl would know what was happening. She would understand what Lionel Kane was doing to him. Jake was landing more punches, he might even be winning on the scorecards, but Kane was beating him deep down, where a spider's web of cracks can spread through a fighter's heart. Boxing people might not see it, but Thelma Pearl would know that he was done in the ways that matter. If he was done in the ring, he was of no more use to her.

In the sixth round, he missed with a left jab and Kane caught him on the nose with a terrific, ripping right cross. It felt like a hand grenade exploding between his eyes, as though bone and shrapnel had blown up into his brain. Jake hit the canvas so hard that he bounced and came down a second time. He rolled over, tried to sit up, felt blood pouring down his chin and neck and chest. The ref stood above him, legs wide apart, right arm swinging back and forth like a metronome.

One . . . two . . . three . . . He could hear Bucky screaming. *Ya gotta get up! Get off the goddamned canvas!* He heard the crowd, their voices far away, as though he was underwater, drowning right next to a crowded beach. *Four . . . five . . . six . . .* He gathered his legs. *Seven . . . eight . . .*

He was up. The bell rang. The round was over. He staggered rubber-legged to his corner, where Bucky was lifting the stool into the ring. Herb Ferren, the cut man, stuffed cotton batting into his nostrils. Bucky tried to sponge away some of the blood. He soaked through one sponge, then another. Jake wondered if a man had ever bled to death in the ring. Bucky wore a white shirt and a black tie and the shirt looked like a butcher's apron. Bucky was in his ear, telling him to jab and move, jab and move, but what he needed was a crowbar.

Somehow, he answered the bell for the seventh. He tried to back-pedal on watery legs, but Kane shoved him into a corner and whacked him where his ribs were cracked. The pain was awful, but he wanted it to hurt. The pain kept him on his feet. He could hear Kane wheezing when they got in close. Kane lived in Louisiana. He wasn't used to fighting a mile above sea level. Sooner or later, his lungs would go and the legs would follow, but it might be too late. Jake survived the eighth and connected with one good shot in the ninth, but Kane answered with a straight jab that burst his eyebrow. When the bell rang, Jake collapsed on the stool in his corner. He was spitting blood from his mouth, his left eyebrow was pumping out a cauliflower of blood, his nose was smashed. Herb Ferren shook his head. "I can't fix that eye. Not so's he can see worth a damn."

"You've had enough," Bucky said. "I'm goin to throw in the towel."

"Like hell you say."

Jake dragged himself back into the ring and took a straight left to the nose. He stumbled to his left and almost went down. His gloves grazed the canvas. He caught his balance, swiveled on the ball of his right foot, put everything he had into the punch, a left uppercut thrown from his shoe tops. The punch flowed from ankles to calves, thighs, hips, torso, through shoulder and forearm and fist until it exploded on Lionel Kane's jaw. Kane was leaping in, eager to finish it, leaning off-balance. Jake's left caught him flush on the sweet spot. Kane's thick, dark body quivered in midair and he fell facedown, so hard Jake felt the ring tremble. The ref began the count. *One . . . two . . .* Kane rolled over onto his back, brushed at his eyes with the back of his glove, trying to wipe the cobwebs away. The ref broke off his count to push Jake into a neutral corner, looked twice to be sure he had obeyed, then started the count all over again. *One, two . . .* Jake stood in his neutral corner screaming at the ref. *Count, goddammit! Count! Don't give him no goddamned Gene Tunney long count!* The ref broke off his count again, pointed a finger at Jake, ordered him to shut up. He sagged against the ropes, needing them to hold himself up. At last, the referee's hand tolled again as he started the count over a third time, like a bell ringing for the dead. *One, two, three . . .* Ten thousand people were on their feet screaming his name *Jake! Jake! Jake!* The ref seemed to be counting in slow motion, *four, five, six, seven . . .* Kane tried to drag himself to his feet, got as far as his knees, collapsed onto his belly.

Eight . . . nine . . . TEN.

14.

All hell broke loose. Wade Wynkoop barked into his microphone, his Adam's apple working like a plunger in a toilet.

That was a dilly of a fight, folks, what did I tell you, a dilly! It looked like Jake McCloskey was done, felled by the thunderous blows of King Kane, but that mighty left hook found its target right on the jaw and Kane is down! Lionel Kane is down! Lionel Kane is done! Thirty seconds into the tenth round and it's over! Jake McCloskey has won by a knockout! They'll be talking about this one from Maine to Monterey!

It seemed like there were a hundred people in the ring. They hoisted Jake onto their shoulders and waltzed him back and forth from one set of ring ropes to another. He felt like a dead man sitting on top of the world. When they put him down, Thelma Pearl was in the ring, looking petulant and bothered. He grabbed her, lifted her up, spun her around. When he put her down, she slapped his swollen mug. There was blood all over her new gold dress. She rubbed at it furiously. Jake tried to tell her over the din that soda water would take it out, but Thelma Pearl ignored him, wet her fingers with saliva, rubbed at a spot. *Damn you, Jake McCloskey. Damn you, you stupid hillbilly. I can't get this damned spot out. Look at this. You've ruined this dress, it's just plain ruined. How can one man have so much blood in him?*

By the time they got things calmed down in the ring, she was gone. Lionel Kane sat on his stool, glowering at Jake while his cornermen waved smelling salts under his nose. Kane had won the fight. No doubt about it. Won every bit of it except that last punch. Jake knew it, Kane knew it. Maybe the damned fools in the crowd didn't know, but Jake knew. Kane and Jake, Bucky Betz and Herb Ferren, Thelma Pearl. Five people who knew he was done, no matter what the papers had to say. No matter what pile of hooey Ed Floate cooked up to keep Moe from cutting his balls off.

Moe Spitzer wasn't one of those who had figured it out. He blew cigar smoke in Jake's face. "Never in doubt, *boychik*. Never in doubt. With a fuckin punch like that, you got to be champ. You had me worried there a time or two, but I knew you'd drop that jig."

Jake grinned a wobbly grin. Moe's face came into focus and faded again. The lights were too bright and the ring was spinning. His legs gave way. He fell, crashing facedown onto the canvas.

When he came to, he was lying on a table in the dressing room with Bucky and Herb the cut man trying to clean him up. He was still there when Thelma Pearl marched in, still mad over the blood on her dress, Moe Spitzer with her. Moe was laughing.

"First time I ever seen the *winnah* carried outa the ring on a fuckin stretcher, I'll tell you that much. The *winnah*! Hey, it don't matter how you leave the fuckin ring, it's what you do when you're in there, am I right?"

Moe handed Jake an envelope with a thousand dollars in cash tucked inside. It was supposed to be fifteen hundred, but Moe had deducted five hundred dollars in expenses for two sparring partners who earned five dollars a day for two weeks. Jake didn't think it added up, but he was too beat to argue. He counted out Bucky's two hundred, but before he could stuff the rest in his pants, Thelma Pearl snatched it out of his hand.

"I'll take this, you big palooka. The shape you're in, you'll lose it. I'll see you at Boodles Speak. Bucky, clean him up. He's enough to make a girl sick."

She turned on her heel, left without another word. Didn't even ask if he was all right. Jake drew back his fist, smashed it into the brick wall, didn't feel a thing.

"Goddamn that little hussy. I swear, one of these days I'm goin to break her up in pieces."

Bucky clucked his tongue, watching Herb work on Jake's split eyebrow.

"I don't know why you're surprised. You know what she is, woman who sits on her moneymaker."

Jake had seen the look on her puss, the look she had worn every day since she got the manacle on his finger. The look that said, *If you start losing, I'll take this sweet little chassis to the first sucker who can keep me in style.* No matter how mad he was, he could never say no to her. She would run a fingernail the color of blood along his zipper. She'd pout those red Clara Bow lips. *Honey, I could do you real sweet right now, but the only thing gets my motor going is if I know I can buy that little red dress you promised me.* What was it they said? *The screwin you get aint worth the screwin you get.* Only with Thelma, that wasn't exactly true. She had a tight little quim, fit like a deerskin glove. Made his eyes cross every time. But she knew he had lost the fight. She would know how bad he had lost and where, all the places he had been hurt. Sooner or later, she would light out for Reno or Salt Lake or Seattle.

Bucky peeled the sweat-soaked gloves off his broken hands, cleaned off some of the blood, slipped his shoes and socks off. Jake sat there in his trunks, his taped hands dangling between his knees, his chest still heaving fifteen minutes after the fight, trying to get enough strength to hit the showers. When he needed to take a leak, his hands were so busted up that he had to ask Bucky to come pull his trunks down. When he managed to pee, he had blood in his urine.

Bucky shook his head. "Damned if he didn't beat your kidneys plumb to hell. You'll be pissin blood for a month."

Bucky cut the tape off his hands. Jake could see himself in the mirror, the bruises on his chest and arms, as though he had been mauled by a Brahma bull. He stumbled into the shower and stood there, letting the hot water run until it turned ice cold without warning, stepped out cursing and toweled off. They found a sawbones in a card game next door who was more or less sober and paid him to sew the cut over Jake's eye. It took nine stitches and hurt like hell. When the doc was done, they walked the three blocks to Boodles Speak. Thelma Pearl had been there and left. The barkeep didn't have to say it. *She left with a man.* Jake saw it plain on his face. For the second time that night, he punched a wall because of her. The barkeep gave him a look. *Easy, buddy.* He ordered a double whiskey, but he was thirsty too, so he asked for a beer chaser and bought one of the same for Bucky. There were fight fans in the speakeasy, dozens of them. Most of them had won money on him. After the first one, they lined up to buy him drinks. He wasn't a drinker, but on this night it went down like water and it didn't dull the pain a bit. Drunks swatted him on the back, hard enough to make him wince. Women ran pink tongues over red lips. He shook his head. *Not tonight, sweetheart. Not tonight.* The night slipped away. By the time Bucky drove him to the little rented house on the edge of Denver, there was a streak of watery gray light out east toward Kansas.

The door was open wide, the lights on. Everything that was loose was gone, even the sheets and blankets and pillows from the bed. She had left with the money Moe gave him, all that he earned from the fight. He would have hit something, but he was too tired. He swallowed four aspirin, curled up on the bare mattress, rolled his jacket for a pillow, fell asleep with his boots on.

* * *

Bucky fronted Jake a double sawbuck until he felt up to going to the bank. Bucky's wife, Vera, brought some bedding, filled up his icebox, looked in every day to make sure he had something to eat. He slept twelve hours a day, took short walks around the block, slept again. The ribs hurt every time he moved, his nose was so swollen he had to breathe through his mouth. Every time Bucky mentioned fighting again, he shook his head. Not now. Maybe not ever.

It was a week before he could walk the ten blocks to the bank. He took the bank book that showed a balance of $4,237.74, filled out a withdrawal slip for fifty dollars, handed it to the teller. She took it, pulled his card out of a file, held it up for him to see.

"I'm sorry, Mr. McCloskey. Your balance is one dollar." She pointed to the figure: $1.00.

"That aint right. I got better than four thousand dollars in this bank."

"It was a joint account, Mr. McCloskey. Your wife? Thelma Pearl McCloskey? She withdrew the money on October seventeenth, 1931. See, that's her signature right there."

It was Thelma Pearl's signature, plain as day. Right under the amount she had withdrawn, $4,236.74. Jake stood there looking helpless. With his black eyes and his swollen nose, he looked like a bum and felt like one.

"You mean she took it all?"

"All except this dollar, as you can see. With a joint account, either of you can withdraw the money."

"That aint right. How come nobody called me?"

The teller blushed. "Well, she came to me with this. It was a lot of money to take out at one time, so I took her to see the manager, Mr. Martz, and she was in his office for a while. When they came out he told me to go into the safe and get the lady's money."

Jake didn't need to know more. Thelma Pearl had ways of getting men to do exactly what she wanted them to do. It was possible she had done something on her knees in the banker's office to get that money, but it was usually enough for her to lick her lips and bat those big eyes. He looked over his shoulder at the manager's office. The curtains were drawn and the lights were out. The teller saw what he was thinking.

"Mr. Martz is away," she said. "He'll be back in two weeks."

Jake shook his head like a wounded bull. He wanted to beat the hell out of this Martz fellow, but he couldn't even do that. For all he knew, she had lit out with the banker who helped her take Jake's money. He felt light-headed, as though another of Lionel Kane's punches had landed on his noggin. He could see the teller mouthing words at him, but she had to repeat what she was saying three times before it registered.

"Did you need anything else?"

"No, ma'am."

He reeled out into the street like a drunk, unable to put one foot in front of the other. He found a park bench, sat down and put his head between his knees, trying to shake that giddy feeling. The numbers swam in his mind. All those fights, a dozen years in the ring. All those paydays, even if Moe Spitzer siphoned off more than his share. All of it gone, down to a single dollar. The thieving little bitch. If Thelma Pearl had come sashaying down the street at that moment, he would have put a whupping on her she would never forget.

Despair turned to black rage. He punched the wooden bench so hard he shattered two of the slats. A well-to-do gentleman in a business suit paused to deliver a lecture. "That's city property you're destroying there," he said. "I should have you arrested."

As he got to his feet, Jake wore a crazed smile. He grabbed the man's shirt and collar with his left hand and punched with his right fist, three, four, five quick blows. He relaxed his grip and let the man slide to the sidewalk, out cold. There were a few other people on the street, but as Jake glared around, they lowered their gaze and hurried away.

He aimed a kick at the businessman's ribs and walked the rest of the way home in a seething fury, fists balled at his sides, hoping someone else would give him an excuse to start throwing punches. Back in the little house he had shared with Thelma, he put three holes in the walls before he reached the kitchen sink, where he washed the blood off his knuckles.

He called Bucky and told him what had happened.

"Why the hell didn't you ask me before you opened a bank account with that dame?"

"Well, I never thought."

"No, by God. You never did think. You stopped thinkin the first time you saw her, now she's cleaned you out neater than a skeeter's peter. What the hell are you goin to live on until your next fight?"

"I thought maybe you could spot me another double sawbuck."

"Spot you, hell. I ought to let you starve, you damned dumb hillbilly."

"That's what Thelma Pearl called me, when I got blood on her dress. A damned dumb hillbilly."

"Maybe she had a point. How can you be so fuckin stupid?"

"I got no idea, Bucky. All I know, I need to get more fights."

"You're too busted up right now. Got to wait a month, anyhow. I'll talk to Moe, see what we can find. He wanted to hold you out, maybe get a title shot before you screw up and lose."

"I can't wait around for no title shot. I got to fight now."

"Like I said, I'll talk to Moe. You still got the De Soto, aint you? And the motorcycle?"

"Thelma Pearl can't drive."

Bucky found a drunken lawyer who worked cheap. The lawyer located a judge who was a fight fan. Jake was granted a divorce from Thelma Pearl on grounds of desertion. Bucky wanted to go out and celebrate, but Jake turned him down. It didn't matter a whole lot if Bucky was right and Thelma Pearl was all the terrible things he claimed she was. He missed her. Bucky went out and got drunk for both of them, starting a bender that lasted a week. Jake went home. By nine o'clock, he was sound asleep.

He fought a dozen times in 1932 and lost two close decisions. The fix might have been in with the judges, he'd never know, but they were losses to men he would have knocked out a year or two earlier, before Lionel Kane. It was harder to get up in the morning to do the roadwork, harder to take the punches. He was casting about for another racket, but a working stiff couldn't earn in a year what a prizefighter could make for one big fight, so he kept fighting two or three bouts a month, sometimes taking fights on consecutive nights in different towns. In the early spring of 1933, Moe Spitzer came by the gym.

"I got a real fight for you, McCloskey."

"Who is it?"

"Big Polack out of Omaha. Looks mean as hell, aint been beat, but you can lick him. I seen him in Cheyenne, he can't fight."

"You told me Lionel Kane couldn't fight."

"You don't listen good. I said Kane was fat. I never said he couldn't fight. I said *fat* and you thought *slow*, which is not the same thing. Now are you going to fight this fuckin Polack or do I got to get one of the niggers to fight him?"

"Do I got a choice?"

"We all have choices, *boychik*."

"Not when that damned dame run off with all my money."

"Good you reminded me." Moe pulled his roll out of his pocket, peeled off a hundred dollars for Jake. "There's an advance on expenses. You get so you got to have quiff, pay for it up front. Stay away from them farmers' daughters. I don't need no crazy hayseed with a shotgun after my fighter, hear?"

"You know me, Moe."

15.

EMALINE WOKE AT DAWN. THE WIND HOWLED OUTside, grit rattled against the windowpanes, dust sifted into the house. She rose, dressed quickly, fought her way out the door. For the three-mile walk to the Arrowhead Diner, she turned up the collar of her coat, wrapped one scarf over her head, wound another over her eyes, leaving just enough room to peer through the slits. It wouldn't keep all the dust out, but it was better than nothing. Outside, she watched a turtledove trying to fly west, into the wind. Hard as it flew, the dove kept getting pushed back in the opposite direction. She worried that the poor thing might die flying backward, but the wind eased a bit and the dove was able to fly at an angle to the wind and into shelter under the eaves of an old barn.

She had walked no more than half a mile when Deputy Sheriff Dexter McGuinty eased his patrol car up beside her and pushed the door open. Emaline got into the car.

"Morning, Dexter."

"Mornin yourself, Emaline. Nasty weather for a girl to be out walkin by her lonesome."

"Thanks for stopping."

"That's Dexter McGuinty, sweetheart. Just the way I am. Always anxious to do a favor for a little lady such as yourself."

He squeezed her thigh.

"How's Estelle, Dexter?"

"Still asleep when I left. She's probably on the telephone right now, telling Syl Whiting the coast is clear."

Syl was a big, shambling deputy who was about two of Dexter in every direction. Dexter's wife, Estelle, was a pale and peaked little thing with a wonky eye. Emaline thought it was unlikely that Syl was after Estelle, but Dexter was sure something was up. One of these days, he said, he was going to sneak home early and catch Syl and Estelle in the act.

"Dexter, I'm sure Estelle only has eyes for you. In a little town like this, he couldn't park his patrol car outside your house."

"Sure he could. People would think it was mine."

"If you want to go on being silly, Dexter, there's nothing I can do about it. But you're wrong about Estelle."

Dexter rolled his eyes, but he shut up. When they pulled up in front of the diner, he put his hand on her thigh again. She slid away, asked if he was going to come in for breakfast.

Dexter shook his head. "No, I think I'll drive by the house. See who's there."

Emaline barely had time to take off her coat and scarf and shake the dust out of her hair before the door blew open. Cecil Narrows limped into the diner, followed by Earl Beckman and Vern Schneider, all of them shedding dust like sod-house rugs. Charlie Naudain glanced up from his cash register and grinned. Customers who paid cash on the barrelhead, all three of them.

"Mornin, Cecil. Mornin, Vernon. Mornin, Earl. Good to see you fellas aint blowed away."

Cecil wiped grit from his eyes. "Not yet, maybe. About another day a this and I'd just as soon blow away. I got about half a some fella's red-dirt ranch up in Wyoming all over my beet field."

Emaline poured three cups of coffee. Cecil took his spot at the end of the counter, still wiping grit out of the corners of his eyes with a hankie. "How do, Emaline?"

"I'm doing, Cecil. I'd be a lot better if it wasn't for this dust all the time. Wet sheets and tape won't keep it out."

"Aint it the truth? Can't imagine what my Betsy would say, if she was still with us. She always kept a clean house."

Hank Crippen hawked and spat into the garbage pail as he scraped his grill. There was music on Hank's radio. *Have you ever been lonely, have you ever been blue.* The song always made Emaline feel lonely and blue. The music stopped, a nasal voice started in on the Iowa hog markets. The farmers paid no attention. Prices were so low it didn't pay to listen.

Earl took the stool next to Cecil and glared out the window at the dust. "A fella can't win for losin. First we got that late freeze, turned the damned ground to cast iron. It warmed up enough to plow, then we got a duster. You put a crop in, and it goes like my flax did last year. Got so damned hot, the seeds cooked right in the ground. I never thought I'd live to see a hundred and eighteen degrees in Nebraska, I surely did not. Might as well try to farm Death Valley."

Cecil chuckled. "Hell, Earl, you couldn't farm the Garden of Eden."

"The hell you say."

"If you was in charge, that apple tree would a shriveled up and died. Eve wouldn't never tasted that apple, saved us all a lot of trouble."

"You got to have dirt to farm. The way it's blowin, them New Dealers will be pickin up Nebraska dirt in Tennessee. Sell it back to us, dollar a bushel."

While they needled each other, Vern Schneider sat watching Emaline with those puppy-dog eyes. He was short and wide and homely. His eyebrows grew together in a line straight and black as a crowbar.

"Mornin, Emaline."

"Morning, Vernon."

"Come with me to the dance tonight, Em?"

"No, Vernon."

"It's because I'm shorter than you, aint it?"

"No, it's because I don't want the stink of your Wildroot Cream-Oil up my nose."

"You say the same thing every week."

"That's because you ask me the same thing every week."

Emaline took their orders, which never varied. Pancakes for Cecil, two poached eggs for Earl. Pancakes, bacon, a bowl of Cream of Wheat, eggs sunny-side up for Vernon.

Emaline handed them their plates as soon as Hank finished frying the bacon and eggs. With the dust storm roaring outside, there wasn't a useful thing the men could do. They sat and gossiped and watched the dust blow. Emaline poured more coffee and Hank grilled more eggs and bacon and they hunkered down to wait it out, the talk a mere rumble over the drone of Hank's radio. Emaline watched an Indian family walk past the diner, fighting their way against the wind and the dust. The man was a big Crow named George White Magpie who worked as a hired hand, earning a dollar a day helping farmers haul hay or thin beets with a hoe. They walked single file, White Magpie leading the way with his long, loping strides, followed by his wife and their five children in descending order of their age and height, each two or three paces behind the one ahead. The youngest brought up the rear. She couldn't have been more than three years old, struggling to keep up on her chubby little legs as they battled against the dust and wind. The others kept walking. Not once did White Magpie or his wife or any of the older children look back to see if the little one was keeping up. They came to an intersection and crossed single file, not pausing to look for cars. In the middle of the road, the little one fell hard and skinned her knees. Emaline started to run out to help her before a car came along, but she bounced to her feet and went on, rubbing her knees. She ran to catch up. Emaline watched them vanish behind a curtain of dust.

Around midmorning, a De Soto coupe crawled along the road in low gear and pulled off to park in front of the plate-glass window of the Arrowhead. Two men got out and dashed into the diner, holding their hats against the wind. All the talkers craned their necks to give these two birds a look-see. One was tall and lean, the other short and wide. The short one walked with a limp, a lit cigarette dangling from his lower lip. The tall one moved like a dancer, light on the balls of his feet, but his nose looked as though it had been smashed by a baseball bat and his hands were lumped with fractures. They sat at a booth by the window. When Emaline brought the menus, the short one wanted a coffee, black. The tall one ordered a half dozen eggs, scrambled, with pancakes and bacon and a glass of milk.

"Hank makes big pancakes. You sure you can eat all that?"

"Hell yes, little lady. Got to, or I'd blow away."

"Suit yourself."

She picked up the menus, brought them each a glass of water. While Hank made their breakfasts, Cecil watched them in the mirror behind the counter. He leaned over to Emaline.

"That tall fella there is Jake McCloskey, the boxer. Had his first bout right here in Scottsbluff."

"Never heard of him."

"I expect you don't pay much attention to the fight game. There was a time they thought he was going to be light-heavyweight champ."

Emaline made a face. "Such a silly sport. I never did understand why people would pay good money to watch men hit each other in the face."

"There's an art to it."

"Oh, Cecil. That's a lot of hooey. It's ugly and it's brutal."

Once he heard who the man was, Earl Beckman had to amble over to say hello.

"Aint you Jake McCloskey, the prizefighter?"

"Yessir, I sure am."

Earl put out his hand and the fighter shook it. Earl winced. Jake introduced his trainer, Bucky Betz.

"Well, aint this a treat," Earl said. "I've got newspaper clippins about you. A couple big write-ups when you beat that colored fella, Lionel Kane. So what brings you two fellas to Scottsbluff?"

"Supposed to fight a big Polack from Omaha over here."

Earl waved Vern and Cecil over, introduced them to Bucky, who squinted at Cecil through a haze of cigarette smoke. "How long has it been blowin like this?" he asked.

"Since about 1929," Cecil answered. "Or maybe it was '28."

"You expect it'll end anytime soon?"

"When they run out a dirt."

Earl got up the gumption to ask for a display of Jake's talents.

"Why don't you do a little shadowboxin for us, Jake?"

"Aw, folks are eatin their breakfast. Aint right to make a disturbance."

"No, they aint. Everybody ate a long while ago. We're just waitin for it to stop blowin."

"Well then, I guess I got to provide the entertainment."

Jake climbed out of the booth. Earl helped Charlie push back some tables and chairs to form a square roughly the size of a boxing ring. Jake rolled up his sleeves and began dancing on the balls of his feet, pausing now and then to throw a flurry of punches. Emaline had never seen a man move like that, so easy and fluid. The speed when he unleashed those punches was a little frightening. That beat-up mug did not go with such easy grace.

After watching for a couple of minutes, Earl suggested that one of their own face off against the boxer. No real punches, just a little exhibition. "How 'bout you, Vernon? You're the youngest and the strongest."

The others took up the cry, shamed Vernon into peeling off his jacket and rolling up his sleeves. He was at least a half a foot shorter than Jake McCloskey but considerably heavier, with short legs, a wide back, long, simian arms. Jake pointed to the deep cleft in his own handsome jaw. "I promise I won't hit you, but if you can land one here, you win."

Earl announced that the two men would box three rounds of three minutes each and he would be the timekeeper. He rang an imaginary bell. Vernon shuffled off after Jake, fists held wrong side up like in the old daguerreotypes Emaline had seen of nineteenth-century boxers like John L. Sullivan. Jake let him get in close and throw as many punches as he wanted to throw, each deftly blocked or dodged. Vernon threw a haymaker at his head, Jake leaned back, let the punch whistle past his jaw, tapped Vernon two or three times in the face with his fingertips to show what he could do if he wanted to. After one round, Vernon's shirt was soaked through and he was breathing heavily. After two rounds, he could hardly hold his arms up. Halfway through the third round, Jake threw a half dozen mock punches that tapped Vernon all the way from the belly to the top of his head. Then he danced out of reach, laughing. Vernon bent over, wheezing, waved an arm to show he couldn't go on.

Earl announced that Jake was the winner by a technical knockout in the third round. Jake held up his arms, spun around, winked at Emaline. She turned her back on him. What made the man think he could get away with winking at her like she was some cheap floozy in a dime-a-dance joint? She noticed that the little trainer didn't even look up while his fighter was showboating for the crowd. He sat with the cigarette dangling from his lower lip, staring into his coffee cup like it was a bill from the undertaker.

An hour later, the wind died abruptly and the dust began to filter out of the air. The farmers left the Arrowhead in twos and threes, pausing to brush the dust from their windshields before starting their jalopies.

Jake and Bucky were the last to leave. When Emaline went to clear their table, she found a dollar under Jake's saucer, more than she made in tips that day from all her other customers put together.

16.

Bucky and Jake checked into the Platte River Motel Cabins that afternoon. They grabbed a little shut-eye first, then Bucky went in search of liquor while Jake headed out to do some roadwork along the banks of the North Platte River. It was familiar territory, the willows and poplars along the riverbank, the big bluff brooding over the town, the broad, flat river itself with its sandbars and eddies, its crawfish and bullheads. He had first come this way after mustering out of the army in 1919. Hopped a freight out of Camp Dix, New Jersey, headed for California, made it as far as Kimball, Nebraska, on the Union Pacific line. He had struck out from there, looking for work with three other veterans of the Great War, found it fifty miles to the north in Scottsbluff, loading sugar beets with a pitchfork. The pay was three dollars a day for a twelve-hour day.

He was slinging beets on a chilly October morning when a long, black Lincoln came crawling into the field and Moe Spitzer climbed out, puffing on a big stogie. Moe was putting on a fight card that night headlined by Curly Sackett, a Denver heavyweight who was supposed to be world champ someday. Sackett's opponent had pulled out at the last minute, so if one of the harvest hands was brave enough to step into the ring with the heavyweight, it was worth one hundred dollars cash money. Any man in that field would have let himself get knocked out for a hundred dollars, but Jake happened to be bigger and younger than most. He was standing up front when Moe made his pitch. Moe didn't mention that Curly Sackett had knocked out twenty-eight of the thirty men he had faced, but it would have made no difference. As far as Jake was concerned, they could carry him out of the ring on a stretcher, as long as he got his hundred dollars when he came to. Moe had found his man.

Jake forked sugar beets all day and barely made it to the arena in time. Bucky Betz taped his hands and slipped on the gloves.

"You ever fight before, son?"

"Not in the ring, but I been fightin my whole damned life."

"Well, keep your hands up and don't lead with your chin. He'll carry you three, four rounds, then when he's ready to end it, he'll wave one hand like he's showboatin. You take one on the kisser and go down. Don't try to be a hero, we don't want nobody hurt."

Jake didn't say a word, but he would be good and goddamned if he was going to lie down for any man. He stepped into the ring, slipped on a patch of blood from another fight, almost fell. There was laughter in the crowd. Jake McCloskey exploded. He went after Sackett, who grinned and backed away from his first flurry. When Jake came in again, he took a hard left to the nose, spun away, came up under Sackett's guard, knocked the man out cold with a right hook to the jaw thirty seconds into the fight.

Moe signed him on the spot. "I don't know if you was just lucky," he said, "or if Curly has a glass jaw, but what the fuck? If you're that good, I'll make you champion of the world." Curly Sackett took the train home. Jake rode to Denver in Moe's Lincoln, with Moe and a bottle blonde who called herself Miniver and licked her lips at him. He stayed at Moe's house in Denver, where Miniver left Moe snoring in bed each night to crawl under the sheets with the young boxer. Jake worried about what would happen if Moe woke up, but Miniver laid a finger on his lips. "Don't worry about him. I slip a little packet in his whiskey every night before bed, so's he don't bother me. I don't like doin it with a fat man, but these times, a gal can't afford to be choosy."

Jake spent three months working in the gym with Bucky before Moe got him another fight. He knocked the man out in the second round and pocketed fifty dollars. He was nineteen years old and he was a professional prizefighter.

It was after dark by the time Bucky Betz got back to the Platte River Cabins. He was a little drunk already, with a gallon jug of bootleg corn liquor dangling from one finger. He offered the jug. Jake propped it along his arm and took a long swig as he reached for his shoes.

"Where you goin in such a all-fired hurry?"

"Out. I got better things to do than to set here watchin you drink corn liquor."

"Well, hell. I thought we'd go back to that Arrowhead Diner, see if that pretty little lady is still waitin tables."

"It's after dark. I expect she's gone home by now. Anyhow, she got me all riled up and I got to do something about it."

Jake was almost to the door when Bucky hailed him back. "Hell, I forgot. Gimme my coat."

Jake handed it over. Bucky dug into a pocket of his overcoat, hauled out an old copy of *Time* magazine. He thumbed through it and found what he was looking for. "This here is called 'Mandolin Murder.'

> 'Last week Denver's leading 'legger, a little grocer named Joe Roma, sat plunking his mandolin in front of a music rack in his home. While a pot of spaghetti was bubbling in the kitchen, some unknown persons called. When they rose to go, they filled Joe Roma with so many .38 and .45 slugs that the police could not count the holes.
>
> 'The sudden death of 'Legger Roma was first thought to be connected with the kidnapping, the week before, of rich young Charles

Boettcher II. 'Legger Roma had just called on Chief of Police Albert T. Clark, presumably to discuss the Boettcher case. Meanwhile Boettcher's father, satisfied by notes that his son was alive and well, promised to pay sixty thousand dollars ransom.'

"Aint that somethin? Aint it? Legger Roma dead. Seems like every fight I ever worked, he was settin there at ringside, now he's shot full a holes."

Jake looked puzzled. "What happened to the rich kid? Did they turn him loose?"

"They don't say."

"What's a mandolin?"

"Somewhere between a guitar and a banjo, I think. Or maybe it's more like a violin. How the fuck do I know?"

"How'd they know a pot of spaghetti was boilin on the stove?"

"They don't say. Them reporters goes nosin around. Maybe they nosed in the kitchen, found the spaghetti boilin."

"I hope it didn't boil over."

"Jesus H. Christ! Did you hear what I said? Will you stop worryin about the goddamned spaghetti? They filled Little Caesar full a holes while he was playin the mandolin. Helluva way to go."

"Is there a good way to go?"

"You goddamned right there's a good way to go. Say you're a hundred and twelve years old and you're richer'n J. P. Morgan. You got a big old yacht, and you're sailin out in blue water. You're drinkin good whiskey and you just finished a two-pound sirloin steak. A sweet little blond chippie is swallowin your pecker. She gets you right to where your eyes roll back in your head, and bang! Your ticker quits while your pecker is still a-pumpin away. Now that's a good way to go. Gettin shot full a holes while you're playin a fuckin mandolin, that aint so good."

"It don't seem right. A man settin there bleedin to death with spaghetti boilin all over the stove. You ever eat spaghetti?"

"I don't eat wop food no more'n you do. Let's forget it, okay? You get all tangled up in the spaghetti, forget what the hell the story is about in the first place."

"It aint right, that's all. Don't that worry you, what happened to the spaghetti?"

Bucky threw a shoe, which Jake had to duck. "Jesus H. Christ. Get the fuck outa here, go get your ashes hauled. Try not to get stabbed and don't get a dose. And don't stay out all fuckin night. We got roadwork at six and sparrin partners at ten."

"*I* got roadwork. *You* don't have roadwork. You couldn't run your sorry ass from here to the damned door. Don't swallow that whole jug a whiskey neither. I aint got the jack for your funeral."

Bucky Betz had his weakness, which was liquor. Jake could take his drink or leave it. Women, though, he had to have women. That pretty little thing working in the diner, say. Sweet as peach cobbler. Nice figure to her too. Something wrong with her arm, crippled up, she was always hiding it behind her hip. But those big dark eyes, the black hair, those high cheekbones, the narrow waist. He was part Cherokee, he could spot Indian a mile off. She got him all cranked up, like there was something wild in her and he was the man to let it loose. Now he had the fever in him and he had to have it somewhere. In his pocket, he had the address, scrawled in pencil by a colored sparring partner in Denver. A place in jigtown where a man could get nickel beer and fifty-cent women. East Ninth Street. Couldn't be hard to find in a town this size.

He slipped out the door before Bucky could draw him into another argument, got directions at a gas station, found the place easy. Red light in the window, curtains drawn, jukebox music from inside. It was one of a row of such establishments along the south side of the street. There was a neon sign in the window: RED'S PLACE B-B-Q. The doorman peeked through a slit. Jake said he got the address from Reck

Towne in Denver, the door swung open. Red's Place was a long, narrow room with a bar along one side, sweet-scented pork barbecue opposite, tables toward the back, a dance floor in the middle. There was a good crowd already, sixty or seventy people, about as many as the room would hold. Men in loose suits and women in tight dresses.

The bartender had a red conk. Red's Place. Jake said howdy to Red, ordered a beer and ended up drinking three, then danced three dances with a slender, cocoa-colored gal who wanted two dollars to go to the room in back. He thanked her for the dances, ordered another beer, took the glare from her man, a thickset pimp, his legs spraddled on a barstool up front. The pimp could give him the evil eye all night long. He wasn't going to pay two dollars for a chippie. Quim always felt like quim, once you were beating around inside it. One visit with Miss Cocoa was four tricks with a fifty-cent harlot.

By the time he was halfway through the fourth beer, he hadn't spotted a likely whore other than Miss Cocoa and he was ready to start trouble. The pimp would do just fine. He wore brown pants and a brown shirt, which made it easy. *Say, where'd you get them shit-colored clothes? Was they always that way, or did you just shit yourself when you seen me comin?* The pimp would come at him quick and low, the knife held blade up. Kick the blade loose, bust him in the face.

Jake drained the beer, set the bottle down, rubbed his knuckles. He was about to head after the pimp when a woman dark and ample as a coal car planted herself between his thighs. The heat of her went straight to his loins.

"Hello, sweetheart . . ."

"Well, hello yourself."

In the back room she washed him with a cloth so hot it made his eyes water, then squatted over a basin on the floor and washed herself. He closed his eyes, thought of the slender, willowy body of the girl working in the diner. The whore mewed like a newborn kitten while she rode him.

It was hot in the little room. They were both soaked in sweat when it was over. She sat up, her chest heaving, wiped her breasts with a towel. "Damn. I aint had it like that since Chester left for Kansas City."

Jake leaned back, pleased with himself. "Is that your pimp out there, the man in the shit-brown pants?"

"Naw, that good-for-nothin leech is Yancy. Only girl he got is Kitty, that high-color gal you was dancin with. My man is Chester, only he been gone a month. They all afraid of Chester. Don't know when he'll come back, so they leave me be."

She moved across his chest to reach for a cigarette. The weight of her breasts got him going again. He reached for his pants and hauled out another fifty cents. "I got to have it again," he said, "but this time, let's make it wrong side up."

"Oh, no, sugar. You want to go up that road, it will cost you six bits."

He paid her another quarter and turned her onto her stomach. This time he was quick and savage. She was so loud he was sure they could hear out in the bar, even over the noise of the jukebox.

She went to wash herself after. Jake tipped her an extra two bits as he pulled on his pants. "That was just dandy. So long, sugar."

"Call me Cherry. Cherry will take care of what ails you. *Any. Time You. Want.*"

"Cherry. Yes, ma'am. See you again real soon, Cherry."

"That was fun, sugar, but next time I fuck in here? This place is goin to have a *fan.*"

17.

Every morning until the big fight, Jake went by the diner at six o'clock sharp, just as Emaline was getting to work. He ran with a towel wrapped around his neck and he threw punches as he ran, usually with Bucky beside him in the De Soto, leaning out the window to egg him on. "C'mon, McCloskey! I know fat ladies who can run faster than that! Do you wanna lick this Polack or not?"

Jake always waved at Emaline as he passed. She would wave back because it was impolite not to do so. Bucky and Jake would climb the hill to the north until they vanished from sight. An hour or so later, they would be back, Jake toweling off the sweat and Bucky lighting another cigarette as they entered the diner for their usual breakfast—coffee and more cigarettes for Bucky, a half dozen eggs with pancakes, bacon, two big glasses of milk for Jake. Emaline had never seen a man eat like that, but she supposed that if you ran for an hour before breakfast it would give you an appetite.

If Cecil and Earl and Vern were around, they would sit with the boxer and his trainer for a while and talk to Jake about the fight game. Was it true that Slapsie Maxie Rosenbloom had ducked him? Who was better, Jack Sharkey or Max Baer? Would a good big man always beat a good little man?

Emaline wearied of the endless boxing talk that had taken over the diner since Jake and Bucky came to town, but it would soon be over—and Jake was the best tipper she had ever seen. Every day he left at least fifty cents under his plate. Once he left a silver dollar. That was the day of the fight, when she found the dollar on top of an envelope under his plate. Inside were two tickets to the boxing card at the arena that night, with his name printed right on the ticket, Jake McCloskey against Dobroslaw Jarogniew. There was a note for her attached to the tickets:

Miss Emaline,
I'd be greatful if you'd come see this fite and bring a frend these here too tikets are on me.

yours truely,
Jake
(the boxer fella)

Emaline showed the tickets to Charlie Naudain.

"Why would he want to leave tickets for me?"

"I expect he thinks you're a good-lookin woman."

"That doesn't mean I'm going to go watch a silly prizefight!"

"Well, don't go, then. I imagine Bobby would love to see the fights."

"Look at this note. He can hardly spell a word. I'm surprised he got my name right."

"I had to tell him how to spell it. There's things in life other than spelling, Emaline. He's a good-lookin fella, just like you're a good-lookin woman. He's maybe ten years older than you are, but I always say a woman should be younger than her man. Takes men longer to grow up."

"Charlie! I would never step out with a boxer."

"No, you wouldn't. And you wouldn't go with me nor Cecil Narrows, because we're too damned old. You won't let Vernon take you dancin because he's short and homely and he dances like a Black

Angus bull. You're going to end up an old maid if you don't quit bein so picky."

"I'm surprised at you, Charlie Naudain. I never knew you for such an old matchmaker. This is one match you are not going to make."

Cecil Narrows came in then, without Earl Beckman for once. He said Earl was complaining of stomach pains, probably ulcers from all that worry about what the New Dealers were up to, stealing Nebraska dirt and all. Cecil tried to convince Emaline that she ought to go to the fight.

"How often do you get out, girl? Once a week to the motion pictures?"

"Once a week! Who can afford that these days? Once a month, maybe."

"So go to the fights, then. At least it's free."

"No, it isn't. If I go, he'll expect something from me. Then it's not free."

"By gosh, you're a hard nut to crack. Aint she, Charlie?"

Charlie shrugged. "Too tough for me. Couldn't get through that one with a brace and bit."

"I swear, you two are getting sillier as you get older. I'm not going to watch a bunch of sweaty men punching each other bloody. If one of you wants to go with Bobby, here's two tickets you can have."

Cecil Narrows said he would take Bobby to the fight. He showed up in his old Model T Runabout, with a box in back large enough to haul a good-size hog. When he came into the house, Emaline almost threw him out again.

"What is that you're carrying, Cecil?"

"Why, it's a rifle."

"I can see that, Cecil. Why are you bringing it into our house?"

"It's a present for Bobby. He's the best shot I know, and I can't shoot worth a tinker's damn anymore. Never could, although I got lucky a time or two. This here is an Enfield M1917 rifle. I carried her in the war. Shot me one fat German. He had to be fat, if I shot him."

Cecil handed the rifle to Bobby, who took it like he was handling the Holy Grail. The rifle was four feet long. It weighed almost five pounds. It had a bolt action and a flip-up rear sight. While Emaline watched, Cecil showed Bobby how to load the five-round fixed-box magazine. He also gave the boy a hundred rounds of ammunition and the original sling with the bayonet and scabbard. Emaline thought it all looked very dangerous.

"Cecil, we can't accept this. Really. Bobby is too young and we can never repay you."

"Don't you fret, girl. He's twelve, but he's a born hunter. I've got no children of my own, so I want to give this to somebody who'll use it right. If you can ever shoot deer in this state again, maybe he can get me a haunch of venison. Then we're square."

"Well, I guess we can't thank you enough. But I want you to go out with him the first time he fires this thing. I want to be sure he knows what he's doing."

Emaline had promised to make an early supper for Cecil if he would take Bobby to the fight. When she told them supper was ready, she had to remind Bobby to put the rifle away first or he would have laid it on the table next to his meat loaf.

It was past eleven and she was starting to worry when Cecil brought Bobby home from the fight. The boy came in wide-eyed and chattering. He said there were eight bouts on the card, but the best one was the last one. Jake fought a Polish guy with a name like a sackful of letters all shook up and knocked him right through the ropes in the fifth round. Some men pushed the other fighter back into the ring, but Jake hit him again, right in the kisser, and he was done, flat on his back while the referee counted him out. Cecil bought peanuts and two cream sodas for Bobby. When the fight was over, Bobby got to meet Jake McCloskey and shake his hand.

"He had this tape all over his knuckles under his gloves. That's what they do, so they don't bust up their hands, but he said his hands are all busted up anyway. He told us how he done it, said he knocked out that Polack with a right to the body that brought his hands down and a left hook to the head. Oh, and he asked how come you weren't at the fight."

"What did you tell him?"

"I told him you didn't care for boxing. He said he was right sorry you wasn't there."

"Well, I wasn't sorry. I'd rather stay home and read a good book. I had my Chekhov stories to read. That beats watching a bunch of sweaty men try to hurt each other, don't you think?"

"Who's Chekhov?"

"He's a Russian writer, honey. He writes wonderful stories. You should read them someday."

"Aw, Sis. You know I aint much for readin. I might like to try boxing, though. It looks almost as much fun as baseball."

"Absolutely not! Never! I will not have my little brother getting a broken nose like that Jake McCloskey."

"But women think he's a swell-lookin fella."

"How do you know?"

"There was two of 'em settin behind us. They kept goin on about how handsome he was. When me and Cecil left, they was still waitin outside the dressing room to talk to him."

When Emaline went to bed, she tossed and turned. She was jealous. Jealous of two women, low creatures who would go to watch a boxing match without a male escort and wait outside a boxer's dressing room just to talk to him. In spite of herself, she imagined Jake with them at this moment, grinning that grin, sitting there with that handsome cleft in his chin and those green eyes and that shock of black hair. He *was* good-looking, there was no arguing that, but he was as untutored as a billy goat. Anyway, the fight was over and Jake McCloskey would be headed back to Denver. There was no point losing sleep over a man who lived two hundred miles away, especially one who could barely spell his own name.

18.

AFTER TWO DAYS OF GOOD, SOAKING RAIN IN early May, the bunchgrass greened some. Three warm spring days without dusters followed the rain. There were leaves on the trees and the sun was shining and the weather made Emaline feel as light as one of those feathery clouds skimming through a sky the blue of cornflowers. When school was out, Bobby took the train to Sheridan to spend the summer on the 8T8. She helped him get his things to the train station, including the Enfield rifle in its scabbard. She wished he would leave the thing at home, but he was as attached to it as he was to his baseball bat. She managed not to cry as he boarded the train, but she would miss him awfully, the way he whistled around the house and sang little bits of funny tunes and told her jokes he had heard at school.

The next time she had a day off from the Arrowhead, she took a picnic lunch and headed for her favorite spot by the river, a place she had often gone to pick gooseberries with Velma. At the last minute, she decided to take along an old fishing pole that had belonged to Calla's husband. If she could catch two or three fish, she and Calla could have something different for their supper. She packed a pork sandwich and a sweet potato and a jar of sweet corn kernels that Velma had canned in the fall. The corn was for the fish.

It was a three-mile hike to her picnic spot. She had to cross the bridge that connected Scottsbluff with Gering, then work her way back to the west, to a sheltered grove of elm and cottonwood. There was a row of weeping willows along the riverbank and she had to search to find a space between the willows where she could get a hook in the water. Bobby always caught fish along here, although perhaps not at this time of year, when the spring-swollen river was roiled and muddy.

Emaline eased her way along the riverbank, her shoes and stockings off, feeling the warm mud between her toes. The river could be a rough place, especially near the hobo jungle. She didn't see any tramps around, but they had built campfires in the grove and the ground was strewn with empty bean cans, bits of torn clothing, shattered whiskey bottles, even a little booklet soaked in the rain and charred around the edges by the campfire. She picked it up, saw a crude drawing of two popular cartoon figures copulating, tossed it away. She turned her back on the mess, took an old blanket from her basket, spread it on the riverbank, sat on the blanket to watch the river flow. She ate half her sandwich and all of the sweet potato. When she tossed a crust of bread aside, a colony of ants moved in, efficient as engineers. In the distance she could hear traffic on the bridge, but it was peaceful down here. She lay back to rest for a while, watching a hawk circle, a speck in the vault of blue sky. She wondered if they could really see a mouse from so far up, but then the hawk turned into a plunging bullet. When it rose, a small animal struggled in its talons.

She sat up, reached for the jar of corn, dropped a handful of kernels into the water to draw the fish, baited the hook with more of the corn, cast her line. Within an hour she had three small perch and a good-size carp wrapped in a towel in her basket. She ate the second half of her sandwich and drank the rest of the well water she had carted along. She had just finished eating when she saw the huge thunderheads building over the bluff and a curtain of rain approaching the river. She began packing up her things, thinking that she had plenty of time to finish before the rain hit, but the storm was coming fast. She began to walk back to the road, but when lightning struck a tree a hundred feet behind her, she dropped the fishing pole and picnic basket and ran all the way to the bridge. She wanted to slip under the bridge to wait out the storm, but a dozen tramps had beaten her to the spot.

"Hey, little missy!" one of them shouted. "C'mon in here, we always got room for a pretty little gal."

She swerved onto the narrow track that led up to the highway. The rain had turned the path into a slippery stream. She scrambled up the bank with her hands and fingers and knees, clutching at brush and brambles to drag herself along, cutting her palms and muddying her dress. A bolt of lightning spurred her up onto the bridge. Her legs felt as though they were made of rubber. She slowed to a walk, her chest heaving. A handful of automobiles crawled over the bridge, their windshield wipers flailing at the rain. She waved her arms, trying to flag someone down. She walked quickly, trying to gather enough air in her lungs to run again. She was halfway across the bridge when she saw an apparition out of a comic book, a man riding through the rain on a bright blue motorcycle, complete with a sidecar. He wore a leather cap and goggles, a long black leather coat, black knee-high motorcycle boots fastened with a dozen buckles up the side, a long, white scarf like a fighter pilot's, now soggy with rain. The rider slowed his motorcycle and eased up next to her, shouting above the storm and the roar of the machine. "C'mon, get in!"

He handed her a rain slicker from the sidecar. She hesitated. He looked familiar, but she couldn't place him with the leather helmet on his head and his face half-hidden by the goggles. The lightning flashed again. She pulled the slicker over her shoulders and jumped into the sidecar. Water sloshed around her feet. He leaned toward her. "Where do you live?"

"Out West Overland. Two miles. Straight ahead, then make a left."

He kicked the motorcycle into gear, did a U-turn in front of a slow-moving farm truck, zoomed off to the north, the tires throwing up a wide fan of water on either side. They made the left turn onto West Overland going so fast that she was afraid they might roll over, then roared down the empty road with thunder crashing all around them. When they were a quarter mile away, she pointed out the little white house on the left. He turned in to the driveway and hit the brakes hard, sending out a spray of gravel and killing the engine all at once, coming to a halt under a towering Chinese elm.

Emaline jumped out of the sidecar and ran in, holding the door open for him. They stood just inside the door, water pouring off his leather coat and her dress and hair, puddles widening on the floor as he peeled off the leather helmet and goggles. "Mr. McCloskey."

"Yes, ma'am."

"Sorry, I didn't recognize you in that getup. What were you doing out there in the rain?"

"Lookin for you. I went by the diner to see if you wanted to come for a ride. Your friend Calla said you went for a picnic by the river, so I was headed over to look for you, but by the time I got to the bridge it was rainin like a cow pissin on a flat rock."

Emaline wrinkled her nose at the crudeness of the man. She wanted to ask him to leave, but she couldn't turn him back out into the storm.

"Thanks for rescuing me from that rain, Mr. McCloskey. The storm gave me an awful fright."

"Call me Jake."

She looked him over warily. She was soaked through and wanted to get out of the wet dress. She ran her hands through her hair, wringing out more water. "I must look a sight."

"Not to me, you don't."

"All right. You may come in. Take off that wet coat and your boots and have a seat on the davenport. Let me change into something dry."

Emaline left him to unbuckle those complicated boots, slipped off her shoes, padded barefoot into the bedroom. She toweled off and ran a brush through her hair before she changed, but she was still damp and breathless when she lifted the lock and stepped into the parlor. He was sitting on the davenport with his long legs stretched out, those big, broken hands resting on his thighs, watching it rain. She had no dry towel to offer him, so she asked if he wanted a cup of tea.

"I'd care for a glass of water if you got one handy."

She fetched him a glass of water and put a kettle on for her tea.

"I have to thank you again," she said.

"You were in quite a state. What happened out there?"

"When the storm came, I wanted to get under the bridge, but there were these tramps under there hollering at me."

"I'll go back right now and give those birds a lickin."

"Oh, I'm sure they're not there now. There is one favor you can do for me when the rain stops. I dropped my basket and fishing pole when I was running to the bridge. If you could just take me back, I'd like to get my things. I don't want to go back there alone."

"Don't mind a bit."

She could see the rain outside, pouring off his shiny blue motorcycle. "That's quite a machine."

"She aint new, but she's a beauty. She's a 1924 Henderson Model K. Royal blue. Eighty cubic inches, all the power in the world."

He looked her square in the eye when he spoke. She liked that. His battered mug seemed more vulnerable now. "How long have you been a prizefighter? A long while?"

"Yes, ma'am. Too long. I've been in the ring since the end of the Great War, more or less. Started right here in Scottsbluff in the fall of 1919. I was a kid, nineteen years old, fresh out of the army. Had about enough of it by now, tell you the truth."

"I'm sorry, I don't know anything about fighters, except I've heard of Jack Dempsey and Gene Tunney. I don't like fighting."

"This aint fighting, it's boxing. They call it the sweet science because there's an art to it."

"That's what Cecil Narrows tried to tell me. I don't see anything sweet about getting hit in the head."

"That aint the sweet part. The sweet part is hittin the other fella."

"So what brings you back here? I thought you'd go back to Denver after your fight."

"We did. I was back there a week and this promoter fella got me another fight here in Scottsbluff. This time, I pulled a trailer behind the De Soto so I could bring the motorcycle."

"I guess it's lucky for me that you did."

The rain eased. When it stopped, she gave him some old rags to dry the motorcycle. By the time they turned around in the driveway and headed east, the sun was out again and there was the long arc of a rainbow on the northeast horizon. He parked on high ground on the south side of the bridge. They slid down the muddy path and picked their way along the bank, skirting the piles of broken bottles and tin cans. They found the pole and the basket of fish and walked along the river until Emaline thought they were too close to the hobo jungle.

"You aint afraid of them birds, are you?"

"Well, not exactly . . ."

"You're with me. Long as you're with Jake McCloskey, there's no need to be afraid of a solitary thing."

After the storm, the sun baked steaming puddles and wet branches and everything seemed to glow. Even the grass seemed vibrant with life. They strolled along the river's edge, found a good place to sit and watched until the sun disappeared behind the battlements of Scotts Bluff. Jake pointed to the summit. "You ever been up there?"

"Oh, yes. Many times. It's a hard climb, but it's wonderful once you're up top. You feel like you're on top of the world. On a clear day, you can see Laramie Peak."

"We'll have to take a hike up there."

She wanted to say they wouldn't be doing that because she couldn't possibly see him again, but it seemed a rotten thing to say at such a time. They walked to the motorcycle and rode back to the little house. Emaline felt she had to invite him for supper to repay him for all he had done for her that afternoon. He scaled and gutted the fish and she fried them with some potatoes. By the time she had supper on the table, Calla was home from the diner. Jake kept them both laughing with his stories about boxing.

When the clock struck nine, he stood abruptly. "I got to get up at five o'clock for roadwork. If I aint up, that danged Bucky has been known to dump a bucket a water in my face."

"It must be hard, training like that."

"Aw, I been doin it so long, I don't think about it much. Worst part is havin to see Bucky's mug that early in the day."

After he left, Emaline warmed a cup of milk to help her sleep, then slipped into her narrow bed. It started to blow around midnight. She lay awake much of the night, listening to the shotgun blasts of the wind blowing grit against the window. Sometimes when the dust started up like that, she thought they were living through the end of the world.

19.

EACH DAY THE FOLLOWING WEEK, JAKE PICKED her up at home and drove her to the diner before he went to do his roadwork. Sometimes Bucky was with him, sometimes he was alone because Bucky had lost a battle with a bottle of corn whiskey. Bit by bit, she learned things about him. He came from a family of eleven children, eight boys and three girls, the girls as rough as the boys. There was a good deal more to him than she had thought at first, but she hadn't changed her mind. She would never get mixed up with a semiliterate man who made his living with his fists.

At the end of the week, Jake asked if she would like to go to the Saturday night dance at the Armory. She started to turn him down with the ritual speech she gave Vernon when he persisted, about how she was run off her feet all week and by Saturday she was too tired to go dancing. Then she remembered how much she liked to dance. She hadn't danced in at least a year. "All right. I'll go to the dance with you. What time are we going?"

He winked at her. "You be ready. I'll be by."

The night of the dance, Jake bought a flask of something fiery off a bootlegger operating from an old Dodge parked outside the Armory. They sat talking in the De Soto, watching the crowd filter inside. He offered the flask. She took a long, bold swallow and felt the liquor like pure flame going down her throat, spreading warmth in her limbs. She felt wild and young and a little giddy.

Inside, they danced three dances to a good swing band. Jake was an agile dancer, long and lean and light on his feet. Emaline was thrilled, her face flushed, grinning from ear to ear as she followed him through a jitterbug, knowing that people were watching the smooth way they flowed together. After a very quick fox-trot that left her breathless and laughing, Jake went to get them both a root beer. She was smoothing her hair down and trying to catch her breath when she saw Bose Hubbard. He was standing with a group of railroad workers in a corner of the dance hall, the bunch of them laughing over some joke. Instantly, she was a terrified girl again, bent over a kitchen table with Bose's hand around her throat.

When Jake returned with their root beers, she grabbed his sleeve and led him toward the door.

"What's the matter with you?"

"We have to leave."

"Why? We just got here. Paid fifty cents to get in."

"I know, Jake. I'm really sorry, but I have to leave right now."

"What's the matter?"

"You see that big man with those fellows over in the corner? His name is Bose Hubbard. He's the reason I have to leave. Please, I want to go now."

They stepped outside into the fresh air, stood for a moment in the shadows of the building listening to the band. Jake took her hand. "You're goin to have to tell me why."

"I can't."

"Yes, you can. You had some trouble with that fella?"

"I can't tell you. I've never told anyone."

"Well, you're goin to tell me if we have to stand here all night. If he did somethin to you, I'll take care of him."

"You can't, Jake. He's too strong. I've seen him take the back end of a Model T and lift it out of the mud all by himself. Let's just go. I don't want to see you get hurt."

"I'm not goin to budge until you tell me what happened. Come on now. Out with it."

She took a deep breath. "When I first came to Scottsbluff, my mother was in the TB hospital in Denver, so I stayed with Bose and his wife one year while I went to high school. When I came home after the last day of school, Nellie was out visiting a sick friend. Bose was drunk and nasty and I was scared to be with him, but I thought he would quiet down if I fixed him supper. He grabbed me while I was at the stove and threw me over a table. He didn't actually do it, you know, but he had a beer bottle. I tried to fight, but he had his hand on my throat and I knew he could break my neck like a chicken. He said if I ever told anybody he'd kill me. When he finally went to sleep, I packed my things and ran out and never went back. Now can we leave?"

"Okay, we'll go. Just give me a minute to take care of this bird."

"It's not your fight. Please don't."

Jake was already striding back into the dance hall. Emaline peeked nervously from the doorway as he crossed the dance floor and tapped Bose on the shoulder. He said something. The big man's face darkened. Jake turned on his heel and strode back toward the door with Bose trailing. As he stepped out the door, Bose leaned toward her, his voice a low growl. "So you couldn't keep your trap shut, huh? Soon as I get done breakin the back of your little boyfriend, I'm comin after you."

Jake waited in the light that spilled out through the windows of the dance hall, rolling up his sleeves and grinning. Emaline thought he looked positively blissful. Bose's friends had followed him out the door. They stood in a circle around the two men. When the word spread that Bose Hubbard was going to crush some poor devil, the dance hall emptied as people rushed to watch the spectacle. Even the band members left their instruments and hurried out to join the circle. Bose grinned and rubbed his thick palms together. He opened his arms, bearlike, ready to swat away this irritating little fly. Then one of his buddies recognized Jake.

"That's Jake McCloskey, Bose! He's a boxer."

"I don't give a damn if he's Max Baer. I'm goin to break him in half."

Bose charged like a bull. Somehow, he missed. Jake danced to the side, out of harm's way. Bose turned like a big old locomotive in a roundhouse. He lunged again. The first blows landed, left-right-left, so fast that Emaline saw only a blur. Bose felt something give between his eyes. Jake had broken his nose. Another lunge and a crisp left jab on the broken nose sent a wave of red pain flowing through his temples. He got one hand on Jake's shirt, took a flurry of blows to his belly that left him gasping for air.

It was like watching a big, clumsy dog chase a bumblebee. Jake wore three or four rings on his fingers. They were cutting Bose to ribbons. The man's eyes were swollen shut and three of his teeth had been knocked out and he had yet to land a single solid punch. It was a terrible spectacle, but Emaline did not want it to end, she wanted it to go on and on. She was screaming, not even trying to mouth words, just screaming. She had been choking down the rage she felt for so long that she hadn't guessed at the terrible, black anger she held inside. She wanted to see this man damaged, destroyed, turned into a pitiful, battered hulk. His nose was smashed, blood flowed from a dozen cuts on his forehead and around his eyes. He had spat out two or three teeth. When he tried to breathe, he gagged on his own blood. Bose lunged again, took a hard left that dropped him to his knees and a smashing overhand right behind the ear that toppled him onto his side. He sagged like a collapsing tent and lay unconscious on his stomach, blood from his nose and mouth pouring over the ground.

Jake stood in the shadows, grinning, waiting for her, flicking the blood off his knuckles. He saw the look in her eye, something wild and feral that had been let loose by the beating. Emaline took his battered hands and held them to her cheek. "Can we leave now?"

Jake heard the distant wail of a siren. "I'd say it's about time."

He held the door open for her, started the De Soto. They sped off, passing a deputy sheriff's patrol car on the way to the Armory. Emaline saw Dexter McGuinty behind the wheel. Jake laughed and banged his palm on the steering wheel. "Dang, that was fun."

When he asked where they were headed, she invited him to come home with her. Calla was away visiting her sister in Torrington, they would have the house to themselves. They slept together in her narrow bed, fully clothed because she wouldn't allow it any other way. Around midnight she woke. For the first time in years, she felt safe. Something had eased inside her, some constriction of the breath and spirit had been released. She was free from the tension that fear brings. The fear she had felt in the orphanage, fear of her stepfather Watson and his drunken rages, fear of Bose, fear for her mother. Since she was a very young girl, there had never been anyone who could protect her. Now she had this fighter who could destroy powerful men with his fists. He had already battered the man who frightened her most, and he did it with ease. It was like living inside a fortress where no one could touch her.

20.

THEY WERE MARRIED IN DENVER ON JULY 1, 1933. Jake wanted it even sooner, but Emaline was not entirely certain she wanted to be married to such a rough, untutored character. Charlie Naudain kept telling her she should go ahead and marry the man, but Calla was firmly opposed.

"His head is always on a swivel," she said. "Every time a pretty girl walks by, he watches her like a hungry fox. And he's got an awful temper."

Jake did have a terrible temper. Calla had seen it one day when Jake got into an argument about religion. He and Bucky had stopped in for supper at the Arrowhead Diner. Walt Deegan, an elder in his church, was at the next table. When Deegan began praying noisily over his dinner, Jake listened for half a minute and then told the man to put the quietus on it.

Deegan opened his eyes and unfolded his hands. "Excuse me, sir, but we always pray before supper. I don't believe that's any of your business."

Jake leapt out of his seat, his face a thundercloud, fists clenched. If Charlie Naudain hadn't quickly stepped between them, he would have destroyed poor Deegan.

Emaline knew that Jake would explode over nothing, but the storm always passed quickly. Above all, he made her feel safe. The fourth time he asked her, she finally said yes.

"In that case," he said, "I got to tell you, I was married before, to a woman name of Thelma Pearl. She left me in Denver two years back, took most every penny I had. I got a divorce on account of desertion, I aint seen her since."

"You should have told me before."

"I know. Tell you the truth, I didn't think you'd ever say yes. Figured there was no point bringing it up."

"Yes, there was. The point was to tell the truth. Do you still have feelings for this Thelma Pearl?"

"Yeah, I'd like to knock her damned head off, only I don't even know where she lives."

"Well, as long as you never want to knock *my* head off."

Jake was to fight a rising light-heavy named Bam-Bam Butterfield three days after the wedding, so they made it a little honeymoon. They drove to Denver in the De Soto, checked into a hotel downtown because Jake had given up his rented house, and walked the three blocks to the courthouse. Emaline wore a bottle green dress that belonged to Calla, Jake a tan suit, two-toned shoes, a straw boater. Bucky and his wife came along to act as witnesses. The justice of the peace was a twitchy little man with a stutter and a two-dollar rug laid cattywampus across his head. Emaline couldn't take her eyes off that hairpiece. It looked like a muskrat pelt, as though it might come alive at any moment and sink its claws into the man's skull. When it was time for her to say "I do," Jake had to elbow her in the ribs to get her attention.

They all signed the papers, Jake paid the clerk three dollars. She was Mrs. Jake McCloskey, swallowed up in all that male storm and ego. She didn't mind a bit. They stumbled out laughing into the glare of a Denver noon, the roar of traffic and blare of automobile horns, the reek of gasoline and diesel fuel, the shadows of the tall buildings, the rush of pedestrians in an almighty hurry. She wondered how people could actually live here without feeling all jumbled up inside. It pulled you in too many directions at once, so that you held nothing in your memory but odd, disconnected fragments, like a child's worn shoe lying in a gutter or a cop lounging in the sunshine on the front fender of his patrol car, ogling the shopgirls as they passed by.

She had hoped that Bucky and his wife would come with them to put off the inevitable moment when she would be alone in that hotel room with her new husband, but Bucky said it was time for the newlyweds to be alone. Emaline and Jake celebrated with lunch at the Woolworth's counter down the block, where Jake bought her a tuna-fish sandwich and a banana split with a cherry on top. He tried to talk her into a cherry Coke as well, but she said that a glass of water would do just fine, thank you, it was silly to waste a nickel on pop.

When they finished eating and he went to the cash register to pay the check, Emaline felt all nervy and short of breath. She had made him wait for anything more than a kiss, now she wished she hadn't. She wished they had gotten it over with in the back seat of his De Soto. She was jittery as a cat on a stove, wanting it and wishing it would never happen at the same time, thinking of that wide brass bed in the hotel room yawning like the entrance to a cave. She told herself that she didn't have to do much, just lie there and close her eyes and wait. It was like dancing, Calla said, the man was supposed to lead. But if he didn't know how to dance, then what did they do? Jake was a superb dancer, he was good at all things physical. He had been married before. He would know what to do. Still, her mind skipped along like a dragonfly over the water, and her heart was beating too fast. She pressed her hand to her chest. *There, girl. Settle down, settle down. It will soon be over and then you'll know.*

At the hotel, the elevator boy closed the iron gate as they stepped into the cage, turned the brass handle. They climbed as if by magic the three flights to their floor. Jake got out the big brass key and turned the lock and the door to Room 14 opened and she thought she would faint right there, facefirst onto the bed. He kissed her hard.

"Here you go, Em. I got to head out. I'll be right back."

"Where on earth are you going?"

"Department store across the street. Goin to get you some little thing to remember our wedding day."

"I don't need anything. I'll remember our wedding day just fine. That muskrat thing setting on that poor man's head, if nothing else."

"Won't take a minute, Em. I know just what I'm lookin for."

"Can't you go later?"

"You go ahead and freshen up. By the time you finish, I'll be back. Don't let any strangers in the room now, hear? Somebody knocks, you peek through this little hole, see who it is. If it aint me, don't open it."

He gave her a peck on the cheek and vanished. She sat on the edge of the bed with her heart beating in her throat. Her nerves made her thirsty, so she poured a glass of water from the vase on the dresser and drained it. She seemed to have a bottomless thirst. She listened to the ticking of the clock. An hour passed and still he wasn't back. She fidgeted and paced, tried to read one of the library books she had packed in her valise. She got stuck on one sentence and read it over and over. Why would a man disappear on his wedding day?

When she got up enough nerve to venture out into the hall and take the stairs down three floors to the lobby, the clerk on duty was not the same kindly, gray-haired gentleman who had checked them in that morning. This one was thin and young and dark, with dandruff all over the shoulders of his dark blue jacket. She walked past him to the entrance of the hotel and peered across the street at the great, looming bulk of the department store. It was the biggest store she had ever seen. She couldn't face the thought of entering that cavernous place to search for him. She headed back to the stairs. The clerk glared at her, but he didn't try to stop her. She had the horrid thought that perhaps he thought she was in the hotel for some illicit purpose. She climbed the stairs quickly, ran down the hall to Room 14, twisted the doorknob, almost sprained her wrist. The door was locked. Of course it would be. Jake had explained it to her when they arrived. The door had a special mechanism that caused it to lock when you closed it. He had two copies of the heavy brass key. One was on the bedside table, next to her library book. The other one Jake had taken with him. Did the hotel clerk keep a third copy? That was an awful lot of keys for one room. Still, she would only know if she asked. She would go right up to that clerk and say that she was Mrs. Jake McCloskey and that she had accidentally locked herself out of Room 14, and would he be so kind to give her another key, please. But how would he know that she belonged to that room? She didn't have her handbag or her coat or anything at all. Just herself, a hick girl from Nebraska, left in a hotel room by a man who'd lured her to the big city and abandoned her. How many times did people who worked in hotels hear that story?

She paced the hallway, back and forth from one end to the other. The sensible thing was to go downstairs. There were two or three davenports in the lobby. She could sit there and wait for Jake. Sooner or later, he would come back. She sat down on the steps, aware that she had another, more urgent problem. She had drunk so much water that she had to pee desperately. She squeezed her thighs together, jiggled her calves, tried to think about something else. She tried to recall whether there were facilities for ladies and gentlemen in the lobby. She couldn't possibly ask that surly male hotel clerk. She needed to go so bad her eyes watered. She hurried down the steps, praying her bladder would not let go in the lobby.

She looked around desperately. There was a narrow hall that led to something behind the main desk, but she couldn't see what was back there. The clerk was helping an elderly couple who were being laboriously fussy over the room they would have. She rushed up the steps to the third floor. For no rational reason, she decided to try the door to their room again, to be certain it really was locked. She pushed so hard that when the door opened, she went stumbling into the room and caught her balance on the brass bedstead. Jake was lying on the bed, his shoes off and his legs crossed, with a newspaper open to the sports pages, trying to read a story about his upcoming fight with Bam-Bam Butterfield. He looked up.

"Where the hell were you?"

"Never mind where I was! Where the hell were you?"

Jake grinned that big silly grin. "I got lost."

"You what?"

"I got lost. Can't help it."

He started to explain, but she cut him off and rushed to the bathroom. She locked the door, turned the water in the sink on as high as it would go to cover the sound, unbuttoned her corset and yanked her drawers down, felt as sweet a release as she had ever known in her life. When she was done, she washed her hands and face, took a deep breath, opened the door.

"All right, mister. Do you want to explain what happened?"

He shrugged. "Put me down in the country and I can walk a straight line for a hundred miles, daylight or dark. Turn me around just one time in a big city and I lose my directions. I tried to ask a couple of folks, but nobody I could find ever heard of this hotel."

"You were gone more than an hour."

"It's a big city, hon. Once you go the wrong way, it's a long way back."

"But you lived in Denver. You couldn't possibly get lost here."

"I only had to know how to get one or two places, mostly to the gym and back home. Usually I had Bucky with me, or Thelma Pearl, or somebody knew where they was goin."

"I don't want to hear about that stupid Thelma Pearl."

"Whoa! You're mad at me, aint you?"

"Who wouldn't be, you big oaf? You left me on our wedding day. All by myself, in a strange hotel in a strange city. I went out to look for you and I locked myself out of my room. I didn't know where you were and I was afraid you got kidnapped!"

"Kidnapped? Who the hell would want to kidnap me?"

"Gangsters. Like those gangsters you told me about in the fight business. I thought maybe you didn't throw a fight you were supposed to, or you owed them money, or you got hit by a streetcar."

Jake laughed until she thought he was going to choke. Emaline was so mad she just wanted to slap the big lug and pack her valise and take the bus back to Scottsbluff. Then he reached into his pocket and pulled out a present wrapped in tissue paper. "Here, girl. This is what I went to find."

She wanted to fling it in his face, but curiosity got the best of her. She opened it cautiously, as though she might find dynamite inside. It was a lovely tortoiseshell comb. She turned to the mirror on the wall next to the wardrobe and slipped the comb into her hair on the left side, pulling it back. He stood and watched over her shoulder, ran his fingers through her hair. She leaned back against him.

"It's beautiful."

"Gawd, I should hope so. I must a walked twenty miles to get it."

She turned to him. "Don't you ever do that again. Don't you leave me alone in a place like this. The rest of the time we're here, I want you within fifty feet of me, is that clear?"

"Then you're goin to have to come to the fight. You said you'd never go nowhere near a prizefight."

"I will this time. I'm not going to stay in this hotel alone."

He took out his handkerchief and wiped away her tears. Then he lifted her easily in those strong arms and carried her to the bed. Her emotions were spent. She hadn't the strength left to be nervous. It was all easy and natural and she was very happy that he knew what he was doing. When they finally crawled out of bed, it was near nine o'clock and they had to walk a dozen blocks to find a diner that was open where they could get hamburgers and pie. She counted the blocks and watched for landmarks so she could find the way back. She had a hamburger and a vanilla malt, he ate three hamburgers with a slice of apple pie. They walked back to the hotel, enjoying the warm air of a summer night and the distant lights winking high up in the mountains.

21.

Bam-Bam Butterfield hit hard and he hit often. Emaline sat with Vera Betz in the second row, directly behind Moe Spitzer, inhaling the smoke from his cigar. It was hard to watch. She peeked through her fingers, covering her face when Jake seemed to be getting the worst of it. He fought well but lost a split decision.

Vera showed her the way back to the dressing room, where Jake sat on a table looking bloody and battered and completely spent. Bucky's cut man was working on a gash on Jake's left eyebrow, the room smelled of blood and disinfectant. Emaline ran her finger over his cheek. "I want you to quit now. I don't want you to fight again."

Jake turned, spat a great gout of blood into a bucket on the floor, threw a towel aside in disgust. "You don't have to talk me into it," he said. "I'm done. I might take another fight or two to pay the bills, but I'm done."

He knew how things were. In the fight game, a man was headed up or out. It wasn't the kind of career where you punched a clock for forty years and then they gave you a gold watch. Every boxing gym had old fighters hanging around, sweeping the floor and doing odd jobs for a few bucks a week and a place to flop. Some of them could still remember their big fights, some couldn't recall their own names. Young fighters ignored the punch-drunk cases and told themselves that was what happened when you weren't good enough. The week of his last fight, Jake walked into the men's room in the Shaughnessy Gym and saw Dink Hudson, a former welterweight only ten years older than himself. When Jake got his start in the business, Dink Hudson was knocking them out in front of big crowds. Now Dink stood at the urinal with an odd, lost smile on his face as a stream of urine soaked his trousers and left a spreading yellow pool on the floor. He had forgotten to unzip his pants.

Jake collected his money for the Butterfield fight and told Moe he was done. Moe shrugged. Jake had been the best fighter in his stable, but he was thirty-three. Another fighter, Moe might have tried to wring a few more dollars out of him. But Jake had made a lot of money for Moe. Moe shook hands with them both and wished them well, then reached into his wallet and pulled out a C-note, a little something to help them get a start. Jake started to protest, but Moe waved him off. It was the least he could do, he said. Jake tucked the hundred away.

"People are too hard on you, Moe," he said. "Way down deep, you're all right."

Moe took a long puff on his stogie. "No," he said. "I aint."

The next morning, they left for Scottsbluff. All Jake's furniture from his rented house made barely half a trailer load. On the drive, they talked it over. Jake wanted to head to California, make a life out among the orange groves. Emaline wanted to take the cash Jake had left, pool it with her savings, buy a little farm in Nebraska.

"We have some money in the bank now," she said, "better to get ourselves a place than to fritter it away."

She didn't mention the De Soto or the Henderson motorcycle, or various other fripperies which he seemed unable to resist. Left to his own devices, Jake would eat in restaurants three times a day. He wasted money on pop and candy bars. He dressed to please the ladies. She had yet to see him in a pair of bib overalls. If they were going to make a go of it farming, he would have to change his ways.

Jake had farmed with his father and brothers. He knew that farming was brutally hard work. No matter how much toil a farmer put in, he could be wiped out overnight by a hailstorm or a duster or a collapse in the price of wheat or barley.

She knew that everything he said was true. Times had never been worse. Even the old-timers couldn't recall when it had been so hot and so dry. Prices couldn't be lower. Truck farmers were dumping their produce in the barrow pit and pouring oil on it because it wasn't worth trucking it to market. Something was wrong with the weather. Clouds would come streaking over the prairie, turn dark and threatening, and then vanish after leaving no more than a few drops of rain. But Emaline reminded him that things always change and that land would never be cheaper.

"Folks always tend to think that whatever way things are, that's how they'll always be," she said. "In good times they think times will always be good. They live high on the hog, get themselves in debt, then they lose it all when times go bad. In bad times, people hunker down. They're afraid to spend a dime. They think there will be drought and depression from now till Kingdom Come, but it won't be like this forever, Jake. The rain will come back and times will get better."

Jake didn't necessarily believe her, but she found an argument he couldn't resist. A farmer was his own boss. He didn't have to listen to some foreman barking at him on the job or find his pay docked because he showed up fifteen minutes late for work. There was no more independent man on this earth than the American farmer. He finally agreed. As soon as they got back to Scottsbluff, they would start looking for a place. He saw himself with a big, lush farm, a brace of prize horses, maybe a purebred bull. A half dozen strapping boys to do the heavy lifting and three or four beautiful girls to help around the house.

Back in Scottsbluff, Calla Plessman and Charlie Naudain organized a little party for the newlyweds. Cecil Narrows was there with Earl Beckman and Vernon Schneider. All her regulars. Somebody invited Dexter McGuinty. He hung around making people nervous with his badge and his twin Colt .45 revolvers. Vernon had a hangdog look, but he shook Jake's hand as if to say the better man had won. Charlie Naudain wasn't sure that was true, but he knew that Emaline would never have married a homely fellow like Vernon. It wasn't in her.

The Sunday after they returned to Scottsbluff, she and Jake drove out to the Lindquist place. Emaline made a roast beef dinner while Lee and Jim walked the farm with Jake, explaining how they did things and why. Lee said a long prayer in Swedish before they ate and she could feel Jake getting restless, but at last the prayer ended and they fell to, the men eating like famished coyotes. Emaline explained what they wanted, a little place with a house in fairly good shape, maybe with some farm machinery in the deal.

Jim knew of one such farm, a place about three miles north of Stegall and twice that far from his own farm. It had been good land before this drought hit. Eldon Duncan, a farmer working a homestead there, was about to go broke. If they moved quick, they could buy a hundred and sixty acres of land and a pretty good house for three thousand dollars.

"Eldon paid sixty dollars an acre in 1928. Now he'll let it go for less than twenty. Another five hundred will get you his team and machinery. That will just about square him with the bank. Anything he has left, he'll use to set up somewhere else."

Jake and Emaline drove out to the Duncan farm early Saturday morning. The farmer met them on the front porch. He was a man barely over forty, with a stoop and a weathered face that made him look twenty years older than he was. Emaline saw his wife watching them through the screen door, a thin, worn-out woman with three kids clinging to her dress and one big, sullen boy who stood off to the side of the house with his cap pulled low over his eyes. They walked around the place while Duncan pointed to this and that, improvements he had tried to make. Emaline worried about the house itself. The front porch sagged, making the house look like it was about to collapse. There was a second house on the land, the original homestead, a basement house built right down into the earth, with the edge of the roof only two feet above ground level and a single window facing south.

The fences were in good shape, as were the corrals and the pigpen and chicken house. The barn looked more solid than the house. Duncan had obviously put all his effort into looking after the farm. Duncan pumped water to show that it was a good well and filled tin cups with fresh water so they could sit in the shade of the one big cottonwood tree while they talked. He rubbed his thumbs along the seams of his bib overalls.

"This place just plumb beat me. I thought I could set it right, just one more year, get a little rain. Prices go up some, maybe. Didn't happen neither way. Had ten inches of rain last year, I don't think we're goin to see that much this year. Wife can't take it no more. She says if she has to watch that dust blow another year, she's goin to take my shotgun and blow her durned head off. Hell, she might want to take me with her. I shore do hope you folks have better luck here, 'cause if it warn't for bad luck, we wouldn't have no luck at all."

When it came time to close the deal, Emaline had almost as much to invest as Jake did. She put in four hundred dollars, which she had saved, a nickel tip at a time except when Jake was her customer, from her job at the Arrowhead Diner. He put in six hundred. They borrowed three thousand from the First State Bank, which was eager to loan money to folks who could put up twenty-five percent cash. When the papers were all drawn up, they shook hands with the banker.

They moved into the basement house to give Jake time to make repairs on the main house before winter hit. From the first day on the farm, they rose with the sun and worked till sundown. Jake managed to make some improvements on the house, but he was no carpenter. He tried to do everything by main force. When nothing else worked, he would reach for a sledgehammer. He might have knocked the entire house down, but a bindle stiff who called himself Colonel Amen came knocking at the door, wanting to work for food. He was handy with a hammer and saw and willing to work hard for three square meals a day. He quoted scripture at the top of his lungs while he worked, but he could drive a nail straight, cut a two-by-four so it fit perfectly the first time, shingle a roof without falling through it. After he had worked for two weeks, the house no longer looked as though it might collapse with the next strong wind. Emaline grew weary of hearing the Revelation of St. John all day long and asked Colonel Amen if he didn't know a few of the Psalms. He recited one or two and went back to Revelation, but it was worth it to see an almost new house emerge from the wreckage of the old. Colonel Amen slept in the barn and refused even to take his meals in the house. Jake said he was a tramp of the old school, a man for whom the road was a calling. As soon as he finished the job, Colonel Amen would be off again, back to riding the rails.

They had lived in the basement house barely two weeks when Emaline woke at first light to an ominous roaring noise. It sounded like a low-flying plane, so loud that she could feel the vibrations in the bedposts. She jumped out of bed just as the roar turned to a scream and heard the impact as something hit the roof. She could see the ceiling tremble as whatever it was went right on over the house. The water jug she kept on a nightstand next to the bed fell and smashed on the floor, scattering fragments of glass in every direction. She ran up the steps and out the door in her nightgown, shading her eyes to peer up at a sky the color of rose water.

The sky was empty, but the roar was coming at the house again, this time from the other direction. She darted around in back in time to see Jake on the Henderson, roaring along the hard-packed dirt track that led to the house, dressed in his motorcycle outfit. He had to be doing at least forty, maybe fifty miles an hour, coming right at the house. She thought he was completely mad, that he intended to crash into the house and kill himself, but then she saw that he had braced a twelve-foot plank from the ground onto the roof and an identical plank on the opposite side. He had detached the sidecar to make the motorcycle lighter. As it screamed toward her, the royal blue machine glittered in the morning sunlight. Then he bumped onto the plank, the motorcycle roared up the north side of the roof and soared into the air, flew fifteen or twenty feet past the south edge of the house, came down onto the dirt track that led to the pasture. Three or four shingles had been knocked loose and came sailing down with the breeze, one of them landing almost right at her feet. Emaline shook her fist at his receding back. "Have you completely lost your mind?"

Colonel Amen came running out of the barn barefoot, his hair full of straw, convinced that the Second Coming was at hand. Even above the roar of the motorcycle, Emaline could hear him start in on Revelation: *His head and hairs white like wool, as white as snow; and his eyes as a flame of fire . . .* The hens scurried wildly to and fro in the yard, panicked by the machine. She wouldn't be surprised if they stopped laying after such a fright. Jake turned and sat on the motorcycle, gunning the engine, revving up for another run. He popped the clutch, stood the bike up on its back wheel for thirty or forty feet, came again, racing up through the gears. This time she saw him wobble a little in the air before he got the machine under control and came down for a shaky landing. He roared off, made his turn, came back again, made three more jumps before he throttled down and eased the motorcycle up to where she stood. He pulled off the helmet and goggles. Colonel Amen headed back to the barn, muttering to himself, disappointed the Apocalypse was not at hand. Jake was grinning like a three-year-old with a toy truck.

"Aint that something else? I didn't know if she'd make it, but she sailed right over the house, easy as pie."

"Are you completely crazy? You scared me half to death. I was sound asleep. I thought we were being bombed or something."

"Aw, don't go gettin upset over nothin. I couldn't sleep last night. I got to thinkin about a basement house like this, how a man on a motorcycle ought to be able to get up enough speed to fly right over. All I needed was planks, we got plenty of those. Had to wait till daylight to give her a try. By gosh, that's a thrill. You ought to climb on the back, come with me. I think I can get up enough speed so it'll carry us both on a jump."

"You *think*? You are completely insane. I will never get on that thing again, much less jump over a house."

"Gee, Em. I thought you'd see how it could be a helluva deal. We could get up a crowd. Sell tickets for a dime apiece. Sell watermelon and lemonade too. On a good Sunday afternoon, we might take in twenty or thirty dollars."

"Honestly. Do you think folks have money to spare to watch you try to break your neck? We're out here to farm, not to run some five-and-dime P. T. Barnum motorcycle stunt show."

She stormed back into the house, leaving Jake to return the motorcycle to the shed. He came whistling in and looked at the stove as though he expected to see his breakfast frying.

"Aint breakfast ready yet?"

Emaline hurled an egg at his head from across the kitchen. He caught it deftly, tossed it behind his back, caught it again with his left hand, cracked it on the edge of the frying pan. He dropped the egg into the pan and tossed the shell into the slop pail for the hogs.

"That's one," he said. "I expect I'll need about five more."

Three weeks later, they woke to find Colonel Amen gone. He had been sleeping rough, tucked into a bedroll on a mound of hay in the barn. The carpenter work on the house was finished, there was nothing to keep him. Jake figured that with the cold weather coming, the colonel wanted to hop a freight for a warmer climate before the first snowfall.

The Lindquist brothers came by and helped them move into the main house. To Emaline, it seemed like a palace. She had a kitchen with a big cast-iron coal stove, a comfortable bedroom, a second bedroom, where the Duncan children had slept, a parlor big enough for a davenport and four chairs. There was a cellar under the house where she could store potatoes and onions and apples, and a pantry off the kitchen where she kept her cream separator, her butter churn, her washtub, the vegetables she managed to can before winter. They had a small barn with three stalls and a haymow, a chicken house, a hog shed, a smokehouse, a tack shed for harness and saddles, two outhouses. Apart from the exhausting, unceasing labor, it was a good place to live.

22.

THEY WERE STILL GETTING THINGS ARRANGED in the main house when Emaline was awakened sometime after midnight by the sound of tires on gravel. It was a hot night, the sheets sticky and uncomfortable, and she had fallen asleep without a stitch on after performing her usual bedtime duties for Jake. As she pulled her nightgown over her head, headlights swept across the south window of the basement house. A car was creeping along the narrow dirt track between the house and the barn.

"Jake?"

He answered with a long snore.

"Jake!"

This time he sat bolt upright. "What the damned hell?"

"There's a car coming. Someone right outside."

He jumped out of bed, peered out the window. "Somebody in a pickup truck."

"Who could it be at this hour?"

"Damned if I know. They better have a damned good reason for bein out there."

He pulled on his boots and overalls and headed out the door shirtless. As she watched from the window, a tall woman got out of the pickup and ran to Jake. The two of them embraced with fervor.

The woman pulled back a tarp to show Jake something in the back of the truck. He nodded and laughed and said something that made the woman laugh in turn, then he took her by the hand and led her to the house. Emaline pulled on her threadbare robe. She was still trying to yank her hair back with the tortoiseshell comb Jake had given her when they burst through the door.

"Look who's come to visit, Em! This here is my sister, Luella, drove down from Rapid City tonight. Luella, this here little lady is Emaline."

Emaline started to shake hands, but Luella wrapped her in a bear hug and lifted her off the floor. Luella was nearly six feet tall and heavier than Jake, with shoulders like a man's. She spoke in a voice that sounded like she was calling hogs.

"How do, girl! My, she is a sweet-lookin little thing, aint she. Where you been hidin her all this time? Honey, I'm awful sorry to come pilin in on you in the middle of the night like this, but I got two flat tires comin down from Rapid City and the second one, I didn't have a spare so I had to get a fella to give me a lift to a garage to get her fixed. Listen, doll, I'm just as pleased as punch to meet you. Now what say we get some coffee goin and get acquainted? We can unload that truck in the morning."

"Jake didn't even tell me he had a sister in Rapid City," Emaline said.

"Well, I only just moved up there six months ago. Before that I was down in Oklahoma."

It sounded odd, a woman on her own in a pickup truck moving from place to place, but Emaline didn't like to ask questions. Jake often talked about his family, but there were so many of them that Emaline couldn't keep them all straight. She seemed to remember that Luella was the youngest of Jake's sisters, but she couldn't be sure. After their wedding, she had written letters to Jake's parents in Missouri and to a sister in Omaha, but she hadn't written to Luella, nor had Luella given them any warning. She had simply dropped in after midnight and expected a big welcome.

Luella was hungry, so Emaline heated some potato soup and sweet corn and sat yawning while Luella told one story after another. At last, she wound down. Emaline made up the bed in the spare room for Jake's sister and went back to bed. After a few hours of troubled sleep, she woke to find Jake and Luella already up and whispering as they dressed and went out. She thought they might stay in bed at least until six, but apparently Luella rose as early as Jake himself. Emaline tried to go back to sleep, but there was something about that Ford Runabout and its contents that troubled her. She got out of bed, tiptoed to the kitchen window, watched as Jake backed the truck up to the barn door and they began unloading what appeared to be big brass pots, sacks of something that might have been oats or corn, lengths of copper tubing, a small stove. It took them twenty minutes to get it all into the barn.

They came in hungry, wanting breakfast. Emaline got going on eggs, bacon, coffee, and oatmeal. Luella told some story about Jake and his brothers when they were young, how they had turned the bulls out to fight while old Ike McCloskey was away. There were seven or eight bulls and they tore up Ike's prized corn planter, purchased brand-new from Chicago that winter. The brothers got the bulls back in the corral and propped the planter up so that it looked as though nothing had happened. It was midwinter and they had almost forgotten the incident in the spring when Ike brought out his team, hitched them to the prized planter and popped his whip. The big draft horses leaned into the harness and lurched forward and the planter fell apart, dumping the old man on his seat right there in front of the house, where he sat bellowing, "Boys, get the hell out here!"

Luella slapped her thigh and laughed her honking laugh and Jake slapped his thigh and they both laughed until they cried. It was not until he came up for air that Jake noticed Emaline wasn't laughing.

"What's the matter, hon? Aint that just about the funniest thing you ever heard?"

"I want to know what that was you put in our barn."

"Why, it was a hog feeder."

"Do you think I'm stupid? Since when do you need kettles and copper tubing and a heater for a hog feeder? You're putting a still in our barn, aren't you?"

"Em, what makes you think that?"

"We had a neighbor up in Wyoming who ran a still. I saw it a time or two when my stepfather went to buy liquor."

"Well, if you know what it is, why do you ask?"

"Because I want to know what it's doing on our land."

"Less you know about it the better, hon, but the main thing is that Luella was getting crowded where she was, so she had to set up someplace else."

"And she picked our barn, is that it?"

Jake was about to answer when Luella butted in. "Listen, honey, it's only going to be for a while. I'll give you two bits out of every dollar I make, just for the use of your barn."

"Nobody can keep a secret around here. The sheriff will be onto you in no time."

"Honey, you let me take care of the sheriff. All you got to do is go on about your business. It's none of your concern."

"It is my concern. It's my house and that's my land. I don't want the kind of people who buy that stuff coming around and I don't want the law crawling all over our barn. Anyhow, I don't know why you'd start up a still now. They're repealing the Volstead Act. Prohibition is going to end by January."

"I know that, honey. That's exactly why I have to try to make an honest nickel right now, before legal liquor comes back and puts little operations like mine out of business."

Faced with the two of them, Emaline felt as though she was banging her head on a wall. She was about to say something else when Jake's fist banged down on the table. "That's just about enough, woman. We need the money, the still is goin in the barn. That's all there is to it. Aint like we asked you to make it, nor drink it neither. You won't have a thing to do with it. You can do somethin around here to help make ends meet, and all you got to do is shut the hell up."

Jake's face was black with anger. Emaline had never seen a man explode so quickly. It shook her.

"So does this mean Luella is staying with us?" she asked.

"Long as she pleases, she is. I told her she can have the basement house as long as she wants. You don't expect me to turn my own sister out, do you?"

Emaline dressed and left the house without saying another word and walked the six miles to the Lindquist farm. She found Lee and Jim out with the team, mowing hay. She sat with them for a time in the shade of a haystack. Jim asked if anything was wrong. She shook her head.

"It might have been a terrible mistake, that's all."

He nodded, looked out into the distance with those blue eyes the way he always did, like he was looking for answers out there somewhere.

"He's a hard man. I knew that soon as I saw him."

"He is. Most of the time he's real good to me."

"Most of the time. Not all the time."

"No. His sister came from Rapid City last night. She's going to be living with us for a while."

"Is that all? You don't like this sister moving in?"

"No. That's not all. She brought a still. She's going to run it out of the barn."

"You'll have the sheriff on you."

"That's what I told her. She says she can take care of the sheriff. I don't know what she means by that."

Jim plucked a stalk of alfalfa, picked his teeth with it. "I have an idea what she means. You aren't going to like it."

"I know that."

"You can stay with us anytime, long as you want."

"Thank you, Jim. I'd like to, but my place is with my husband."

Jim drove her back to Pancake Flats. The Ford Runabout was gone. There was a note on the kitchen table in what had to be Luella's hand.

Emaline,

We're going to be gone for two or three days, honey. You take care of things here and we'll see you real soon. Lots of love from your sister-in-law.

Luella

The nerve of the woman, telling her to take care of things on her own farm. Wherever they'd gone, they were up to no good, she was sure of that.

They were away four days. Emaline would have left the farm, except that someone had to look after the livestock. The De Soto was still parked under the little shed Colonel Amen had built for it, but Emaline couldn't drive. When she needed some things on Saturday, she walked to the Lindquist place and caught a ride into town with the Swedes.

When Jake and Luella returned, it was around midnight. Emaline saw the pattern. Luella drove at night because she figured there was less chance she would run into the law. This time, they unloaded whatever was in the back of the truck before they came into the house. Emaline waited until they were alone the next morning to confront him.

"Where have you been?"

"Way down in the southwest corner of Colorado."

"What was that in the truck?"

"Load a broom corn."

"Like they use to make brooms?"

"They used to. Don't anymore. Found better uses for it now."

"Like what?"

"To feed the hogs."

"Why would you have to drive all the way to Colorado to get hog feed when we've got plenty of corn right here?"

"Not broom corn, we don't."

"You're not going to feed it to the hogs at all, are you?"

"No, Em, we aint. The less you know about it, the better. We got a banknote to pay off. The quicker we get it paid, the better you'll sleep at night."

"I won't sleep at all if you're in jail."

"Didn't Luella tell you she'll take care of the sheriff?"

"I don't know what that means and I don't think that guarantees you won't go to jail."

"It's only a few months, woman. When Prohibition is done, we're done runnin that still. Now just look the other way and don't worry so damned much. I never seen such a woman for worry. If you didn't have nothin to worry about, you wouldn't know what to do with yourself."

"Well, mister, I'm beginning to think that any wife of yours has plenty to worry about. You got lost on our wedding day. Then I woke up one morning to find you jumping a motorcycle over the house. Now your sister is running a still on our land. If I had known you were going to do all that to worry me, I would have told you to stick to boxing. At least when you were fighting, I knew where you were."

It wasn't long before Emaline learned how it was that Luella could get away with running her still. At two o'clock one afternoon, Sheriff Orie Bassett pulled into the driveway in a big black Buick and honked his horn. Emaline was about to go out to see what he wanted when Luella came out of the barn. She went around to the passenger side and opened the door and slid onto the seat next to the sheriff. They talked for a bit, then Luella's head disappeared from view. She came up two or three minutes later, shook hands with Orie, gave him a peck on the cheek, sauntered back to the barn. As he pulled out of the driveway, the sheriff tipped his hat to Emaline.

The next day it was Dexter McGuinty at the door, shuffling his boots and looking sheepish.

Emaline peered at him through the screen. "Well, hello, Dexter. What brings you way out here?"

"How do, Em. I was just lookin for Luella."

"I think you'll find her out in the barn."

Dexter disappeared into the barn and came out twenty minutes later, whistling and zipping up his pants. Emaline waited until he was out of sight, then stormed out to the barn and got her fist right up in Luella's face.

"Listen, woman. I put up part of the money for this place. It's mine as much as it is Jake's. Maybe I can't stop you from running a still out here, but if you have to have visits from the law, can you confine it to the basement house and not be fooling around in cars or rutting in the barn like a filly in heat?"

Luella drew herself up to her full height. "You got no call to talk to me that way, little girl."

"I'm not a little girl. I'll talk to you any way I please. You're running a still and behaving like a harlot. You put on all these airs but you're nothing more than a common criminal."

"By God, you got a mouth on you, girl. You keep runnin it and I'll whale the tar out of you."

Emaline picked up a pitchfork. "You aren't going to whale on anyone around here. You touch me and we'll see if Jake is strong enough to pull this pitchfork out of your guts."

Luella laughed. "Well, aint you the feisty one. Listen, I do what I got to do to keep the law off my still, but from now on, I'll tell the fellas to meet me down at the basement house. Would that satisfy you?"

Emaline was about to agree when Jake burst into the barn. He had been down working a horse when he heard the commotion and walked in to find his wife holding a pitchfork aimed at his sister.

"What the hell's goin on?"

Luella waved him away. "Not a thing, Jake. Me and Emaline had a little difference of opinion, but we got it all worked out. You never told me she was such a little spitfire."

After that, Dexter McGuinty came out to the farm once or twice a week. Orie Bassett always turned up on Mondays and Fridays. Dexter would come Tuesdays and Thursdays. Once in a while, one or the other would arrive on a Saturday. Never once did Syl Whiting appear. Emaline's opinion of Syl went up considerably. With Luella's carrying on, Emaline felt that she had no choice. She sent a note to Bobby explaining that she and Jake were still trying to get the main house livable. She suggested that maybe it would be better if he stayed in Wyoming and went to school with Eli's kids for this one year.

With the end of Prohibition that winter, factory liquor was flowing again and the market for corn liquor dried up overnight. Luella broke up her still and sold it for parts. The following spring, she went to a camp meeting and came back full of religious fervor for Aimee Semple McPherson and the Foursquare Gospel church. She took the train to California, stayed six months, and returned to the North Platte Valley as an ordained Foursquare Gospel minister, trusted to carry the word of the Lord to the sinners of the world. Luella was a born preacher. She had fervor, the gift of gab, a ready-made tale of a woman who had sold her soul to the devil in order to manufacture demon rum until Aimee Semple McPherson showed her the error of her ways. One of her first converts was Sheriff Orie Bassett. He became Luella's third husband.

23.

THROUGH THE LONG, HARD WINTER AND INTO the spring of 1934, Emaline clung to the radio and the mail. On the radio, she followed the titanic struggle waged by President Roosevelt and his top aide, Harry Hopkins, against the ravages of the Great Depression. The president had moved with stunning speed from the day he entered the White House, acting in hundreds of ways to restore confidence in the banking system, to put the unemployed back to work, and to bring federal relief to those who needed it most. A quarter of a million young men were put to work through FDR's brainchild, the Civilian Conservation Corps. They were improving the national parks, building bridges and hiking trails on public land. The Federal Emergency Relief Administration was bringing help to the truly desperate, or at least trying to. Every day she listened to the radio news in the morning and again in the evening, catching snippets of the great struggle, trying to piece it together, to understand whether it was all tipping toward some horrifying final collapse or whether the nation and the world beyond were beginning to crawl out of this morass.

She didn't need the radio to know how bad things were. Almost every day, reminders turned up at the farm. If they didn't hear about the depression, the depression came directly to them. Colonel Amen was the most capable of all the hoboes passing through, but men and boys came by every week, wanting work, even in the dead of winter. They almost never asked for handouts. Like most of the desperate poor, they were looking for any job at all. They would muck out the barn, fix fences, build corrals, paint, help with the livestock. The most they asked in return was a dollar a day or a square meal or two.

Most times, Jake found something for them to do. As much as anything, he liked to have someone around to talk to. The first question he always asked was whether the man played checkers. The game was his third passion, right after boxing and horses. For a good checkers player, he could always find at least a week's work.

Jake could barely read, but he possessed a restless curiosity, and the men who came through could tell him how it was in Washington or Texas or Pennsylvania. The tales they had to tell were disturbing. Many of the men who came through had ridden the rails, as Jake once had, but hopping a freight was getting more difficult. With millions of hoboes as young as twelve or thirteen riding freight cars all over America, the railroad bulls had been turned loose. The hoboes who were caught were lucky. They were handed brief sentences for vagrancy in the city jail. If they were less fortunate, they could be sentenced to six months or more on a chain gang for the "crime" of wandering the country, looking for work. In some places, tramps were savagely beaten or murdered. Even so, white hoboes didn't face the horrors that greeted blacks on the road in places like Oklahoma, where in some towns if a black man so much as stepped down off a boxcar, he would simply disappear. There were also tens of thousands of women and young girls riding the rails, some with babies in their arms. They would run to hop a train, toss a child up into a moving freight car, hope that someone would be there to catch the baby, then try to swing up themselves. There was no way of knowing how often they failed.

When men stopped at the farm to work, whether for a day or a month, they ate at the kitchen table with Jake and Emaline. Now and then, Jake would have to let a man know that he wasn't welcome unless he climbed into the stock tank and cleaned up before he came indoors, but they would never allow a hired hand eat in the barn while they ate in the house. It was a small thing they could do for a few unfortunates in this mobile army of the poor, but it was better than nothing.

Emaline sent news from their small Nebraska farm all over the country, writing a steady stream of weekly letters to all her aunts, Tavie in Jackson Hole, Ruby on Sheep Creek, Marguerite in Valentine, Kate in Bellingham. They were all literate, intelligent women. Their lively letters kept her up-to-date on the world outside the Nebraska panhandle. She also wrote two or three letters a week to Bobby and Ben.

In February, Ben wrote a short note to say that Ida Mae Paint had died of heart failure in the State Hospital in Evanston and would be buried in Sheridan. Emaline had mixed feelings when she heard the news. She tried to be charitable to everyone, but Ida Mae had made life very difficult for Velma and her children. Someone else might want to mourn the woman. Emaline never would.

They had moved onto the farm too late in the summer to plant or to do much of anything with the land other than try to save some of what was left of Duncan's crop. With the spring, they would be able to try their own luck. Emaline wrote to the Department of Agriculture in Washington, D.C., and to the University of Nebraska to order every pamphlet, booklet, paper that might help them decide what crops to plant, how and when to plant them, how to keep the soil from blowing away, how to irrigate in the absence of rain or to use the irrigation water that was pouring down from the Guernsey Dam in Wyoming.

She was able to engage Jake's attention only now and then. The agricultural pamphlets were far too difficult for him to read, so Emaline would take notes for him and boil it down to simple instructions. Plant this, don't plant that. Plow to a depth of eighteen inches. Plant in strips fifty yards wide, allowing one strip to lie fallow while you planted the other. Chicken manure makes the best fertilizer for a truck garden. Create a windbreak by planting a row of poplar trees. She learned to tell him what she had to say in five minutes or less. Longer than that and his attention would wander. He'd tap his foot, gaze out the window, pace back and forth. He was so perpetually restless that at times she wondered if it hadn't been a mistake for him to retire from the ring. During the winter, he played checkers, listened to the big fights on the radio, worked horses on the coldest days, argued politics and religion with anyone who cared to argue. He also made it to every Saturday night dance in town, no matter what the weather. Emaline watched it all and fretted. Those dances were expensive. She went along with him at first, but they never got home before two or three o'clock in the morning, with cows bawling to be milked at six. He could do it, but if she tried to get through a Sunday on two or three hours' sleep she would be exhausted for days.

In the spring of 1934, Jake did the plowing with the team, then swapped the draft horses and a hundred dollars for a used Farmall tractor from the International Harvester company. The tractor had been fitted with rubber tires and it had the narrow tricycle wheels on the front so that it could be driven between the rows. He also swapped the De Soto straight up for a little Ford Roadrunner pickup, a truck that would be a good deal more use on the farm than the automobile. Emaline wanted him to sell the motorcycle as well, but Jake refused to part with the machine.

The harrowing would be the first job for the tractor. By three o'clock in the morning, Jake was up every fifteen minutes, checking the clock, anxious to get the tractor out with the twelve-disk harrow. As soon as it was light enough to see, he made one pass through the field and realized it was too much for one man. There was a seat on the harrow for an operator who could lift the disks at each turn so he didn't have to stop at the end of each row and do it himself, then stop again to lower them after he had turned around. He also needed the extra weight. The harrow was heavy, but it wasn't biting as deeply as it should. He came back to the house for Emaline and told her to tie a scarf over her hair to keep out the dust. The scarf helped, but the wind still blew grit into her face along with the fumes from the old tractor. Jake was running it fast. It was a bumpy, jouncing ride, the big clods and occasional rocks in the soil tossing her around like a twig on an ocean.

Still, the work went on. She had to admit it was faster with the tractor. By eleven o'clock, they had only two more passes to make and the field would be done, a job that might have taken until sundown with the team. Jake was going faster and faster, partly because he was hungry and partly because he wanted to see just how fast he could work with the tractor. As he came to the turn for the last pass, he sped up instead of slowing down and set the brakes on the left side of the tractor hard to bring it back in a very tight turn. In order to turn in as short a radius as possible, the machine was equipped with brakes for both the front and back wheels. By setting them both on one side, the operator could bring the tractor right around on itself, freezing the left side while the big driving wheel on the right kept spinning. The tractor worked beautifully, but the turn was much too tight and too fast for the harrow. It flipped over, twisting the heavy, cast-iron tongue that connected it to the tractor into a corkscrew.

Emaline was thrown from the seat and landed facedown in plowed earth an instant before the harrow came crashing down on her left leg just above the knee. With the roar of the tractor, Jake didn't notice what had happened until he was a hundred feet up the row. Then he glanced back and saw that the harrow was upside down. He killed the engine and ran back to her. She cursed him. "You were going too damned fast, you damned idiot. You broke my leg."

He picked her up, carried her at a jog all the way to the truck, eased her onto the seat, drove sixty miles an hour all the way to the hospital in Scottsbluff, with Emaline screaming at every bump. By six o'clock that afternoon, she had a cast on her leg from thigh to ankle.

It was a week before Doc Baker would let her leave the hospital. She spent the first four days with the leg in traction. It was broken in three places between the ankle and knee. She would walk again, but the leg would never be the same.

Jake was too restless to sit quietly when he came to visit. He ranged up and down the halls, flirted with nurses, argued with farmers and ranchers, played checkers with other patients. He was apologetic, but not in a way that dimmed her anger. He had been pulling the harrow the same way he did almost everything, in a frantic hurry. Getting something done was always more important to him than doing it right. Now she was the one who would be in pain a good, long time because of his haste and carelessness.

One morning, she woke to find him right outside the door of her room, leaning down to whisper in the ear of a pretty, dark-haired nurse. He had left a vase of wildflowers on Emaline's bedside table while she was sleeping. She was tempted to hurl the flowers at his head, but a public display of anger was not in her character. She had to call him twice before she got his attention. He pulled himself away from the nurse and came to sit on the edge of her bed.

"Was there somethin you needed, Em?"

She answered in a whisper. "I need you to stop flirting with that nurse and sit with me for a while. You're the reason I'm lying here with my leg broken, the least you could do is pay a little attention."

"Hell, you don't have to get jealous. I was just sayin good mornin to the little lady. You're just cranky cause that cast is itchin your leg."

"It is itching me, but I have a great deal more than that on my mind. If all you're going to do here is flirt, you should go do the planting."

"Now, see? That's just a plumb jealous thing to say. I come in here to see you, I visit every doggone day, and you're worried because I was sayin hello to a nurse. If that don't beat all."

He stormed out, leaving Emaline to worry about the mounting hospital bills, the spring planting, the mortgage on the farm, the health of her leg, life with a man as difficult as Jake McCloskey.

24.

EMALINE CAME HOME TO A MOUNTAIN OF DIRTY dishes and a filthy house. Every moment she was on her feet was anguish. She hadn't the strength even to lean on her crutches and wash the dishes. She managed to sit up in bed and write a letter to Ben and Bobby telling them what had happened, but even that tired her out.

She was resting on the davenport on a hot, dusty afternoon when someone knocked at the door. She peered through the screen and saw a tall, slender, dark-skinned woman with long black hair.

"Don't get up, please," the stranger said. "Are you Emaline McCloskey?"

"Yes, ma'am."

"My name is Juanita Barrios. I work for Eli Paint, on the 8T8 ranch up in Wyoming."

"Oh, yes. My brothers told me about you. Do you mind letting yourself in? It's hard for me to get to the door."

Juanita stepped inside and paused a moment, letting her eyes adjust from the noon glare outside. "Bobby told me about your accident. I'm a nurse. I have some experience getting Eli back on his feet after he broke his leg, so I have come down to see if I can help."

"Eli didn't have to send you."

"He did not send me. I came because I decide to come. I know it is very hard when you have a broken leg. I can perhaps help you to walk again."

"I think that's going to take a long time."

"Not so long as you think. Perhaps a month or a little more. Until you can use a cane. It is better if someone works with you. You will walk more quickly."

Emaline was in too much pain to argue. Juanita seemed to have everything she needed in a small valise. She moved into the spare room and took over. Before Jake returned from wherever he had been, she had washed the dishes, washed Jake's dirty work clothes, made a good supper from what she found in the cupboard and the icebox.

Emaline took an instant liking to Juanita. The two women got along like old friends from the beginning, but when Jake came back from the fields and found a beautiful woman looking after his wife, he couldn't hide his reaction. Emaline noticed, but she noticed also that Juanita parried every attempt he made to flirt. It didn't matter. Jake behaved like a dog in heat, but Juanita was having none of it. She drew a line and would not allow him to cross it.

As the days went by, Juanita began to rule Jake in other ways. He was in the habit of strolling into the house with his boots on, tracking in manure from the corrals. Horse manure, cow manure, sheep manure, pig manure. Emaline had tried without success to get him to use one of the three bootjacks on the back porch to take his boots off. After a single day of sweeping and mopping the floor every time Jake came in, Juanita had put her foot down. The next morning, when he returned to the house after milking the cows, she met him at the door.

"Take off your boots."

"What?"

"You heard me. I said take off your boots."

She had been cutting slices of ham for breakfast, so she had a butcher knife in her hand. She didn't threaten him with it, but she didn't look defenseless either.

He started to push his way past her. "I'll be damned if a Mexican housekeeper is goin to tell me what to do in my own house."

Juanita took him firmly by the shoulder and pushed him toward the porch. "If you don't take off your boots, you don't come into this house. We are not going to clean up after you a dozen times a day. You track manure every place, even into the bedroom. No more."

Juanita's black eyes flashed. She held firm to the butcher knife. Had she been a man, he would have knocked her down, but he was not inclined to hit a woman, especially not a beautiful woman holding a sharp knife. He backed away in search of the bootjack, making like it was all a big joke.

"Hell, if you want me to take my boots off, all you got to do is say so. I aint goin to argue with a woman pretty as you."

After that, he made a show of removing his boots each time he came into the house. It was a small victory, but it established one thing. If you were sufficiently stubborn and determined, Jake McCloskey would sometimes back down. Once she was back on her feet, Emaline decided that she would have to try to assert herself more with him, because since the first day they were married, he had done exactly as he pleased. Not for one moment had he behaved like a married man who had to consider her feelings, not even when she was flat on her back in a hospital bed because of his carelessness.

Despite their different backgrounds, Emaline and Juanita had a great deal in common. They had both been through tragedies, they had seen much and forgotten little, they were trying to make the most of a hard life. They both loved to read, they took an interest in politics and the world. Like Emaline's aunts, Juanita knew at least a little bit about a good many things. During her years with Dr. Hodgson, she had picked up smatterings of his Harvard education. She knew about medicine and books, she knew a great deal about the hidden chambers of the human heart. Gradually, Emaline began to confide in Juanita. With her, Emaline felt she could ask questions she could not ask of anyone else. She told Juanita about how Jake was after her all the time. Even her broken leg hadn't eased his sexual demands. As soon as she was home from the hospital, he wanted her two or three times a day. "I was just wondering. Are all men the same way?"

"No, they are not. Dr. Hodgson, he would never touch me unless I did something to get his attention. He always had his mind on his work, nothing else. And he was a very shy man, too shy to demand things. He would crawl into bed at night and before I could get undressed, he was asleep. Sometimes I wished he would be a little more like your Jake. But we were working together for twelve years before we were married and he seemed never to think of lovemaking, so marriage did not change him in that way. Have you asked Jake not to be so 'at you,' as you say?"

"I've tried to tell him it's too much for me. It gets to where it's just another chore, like feeding the chickens or doing the washing up."

"Then you have to be firm with him. Tell him it's too much."

"If I do, I'm afraid he'll be off after someone else. You've seen what he's like. Head always on a swivel, my friend Calla says."

"I'm sorry, I do not know this expression."

"It means he's always looking at other women. You see the way he is with you. When you first came, it was like his tongue was on the floor all the time."

"I have seen how he looks at me. But I see also that he loves you very much. He is very tender with you."

"Not enough to be careful when he has me riding the harrow."

"That is different. That was careless and stupid. He feels very bad about this, so perhaps it will not happen again."

"It's the way he is. He doesn't see danger. When we first moved here, we were living in the basement house down the hill. I woke up one morning and he was jumping the motorcycle over the house."

"Over the house? That is not possible, is it?"

"It is. He put planks up one side and down the other. Then he came roaring up doing fifty miles an hour, hit one of the planks and took off. I thought he was going to kill himself or tear the roof apart, one or the other."

"He is an interesting man, this Jake."

One evening as they sat on the porch together, watching the sun go down in a red sky, Juanita put her hand on Emaline's arm. "I have something I must tell you. I am with Eli. For more than a year now, since the car accident."

"With him?"

"Like man and woman. Man and wife, except that we are not married."

"I thought perhaps you were. The way you talk about him."

"Yes. I wish you knew him better. He is a good man. He pushed so hard for so long because he did not know another way. Now he is beginning to learn, but it takes time. He is very sorry for the way he was with your mother."

Emaline nodded. "I know. I thought about that after Ida Mae died, how she was always the one pushing him to keep my mother away from the ranch. Now that she's gone, maybe I can come up to visit someday."

"He would like this very much."

"What are you and Eli going to do? Will you get married?"

"This is what he wants. Very much. I tell him that in all ways we are married, why does it matter? Even his children accept it, they are very kind to me. But he wants this. I tell him I want it too, but I cannot marry a rich man, because if I do they will say I am a poor Mexican who wanted to catch a rich man for his money. He says things are very bad in the whole country and he will soon be poor like everyone else, so I say, 'If you are poor, then we will marry!'"

Emaline laughed. "Then I don't know what I should wish for. For Eli to be poor so you can marry him, or for him to stay rich."

"He will be happier when he is poor. Then he can start over again. This is what he is like. He is not happy to succeed. It is trying to make something, this for him is the important thing. He must be doing the impossible. This is what he is made to do."

On May 9, 1934, the day before Juanita was to head back to the 8T8, a duster began as a series of whirlwinds in eastern Montana and the Dakotas and swept east like the vengeance of an angry God. It swirled so high in the air that pilots had to climb to fifteen thousand feet to avoid it, because they couldn't go around it. The storm was nearly two thousand miles wide and carried 350 million tons of dirt. It fell over Chicago; Boston; New York; Washington, D.C.; and ships three hundred miles out to sea. The New York harbor turned gray, the tulips and grass in Central Park were covered with a fine coating of sand. People atop the Empire State Building stared into a dust soup, unable to see the street below. The dust even seeped into the White House, where President Roosevelt was discussing drought relief.

Emaline and Juanita listened to the radio reports describing the dust filtering into the NBC offices in New York City. Some of the farmers saw it as revenge on the easterners who had not suffered from the ravages of the Dust Bowl. To Emaline, the great dust storm confirmed her deepest fears.

"Do you ever feel as though we're living at the end of the world, Juanita?"

"Yes, I do. It is bad at night when you lie there listening to the wind and you think it's all going to blow away. Everything. There will be nothing left here but sand dunes and the wind will blow night and day forever."

"It's good to know I'm not the only one. I thought perhaps I was going mad."

"Perhaps we are all going mad, Emaline. The times make us so."

25.

EARLY ONE MORNING IN THE SPRING OF 1936, Emaline staggered up from the well, carrying a five-gallon bucket of water in her good left arm, her weight balanced against it. She wore a man's castoff shoes and a man's old overalls under a linsey-woolsey dress worn thin from too many washings, a scarf tied over her hair to keep the dust out. It was an unusually warm day for March and she was not feeling well. She would have to make the usual half dozen eggs for Jake's breakfast. For some reason, the thought of eggs made her want to vomit. The sun was barely up, the cows were bawling to be milked. Jake's Hampshire hogs crowded around the trough waiting to be fed. They nosed at her legs and knocked her off-balance. The horses leaned patiently against the fence, waiting for her to fork hay into their manger. The rooster crowed again. He was so much like Jake, strutting and crowing, gussied up, with his tail feathers fanned out for the neighbor ladies and raising a racket before dawn. She hated that rooster. One of these days, she'd turn him into a chicken pie.

Jake hadn't done the chores because he was out in the pasture, working a horse for a neighbor. The horses took more and more of his time. The neighbor had no money to pay him and Jake knew it, but it was an excuse to fool around with a horse instead of fixing fence, dragging the rusty old corn planter out of the field, or doing something about that wrecked Model A that had been plugging up the irrigation ditch since they bought the farm. He was up and out of the house before four o'clock every morning, but when he was working a horse he left feeding the livestock and doing the milking to her. When he came back around six, he'd want his coffee and breakfast on the table.

She emptied the bucket into the basin in the kitchen and put coffee on the stove to perk, then went back out to fork hay to the horses and cattle and scatter slop in the trough for the hogs. When she had finished the first round of chores, she stood stroking the neck of Maudie, her bay mare. The mare's dark, wet eyes watched her, the way old friends watch to make sure everything is all right. Flies settled on the Roman nose, the long black tail flicked like a lash, the hide rippled where the flies landed. The mare was so heavy with foal that she looked as though she had swallowed a barrel. Emaline scratched her nose. *Any day now, girl. You're going to have a prize colt and keep us in money for flour and sugar all winter long.*

She left Maudie gulping water at the stock tank and went back into the house to start Jake's breakfast. It was too hot indoors, so she kicked off the loose-fitting brogans and peeled off the overalls and stood at the stove in her thin dress with nothing underneath. She put on the radio to keep her company. There was nothing on but the hog and cattle markets. Jake would be back soon. Knowing that made her want to scream. She shrank from him, but in this small house there was nowhere to hide.

She had to fight the urge to gag as she cracked the eggs, but she had his breakfast almost ready when she heard the horse coming up the lane from the county road. She braced herself. Moments later, he came striding into the house with his boots on. He smacked her bottom so hard it stung. Watching him eat, she was reminded of the hogs. Like them, he ate with his nose to the trough and his mouth wide open, shoveling it in as fast as he could inhale.

He finished eating and shoved the plate across the table at her. A golden yellow trickle of egg yolk dripped from his chin. He backhanded it away, rose without a word, and headed to the outhouse. She picked up the dishes and set them next to the washbasin. She had finished the washing up by the time she heard him whistling on his way back. He stepped into the kitchen again and came up behind her. She tried to twist away from a rough, stubble-cheeked kiss, then let her body go limp. When he was done, he kissed her roughly on the neck, slapped her bottom again, went whistling out the door.

She did the washing up and walked to the outhouse. She slipped the hook into the U-shaped nail that held it and sat on the smooth boards, watching a fat spider climb its web. It had a dozen flies trapped, bottle green prisoners waiting to be eaten. Outside she could hear a tractor gargling and farting off in the distance. She cleaned herself with three pages from the shrinking Monkey Ward catalog on the floor and flipped through what was left, looking at things she would never be able to afford. A slip for three dollars. Who could pay three dollars for a slip?

The tears came. They always did. It helped to bawl a little, to let it out. She could still hear her mother saying *Don't stand in the corner and bawl for buttermilk,* but sometimes she couldn't help it. If she didn't let go, she would go crazy. She let the tears flow until she was empty, then straightened up, smoothed her dress, dabbed at her eyes with a corner of her apron. There was work to do, a whole day of chores ahead. She had walked ten feet from the outhouse when a sudden, violent nausea overtook her and she went down on her knees and vomited into the weeds until the last spasm passed.

She walked back into the house and pulled her overalls on. There was a section of fence almost down on the south side of the pasture. They didn't dare turn the cattle in to that pasture because there was green alfalfa starting to come up on the other side. If the cows got into it, they'd founder and bloat and die, unless Jake could get to them with a knife quickly enough to open holes in their swollen flanks to let the gas escape. It was just like him to be quick and deft at a job like that but incapable of fixing the fence. She tucked a claw hammer, vise grips, a come-along, and a supply of wire staples into her pockets, saddled Maudie, rode out.

She threw up again the next morning, and the morning after that. After a week, she got Jim Lindquist to drive her in to see Doc Baker. The doctor confirmed what she already knew. She was carrying Jake's child. She cried all the way home.

When she told him, Jake threw his straw hat ten feet in the air, whooped and hollered and talked about what a fine prizefighter this boy was going to make. He wanted to throw a wingding on the spot, but Emaline persuaded him to hold off until the crops were in.

After that, her days took on a clarity she had never known. Everything now was for the baby. Each day, the child inside her grew, by how many fractions of an ounce she did not know, but surely it weighed more than it had the day before. Her hopes grew with it, until it seemed that her aspirations spanned the universe. This would be her magical baby, her salvation, a child of such wondrous talents that its ability to alter the known world for the better would be without limit. She would become a doctor and cure terrible diseases and write symphonies as a sideline. Emaline knew that her dreams for the baby were giddy with excess, but they took her away from this brown, dusty place. She was as happy as she had ever been, all her being now functioning like her body, at the service of this unborn infant.

Even Jake seemed to change. He was quieter, less explosive, less rough when he took her. He tried to do the heavy lifting around the farm so she wouldn't have to do it, and his hopes were every bit as large as Emaline's, although they lay in a different direction. He bragged to anyone who would listen, telling them that Jake McCloskey Jr. would be heavyweight champion of the world.

In late May, Emaline said maybe it was time they had that wingding. They had survived drought and dust storms and crop prices that wouldn't keep a hummingbird alive. Farms were still going under by the thousands all over America, but they had staggered from one dry season to the next. A week of rain was a sure sign that they were about to be blessed. They would invite all the neighbors for a potluck. They would sing and dance and laugh and forget the hard times. She would feel the baby move inside her and hold her hands over her belly and feel as happy as she had ever been.

26.

IT WAS A BEAUTIFUL JUNE EVENING, SWEETER BEcause it happened to coincide with Emaline's twenty-sixth birthday. Charlie Naudain and Calla Plessman drove out from town, the Lindquist brothers came in their Dodge Brothers truck, Vern Schneider arrived with Cecil Narrows and Earl Beckman, Luella came with Orie Bassett still in his sheriff's uniform. Even Dexter McGuinty turned up sporting his pistols, although he hadn't exactly been invited. Bo Willoughby brought his harmonica, Leif Hansen his fiddle, Leif's brother Karl and Mink Provo had their battered guitars, and Pete Southern his banjo. Kitty Perks, who could sing like an angel and was so pretty everyone said she should be in the movies, performed a dozen songs with Leif and Bo and Jake doing harmony.

After Kitty sang, someone got a square dance going, with Leif doing the call and the couples clapping and swaying through the steps. After she had finished eating, Emaline poured herself a glass of wine. She usually didn't drink at all, but she felt that she deserved a little reward after all the hard work of the spring. She danced with Jake, but with her belly beginning to act as an uncomfortable counterweight, she didn't mind sitting down after a couple of dances. He danced a half dozen more dances with other women, then vanished just when the square dancing was getting started.

When he had been absent for half an hour, she got up and wandered into the house. She didn't see him in the kitchen or the parlor, so she thought he must have gone out to the corrals to check on the horses. She wandered out to look. The horses were there all right, but there was still no sign of Jake. Maudie and her foal came to the rail. Emaline scratched the mare's nose, feeling sorry that she hadn't brought the usual apple tucked into her apron as a treat for the horse.

She was a little peeved with Jake. He was the fun-loving character who could never resist a party. This wingding had been his idea, he should be with their friends and neighbors. She was about to head back to the house when she thought to check the barn. She saw nothing at first, but she heard a noise from up in the haymow and climbed the ladder cautiously, afraid that a rat would jump out of the dark. She was halfway up when she saw Kitty Perks kneeling in the hay with her dress carefully folded beside her and her slim hips exposed. Jake was behind her, his dark brown hands on Kitty's rump, pulling her to him. Kitty's long, reddish brown hair was undone. It fell down over her face, her breasts swayed in rhythm to the slap of Jake's groin against her behind. Kitty made a high, whining sound in her throat and seemed to enjoy it much more than Emaline ever had.

The fragments came together. Jake and Kitty, Kitty and Jake. Of course. Kitty loved horses and they often rode together when he was out working a horse, if that was what he was really doing, all those mornings when he was gone for hours and left Emaline to look after the farm.

She backed cautiously down the ladder until her feet were on solid ground, then whirled and ran. She could not go back to the party, that was the last place she wanted to be. She ran the quarter mile to the county road, one hand on her belly, supporting the weight with her good left arm, used her right for balance. The moon was full, a fat yellow moon. A moon pregnant as she was. It was in the light of that moon she had seen them, light spilling through the upper hatch in the barn where they pitched the hay.

The first vehicle she saw on the road was a farm truck, running without headlights, grinding along with a heavy load. She stepped into the center of the road, directly in front of the truck. She waved her arms frantically to flag him down. When she realized that he hadn't seen her, it was too late. She tried to spin out of his way, but the right front fender caught her in the belly with a sickening *whump!* She cartwheeled through the air, flew head over heels into the barrow pit, landed face first in fetid water.

The truck fishtailed to a halt, its brakes groaning. The driver in his panic forgot to hit the clutch and killed the ignition. A lean, long-geared farmer with the legs of a stork came scrambling down the bank after her.

"Oh migawd, miss, I'm sorry, but what on earth was you doin in the road like that? Aw hell, I didn't mean to do a thing like that, miss. Are ya all right? Are ya all right at all, missy?"

He grabbed her forearm, heaved her up out of the muck without pausing to see if anything was broken. She came up onto her knees, gasping for breath, and vomited everything she had eaten all over his brogans. The man was Alf Muzzy, a farmer who used to drop by the Arrowhead Diner when he was flush, which wasn't often.

"Migawd, Miss Emaline, it's you. Oh, gawd, I am sorry. I shore am so sorry. What a awful thing to have done to you, Miss Emaline."

She was still fighting for breath. "It's all right, Alf. Not your fault. I shouldn't have jumped in front of your truck. I thought you saw me."

She turned away and vomited again, wretched until nothing more would come. Alf stood back, waiting with his eyes averted, trying to rub off what she had vomited on his shoes by swishing his boots around in the tall grass so as not to embarrass the lady. At last she wiped her mouth on the hem of her dress and he helped her get a foot on the running board and climb up into the cab of the old truck.

"I don't know where you was headed, but expect I better get you to the hospital, little lady. Don't look like nothin's busted, but we'd best get a doc to check you up. It's a lucky thing this old truck won't go no faster than she will. Speedometer's busted, so I can't say exactly, but it can't have been more'n ten miles a hour. Fifteen the most. I was goin real slow, and then you was just there. Migawd, Miss Emaline. You of all people. You who was always so sweet to me when I come in with two nickels for breakfast and it cost fifteen cents. You would always get me something, you felt sorry for me, I know."

She put a hand on his arm. "It's all right, Alf. It was my fault. I shouldn't have been in the road."

"What on earth was you doin out there this time a night? Shoot, most folks is in bed by now. That's why I wasn't watchin for nobody this late. What was you doin out there?"

"I had a little trouble at home, is all."

"With Jake? Jake McCloskey? That man dotes on you. I seen him at the feed store last month, he was just goin on and on, how this Emaline is the most wonderful woman on the face of God's green earth. He said the two of you was goin to have a baby and that child would be heavyweight champion of the world. Kept talkin about how lucky he was to marry a fine woman like you. Jake, he's plumb crazy about you."

"Well, maybe he isn't crazy enough. Or maybe it's just that I'm not the only one he's crazy about."

"Now that's been known to happen. A marriage aint no footrace. It's more like a long crawl, and sometimes you're a-crawlin one way, and other times you're a-crawlin another way. Me and the mizzus, we had our ups and our downs. I don't mind tellin you, there was times I was ready to up and leave that old woman. She'd get nasty, raggin on me about this and that, and I'd say, 'Woman, that's a damned nuff. I've had all I can take. Now you are goin to shut it or I'm goin straight down that old road and I aint never lookin back.' She understood she had to shut it, because I wasn't goin to take no more. I'd a gone right down that road and she would never see this face again. Okay, I aint much to look at, but I'm a provider, I am. Maybe I don't put no roast beef on the table ever night like some, but we aint gone hungry, nosir. Not even in these hard times, with folks a-starvin to death all over the country. You see my old woman with a back bumper on her wide as a barn door and you know she aint gone hungry, not for a solitary minute of her life. If she wasn't fertile as new-plowed ground, we'd have a-plenty to eat. It's them nine little ones that make us have to stretch ever meal. Ever time I get a sniff of that woman, she's got her belly stickin out again."

Emaline was grateful for Alf's chatter, for the roar of the old truck engine, for the cab with its reek of hay and sweat and axle grease, for anything to take her mind off what she had seen in the barn and what might be happening inside her.

By the time they arrived at the hospital, she had passed out. Alf Muzzy lifted her out of the truck and carried her tenderly into the emergency room. The first nurse he saw was in a hurry, but he stopped her in her tracks.

"This here little lady, miss? I run her over with my truck."

27.

When she woke, it was midmorning. Sunlight flooded the room. Doc Baker bent over her, feeling her pulse. She could see the truth in his eyes. "I lost the baby, didn't I?"

"I'm afraid so. We couldn't save him. I wasn't too sure we were going to save you either. You lost a lot of blood."

"You said you couldn't save *him*? It was a boy, then?"

"Yes, ma'am. It was a boy. I'm real sorry. But you're a healthy young woman, no reason you can't have another one."

She tried to stifle the cry in her throat. The doctor had to examine her, then he explained how she should care for herself.

"You'll have to guard against infection, Mrs. McCloskey. And you have to avoid overdoing it the next few days. You rest here now, I'll let you know when you're ready to go. Once we release you, you won't be able to have relations of any sort with your husband for at least a month. Now I have to ask, I know he didn't bring you in. Does he know you're here?"

"He does not."

"Would you like us to get in touch with him for you?"

"I would not."

"I'm afraid we're going to have to contact him sooner or later, Mrs.

McCloskey. He was the father of the child you lost and he is your next of kin."

"All right. Call him on the farm if you want."

Doc Baker didn't have to call Jake. Alf Muzzy had driven over to the McCloskey place as soon as his chores were done. He found Jake still in bed, the cows bawling to be milked. The farm women had tidied up the house before they left the party. They decided that Emaline in her condition must have tired early and gone to bed, so they cleaned up for her and left quietly, but they couldn't do anything about Jake. He was still asleep at eight o'clock in the morning, and he reeked of liquor. Alf dragged Jake outside, made him peel off his stinking clothes, pumped cold water on him straight from the well. Jake shivered and howled, but Alf kept at it with grim determination. When Jake was thoroughly soaked in icy water, Alf pushed him back inside and set coffee on to perk. Jake was still so drunk he hadn't thought to ask where Emaline was or why a neighbor he barely knew was bossing him around. Alf waited until he had downed half a cup of black coffee. There was no point beating around the bush.

"Your wife come a-runnin outa your place last night. Tried to flag me down on the county road yonder. Stroke a luck that my old truck won't get outa second gear loaded or I might a killed her. I didn't see her at all until I run into her with the front fender. Knocked her right down into the barpit. I pulled her out and cleaned her up some, took her into the hospital in Scottsbluff. Time we got there, she was out cold and bleedin bad. I hung around the hospital until near four o'clock this mornin, when I had to get home to do my chores. Last I knew, it looked like she was goin to live through it all right, but they couldn't save the baby. They told me she lost that child."

Jake grabbed his hat and was ready to jump in the Ford and head to town when Alf mentioned the livestock. Maybe somebody ought to milk those poor bawling cows and fork them a little feed first? Alf would have done it himself, but he was too disgusted. He left Jake to look after himself. If he made it into the hospital, that was fine. If he never got there at all, that poor girl might be better off.

By the time Jake was through with the chores, he was sober enough to know that something real bad had happened.

Jake brought a bouquet of wildflowers he had picked alongside the road. Emaline dropped them on the bedside table without looking. She lay with her back turned to the window. Late spring sunlight came pouring through, dappling the sheets. The window was open, there was just enough breeze to stir the curtains. He found a chair against the wall, pulled it over next to the bed, touched her shoulder. She pulled away from his touch like a woman avoiding electric shock.

He cleared his throat. "I'm right sorry, Em."

She said nothing.

"Maybe you didn't hear. I said I'm sorry."

She turned on him, her dark eyes burning.

"Sorry isn't going to do it this time, Jake. This isn't our wedding day, when you got lost. It's not the time you were running the harrow too fast and flipped it over on me and broke my leg. It's not the way you flirted with the nurses the last time I was in the hospital. I saw you with Kitty, Jake. Snorting like animals in the hay. I *saw* you!"

"I don't know what the hell you think you saw."

"Don't, Jake. Don't try to kid me. I know exactly what I saw. I climbed the ladder in the barn right up to the haymow. There was a full moon and the hay door was open. It was plain as day. How long has this been going on? You've been riding out with her for more than a year now. Where do you go? That old cabin down by the creek? I know there's a little bed there, made up nice. I was wondering who used it. Now I know. It's you and Kitty. She's your little whore, isn't she?"

"Aint no call to talk like that, Emaline. I don't know what come over me last night. Too much to drink, I suppose. That's the only time anything went on. I done said I was sorry. I don't know how many times I've got to say it."

"Until I get tired of hearing it."

"It still don't make sense, what you did. Runnin into the road like a damned fool."

"I ran because I wanted to get away. I was so shocked. I ran and I got hit by Alf's truck and I lost our baby. That child is gone forever. The one thing I wanted more than anything in the world. I don't ask for much, I don't complain that we're poor. I don't care that we can't eat a meal without swallowing dust with every bite. I don't mind that I get up every morning at five o'clock to make your breakfast and work until I drop. But I want it to be *for* something. It was all going to be for that child. Now he's gone."

"Hell, taint all my fault, woman. You're the one did a fool thing and run off."

"Why can't you understand? I ran because I saw my husband with Kitty Perks. In *our* barn, during *our* party. I should have stuck one of you with a pitchfork. Are you a dog, that you have to do it in the street?"

"Aw, hell. She's a pretty gal. Never happened before. We had a bit a wine and danced a little, then she wanted to go for a walk, one thing led to another."

"Oh, Jake. Do shut up. Do please just shut up. I don't want to hear your stupid excuses. Our baby is gone."

She fiddled with her gown, listening to the hospital sounds. The rush of nurses, a bell somewhere, farmers and ranchers in the hallway chatting about the drought, the price of wheat, the dusters. She was on the same floor where Velma had died in 1933. That awful January, the long vigils. Nights listening to the rattle of her mother's breathing, tuned to every slightest change. Waking to find Velma dead. She had lost a mother in this place, now she had lost a baby. All she wanted was to get away from this hospital, this town, the farm, this man. She decided she might as well tell him and get it over with.

"When I can travel, I might go stay on the ranch."

"In Wyoming?"

"That's where the ranch is, isn't it?"

"Well, I dunno. You're comin back, aint you?"

"I don't know, Jake."

"What does that mean?"

"It means that I don't know."

"It aint that difficult a question. Are you comin back or aint you?"

"I said I don't know. I saw you with her, I got hit by a truck, I lost a baby. That's a lot to think about. I need some time. Maybe I'll go cook for Ezra and the boys."

"There aint no need to go runnin off. You know I'm sorry for what I done. I didn't know it would bother you, or I never would a gone into that barn with Kitty."

"What you did was bad enough. Don't make it worse by lying. I know you're a hopeless, ignorant hillbilly, but nobody can be that stupid. You had to know it would bother me."

"It aint a lie. You never seemed to care for it all that much. You go at it like it's a awful burden. I thought you'd be relieved if I was hammerin at somebody else for a change."

"I used to like it all right. I don't care for you going at me three or four times a day when I'm tired and there's work to do."

"All the same, I swear to God. If I knew that you cared one way or t'other, I wouldn't a done it."

"I don't know whether you're the stupidest man who ever lived or the biggest liar. All I know is that if I decide I want to go to the ranch, I'm going. After what you did, you have no claim on me."

"You're my damned wife, that's what claim I have. You're my wife and you'll do as I say."

"Like hell I will."

"If you think I'm goin to set still and let my wife leave me, you got another think comin."

"I didn't say I was leaving you. I said I might go to Wyoming."

"If that aint leavin, I don't know what is. It sure as hell aint stayin."

"Please give me some peace, Jake. I need to rest. Don't keep going on at me. I'm going to need some time, then we'll see."

"How much time?"

"I don't know. Time. A month, six months, I don't know."

He got up, paced to the window and back. "I'm not goin to allow it. No way, no how. Soon's you're well enough, you're comin back to the farm."

"No, I am not. Not until I'm good and ready, if that day ever comes. I'm going to go someplace where I can think for a while. That's that."

"No, it aint. I'm your husband and you'll by God do as I say."

"I will not. You will not order me around like a servant anymore. You've done that long enough. When I saw you with that woman, that was the end of it. If I choose to go, I will go."

He leaned over her, his face black with fury.

"No, goddammit. You will do as I say. *Exactly* as I say. When you get outa this place, you're goin to learn to behave like a proper wife."

"I have been a proper wife, you fool! What do you want? A woman like Thelma Pearl? Was she a proper wife?"

"Thelma Pearl was a goddamned she-bitch, and that's exactly how you're actin right this minute."

She spat in his face. There was an instant of disbelief, then the rage turned to thunder, his right fist drew back like a piston, the row of broken knuckles poised to strike. She heard someone moan in pain. A baby's cry. Laughter down the hall. Hurried steps. So much suspended in that moment, as they both waited to see what would happen.

There was a swift ripple of shoulder muscle as he drove the fist into the palm of his left hand, the sound like the crack of a whip. She lay trembling with fear, refusing to waver, staring him down, daring him to do his damnedest.

"Go ahead, you sonofabitch. Do it! *Do it*! Hit me! *Hit me!* Hit me and go straight to hell!"

They were motionless, their faces six inches apart. Emaline sitting halfway up in bed despite the pain. Jake bent over her, his fists still cocked. She saw movement behind him. A nurse had heard the commotion and summoned three big orderlies, wide men accustomed to moving what needed to be moved. They eased up behind, but Jake heard them coming and whirled to face them, weight shifting to the balls of his feet, fists up. "Come on, you sons of bitches. You want to dance, let's dance."

The orderlies sized him up in an instant and backed away. Jake turned to face Emaline again, so angry the tendons in his neck bulged.

"You've got to be the damnedest woman I ever knew."

He picked up his hat. The orderlies fell out of his way, and he stalked between them. She heard his boot heels echoing down the hall. He was gone.

Emaline sank back into her pillow, and the nurse rushed to see if she was all right. Her name was Elizabeth, but they called her Beth. She was an older woman who had been kind when Velma was dying. Emaline held on to Beth's shoulders and wept until she was empty and dry. Doc Baker gave her a sedative and she fell into a long sleep. She woke deep in the night and felt the sorrow wrapped around her belly like the tentacle of a jungle plant, tight and unrelenting. She tried to weep but the sedative took hold again and she dropped over the dark edge of a cavern, into a dreamless sleep.

When she woke the next morning, her abdomen hurt terribly and she was doubled up with cramps. Her breasts were engorged with milk and leaking. Beth brought her something for the pain and bags of ice to ease the discomfort in her breasts. Emaline asked her to put in a call to Calla Plessman at the Arrowhead Diner. When she was well enough to leave the hospital, Charlie Naudain picked her up and took her back to Calla's little house on West Overland. While Emaline dozed on the davenport, they drove to the farm to get her things. Jake was out when they pulled up. It was the time of day when a farmer should be working in the fields, but the old Ford was gone. Charlie parked in front of the house and stood guard while Calla dashed inside with the valise to pack Emaline's things. She couldn't believe how little the woman owned. Two threadbare dresses in addition to her good dress, which had been ruined when she was hit by Alf Muzzy's truck. Enough underthings for three days, no more. Two slips, stockings, a jar of cold cream, a bottle of rose water, a pair of man's overalls, worn brogans, which she obviously wore to work in the fields. Calla found Emaline's ancient winter coat in the closet, but even with that and the overalls and the brogans, the suitcase was only half full.

28.

THE KNEELING BUFFALO, NEARLY AS VAST AS THE bluff itself, offered comfort and consolation from the far side of the river as Emaline recovered. As a girl newly arrived in Scottsbluff and miserable with longing for Wyoming and the Bighorns and the rush of Little Goose Creek, she had discerned in the pattern of sage, buffalo grass, and yucca that grew up the north flank of Scotts Bluff a kneeling buffalo two hundred feet high facing to the west, its head and hump clear in outline. The great buffalo was like the Burning Man of her dreams. It also communed with her without speaking, offered a vision of something beyond time and death, untouched by the squalor, mendacity, greed, and chaos of human existence down below.

Each morning when Calla left for work, Emaline took a cup of tea out to the back porch, sat on the rocking chair, watched the light of the rising sun strike the bluff and the buffalo. She would go out again in the evening to watch the sunset, but at midday when the sky went the palest blue of river ice she remained indoors. The pale summer light was too harsh. It reduced the great bluff to mere dust and clay and the buffalo looked parched and thirsty. Then the long shadows would stretch over the clusters of sage and the light would soften and in the long fiery streaks of cirrus clouds the vague yearnings would be born again as she sat and rocked and watched the buffalo vanish into darkness.

Calla, soaking her bunions in Epsom salts after a long day at the Arrowhead Diner, had more mundane matters in mind. "You know, Charlie Naudain would take you back at the Arrowhead as soon as you're able to work."

"Thank you, Calla. That's good to know."

"I'm run off my feet there and you know how Charlie feels about you. He'd always make a place for you at the Arrowhead, if he had to fire me to do it."

"Goodness! I would never let that happen."

"I know you wouldn't, but Charlie would. I think he's in love with you. When you think about it, you could have done worse than to marry old Charlie. He aint much to look at, but he's got money in the bank and he's as kind a man as I ever met. Him and Cecil Narrows. And here Charlie is a bachelor and Cecil is a widower and the both of them plumb crazy about you, and Vern Schneider mooning around over you until you married Jake and then he up and married that woman Connie Ballew. But Charlie and Cecil, they would have married you anytime. They're older fellas, but neither of them would have done you as Jake did."

"You could marry one of them, Calla."

"Me? Not in a coon's age. First place, neither of them fellas has ever looked at me twice. In the second place, I spent enough years pickin up a man's dirty underwear. I've kind of taken to lookin after myself and nobody else."

"You're looking after me."

"No. You're stayin with me. It's not the same. You look after yourself, even when you're hurtin, like now."

"Thank you, Calla."

"I'm sorry, honey. But it's better to know the truth about a man. You're goin to have some hard decisions to make. It won't help if you try to kid yourself. For the rest of your life, you're goin to blame him for that baby. That's a hard thing to have between you."

"When I was in the hospital, I kept thinking about what you told me before I married him. That his head was always on a swivel."

"I did say that, didn't I?"

"You did. And I should have listened."

"Oh, you can't talk to a young girl in love, sweetheart. My mama tried to warn me about Hank Plessman before I married him. Said pretty much the same thing. *He'll leave you, dear, mark my words. Leave you high and dry.* And that's exactly what he did. Thank God my dear old mother, rest her soul, didn't live to see it. But Jake didn't leave you. He just made one mistake."

"Is that what you think? Jake goes out riding every morning early, before first light. Even in cold weather he doesn't miss many days. He rides down to the creek where he can work a horse in the soft dirt. Tires the horses out a little and they listen better, he says. Anyway, Kitty likes to ride too. I know they ride together. I never thought about it much until I walked into that barn. But there's an old shack down there where he goes to work the horses, still has a cot in it and a stove. Somebody has kept it clean and tidy. I always wondered who it could be. If Jake and Kitty were looking for a place where nobody would be likely to spot them, that would be perfect, down in a swale in a stand of cottonwoods where you don't see it until you're almost right on top of it. Sometimes when he came back from riding I would smell something on him, but I thought it was just my imagination. Now I know better. I think it was her all along, but almost every time he came back, he wanted me. I wish I knew more about what men are like, if they could come fresh off one woman and want another right away. I know I wouldn't want another fella right after Jake gets done with me."

"I don't want to make you more suspicious than you are, girl, but that's exactly what men are like. They get a sniff of one and they just want more. Like a bull elk with a herd of cows, they level them antlers at any other bull comes around and service the females one by one. That's what you're dealin with when you marry a man, unless you find one like poor Stanley Perks, who is off in some world all his own. I could never figure why a beauty like Kitty would marry a wet dishrag like Stanley. Maybe it's because he's not enough of a man to question what she does."

Emaline didn't tell Ben and Bobby about the miscarriage or the fact she was living with Calla. She wrote only one letter telling the truth about what had happened. That was to Juanita Barrios.

Jake came by twice while she was at Calla's and brought a little bunch of wildflowers each time. The first time, she was frightened when she saw him at the door but he was quiet, chastened, utterly unlike the man who had almost hit her while she lay in a hospital bed. When she asked about the farm and her garden, he said everything was doing fine and left it at that. He didn't try to bully her, didn't ask when she was coming back. Just as well, because if he had he would have driven her away forever. He would sit next to her on the porch for a time and ask how she was doing, pat her hand, ask if she had visited the doc again and whether she was getting her strength back. Then he would stand up and say it was time to get back to do the chores. After his second visit, Calla arrived just in time to see his old truck pull out of the driveway. She hurried into the house and found Emaline thoughtfully sipping her tea. "I just saw Jake pull out. What was he doin here?"

"He came by to see how I'm making out. He brought those flowers. I don't know what's gotten into him."

"I know. He's found out how hard it is to get along without you. He wants you back, is all. What are you going to do?"

"I don't know, Calla. He seemed so pathetic. There was a rip in his pants hanging open. I wanted to ask him to take them off so I could sew it up for him, but I know what happens if he gets his pants off around me."

"Don't you dare mend that man's trousers! That's the worst thing you could do. He doesn't realize how much you do for him. Let him miss you for a while, it will do him good."

"I know. I miss him at times, but he's a hard man to live with. A hard man, period. You can't imagine how hard he is. A few weeks ago, he was waiting for me to bring him a hammer so he could pound in the bolt that holds the tongue for the harrow. I was too slow fetching it to suit him, so he drove that bolt in with his fist. When I got back with the hammer, he was licking the blood off his knuckles."

29.

A WEEK AFTER EMALINE WAS RELEASED FROM THE hospital, Juanita pulled up in front of the house, driving Eli's Pontiac. She held Emaline in a long, firm hug, then pushed her away briskly and looked her over.

"All right, honey. You look ready to travel, so I'm going to help you pack. You're coming with me and you're going to stay with us on the 8T8 for a while. If you feel like you have to earn your keep, you can always cook for Ezra and the boys, but I'd rather you stayed with me at the big house."

"I don't think I can go, Juanita. I really haven't decided what I'm going to do next."

"You can think about it on the ranch. You're going to see some beautiful country, visit with us, catch up with your brothers, forget about your troubles for a while. When it's time, you'll know what to do, one way or the other."

"I would love to come, Juanita. But I'm so worried about the farm."

"Honey, with what you've been through, the farm is the last place you should be. If you go back there, I know what you'll do. You'll work fourteen hours a day until you end up back in the hospital."

"I'm afraid I'll have to go back, sooner or later."

"Then you're going to have to make it later, because I'm not going to get married without you."

"What?"

"Eli and I are getting married. I would not do it without my best friend there to see it."

"You finally said yes?"

"I did. Eli is still not poor enough, but it's been more than three years that we have been married in every way but on paper, so we will have a wedding and then we will do one of those things, what does Jake call it? A *wingding*."

Emaline laughed at the way Juanita pronounced *wingding*. "I'm so happy for you, Juanita."

"Good. So you will come with me now and stay for the wedding?"

"Well, I can't say no, can I?"

"No, you cannot. Now are you ready to start packing?"

Emaline could not think of more reasons to refuse.

"Okay, Juanita," she said. "Let's go."

The two women embraced again, long and hard, then started gathering Emaline's things. On the way out of town, they stopped at the Arrowhead Diner so that Emaline could tell Calla she was leaving. Then they were on the road, the tires of the Pontiac popping over the tarred cracks in the pavement on U.S. Route 26, speeding west.

They arrived at the 8T8 near suppertime. Eli was sitting on the veranda in his rocking chair when they pulled up. He stepped out to meet them, followed by Ben and Bobby, and all of Eli's younger children from his marriage to Ida Mae—Calvin, Seth, Jenny, Mabel, Anna, Leo. She said hello to all the children, let Calvin and Seth tote her things inside, hugged Bobby and Ben, walked hand in hand with them into the house. She had just stepped into the enormous parlor with its twenty-foot ceiling and the long, winding staircase to the upper floor when Ezra came in, fresh from looking after the Appaloosas. It was the first time she had seen him and Eli together. She found it uncanny that two men could look so exactly alike and be so different.

The girls had made a big roast beef dinner to welcome Emaline to the ranch. They sat down at the long, long table, Ben and Bobby on either side of Emaline, Juanita and Eli facing her across the table, the two of them canoodling like schoolkids. Emaline had never seen so much food on a table at once. She didn't realize how hungry she was until she started to eat, then she was embarrassed when she realized she had polished off her entire dinner while everyone else was still eating. Juanita heaped seconds on her plate. Eli didn't say much at dinner, but from what Emaline understood, he never did. It was strange to be so close to him, stranger still to find herself feeling something like affection for this man she had hated for so many years. It was Juanita who had changed Emaline's opinion of the man. If, after all the years she had worked in his employ, Juanita cared about Eli enough to marry him, then he must be very different from the remote, uncaring grandfather she had always pictured.

Emaline was pleased to be on the ranch at last, but she was also exhausted. She chatted with Ben and Bobby a little after dinner, but soon she could barely keep her eyes open. It was only as Juanita was showing her the room where she would sleep that Emaline thought to ask what day the wedding would be held.

"Oh, that's not till the last day of July," Juanita said.

"But you said I had to come up right away."

"No, I didn't exactly say that. I knew that if I told you it was still a month away, you would probably go back to the farm and work yourself to death. I had to get you up here so we could look after you."

"Well, you all made me feel really good tonight. I think this will be good for me."

"Of course it will. I wouldn't have dragged you up here otherwise."

✦ ✦ ✦

Juanita wanted her to stay at the main house, but Emaline could not bear to be in a place where she wasn't earning her keep. Eli's daughter Jenny was eighteen, Mabel was seventeen, and Anna was fourteen, so Juanita had more than enough help to run the big house and Emaline would just be in the way. She also wanted to spend as much time with her brothers as she could, so the next morning Ben picked her up in the old truck and drove her to the cabin.

Ezra had a cot for Emaline in a room where he kept a gathering of old saddles, blankets, bridles, lariats, spurs, halters and harnesses, hackamores and martingales, short-handled quirts, a pair of the long black bullwhips they had used when he and Eli were freighting with ox teams in South Dakota with their father, Eb Paint. Most of it was worn and battered beyond use but rich with the memory of old trails, wild horses, fall roundups. Emaline slept among the rich odors of leather and lathered horses. From her bed, she could reach out and touch the bark on the logs of the cabin. The one small window in the room faced west, toward the Bighorns, and each morning when she rose, she could look out at the mountains.

There was plenty for her to do to earn her keep. She was a light sleeper, so she climbed out of bed when she heard Ezra get up, set the coffee to perk, started breakfast while he finished the chores, then woke Ben and Bobby. It took her until the Fourth of July to clean the layers of grime off the kitchen, to scrub pans that had never had a proper washing, to wash floors that looked like they belonged in a stable. Ben took her into Sheridan to buy a few kitchen things, including a big pot for soup, a ladle, extra cups and plates, forks and knives. She crocheted rugs for the floor, sewed curtains on Juanita's sewing machine, began new quilts for winter.

Bobby was fifteen and still slender as a reed, but he was now as tall as she was. He had become a very good horseman under Ben's tutelage, but his greatest pleasure was to ride over to the main house and spend time with Leo. Ezra called them "the twins" somewhat sardonically, given that Leo was big-shouldered and dark and over six feet tall. He meant that they were nearly as close as he and Eli had been when they were in their teens. He didn't demand too much of Bobby because most mornings the boy rode off to see Leo right after breakfast and wasn't seen again until evening. Bobby did his share of work on the 8T8, but he did most of it for Eli.

Emaline and Ben, separated for much of their lives, had grown close again, talking through the long summer evenings about old times and all the things they had been through in their lives. She and Ben rode out almost every day, Ben on one of the horses he was working and Emaline on Popcorn, a lively little Appaloosa filly that Ezra had given her to ride. Emaline wrote to Jake as soon as she got settled, telling him that she was in Wyoming and she would be there for some time. Ten days later, she received a note from him.

Dear Em,

I know you are mad as hell at me and I dont blame you. I already knew you was in Wyoming, Calla told me. If you want to come back here to the farm, I'd sure be glad to have you.

Jake

She waited a few days to answer, because she wanted to think it over first. When she did write, she was cautious.

Jake,

Life is good here on the ranch, it is so good to be with Ben and Bobby and Ezra and Juanita and I am even getting to like Eli. It's the first time in my life that I've been around my grandpa and he's not so bad after all.

I can't tell you much more than that. Eli and Juanita are getting married July 31 and I have promised that I will look after Eli's children while they take a trip to Seattle after the wedding, so it will be some time before I can even think about leaving here. After all the things that have happened in the three short years we have been married, I am in no rush to get back.

I can tell you that if I ever do take a notion to come back to the farm, I am not going to accept the smallest part of the things I have put up with until now, beginning with Kitty Perks.

Now I have work to do. I hope you are taking good care of the farm. Have you found someone to buy the collie pups? Please do look after the garden, I hate to think of it going to waste.

yours truly,
Emaline

30.

Even though Juanita had promised a "wing-ding," it was a quiet little wedding. A few friends and neighbors, the hired hands, Two Spuds and Jenny Hoot Owl, Eli's children, Ben, Bobby, Emaline, Ezra. The Reverend Cletus Barnwell said a few words and pronounced Juanita Barrios and Eli Paint man and wife. Ezra barbecued a steer. The men all played a baseball game, but only Two Spuds could get a hit off Bobby when he was pitching. Two Spuds hit the ball so far they couldn't find it and had to give up the game.

Emaline helped Eli's girls in the kitchen, preparing endless pitchers of lemonade and platters of baked potatoes, sweet corn, sweet potatoes, peas, snap beans, carrots. She had also baked a half dozen pies and made a cake for the newlyweds. When everyone had finished eating, she sat by the fire next to Bobby, feeling that she had at last found a place where she belonged, where she was surrounded by people who cared for her, where life was something other than a pitched battle to survive. As happy as she was for Juanita, Emaline envied her all this, the peace of it, the absence of strife, the plain affection in which she and Eli held each other.

When the games were over and they had all eaten their fill, they sat around watching the fireflies wink as the night settled in. Zeke

Ketcham played his guitar, Leo and Bobby sang a couple of Eli's favorite songs, Juanita sang an old Mexican tune. Two Spuds and Jenny Hoot Owl sat holding hands. In the gathering darkness, Emaline watched Eli with Juanita. They were newlyweds, but they had been together for a good long time now and there was a warmth between them that she had rarely felt with Jake. Eli and Juanita treated each other with such tenderness that it seemed to spread to everyone around them.

Emaline could not imagine a way that her life with Jake would ever be anything like this. If she went back to him, there would always be arguments and explosions, hard times caused by his fecklessness, the absence of trust. More than anything, she sensed that Juanita and Eli trusted each other. Each knew the other would do the right thing in difficult situations.

The morning after the wedding, Eli and Juanita left early to take the train to Seattle. They were going to visit Eli's youngest daughter from his first marriage, Emaline's aunt Kate, and they were going to see the Pacific Ocean, leaving Emaline to run the house in their absence. Emaline had very little to do while they were gone. The girls had their routines, the house seemed to run itself. She read, she went out riding with Ben and Bobby, she thought. It took time, but when Eli and Juanita returned in mid-August, Emaline knew what she had to do.

She explained it to Juanita as well as she could. She had decided to go back and try it with Jake one more time. She couldn't bear it any longer, the constant worry over the farm. They might lose it anyway but she did not want to lose it without a fight. It was hard to separate Jake from the farm but in her mind they were separate. She had to try to save the farm.

Juanita understood. "I would prefer that you stay here. I know how hard it will be for you but I can see that you have to try. I would do the same. If it doesn't work, there will always be room for you here."

Juanita offered to drive her back to Nebraska, but Emaline insisted on taking the train. "You have put yourself out enough already on my account," she said, "and anyway, if I'm going back, I need some time to prepare myself. I can do that on the train ride."

Emaline spent her last night on the ranch in the big house and rose early. When she came out onto the veranda, Eli asked if she would take a walk with him. They strolled down past the corrals where the horses were just beginning to stir, up the rise and out into the pasture where the meadowlarks sang. Emaline was trying to think of some way to tell him how she felt, but Eli spoke first.

"This here is just about my favorite spot on earth," he said. "When we were walking by the ocean out in Washington, it was a sight like I have never seen, the big waves coming in, seagulls flying everywhere. But I'd still rather be here. Aint no place like it, the Bighorn Mountains and the High Plains. I've loved it since I was a kid and I still do."

"It's also home."

"It is that. Bad times or good times, everybody needs a home. I can't blame you for wanting to go back to yours."

"The strange thing is, Grandpa, since I came up here I've found that I feel more at home here than I ever have in Nebraska. The years we lived in Sheridan and up on Little Goose Creek, I got so used to the mountains. Somehow, I've never felt at home in Nebraska. But I have to try to make it work."

"I expect you do, girl. I wish you all the luck in the world, but I'm going to be awful sorry to see you go. I'm like Juanita that way. I find it real pleasant to have you around."

"Thank you, Grandpa. Thank you for taking me in too. It was a bad time for me, but I feel better now. You've taken such good care of all of us, Ben and Bobby and me. That's what I wanted to tell you before I left. We owe you so much, you and Ezra and Juanita. I still believe there are many things you should have done for Velma before she died, but I know you've tried hard to make it up to us and I'm grateful for that."

"Gosh, girl. It sounds like you're close to forgiving this old man."

"No, Grandpa. I'm not close to forgiving you. I have forgiven you. It's time. All that is over and done with. It's been more than three years since that day I went to Mama's grave with you. She would have forgiven you long ago, that's just the way she was, and now I've forgiven you too."

"That's as good as hearing it from Velma herself."

"Well, I should have said it a long time ago. Juanita loves you and I think the world of Juanita, you know that. If you were an awful man, she wouldn't care about you the way she does. Now I've seen how you are. I think I understand how things looked to you when you forced my mother off the ranch. You were a man alone with five girls and a blind son to raise and you couldn't be weak, right?"

"Something like that."

"You felt that if you weren't strict with Velma, you'd set a bad example for the others."

"I did, but I don't see it that way now. I should have kept her and Frank on the ranch, where I could have watched you and Ben grow up. When I see how you are now, what a fine young woman you've grown up to be, it's just a shame I missed so much of that."

"It's a shame we missed you too. You're a strong man, but you're never mean or cruel and you don't try to use your power to hurt people. Everyone relies on you so much, even Ezra."

"I guess that's true. People rely on you too. You know that. You're a strong woman."

"It's never been easy, but I wasn't raised to do things the easy way. That's why I have to go back. I don't want to go. I want to be here, I want to stay close to everyone, but I can't. I have to try to save our farm the way you saved this ranch."

"Well, if things don't go the way you want, you've got a place here as long as I have a place to offer, you know that."

"Thank you, Grandpa. You've been real good to us. I know a person can't go back in time to fix all the things you'd like to change but you've done the next best thing."

"That means a whole lot to me, to hear you say that."

He held her for a good long time in those strong arms. Emaline wished she could stop worrying about the farm, surrender herself to Eli's protection, live on the 8T8 forever. But she had made up her mind to go back and once she had set a course, she was not one to change it.

PART III

The Great Divide

1936–1938

31.

THEIR LAND, WHEN SHE RETURNED, LOOKED AS though it had been blasted by a terrible scourge. Tumbleweeds clung to the barbed-wire fence along the county road, the oat field had withered, scattered clumps of sugar beets grew between cracked patches of bone-dry earth. Corn that should have been knee-high by the Fourth of July was ankle-high now, in mid-August, and so sparse it might have grown there by accident. The fence between the beet field and the cow pasture had sagged so that the cattle stepped over it and stood, dumb as clods, mouthing the tender beet leaves. The cattle guard was clogged with weeds and the dust had silted it over and almost buried the two old wagon wheels that marked the entrance. The culvert under the lane that led up to the house was blocked with more tumbleweeds and stagnant irrigation water had flooded part of the road.

Emaline had spent the night in town with Calla before Charlie Naudain drove her out to the farm. He offered to stay and help, but Emaline said this was her mess to clean up and she would do it on her own. She watched his old Nash until it turned onto the county road, waited until he was out of sight to sit down on the stoop and bawl. The prolonged spasm of collapse that was the Great Depression meant nothing here. This was her personal ruin, two months of neglect that had transformed a working farm into a grotesque wreck.

It was barely eight o'clock on a Sunday morning, but the Ford Runabout was nowhere to be seen. Jake was out, the cattle were bawling. He was still the same Jake McCloskey, tomcatting around the county, living exactly as he pleased, counting on someone else to clean up the mess.

She cut across the alfalfa field to close a gate that had been left open. The short spikes of fresh-cut stubble hurt her feet through the thin soles of her good shoes. She accepted the discomfort as her penance for having neglected the farm and walked a wide circle, taking stock. The worst of it was her garden, now acres of weeds and withered plants. If Jake had watered it even a single time, it didn't show. He plainly had not pulled a solitary weed. Here and there her crops peeked through, but another few days without water and there would be nothing left that she could salvage. She marched into the house, dug her bib overalls and brogans out of her valise, went to work. She milked the cows, fed the chickens and the ravenous hogs, forked hay to the cattle and horses. Molly the collie was wildly happy to see her. The pups, grown so large they would be hard to sell, jumped all over her.

She had finished running the milk through the cream separator when she heard the crunch of tires on gravel. She peered out the door to see the truck coming slowly up the lane. Jake parked next to the well, jumped out, primed the pump, and stuck his head under the icy water. She walked out and watched from under the shade of the cottonwood tree, waiting for him to notice her. He didn't see her until he rose to smooth his hair.

"Well, hello, Em. When did you get back?"

"Where were you?"

"There was a wingding over at the Nordstrom place. Danced till two o'clock and then I went to sleep in the back of the truck, cause I didn't think I ought to drive home."

"Did you forget that you have livestock to look after?"

"Nope, I figured it was better to sleep it off. I wasn't expectin you."

"I can see that."

"Now don't get all riled up, Em. I'm right glad to see you."

"I'm sure you are. I did your chores for you. The cows hadn't been milked and I don't believe the hogs were fed last night. I thought they were going to eat me alive. Those collie pups are so big, they should've been sold by now."

"I didn't find nobody wanted to buy them pups."

"You didn't try. We never had trouble selling them before. You didn't touch that darned garden either."

"I can't do it all by my lonesome. That garden is your lookout. I don't suppose you'd make a fella a pot of coffee, would you?"

She turned toward the house. "You can drink a gallon of coffee if that's what you need. Then we're going to get to work."

That evening, exhausted after a long day trying to put the farm back in some kind of order, they came as close to talking as they ever would. Jake asked what made her decide to come back.

"You didn't hit me that time in the hospital, that was part of it."

"I had no business bein mad at you. I was the one in the wrong."

"Yes, you were, and I'm not about to forgive you for any of it. I didn't want to see all our hard work go down the drain. If you want me to stay, though, you're going to have to put a curb bit on that temper. I'm not going to live the rest of my days afraid of my own shadow."

"I'll do my damnedest."

"You had better. I don't know where you were last night and I don't care, but no more women. You have to promise me that. I'll make allowances this time, because I wasn't here. The way you were raised, I suppose it's possible you really didn't know how upset I would be when I found you with Kitty. But no more. If it happens again, I'll leave and I won't look back."

"Yes, ma'am."

"For everything else, you're going to have to wait and be patient with me. A thing like this, losing the baby, it's going to take me a very long time to get over it. We have plenty of work to do if we're going to save this farm. The rest of it will come if you just give me time."

Emaline went to bed while it was still light outside. She lay awake a long while, listening to the crickets, watching the evening dark settle over the little house. When at last she fell asleep, she slipped into a long, soaring dream. The great Lakota warrior who was her Burning Man led the way over the endless snow, his hair rising to the heavens in coils of fire.

The balance of the summer was an unending haze of work. Emaline was intense, a thin lash of anger. She didn't scold or reprimand Jake any further, unless you counted the set of her shoulders, the pressed line of her lips, the way her black eyes flashed when she told him to leave the horses alone and get back to fixing fence. She even got a hoe in his hand and made him scrape weeds from her garden until the blisters broke and bled. If he faltered at all, she would remind him that she was putting in days just as long and hard as his. The fences were strung taut again, the sagging barn door fixed with new hinges. She got him to train the collie pups so they could be sold and insisted the irrigation had to be done the right way. When the ditch rider came through at two o'clock in the morning to signal that he was about to let loose a head of water, they had to be ready, working up to their knees in the heavily alkaline water to plug gopher holes, set canvas dams, divert the water to the right field, siphon it to row after row of corn or sugar beets or let it seep through the alfalfa field. They worked until their backs ached and their hands were cracked, ignoring the hard little deerflies that left tiny cuts wherever they bit. When the irrigation water got to the crops, it worked magic. The corn grew, the sugar beets recovered. The crop was going to be late, but as long as the frost held off they would have something to market. With the dryland crops, they could do nothing but pray for rain and the rain did not come. The wind did not blow quite as much, the dusters eased a bit, but the drought was as bad as ever. The barley died, the oats died, the pasture appeared to be on the verge of turning to desert forever. Half the cattle were sold while there was still enough alfalfa left from the first cutting to keep the ribs from showing through their hide, but the remainder were barely scraping through.

By driving herself without mercy, Emaline managed to salvage a third of her garden. By harvest time, she was thin and brown and wiry, a dozen pounds lighter than she had been in the spring. There were enormous calluses on her hands and she went to bed each night with an undefined ache that seemed to encompass every muscle and bone in her body. No matter how hard she worked, it was beginning to slip away. They wouldn't have a crop of oats or barley so that they could put some aside for seed. They had fewer cows, so they would have fewer calves. There would be no income from the garden. For most of the summer, they had forfeited the cash she made from the creamery for her eggs and butter. Their cash reserves were thin. When those were gone, they had nowhere to turn unless the sky opened up and started raining money. Sooner or later, a gentleman from the bank would come calling, with or without the sheriff in tow, and that would be an end to it.

They did a little better in 1937. For the first time since they moved onto the farm, Emaline thought they might just squeak through, get past the drought and the depression and hang on until times improved. The garden was thriving. This time there was enough moisture for the dryland crops and Jake was less clumsy with his irrigating. They were expecting a bumper crop until a hailstorm in August destroyed half of their sugar beets. The harvest was still their best. Without the hail, they might have made it. As it was, they managed three mortgage payments but could make no more. The first snow fell. Emaline rationed the kerosene and kept them in semidarkness in the evening until Jake fell asleep around eight o'clock, then turned up a single lantern just enough so that she could read her Chekhov and Balzac as she listened to the wind howl.

32.

TEN DAYS BEFORE CHRISTMAS IN 1937, A BEAT-up Studebaker came slipping and sliding up the muddy, half-frozen track from the county road. Jake was off at Corky Dishman's getting some work done on the Ford Runabout and Emaline was in the house baking Christmas cookies. A petite, well-dressed woman stepped out, smoothing her red hair and adjusting her hat. Emaline put aside her rolling pin, wiped the flour off her hands, went to the door in time to see the woman coaxing a boy about five years old out of the car. Emaline opened the door and stood waiting at the top of the steps. The woman was wearing heels and the steps were slippery, so she took her time, helping the boy up with one hand and holding the crude railing Jake had rigged with the other. When she reached the top, she put out a gloved hand.

"You must be Emaline."

"That's right. Emaline McCloskey."

"My name is Thelma Pearl. Thelma Pearl Perkins? I used to be married to your husband, Jake McCloskey? And this little boy here is Jake Junior. Jake Stuart McCloskey. I call him Junior. He's Jake's son."

Emaline thought she might fall right over. She stood there gaping at the two of them, mother and boy, standing on her front porch with big snowflakes drifting down on their shoulders.

Thelma offered an apologetic smile. "I'm sorry if we're bothering you. I know it's a surprise. It's just that if I phoned Jake, I was afraid he'd tell me to go to hell."

Emaline collected her wits. "No, no. You're not bothering me. I was just baking some cookies. Maybe this little man will have some. Come in, come in, it's cold out there. Jake took the truck into town to get it fixed. I don't expect him back for a while."

Thelma Pearl and the boy stepped into the warm house, the delicious smell of cookies in the oven. She helped the boy take off his coat and galoshes and hung their coats on the pegs by the door. She was a tidy, trim little woman. Emaline was surprised to see that Thelma Pearl was older than Jake, probably close to forty, but with her red hair, small features, wide Clara Bow lips, trim figure, she could have passed for twenty unless you took a close look. She was well-dressed, except that her dress looked a little frayed in one or two places, but she looked completely worn-out.

Emaline showed the boy to a seat at the kitchen table, poured him a glass of milk, told him he could try the first batch of cookies while they were still warm. He looked to his mother to see if it was all right. Thelma nodded. He grasped a cookie and nibbled at it. Emaline kept stealing glances at him. He was a handsome boy, with skin like fresh cream and that rich, wavy red hair. He was small-boned and slender and seemed to take after Thelma Pearl in every way except for the cheekbones and the unmistakable jaw with the deep cleft in his chin. Jake might have tried to deny the rest of that angelic face, but he could not deny the cleft chin.

Jake had always called Thelma Pearl a man-eater and maybe she was, but seated here so prim and proper at the table, she seemed small, nervous, frightened, embarrassed, vulnerable. In spite of herself, Emaline's heart went out to the woman.

"How did you find us?"

"It's the oddest thing. I never had any idea what became of Jake. I went home to Salt Lake City after we split up. When I wanted to get married again, to Mr. Perkins, I checked with the courthouse in Denver to see what I had to do to get a divorce and that's when I found out that Jake had divorced *me*, on grounds that I deserted *him*, which I guess I did. Then when I split up with Mr. Perkins and we moved back to Denver, I went looking for Jake's name in the phone book, but it wasn't there. I forgot all about trying to find him until last week. I was working in Denver Dry Goods, that's a big department store, and in comes Mr. Bucky Betz. You know Bucky? Used to be Jake's trainer? Anyhow, I hadn't seen him in a coon's age. He was looking to buy something for his wife for Christmas, only he don't know me. So I says, 'Bucky, it's me!' And he says, 'Me, who?' and I says, 'Well, don't that just beat all. You don't remember little Thelma Pearl? After we used to have so many laughs together?' So we get to laughing and talking, and then I ask if he knows whatever happened to Jake McCloskey, the prizefighter. And he tells me Jake is married to a real fine gal named Emaline and they have a farm by Stegall, Nebraska, which is west of Scottsbluff and only two hundred miles from Denver. So we left this morning and drove over. I found the little store here in Stegall and they gave me directions to your place. It wasn't hard at all." She turned to the boy. "Honey, watch how you eat, you're getting crumbs all over the place."

She brushed the crumbs from around Junior's mouth. If Emaline hadn't stopped her, she would have jumped up and grabbed a broom to sweep around his chair. Emaline asked Thelma Pearl if she wanted coffee and she turned it down. "Never touch the stuff. I'm the nervous type as it is, see. Mr. Perkins, that was my second husband, he used to say I'd make coffee nervous. But I wouldn't say no to a glass of milk and one of those cookies myself. Wipe your mouth, Junior."

Emaline poured the glass of milk for her, refilled Junior's glass, and told them to help themselves to more cookies.

"I'm sorry, I'm a bit stunned," she said. "So Jake never knew that he had a son?"

"Not a bit. I ran out on Jake, it was six years ago in October, and I never thought to see him again. I had been in Salt Lake City two months when I figured out that I still had a little bit of Jake with me, if you know what I mean. It was little Junior here, he's such a sweet boy, couldn't be sweeter, aren't you, honey? But by the time I knew what was what, I was hooked up with another fella, that would be Mr. Perkins, and I didn't know what became of Jake. I thought it was best to leave him be and I married Mr. Perkins, but it didn't last but three months once he found out I was already with child when we got hitched, because I hadn't let him take any liberties, if you know what I mean. Then I moved back in with Mama in Salt Lake and Junior was born. This is 1932 I'm talking about, Junior's birthday is in April, he'll be six years old. Everything would have been fine, but Mama died two years ago and since then it's been real rough, on account of I didn't have nobody to look after Junior. We moved back to Denver, but I can't make enough money to pay somebody to mind him and if I don't work, we'll just about starve to death."

"Sounds like it's been a hard life for you."

"Oh, no, honey. I don't want to be one to complain. I've knocked around some, but I've seen some swell places and done some swell things. I wanted to find a fella who could look after a gal, which is where Mr. Perkins came in. If it wasn't for my tummy starting to stick out before it should have, he would never have been the wiser. Nobody's fault but my own."

Emaline glanced at the boy. He was watching them both, eyes big as saucers. Poor little fellow.

"Is there anything we can do to help?"

"Honey, I got no right to ask you a thing. Not a solitary thing. Nor Jake neither, even if this boy is his son, I don't think anybody can argue that, just have a gander at that jaw. Nobody but Jake has a chin like that. I just thought, seein as you have this nice farm that would be perfect for a boy and all, well, maybe you and Jake could look after Junior until I get back on my feet?"

"You mean keep him with us?"

"Well, yes. He don't eat much, and he's real quiet and he'll mind his manners. And he is Jake's son and I never asked Jake for a thing for him all these years."

"I don't know what to say. It's fine with me and I don't see why Jake would object, but he'll be pretty shocked."

"I expect so. Sometimes I wonder why I waltzed out on him."

"He says you left because you knew he wasn't going to win the big fights anymore."

"He does? That was part of it, for sure. But I always knew he had an eye out for other women. He didn't think I knew, but I knew. I had a lot of friends in Denver and stories would get around. He used to go with these two gals, the Barlow twins? They couldn't keep their eyes off prizefighters. Two of these little gals at once and them sisters. I'm sorry, I don't want to shock you, honey, but Jake when he was young was a real tomcat, I'm sure he's not like that anymore."

Emaline smiled ruefully. "There are two sides to every story."

"There sure is, girl. There sure is. Anyhow, what do you say? Are you game to look after Junior for a while?"

"How long did you have in mind?"

"A month, maybe two months? After that, maybe we can work something out so little Jake can spend summers with his papa. You'd like that, wouldn't you, Junior?"

The boy looked from his mother to Emaline and back. He nodded, but Emaline thought he was going to cry.

"Well, sure, he can stay with us. I'd be happy to have him. Once he gets over the shock, I think Jake will be pleased. He always wanted a boy."

"That's swell, if Junior can stay with you. Isn't it swell, snuggums?

You're going to stay with this nice lady Emaline for a while, because Mommy has to work. When I get back on my feet, I'll come to get you."

Before Emaline knew it, Thelma Pearl had darted out to the car. She returned dragging a heavy trunk which seemed to contain all the boy's things, even some of his old baby things. Emaline thought it odd that she was bringing so much if she only planned to leave him for a month, but she didn't say anything. She asked Thelma Pearl to stay for supper and wait for Jake to come home, but Thelma said she had to get back to Denver to work the remaining days before Christmas at the dry goods store.

"Tell you the truth, I'd like to get out of here before Jake comes back, if you don't mind. If he sees me here and he finds out he had a son all this time that he don't know about, I'm afraid he'll just plain explode."

Even as she said it, she was pulling on her coat. She kissed the boy, left lipstick on his cheek, walked hurriedly to her car. Emaline held Junior up so he could wave to his mother from the window, but Thelma Pearl never looked back. She turned the Studebaker around, got it started down the road, drove out of sight. Emaline thought then the boy would start crying for sure, but all he said was "May I have another cookie, please?" She had the impression that he was accustomed to being dumped with various people here and there. She spent the afternoon baking more cookies, chatting with him, trying to draw him out. The boy was well-spoken, but it was hard to get him to say more than three or four words at a time. By three o'clock he looked tired, so Emaline took him to the bedroom and said he could curl up for a nap. He slept for an hour and came out looking baffled and confused.

"Where's Mama?"

"She went back to Denver, honey. You're going to stay with us for a while. Your daddy will be home soon."

"I want my mama."

"Well, not just now, little man. You stay here with me and you can help me make some more cookies. Would you like that? I'll roll out the dough and you can help me make the shapes."

The boy nodded, but Emaline could see the tears in his eyes. She wanted to cry for him. She had been left at the orphanage when she was about the age he was now. She could still feel the hurt and confusion, wondering how it was a mother had to go away. The only thing she could do for him was to offer a great deal more tenderness than the nuns had ever given her.

The two of them were rolling dough together when Jake came home. He had his boots and coat off before he noticed the small figure seated at the kitchen table.

"Well, who is this little lad?"

"Who does he look like?"

"Gosh, I dunno. He looks like a kid. What's your name, son?"

"It's Junior."

"Junior who?"

"Junior McCloskey, sir. Are you my daddy?"

"That's your name? Junior McCloskey?"

"Yep."

"That's funny. That's my name, McCloskey. Jake McCloskey."

"That's my real name too. Jake McCloskey."

"Whoa! Now who goes around givin that handle to little fellas like you?"

"My mama."

"And who is that?"

"Mama."

Jake looked at Emaline. "Okay, what's goin on here? Is this somebody playin a joke?"

"I don't think so, Jake. It seems this is your son. I wouldn't believe it myself, but all you have to do is look at him. He's got your chin."

Jake squatted on his heels to get a closer look at the boy.

"Well, I suppose you might say that. I wouldn't swear to it in a court of law. How did he get here?"

"Thelma Pearl brought him this morning."

"Thelma Pearl? *Thelma?* Thelma was here? What the hell was she doin here?"

"She drove him over from Denver. Said she can't look after him right now because she has to work and she can't afford a babysitter. Apparently she was carrying this child when she left you."

"Well, I'll be damned. You're Thelma Pearl's boy?"

"He's yours too, Jake. You've got a son."

"Well, I'll be gosh damned be go to hell."

"And the first thing you're going to have to do is stop swearing around him."

Jake let the boy tag around after him when he did the chores, but the third day he was with them, Junior left the gate to the pigpen unlatched. Two of the hogs got out and Jake exploded, shouting until the boy crumpled in tears. It was easy enough to catch the pigs again, but it took Emaline half the day to calm the child, who plainly wasn't accustomed to such explosions. After that, every time Jake raised his voice, the boy cringed.

As long as he kept his temper, Jake was good with the child. He told him stories about horses and boxers and the war in France and riding the rails with the hoboes. He carted him around on his shoulders and talked a neighbor into loaning him a Shetland pony for the boy to ride. But he insisted on calling the boy Red instead of Junior. Emaline didn't know if that was because he liked the nickname or because he refused to admit that a child so small and slender could be his. Now and then she would catch him rubbing the cleft in the boy's chin as if to test it, to see if this red-haired, fair-skinned child could really be his offspring. Jake was not one to want to look after another man's spawn, but he couldn't argue with that cleft. Red might be unlike Jake in every other way, but he bore that McCloskey stamp as surely as if he had come out of the womb wearing boxing gloves and winking at the first nurse he saw.

Emaline hoped Thelma would send the boy some little gift for Christmas. Nothing came, so she made him a toy scarecrow out of ropes knotted together and told him his mother had sent it and Jake gave him a little Ford truck he had bought in town. After two weeks, there was still no word from Thelma Pearl. The weeks went by and January turned into February. Now and then, Emaline would see the boy peering down the lane as though hoping to see the beat-up old Studebaker, but it never came.

33.

Jake said it was like trying to hold on to a greasy rope with a bull on the other end. No matter how hard they fought, the farm just kept slipping away. After they missed mortgage payments in February and March 1938, Calvin Cox called from the bank and asked if they could come in to talk things over. Emaline had gone to high school for a year with Calvin. She knew that he was a decent man who hated having to foreclose on his customers, but he had no choice. He had carried them as far as he could go. If they were able to sell some machinery or some livestock to catch up with the mortgage payments, they could go on and hope for a bumper crop and better prices in the next harvest. If not, he'd have to foreclose. Emaline had to do the talking, because Jake got too angry when he was dealing with bankers, even bankers as nice as Calvin.

"If we sell the machinery, we won't be able to get a crop in."

"Maybe your neighbors would help. Or Jim Lindquist, with his team."

"Even Jim has a tractor now. He'd help all he could, but they're in the fields just about every day through the spring as it is. Same with everybody else."

The banker shrugged. He was sympathetic, but it was not his problem. They tried to find a buyer. They spoke to the neighbors and asked Jim

Lindquist and Cecil Narrows if they knew anyone who might be interested in buying the farm before they went into foreclosure. Emaline tried to prepare herself for the inevitable. It had happened to tens of thousands of farm families all over America. Why should they be different?

Jake wanted to pull up stakes and go to Oregon, join the great migration to the coast with all the thousands of miserable Okies who had been in search of any work they could find since the beginning of the depression. Every year they got a Christmas card from Clay Tatro and his wife Alice, who lived in a mill town outside Portland. Tatro had been Jake's sergeant in the army. Despite the difference in rank, Jake and the sergeant had formed a strong friendship, probably because Jake had been the only man to put the bull-necked Tatro on his back when the men tried a little bare-knuckle boxing. The last two years, Tatro had included a note with the Christmas card, saying that he could really use a man like Jake at the sawmill, where he was the shop steward for the union. Emaline thought Tatro wanted Jake to be hired muscle.

"Beats workin for a living," he said.

"Not if you get your head broken in a strike."

"That's not going to happen."

"You don't know that. It sounds dangerous."

"It's only dangerous if you don't know what you're doin. I can take care of myself. Hell, there's all kinds of folks headed to the West Coast these days, but we got a place to go and a job, guaranteed. If we lose the doggone farm, we're goin to Oregon."

They were out trying to dig a new culvert on a bitterly cold day in March when Calvin Cox came tromping across the frozen beet field in the company of Deputy Sheriff Dexter McGuinty. Emaline knew as soon as she saw them that it was over.

Cox was apologetic. "You're good folks and I know you worked hard," he said. "I've carried you longer than I would with most, but I'm going to have to foreclose if you can't catch up on your mortgage payments by the first of April. If you're still behind, everything will be sold at auction."

Jake leaned on a fence post, looking like a boxer who is about to go down for the count. Dexter, seeing that Jake looked beaten and feeling safe behind his pistols and his badge, couldn't keep his mouth shut.

"Teach you to marry a prizefighter, Em," he said. "I don't think Jake here was meant to farm."

He was down and bleeding before he could say another word. Dexter staggered to his feet, fumbling for his pistols. Jake yanked them out of his hands and hurled both guns as far as he could throw them in opposite directions.

"You just assaulted an officer of the law," Dexter screamed. "You're goin to prison for that! Straight to prison!"

The banker turned on him. "He aint goin nowhere at all, Dexter," he said. "You're the one caused the problem. If you try to prosecute this man, I'll swear you hit him first. It's bad enough, a man losin his land, without a sonofabitch like you runnin his mouth." Calvin turned back to Jake. "I'm real sorry about that, Jake. I tried to get Orie Bassett to come, but he was feelin poorly this morning. His gallbladder. Luella said I ought to bring anybody but Dexter, but Syl Whiting was takin a prisoner to Lincoln and there wasn't nobody else."

Jake nodded. "Just don't let that sawed-off bastard out here again. Next time, I'll kill him."

It took Dexter ten minutes to find his pistols and clear out. He tried to swagger as he got back into his squad car, but he couldn't pull it off with blood pouring down his shirt.

Orie Bassett came out three days later to have a little talk with Jake about how it wasn't smart to knock down a deputy sheriff, even if it was a cocky little pissant like Dexter. Jake was still fuming. Orie was lucky to get back into town himself without a broken nose.

Before the foreclosure notice came, Emaline had begun to hope that they would never hear from Thelma Pearl again. Now they had to try to locate the woman. Thelma hadn't answered any of her letters. The last two had been returned, marked "No forwarding address." Emaline called information in Denver and was told that a number for a Thelma Pearl Perkins on South Julian Street had been disconnected two months earlier. There was no new number. She called Denver Dry Goods and the switchboard operator put her through to the women's department where Thelma Pearl had worked. A woman there told her that Thelma had been laid off right after Christmas and hadn't been seen since.

In early April, the mailman brought a letter addressed to Master Jake McCloskey. Emaline checked the envelope: There was no return address. Inside was a five-dollar bill and a brief note from Thelma Pearl.

Junior,

It's going to be a while before Mama can get back to Nebraska to see you. Things have been real tough lately, but I think about you all the time. I'm sending some money so your daddy can get you something real nice for your birthday. You tell him your birthday is April 16, and maybe that nice Emaline will bake you a cake. Already six years old! You must feel like a real big boy.

Well, Mama has to go now. I don't know when I'll see you again, honey. You buck up and be a good boy for Emaline and do what your daddy tells you. He should be real proud to have such a fine, smart son. I'm sure he's happy to have you with him and that Emaline is about as sweet as any lady I ever met.

Big wet kisses to my little snuggums,
Thelma Pearl

The letter was postmarked Santa Fe, New Mexico. There was no other clue to Thelma's whereabouts, so Emaline phoned information in Santa Fe. She wasn't surprised when she was told there was no Thelma Pearl Perkins in the phone book, or Thelma Pearl McCloskey either. Red watched her put down the phone.

"You can't find Mama?"

Emaline hugged the boy. "No, honey. Not yet. I'm sure she'll turn up sooner or later. She's just real busy trying to find a job and all. Once she gets a job, I'm sure she'll send for you."

"I don't think my mama wants me."

"Of course she does, sweetheart. Any mama would want a sweet boy like you. She just can't take care of you right now, is all. Now wash your hands and slick your hair down. It's almost time for supper."

She and Jake talked it over that night after Red was in bed. They couldn't find Thelma Pearl, so the only choice was to take him to Oregon. Emaline already thought of the boy as her gift from the God she didn't entirely believe in, paying her back for the loss of her unborn child. She was taking care of him the best she knew how. The worst thing that could happen to her would be for Thelma Pearl to show up at the door and take the boy back. He had a new mother now and Emaline McCloskey had the child she had always wanted.

When they were alone together the next morning, she told Red that he'd be coming to Oregon with them. "It's a beautiful place, honey. We'll take you right to the Pacific Ocean. That's the biggest ocean in the world, waves taller than our barn."

"Will I see a whale?"

"Maybe. You'll see tall trees and mountains and a whole lot of beautiful country."

"But I won't see my mama, right?"

"I didn't say that, honey. We're going to leave our address in Oregon at the store in Stegall. She'll know to go there to find us when she comes looking. Until she gets back, I'm going to have to be your mama, okay?"

"Okay, Mama. I like that. You're a good mama."

He was smart, this boy. Smart enough to see right through her. When she hugged him, she felt the slingshot tucked into his back pocket. Jake had made it from a forked tree branch and a strip cut off an old inner tube. Red never went anywhere without it. He used it to zip rocks at every magpie and blackbird and gopher on the farm. He was still too young to hit anything, but in the determined set of his jaw when he went after them, he was just like Jake.

They spent the day of the foreclosure auction at Jim Lindquist's farm, saying good-bye to Lee and Jim. Some farmers watched the auctions with their families, wanting to know how much each item brought before the auctioneer's gavel came down. All Emaline wanted was for it to be over, to find out how much they would have left to get to Oregon, if they would have anything at all. She had eighty-five dollars in butter and egg money, carefully saved over the years, but they would be hard put to make that stretch all the way to Oregon.

The auction came out a little better than they expected. Floyd Spracklen, a neighbor who already owned three hundred and twenty acres adjoining their land, won the bidding for the farm and most of the machinery. He spoke with Emaline and told her to take her time vacating the house. He would take possession when they were ready to leave. Apart from the things they planned to take to Oregon, everything on the farm was sold except Molly, even Emaline's old bay mare. Because they had made a substantial down payment when they purchased the farm, they fared much better than most. Calvin Cox wrote them a check for $1,072.57 and wished them luck. Jake cashed it immediately because he was afraid the bank would fail before they got to Oregon and the check would bounce all the way back to Nebraska. But they had more than enough to take them to Oregon, perhaps even to make a little down payment on a house once they got there.

Three days before they left, Corky Dishman, the only mechanic Jake trusted, convinced him that the Ford Roadrunner would not make it to the West Coast. Corky just happened to have a 1928 Dodge Brothers sedan fixed up and ready to go. The Dodge was a pretty cream color with brown fenders, but it was ten years old and it looked pretty beat-up. It had an engine which ran thirty-five horsepower to the rear wheels, a floor heater and automatic windshield washers, all of which would come in handy pulling a trailer up and over the Great Divide.

Emaline thought it would be nice to have the car instead of the three of them being crammed into the truck cab all the way to Oregon, but she did not care one bit for the suicide doors in the back. The doors were hinged at the rear and opened in the center, so that if one flew open while the car was in motion, the wind would tear the door back and sometimes fling the occupant of the back seat onto the pavement. She didn't want Red and Molly back there unless Jake could rig some way to keep the doors from opening while the car was moving. He cut a couple of six-inch blocks off a two-by-four and wedged them tightly inside the door handles so they couldn't be moved. Emaline looked at them doubtfully, but Jake had whittled the blocks until they were so snug that he was the only one strong enough to pull them out.

34.

THE DAY THEY LEFT, EMALINE COULDN'T BEAR to look back as the sedan groaned down the lane to the county road. Red was excited, jumping up and down in the back seat while Molly tried to lick his face, but Emaline wanted to bawl. The cattle were gone, the horses gone, pigs gone, chickens gone, turkeys gone, pasture gone to dust. She hadn't bothered to plant a garden for someone else to raise. A few things had come up on their own, but they were already losing the battle to the weeds. The house, which Colonel Amen had painted fresh back in 1933, was scoured almost to bare wood on the north and west sides by sand and grit from the endless dusters. Tumbleweeds had drifted thick against the fences, because it was no longer worth the trouble to clear them, and dust was piling into the web of the weeds. It was easy to imagine dunes and deserts here, much harder to conjure up an oasis. But they had been lucky. Folks with decades on the land often lost it all and left with barely enough money for gasoline to get them to the next town.

It was April 30, 1938. She had been married to Jake McCloskey for nearly five years and this was all she had to show for it, a son who wasn't hers and a ten-year-old Dodge Brothers sedan with everything they had left piled on the trailer in back and a job waiting for Jake in Oregon, if they could get there. A thirteen-hundred-mile trip ahead and they had a hard time even making it the fifteen miles to the Wyoming state line. After two flat tires and the Dodge overheating once, they still weren't out of Nebraska. At this rate, it would take them a month to get to Oregon. With the first flat, Jake was able to change the tire, but he had only the one spare. When the second tire went flat, he had to find the leak, patch it, pump the tire up again, put it back on the axle. The overheating worried him more. They were on level ground and the temperature was around sixty degrees. Climbing the mountains on a hot day would require gallons of water. He already had a dozen canvas water bags stuffed into every available space on the car and trailer and dangling from the mirrors. Even that might not be enough. It was awkward driving with the heavy trailer attached. On the slightest downgrade, he could feel the trailer pushing them along and it would be hard to slow the rig going downhill without burning the brakes. If he got up any speed at all on level ground, the trailer started whipping back and forth. Even at thirty miles an hour, it seemed that it might careen off the road into the barrow pit and drag them along with it.

Between the flats and the overheating, it took them three hours to drive as far as Torrington. They made a late start because Jake had decided at the last minute to repack the trailer. It was already well into the afternoon. Emaline wanted to make for her aunt Ruby's little ranch on Sheep Creek, but Jake wouldn't hear of it. He wasn't going to go fifteen miles from the highway and fifteen miles back dragging the heavy trailer, so they paid twenty-five cents to stay at a campground. The next morning, Jake was up at four o'clock and they were on the road before five. At Guernsey, they could glimpse Laramie Peak, the first shadowy blue hint of the Rocky Mountains. There was more sagebrush and an occasional skittish antelope far off in the distance. There were a few small irrigated farms south of the highway, but to the north there was only empty pastureland. There were few cattle, the grass was sparse. It was the first of May, the time of year when the land should be as green as it would ever be, and all Emaline could see from the window of the Dodge was brown and more brown. As the day warmed, she opened the window visor to get a little air, after a brief shower the breeze was rich with the scent of sage. Jake sang as he drove, barbershop songs or songs from the war, to keep them entertained. After two more flat tires, they had made it only as far as Douglas. They had to stop every ten miles to let the radiator cool and still the Dodge overheated twice. As darkness fell, Jake pulled into a campground and they paid another two bits for a spot to pitch their canvas tarp near running water and an outdoor toilet.

There were twenty other families with their vehicles parked in the campground that night, all of them refugees on the road like themselves. The men were union men and around the fire that night, they sang songs about Joe Hill and the other martyrs of the union movement, too many of whom had been sent to early graves. Every car and truck was piled high like theirs, with everything from live chickens to pianos and organs. The migrants all had the same hope, that things would be better in Washington or Oregon or California. They were chasing rumors that the shipyards were hiring or there was work picking apples in Oregon or hops in Washington. Most had children, some as young as a few weeks old. The kids were ragged but not dirty. Their mothers worked hard to keep them clean, even on the road. Some families also had weary-looking grandparents along, holding in their aches and pains and trying not to be a nuisance. They were better off than many of those who had been streaming west since the beginning of the 1930s, because these people could afford the two bits for the campground rather than squatting somewhere along the road without even the comforts of running water and a toilet. They had a good time singing around the fire that night, shared food back and forth and swapped stories, but to Emaline it all seemed very subdued. People had been down so long, they didn't know how to get up again.

It took them three more days to wind their way along as far as

Riverton, the first town of any size they had passed since Casper. They made it to Dubois early the next afternoon and decided to take it easy and make the crossing over the Great Divide through Togwotee Pass in the Absaroka Mountains early the next morning. They found a campground two miles out of Dubois and paid another fifty cents for a place to spend the night. It was pretty country, with more timber than they had seen anywhere else. Emaline wondered if it would be like this all the way to Oregon, more and more forest until finally you were in the great north woods, where they claimed you couldn't see the sky because of the canopy of trees.

35.

Around two in the afternoon, Emaline and Red drifted off to sleep under their tarp. Jake fiddled with the Dodge awhile, checking the oil and the radiator and the battery, pumping up the tires. He was restless as a coyote, prowling around the campground, looking for something to do. Finally, he decided to walk the two miles down into Dubois for a look-see. Apart from the Wind River Range in the distance, there wasn't a whole lot. Dubois was a pretty little mountain town with a scattering of log houses, the Yellowstone Texaco service station, the Rustic Pine Tavern and the Branding Iron, a long, low-slung log house run by Les Wright and Tom Hewlett. It had a forty-foot log bar at the back and a dance wing that was open only on Saturday nights. When Jake strolled in, Hugh Cheney was sitting at a booth, nursing a whiskey and staring out at the road, wondering how things could have gone so sour. Big Hugh was having a bad week in a bad year. He considered himself a better-than-average grifter, a fellow whose nose for a mark had made him a wanted man in seven states and the territory of Alaska. There his attempt to run a con on the widow of a millionaire rube ran afoul of a team of sled dogs, a gallon of rotgut whiskey, an Eskimo woman who called herself Roxanne and a number-16 bear trap. Hugh Cheney didn't talk about Alaska unless somebody happened to ask why he was missing three fingers and had a list to the left when he walked. He had escaped on a freighter making the Anchorage-to-Seattle run, kissed the ground when he reached Seattle, bought a jalopy and headed for Nevada, a state where he had always found easy pickings and a noticeable lack of sled dogs, bear traps, and Eskimo women.

In Carson City, Cheney teamed up with Maisie, a born grifter so slick she had run a con on Big Hugh himself. She convinced him that she was a helpless sixteen-year-old waif trying to put together enough money to get home to her sweet mother in Sacramento. It turned out that she was really twenty-eight, she was wanted in almost as many states as he was, and she had ditched at least two husbands along the way. A month with Maisie and he was a lovesick fool. Maybe that was what accounted for the losing streak he'd been on since they left Nevada. A grifter needs a cool head and the heat he felt for Maisie was affecting his judgment.

Big Hugh was sitting there drinking whiskey and trying to come up with a plan when this tall bird in a beat-up old cowboy hat walked in and stood at the bar. Cheney never forgot a face and this was not a face that was likely to slip your mind. He had seen the fellow somewhere before, he just couldn't think where. It was not until he saw Jake crack his knuckles that Big Hugh's memory clicked. The fall of 1931 it was, Jake McCloskey in the ring with a colored fellow they called King Kane. McCloskey had thrown a haymaker from his shoe tops and dropped Kane for the count in the tenth round, earning a quick two hundred dollars for Hugh Cheney. The boxer didn't look like he had a dime left to his name, but Cheney figured he might as well buy him a drink for old times' sake. He wandered over, perched on the next barstool. "You're Jake McCloskey, right? Used to fight light-heavy outa Denver?"

"I'm your man."

"Well, I'll be damned. I saw you knock out Lionel Kane. Best damned fight I ever saw. Folks call me Big Hugh. Let me buy you a drink."

By suppertime most of the hangers-on in the Branding Iron had drifted home to their wives and the evening crowd hadn't started coming in yet. Cheney suggested that Jake join him in the booth by the window, where they could sit comfortable and watch the world passing by. After two or three more rounds, Jake said it was his turn to buy. When he reached for his billfold, Hugh caught a glimpse of the roll he was carrying. It had to be close to a thousand dollars, easy. Damned fool with that kind of money riding on his hip pocket deserved to lose every dime. McCloskey no doubt figured that no one would try to rob a prizefighter, but there was more than one way to separate a man from his money.

Cheney knew that he was not the smartest grifter around. As a rule, he borrowed tricks worked out by smarter operators. His gift was that he was such a big, convivial cuss that people trusted him by instinct. Grifters weren't supposed to be burly and amiable. People expected them to be thin little men with patent-leather shoes, shifty eyes, and pencil mustaches, but Hugh Cheney seemed like a good old boy, dangerous as a puppy and none too bright. Men a lot smarter than Jake McCloskey had been taken in because they failed to see Cheney for what he was until it was too late.

Just as Hugh was racking his brain for the best grift to run on McCloskey, Maisie came through the door and sashayed over to their booth. "Hey, fellas! How do?"

Jake took one look at Maisie and Cheney could see the hook was in deep. She could do that to a certain kind of man and it looked like McCloskey was that kind, the kind who let himself be led around by his pecker. Hugh made the introductions. "Jake, this here little filly is my business partner. Maisie, this is Jake McCloskey. Used to be the best light-heavyweight in the Rocky Mountains, maybe in the whole country. I saw Jake knock out Lionel Kane back in 'thirty-one. Won some good money on that fight too."

She gave Jake her best helpless waif smile. Cheney saw his opening and gave Maisie her cue. He always said Maisie was so quick she could turn the light off and be in bed before it got dark. She didn't let him down.

"Maisie, I was just about to tell Jake here about Nevada."

She turned on him, suddenly fierce. "You didn't offer to sell any more shares in our mine, did you? Tell me the truth! If you did, I'm goin back to Sacramento right this minute!"

Cheney looked around. "Keep your voice down, Maisie. You want them fellas at the bar to hear? Then everybody will want in. Don't you worry, I didn't offer our shares to nobody."

Jake perked up. "What shares are these?"

"I can't say, Jake. Maisie won't let me say a word."

She looked at Jake and pursed her lips as though she was sizing him up to see if he could be trusted. "I don't care if you tell this fella, Hugh. He seems okay. Just don't go sellin any shares. You promised me we'd keep all the rest for ourselves."

Hugh lowered his voice so that Jake had to lean forward to hear. "I inherited this piece a land outside Carson City from my grandpappy. Wasn't worth a damn. Nothin but cactus and rock. Little cabin on it, I used to stay there now and again when I wanted piece and quiet. Anyhow, I'm settin there minding my own business one day when a fella comes through, says his name is Cyrus Cunningham. He's a expert on locating mines, found some of the best silver deposits in Nevada. Old Cy, he tells me the silver in Nevada is about played out, but he's on the trail of a lead deposit that might be worth five, six million dollars. Maybe more. He aint sure, but he thinks the mother lode could be right square on my land and he wants to know, is it all right if he takes some samples? I figure I got nothin to lose, so I tell Cyrus to go right ahead. He sniffs around for two, three weeks. Finally, he's sure. I got a seam of lead runnin straight across my land would make me as rich as Rockefeller, only it's down deep. Three, four hundred feet. We got to drill and we need big money to drill. So we set up a company, sold some shares, found our investors in Chicago. We're headed back to Carson City, goin to get that heavy equipment in and get to work. I figure three months tops until that mine comes in."

"Damn. I'm sorry I didn't find you folks before you got them investors."

"Hell, it's a shame, Jake. Fella like you, took care of Lionel Kane and all, I'd love to have you aboard. But Maisie here, she won't let me sell any more shares."

"How much was it for a share? Just outa curiosity?"

"Hundred dollars a share, but we only sold them in lots of ten or more. We kept fifty percent of the company for ourselves, twenty-five percent goes to Cy Cunningham, the rest we sold. Took a week to sell a thousand shares, but the fellas who got in on the ground floor like that, they'll make ten, twenty times their money the first year."

"I'd sure as hell like to get in on that."

Maisie leaned into Jake's arm a bit, let the perfume from between her breasts spill over him. "I don't know, Hugh. Maybe we could make an exception, just this once. Jake is such a fine fella and all. How many shares were you thinkin to buy, Jake? Ten? Twenty?"

"Hell, I'd love to buy a hundred, but at a hundred a share I couldn't manage more'n ten shares. I sold a farm back in Nebraska and I'm on my way to Oregon, y'see."

Maisie made a face as though she was thinking it over. "I dunno, honey. See, we already sold all I wanted to sell. I got my heart set on a big old mansion up on a hill in San Francisco. Why don't you take a look in that billfold of yours and see how much you got?"

Jake was about to start counting money right on the table when Maisie grabbed his arm. "Not where everybody can see, sugar! I don't want all those birds at the bar gettin curious."

Maisie spread her legs a little and he counted the bills into her lap, feeling the back of his hand brush her warm thighs with every double sawbuck. She counted with him, right up to the last two dollar bills he tugged from his front pocket. It came to one thousand and seventeen dollars. Jake said he should probably hang on to the seventeen and leave himself enough money to get to Oregon. First he'd have to walk back up to the campground and check with the missus, make sure she didn't object to him investing the money from the farm.

Maisie clucked her tongue. "Gosh, Jake. That's a tough one. You struck me as the kind of man to wear the pants in the family. I didn't think you'd have to get the little lady's permission to get in on the best deal you'll ever see."

Cheney jumped in then. "Shoot, a name like Jake McCloskey, that's worth somethin. People know who Jake is, smooths the way for all kinds a deals, Maisie. We could make Jake here a company director, put his name right up top with you and me and Cy Cunningham. You wouldn't object, Maisie?"

Maisie's fingernail traced the seam of Jake's trousers. "I'd just love to have this big, handsome fella come along with us. It can get real dull out on that place in Nevada, just sittin around all day long waitin for lead to come outa the ground. But then he probably couldn't come to Nevada anyway unless he gets the woman's okeydokey."

"Hell, yes. I'll go where I please."

"Well, I hope so. First you got to show me you're a man and close this bargain on your own. Imagine how surprised she'll be when she finds out you're goin to be rich!"

"Tell you what, Jake," Cheney said. "Seems Maisie has taken a shine to you. She don't like many fellas, so I'm goin to sell you these shares for a thousand dollars, even. A man can't say no to a deal like that, especially when your shares are likely to be worth twenty times that much by Christmas."

Jake squirmed a little. He knew that Emaline wouldn't like it, not being consulted and all. But a man only got so many shots at the big time. Sometimes you had to strike while the iron was hot. He reached out a hand to shake on it. "You've got yourself a deal, Big Hugh."

"Well, then, why don't you run over to the lodge and grab these share certificates for Mr. McCloskey, Maisie. I'll buy us another drink to celebrate."

Maisie was gone less than five minutes. When she left, Jake put his hand down and felt the warmth where her bottom had perched on the seat. She came back a little breathless and handed him some very official-looking share certificates. When he gave her the cash, she tucked it between her breasts, making a little show of putting the money away carefully. She pointed to an address in Carson City that was printed on the certificates.

"See, honey? This is where you can find us. You come on down when you're ready."

"You can be sure I'll do that."

"That's swell, sugar. I can't wait to see you again. Now me and Big Hugh got to turn in so we can get an early start tomorrow. Don't you go tellin folks you're about to get rich, y'hear?"

"No, ma'am. I won't tell a soul."

Jake shook hands with Cheney. Maisie gave him a long, sweet kiss on the lips, left a trail of lipstick.

"You will come right on down and see us, won't you, sugar? You're not the type to keep a little gal waitin, are you?"

"Aw, hell no."

Jake watched from the window as they left the bar and strolled toward the lodge, the twitch of her tidy little behind. Sure enough, the lady was ripe to be pried away from this bird Cheney. He was going to get rich and he'd get a little bit of this Maisie woman to boot. It was the best day he'd had in a good long while. He was feeling so good he ordered a whiskey and a beer chaser to celebrate.

It was near nine o'clock when Jake staggered back up the hill to the campground. He knew that Emaline would be having a conniption fit, but she'd brighten right up when she heard how rich they were going to be. He whistled along, happy as a clam because he had the share certificates for the Carson City Lead Mining Company tucked safely into his shirt pocket. When he reached the camp, Emaline was waiting for him, pacing back and forth in front of the Dodge.

"Where on earth have you been? Every time I turn my back, you disappear somewhere. It smells like you've been drinking."

"Now, now. Settle down, Em. I only had the one or the two, and I struck a deal that's goin to make us rich by the end of the year."

"What on earth could that be? Did you find a better job?"

"Nosir. I bought shares in what is goin to be the biggest lead mine in Nevada."

"You did what?"

He reached into his pocket and hauled out the shares with elaborate ceremony. "This here, sweetheart, is your ticket to a mansion on the hill."

Emaline took it, glanced over the share certificate. "Look at this, you fool! It says 'led mine.'"

"That's exactly what it is. We got ten shares in a lead mine."

"No, silly. Look how it's written: L-E-D. That's not how you spell *lead*. You spell *lead* with an *a*. These aren't even good forgeries."

"Just cause they don't know how to spell don't mean they aint got a mine. There's plenty of rich folk can hardly spell their own names."

"How much did you pay for these, Jake?"

"A thousand dollars. And they're goin to put my name on the board of directors or some such, me bein a prizefighter and all."

Emaline felt her legs go weak. She sat down on the running board of the Dodge, trying to catch her breath.

"No. Please don't tell me you gave them all our money. Not the whole thousand."

"Well, hell. They wasn't goin to give me them shares for nothin. Not in a gold-plated deal like this."

"Oh, my God. What were you thinking? This isn't gold-plated, it's lead! It's pure lead. Those shares aren't worth ten cents apiece."

"Well, of course they are. They're worth a hundred dollars each. Says right there."

"How stupid can you be? They can print anything they want on a share certificate, especially when they don't even know how to spell. I knew you could be a fool, Jake McCloskey, but not this big a fool. You march right down there now and get our money back."

"What if they don't want to give it back?"

"Beat it out of them, then! You're good at that, aren't you?"

Jake wanted more than anything to crawl into his sleeping roll and go to sleep, but he was beginning to feel a little anxious himself. Big Hugh seemed like a fine fellow, the girl too. Not the type to steal from a man, although Maisie did remind him an awful lot of Thelma Pearl. In his mind, he was still trying to figure out how to spend his million dollars.

"Did you get a name, at least?" Emaline asked. "What did this fellow say his name was?"

"Big Hugh."

"Big Hugh? That's all? Not even a last name? You are truly the dumbest damned hillbilly idiot I have ever known in my life. Now get down there and get our money back!"

Jake hurried down to the lodge where Hugh said they were staying, running most of the way. He had to step over a Rottweiler dog to get in the door. The night manager was a nasty-looking specimen with long, greasy hair, sitting with his cowboy boots propped up on the desk. He had a big hole in the sole of the left boot.

"You need a room, buddy?"

"My name aint buddy. I'm lookin for a fella name of Big Hugh and the woman who is with him, Maisie."

"Don't have nobody here goes by them names."

"Big fella maybe forty years old, heavyset. Little woman with the biggest dark eyes you ever seen, pretty as a picture. Don't look more than eighteen, although I expect she's older'n that."

"Oh, them. That's John L. Jones and his wife, Mary. They checked out a hour ago. Settled up their bill in some kinda hurry and left. They was way behind on the rent till they paid me."

"Sonofabitch! Did they say which way they was headed?"

"No sir, they did not. But they seemed in a big hurry to get someplace, checkin out at this time of night."

Jake had one last hope. Perhaps the two had gone back to the Branding Iron to celebrate their good fortune. The bar was jumping, but there was no sign of Maisie and Hugh. Tom Hewlett was still behind the bar. Jake had to shout to make himself heard.

"Them two I was with, the big fella and that little lady, have you seen them?"

"No, they been in here most days for two weeks, but last time I saw them they was sittin with you."

"Two weeks? They told me they was just passin through town on their way back to Nevada."

Hewlett shrugged. "From what I know they were comin *from* Nevada. They said they were headed east."

36.

EMALINE WOKE TO A BITTER ACCOUNTING. WHILE Jake slept, she counted the few greasy bills she had and counted them again, as though counting would make them multiply. Before they left the farm, she had handed over to Jake almost all of her own butter and egg money as well as the money he had from the sale of the homestead. All she had left was thirteen dollars rolled in a stocking. Jake had the seventeen dollars the crooks had left him. They had nine hundred miles to go to Portland, gasoline cost twelve cents a gallon. With the heavy load it was towing, the Dodge was getting less than ten miles to a gallon. That left almost nothing for food, for the twenty-five cents a night campgrounds were charging for a little fresh water and a place to stretch their tarp, and for the inevitable emergencies and breakdowns.

Red sat beside her as she counted the money. He had heard them quarreling in the night, and he was quiet and anxious. She hugged the boy, but she had little to offer in the way of comfort. It seemed that with Jake McCloskey, there was always another disaster waiting around the bend. She was stunned almost beyond anger. She had not objected when Jake tucked the cash from the sale of the farm into his billfold, because she assumed he could protect their money with his fists. She forgot that he had always been gullible. He had been cleaned out once by Thelma Pearl because he was far too trusting. Now it had happened again, at the worst possible time. Grifters like this fellow counted on stupidity and greed. Jake had been foolish, but he had also been greedy, all too willing to believe that they would get back ten times or a hundred times their money if they invested in a preposterous lead mine in Nevada.

She thought of a hundred questions she would have asked had she been there. Why were these two potential mining millionaires stuck in a burg like Dubois, far from Carson City? Why did they have to seek out investors if the mine was such a sure thing? Why were they making cash deals in a drinking establishment? It seemed so obvious. But Jake had been a little drunk and this Maisie woman was a looker, she had to be. Emaline had seen the smear of lipstick on Jake's mouth. Lookers were born knowing how to manipulate men like Jake. Thelma Pearl and Maisie were the same woman in different incarnations, both of them knowing exactly how to get what they wanted. *Damn, damn, damn that man! What a blessed idiot!*

There was no point going over it. Their money was gone. The grifters were gone. North, east, south, west. Jake could rage about it all he wanted, promise to beat the living hell out of the man if he caught him, but the truth was that they would never be caught, not by Jake McCloskey or anyone else. Jake had spent two hours the night before sitting with a deputy sheriff, going through photos of grifters known to be operating in Wyoming. Neither Big Hugh nor this woman who called herself Maisie had turned up anywhere. Jake's fecklessness had forced them to sell the farm, now he had handed over most of what they had left to a couple of con artists in a bar. It was enough to make her want to throttle him as he slept.

After calculating to the penny what they would need to get to Portland, she prodded Jake with a toe. "Come on, mister big-shot lead-mine millionaire. If we're going to Oregon, we'd best get started."

Within an hour they were on the road, riding in bitter silence in the

Dodge, Red and Molly the collie asleep in the back. As they ground their way up into the Absaroka Mountains and toward Togwotee Pass, the barren landscape changed dramatically. Trees crowded the narrow road, limber pine, whitebark pine, Douglas fir, Colorado blue spruce. They were climbing from one switchback to another toward the Great Divide, nearly ten thousand feet above sea level. The Dodge was in first gear, grinding along with the shift lever vibrating hard. Every few hundred feet they had to stop to let the radiator cool. They were still a quarter mile from the summit when the sedan ground to a halt. The grade was too steep. Jake was about to step out to put blocks behind the wheels when he felt a nudge from in back of the trailer. An empty logging truck was giving them a push, unasked. He waved an arm out the window, dropped the transmission into neutral, let the truck do the rest of the work.

"That's one thing about this country will never change," Jake said. "A workin man will always help another workin man."

Emaline made a face. "Unless he's the kind of working man who makes his living cheating other men."

As they neared the summit, Jake put the Dodge in gear and pulled over into a turnout to let the truck pass. The driver honked and waved. Jake tipped his hat in gratitude. All they had to do now was get down off the mountain. At the summit, they found a wide spot in the road to pull over and let Red and Molly out for a romp. As they climbed back into the car, Emaline noticed that the sky had turned the color of dirty dishwater. Jake looked up and declared there was a snowstorm coming.

"Don't be ridiculous," she said. "It's almost summer."

"Not up this high, it aint summer. Up here you can get a blizzard most any time of year, except maybe the month of July."

They started down the long, steep, winding grade to Moran Junction. They didn't make it half a mile before the first snowflakes started to fall. Another half mile and it was snowing hard. The road was slick and their vision down to no more than a couple of hundred feet, although Emaline had a good view of the sheer drop off the side of the road. In some places it looked as though the car would plunge a thousand feet or more if it went over the edge.

Jake used the transmission to slow them down as much as he could, holding the Dodge in second gear, trying not to overheat the brakes. It was tricky, delicate work. What they needed was a turnout where they could pull over until the storm passed, but there was nothing but narrow, winding road, pine and fir trees already white, their branches drooping with the heavy snow. Jake had tire chains in the trailer, but he didn't dare stop to put them on. It would be far too easy for one of those big trucks to pile into them and send them flying over the edge. There was nothing to do but keep going.

Emaline breathed a silent prayer. Jake knew every trick there was for getting a vehicle down a steep grade in a snowstorm, but when you couldn't see where you were going, nothing helped. She did all she could, leaning forward to peer into the driving snow, looking desperately for a place where they could turn off. There was nothing, just one switchback followed by another, and through it all she could feel the heavy trailer behind them pushing, pushing. It felt almost as if the thing was trying to heave them off the road.

It was twenty-five miles from the summit of Togwotee Pass down to Moran Junction, and every foot of it was so tense that she dug her fingernails into her palms until they bled. Twice the Dodge lurched so close to the edge that it seemed they were about to go over. Both times, Jake was able to bring it back onto the road. They eased along through curve after curve, down switchbacks so tight that at times she could almost reach out and touch the trailer in the middle of a turn. With each twist in the road they strained to peer into the driving snow, longing for flat ground, a bit of straight road, even a spot where they could pull over.

The only mercy was that Red and Molly had fallen asleep, the two of them curled up in the back seat. The perilous trip down the mountain took well over an hour. At last the road leveled out a mile from Moran Junction, where the state patrol had set up a roadblock. All vehicles heading east toward the pass were being turned back. Jake pulled up next to one of the troopers and asked what was going on.

"They're calling for at least three feet a snow up there, probably more. We're closin the road. You folks was damned lucky to make it down, haulin that trailer and all."

It was still snowing lightly at the roadblock, but by the time they got into Moran Junction it had stopped snowing and the sky was beginning to clear. The snow on the hood of the Dodge steamed in the sunshine. The clouds lifted off the mountains.

They camped ten miles south of Jackson that night and ate a quiet supper with other families who were huddled around bonfires. Most had also come through Togwotee Pass. They sat quietly, not talking or singing, worn out by the crossing. Even Jake was quiet and glum. Emaline was grateful for the boy, who lay with his head in her lap as she sat by the fire. As weary as she was, he was a line cast into the future, a reason to go on.

From Wyoming, they followed the beautiful Snake River west into Idaho, the winding river between its high banks so lovely that it temporarily lifted their spirits. Idaho started well, with the river and the mountains, then petered out into flat potato fields, a plateau as flat, dry, and dreary as Nebraska, even if they could look out onto cultivated potato fields rather than sagebrush. Emaline longed for tall trees, shade, wide rivers, and rain, all the things she associated with Oregon. It seemed as though they were making no progress at all, running on a treadmill to nowhere. They limped along from camp to camp, stopping again and again to patch tires on both the Dodge and the trailer, overheating again and again or pulling over to let the brakes cool. Emaline tried to remind herself that the pioneers had come this way by oxcart, but that was small consolation. At least an ox would never get a flat tire.

Despite the flats and overheating, the Dodge held out, which was a mercy because they had no money to fix it if it broke down. They spent two nights resting in a campground east of Boise and crossed into Oregon on May 22. Emaline felt a temporary elation in the Blue Mountains of eastern Oregon. The trees brought relief from the heat and the monotony of the bare, brown landscape. This was the Oregon that Alice Tatro had written about, tall trees and mountains to block the ceaseless wind that blew on the prairies. The drive from La Grande to Pendleton was as spectacular and nearly as difficult as their crossing over the Great Divide. Once again, Emaline was disappointed when the mountains slipped away and Pendleton turned out to be a cowboy town set amid bare, windswept hills, a landscape that could have been Wyoming or Montana or the Nebraska sandhills.

Jake talked to a man in a camp outside Pendleton who told him about a danceland bar outside town that hosted a boxing tournament on Saturday nights. It cost a dollar to enter, but the winner of each bout made three dollars and the champ at the end of the evening earned an extra ten. Jake rummaged around in the trailer until he found his old boxing gloves and shoes and trunks, unhooked the Dodge from the trailer, drove to the bar early on Saturday evening. He was back at midnight, tired and sore and with his left eye swollen shut from a head butt delivered by a brawny blacksmith, but he had won all six of his bouts and the championship bonus. He had come away with twenty-eight dollars. It was enough to keep them in food and gasoline the rest of the way.

37.

THEY LEFT PENDLETON EARLY THE NEXT DAY, passed through Bucks Corner and Umatilla and came at last face-to-face with the Columbia River at the town of Boardman. They climbed out to admire the great river, even here the widest and most powerful stream Emaline had ever seen. Somehow, the river made her hopeful. If they had reached the Columbia, the Pacific could not be far away, their endless trek across the western half of America taken as far as it could go without a ship. When they reached Celilo Falls the following day, they were dazzled by the great slabs of black basalt rock on either side where the river narrowed, the roar of water over the falls so loud they could hear it inside the Dodge even with the windows rolled up. Flocks of ducks and geese wheeled above the Columbia, clouds of spray and mist rose where native dip-net fishermen had erected elaborate scaffolding. The fishermen leaned over the black eddies in the turbulent waters with their dip nets on long poles, risking their lives to haul in forty-pound salmon from the Chinook run. Jake pulled the Dodge over to the side of the road. They got out to watch the salmon hurtling themselves out of the water and the agile fishermen yanking them from the air as children and old women with no one to fish for them waited to share in the catch. An old man, his face a spiderweb of lines from his years working the dip nets, told them that bands of Indians from all over the Pacific Northwest had fished here for ten thousand years, perhaps more. He was from the Umatilla tribe, but Celilo Falls was also a fishing ground for the Yakima, Nez Perce, Wasco-Wishram, and a dozen other bands. The falls had always been a marketplace where the tribes came together to trade their wares. There was talk the white man might destroy it all by building a great dam downriver near a place they called The Dalles, but he didn't believe that even white men could be that foolish. He let them try bites of salmon from his leather satchel. It tasted of smoke and fresh water.

Emaline would have liked to stay longer at Celilo Falls, but Jake was anxious to go. They pushed on and stayed for the night close enough to Portland to see the lights of the city winking in the darkness. The next morning, they wound their way up through Scappoose and Columbia City to Millwood, the company town that would be their home. It was a depressing little burg compared with some of the Oregon towns through which they had passed, with rows of identical little houses packed too close together. They drove on until Jake spotted Clay Tatro's address, the only one painted yellow in a row of white frame houses. It had taken them almost a month to travel thirteen hundred miles.

Tatro was at the mill, but Alice came out to greet them, followed by three of her six children, including a boy Red's age. She was a short, blocky woman, nearly as wide as she was tall, with a beaming smile and a strong handshake. She explained that her husband had arranged for them to rent one of the company houses down the street for twenty-five dollars a month. Until they moved in, they were welcome to stay with the Tatros.

Clay Tatro knocked off work early and greeted Jake with a bear hug. What hair he had left was mostly gray and he had put on at least fifty pounds since the war, but he was a big, powerful man who looked as though he had fought a thousand battles. Tatro had taken part in the Bonus Army march in May 1932, when unemployed World War I veterans formed what they called the Bonus Expeditionary Force and descended on Washington to demand the bonuses that had been approved by Congress in 1924 but never paid, amounting to $1.25 for each day served overseas. Over forty thousand people, including veterans with their wives and many children, had camped at Anacostia Flats across the Potomac River from Washington in a festive atmosphere which included a generous dose of military discipline. The bill to give the veterans their money passed the House but was soundly defeated in the Senate. After the veterans clashed with police trying to clear them out and two of the marchers were killed, Herbert Hoover ordered the U.S. Army to clear the flats. Troops led by Douglas MacArthur, Dwight D. Eisenhower, and George Patton were dispatched, along with a half dozen tanks. Patton's cavalry charged first, attacking unarmed men, women, and children. Soldiers with fixed bayonets followed, firing tear gas into the crowd. Two veterans and two babies in the camp were killed and a thousand civilians injured. The hospitals filled with casualties. The unarmed veterans of the Great War were routed.

The Bonus March taught many lessons to men like Tatro, including the lengths to which men like Herbert Hoover would go to avoid offering relief to the working poor. The same men who had been cheered as heroes when they marched down Pennsylvania Avenue after the war were attacked by the army for which they had fought, for the crime of camping on public property. Tatro returned to the northwest and began organizing for the Sawmill and Timber Workers Union. Strikes in the summer of 1935 shut down half the sawmills and pulp mills in the northwest before the workers won some important concessions at some unionized mills, but three years later, the union was still trying to organize the remaining sawmills. At Millwood, the Columbia River Lumber Company ran one of its larger mills, with a hundred and fifty workers. Columbia River had avoided the 1935 strike by paying fifty cents a day more than most of the mills, but its owners still refused to recognize the union or its right to strike. If there was a strike, the company threatened to throw out the union and bring in scabs. That was why Tatro had been trying to get Jake to come work at the sawmill. By hiring a few men who were capable fighters, Tatro hoped to strengthen the resistance of the other workers.

"They're good men, strong and tough," Tatro said of the sawmill workers. "They're just not used to fighting. If the company tries to bring in scabs, they come armed with axe handles and crowbars. I've seen what happens. They jump out of the trucks and charge, or sometimes they'll try to drive the trucks right through the picket line and run over anybody who gets in the way. All we need is a few men who aint afraid of a fight and know how to go about it. Best thing I've found is to go right at 'em, don't wait for them to come to you. Same as a street fight or a bar brawl. Guy who hits first is generally the one standing at the end."

"Unless the other fella knows what he's doin."

"That's where you come in too. Some of the fellas, they're willing as all hell, but they need to be taught. I got fifteen or twenty men I've picked out, the youngest and strongest. I want them to work with you and learn how to box. You've been in plenty of street fights too, you can teach them how to fight dirty. There aint no rules once the strikebreakers wade in."

"Be a pleasure. Got to earn my pay somehow."

"You'll earn it all right. Once we call a strike and they come in to bust it up, you'll earn every last dime."

Alice fixed supper for them that night. They ate at a long table presided over by Clay Tatro. The children were so noisy they could barely hear themselves over the racket. Even quiet little Red was happily chatting away with the Tatro kids. Emaline thought they might enjoy having neighbors so close after the isolation of the farm. Alice said most of the families in Millwood had children and there were plenty Red's age.

That Sunday, they took all the children in both cars and drove all the way to the ocean, to a little town called Seaside. The children frolicked with Molly in the surf while Emaline stood gazing out at the mighty Pacific. She had spent most of her life in places where water was in short supply. Here it was infinite, with a breadth and power she could not have imagined. To live here, within an hour's drive of such a place, made their long and difficult journey seem worthwhile. The water was still chilly, but she kicked off her shoes and waded with the children, barefoot in the surf. It felt like the beginning of something. She took Red by the hand and led him to where they could look down over the beach and the sea from a low hill. They could see the breakers building far out in the ocean, the powerful waves rolling in one after another until they crashed in the surf.

"Mom," the boy asked, "is that ocean going to drown us?"

She tousled his hair. "No, silly. Not unless we're fool enough to try to swim to Japan, and we're not going to do that."

"What's a Japan?"

"It's a country way on the other side of the water."

"Do boys there have slingshots?"

"I'm sure they do."

"Oh, boy! Can we go there sometime?"

"Maybe when you're all grown up. Right now, we're in a beautiful place, don't you think?"

"Yeah. It's beautiful. But I'm hungry."

The following week, they moved into their rented company house and Jake started working at the mill. His job was outside, where the huge logs were pulled up from the river and into the mill. Tatro asked him where he wanted to work and Jake asked for something where he didn't have to be inside all day, deafened by the clatter of machinery. It was dangerous work, but all the jobs in the mill were dangerous. Men lost fingers, arms, hands, legs, sometimes their lives when they were caught in the powerful saws or crushed by falling logs. Most of what pay they earned went to rent company houses or to buy food at the company commissary. Many of the men with large families were so in debt to the commissary that without a significant change in wages they would never be able to square things.

They lived constantly within the sight, sound, and smell of the sawmill, but to Emaline it was worth it to be in a place where rainfall was never going to be a problem, where they could always count on shade from the tall trees, where the land wasn't blowing away, where Red had other kids to play with. The men worked long, hard hours, so during the day the little town belonged to the women and children. Women with children too young to go to school tended to group together, talking and gossiping while the children were given a pretty free hand to run about as they pleased. Emaline was afraid of children falling into the Columbia, but they tended to stay around the town, far from the river. The men worked ten-hour shifts, six days a week. With Jake training men to box in the evenings, he was gone almost all the time. Red blossomed in his father's absence. He was more talkative and less nervous. When he wasn't playing with the other children, Emaline took him for long walks. It was fascinating to her as much as to the boy, because so much of this was new, the trees and flowers and birds, even the little animals they saw in the forest.

They had been in Oregon less than a month before Jake started complaining about the job, saying that he was never meant to carry a lunch bucket and punch a clock and do the same thing day in and day out for thirty years. When Emaline pointed out that he hadn't even been doing it for thirty days, he stormed out of the house and went to go hit the heavy bag at the makeshift gym. He was talking about going back into the ring, but Emaline said she would not put up with even one more fight. He was nearly thirty-eight, old for a boxer, he had been out of the ring for five years and his skill and speed had eroded, even if it wasn't obvious when he was working with amateurs. Above all, he now had a six-year-old boy to raise. If nothing else, he owed it to Red not to go out and get himself hurt. He agreed, but as the summer went by and the promised strike failed to materialize, he grew more and more restless. When Clay Tatro finally announced on the first day of October that the strike was on, Jake was the happiest man in Millwood. He wasn't exactly spoiling for a fight, but a fight would be a welcome change after the daily drudgery of the mill.

For three weeks, Jake walked the picket lines in front of the silent mill until at last the word came. The owners of the Columbia River Lumber Company said they were going to get the mill up and running one way or another. That meant bringing in scabs. Scabs would mean a fight.

38.

THE MEN BEGAN TO GATHER OUTSIDE THE MILL early in the evening. They had pitched tents at the beginning of the strike. Clay Tatro had set up his headquarters at an old foreman's shack just outside the gates. There was no telling what the owners would do. They might send in replacement workers who were no better armed than the strikers. They might come with police officers or hastily deputized thugs armed with pistols or even shotguns and submachine guns. If the labor movement had learned one thing during the Great Depression, it was that the bosses did not fight fair. Many a strike had ended with casualties when police or hired thugs opened fire on unarmed workers. Tatro knew that a murdered striker or two could be very useful in drumming up public sympathy and turning people against the bosses. Even when workers lost a battle, they could sometimes use their casualties to win the war.

Rumors flew all night long. Forty strikebreakers were on a bus up from Fresno. Canadian scabs were on their way down from Vancouver. The sheriff had signed up two hundred deputies and was passing out shotguns. The president was going to send Harry Hopkins out in person and ask old Harry to sort out the mess. Someone heard a waitress in a diner at The Dalles say that she heard from her cousin they were sending strikebreakers over from Pendleton. Most of the men were too nervous to sleep, so they kept themselves busy by passing around the latest fourth-hand information. Jake slept soundly until three o'clock and crawled out of his tent into a fog so thick he could hardly make out the outlines of the next tent over. Most of the men were still trying to sleep, some in the tents, some in sleeping rolls on the wet ground.

Tatro had been up all night, trying to get some information he could rely on. He had four or five men out scouting around, but the three who had reported back hadn't seen hide nor hair of the scabs. Everyone knew they would be coming. No one seemed to know where they were coming from, how many there would be or when they were likely to arrive. There was no way they could surprise the strikers anyway. There were only two ways in, by the long, twisting road up the hill or down the river and they weren't going to come rafting down the Columbia. The trees were so thick an army could get lost in there, so that left the road. They would have to come up the road, truckloads of strikebreakers moving single file, and then they would have to get out of the trucks and assemble before they could get into a fight. Tatro was not going to give them that opportunity. The strikers were sure to be outnumbered and the company men would expect them to wait for the usual parley before they started swinging the axe handles. But if the strikers jumped the scabs as soon as they started climbing down from the trucks, they'd have the element of surprise on their side. They could isolate the strikebreakers and beat them up in twos or threes before they got organized.

There was one false alarm around five o'clock when a single old truck labored up the hill. Jake was trying to see who it was when shouts went up from the men in front.

"Why, it's Gunny!"

"It's old Gunderson, come to join us."

"Gunny, I'll be damned. Did you bring the turkey dinner, Gunny?"

Gunderson pulled an ancient pickup over to the side of the road and got out. He was at least seventy years old, with long, stringy gray hair that looked like it hadn't been cut in two years. He had the stoop of an old working man and two missing fingers on his left hand. Gunderson reached into the back of the truck, pulled out a crowbar, jogged over to join the rest of the pickets. The men lined up to shake his hand.

"Gunny was one of the reasons we got a union here," Tatro told Jake. "He worked in this mill for thirty years. Then they fired him cause a foreman found him asleep on top of a pile of logs. Thirty years and you're out because of a catnap. That's the way them bastards used to operate. It's dumb, because if they'd treat men like human beings, they wouldn't have to deal with a union."

Tatro introduced Gunderson to Jake. "Gunny, this here is Jake McCloskey, army buddy of mine. Used to be a top light-heavyweight. If things get nasty, you stick close to him. I don't want you gettin hurt up here."

The old man guffawed. "Hell, like as not you fellas will have to hide behind me. I never run from a fight in my life."

"I know you didn't, Gunny. That's why you don't have to fight this time, but you're welcome aboard. Comes to a scrap, we'll need all hands on deck."

Tatro assumed the scabs would attack at daybreak. He had the men up and ready as the first light filtered through the fog and drizzle, but the strikebreakers did not appear. The millworkers fidgeted and shivered, cursed the cold and the damp, and flexed wet fingers cramped from holding on to axe handles, crowbars, baseball bats, and three-foot lengths of concrete rebar. The men milled around, huddled under their rain slickers. They talked in tight little knots, disappeared into the shed for endless cups of coffee, gnawed at soggy sandwiches.

By eight o'clock the trucks had not appeared. The pea-soup fog did not lift. They could see down the hill only as far as the first curve in the road, the wet asphalt shining in the rain until it vanished between thick-trunked Douglas firs a hundred feet tall. Tatro toyed with a set of brass knuckles, moving them from his left hand to his right and back again like an uncertain, married man toying with his wedding ring.

"Let the bastards come, by God. Sonofabitch scabs. I've been fightin them since the war. They're the same as us, workin men, but they take the jobs of other men and make it worse for everybody. They can't get it through their damned heads that the only way to win this thing and get a better life for all of us is to stick together. If we do that, there's no bosses anywhere can beat us."

Tatro knew he was preaching to the converted, but he felt he had to say something. It was a lesson he had learned in the Great War. It was hard to keep men geared up for a fight for more than an hour or two. After that, they started to lose their nerve.

By ten o'clock, Jake felt the men were at the point where their nerves were going to break. They were so tense that little scraps were breaking out, men swinging at each other because one had stepped on another's toes or taken the last cup of coffee from the pot. At last, a murmur went up and down the line. "Hush, what's that? You hear that, boys? Somethin out there. Listen close."

They fell silent, peering intently into the fog, listening. Jake heard the sound, like the ringing of cowbells only pitched a little higher, coming up the road. The men dropped their coffee cups and shouldered their way back into formation. Maybe the strikebreakers were marching up on foot, but why the bells? If they had decided to sneak in without the trucks, why would they announce their arrival? The little bells echoed up the hill, a thin, tinny sound drifting through the rain and the rolling layers of fog.

Jake felt himself tense, felt the hairs on the back of his neck stand on end. He clenched and unclenched his fists, bounced a little on his toes, threw a combination to get loose as he would have in the ring.

A big blond kid standing next to Jake had to pull out of the line to vomit. The men hooted and laughed as he retched.

"What's the matter, boy? Nerves got to you? Never been in a fight before? Say, maybe Tatro will let you go home to your mommy!"

The kid wiped his mouth and stepped back into the line. Jake saw his hands shaking. He leaned over and clapped him on the shoulder.

"Don't listen to them bastards hollerin at you," he said. "They're as scared as you are. I had seventy fights in the ring and I was scared before every single fight. If you aint scared, you aint ready. Soon as you hit somethin, you'll feel a whole lot better."

The kid gave him a grateful smile. He was six foot four and well over two hundred pounds, but he was no more than eighteen or nineteen. *Like the soldiers they sent into combat in the war,* Jake thought. *Always too damned young.*

The bells came closer. Jake heard the shuffle of work boots on wet pavement, men getting set for battle. There was something ghostly about the tinkle of the bells in the fog, worse than the growl of trucks or the shouts of men ready to do battle. Jake could recall priests ringing bells at the head of a procession in a little village in France during the war. Maybe the strikebreakers had priests with them, ready to bless the carnage they were about to inflict. Or goats. Didn't goat bells sound a little like that? Whatever it was, the approach was painfully slow, a crawl up the hillside. Tatro took a few steps forward. The men, unable to bear the stress of waiting, followed. It was better to move toward the thing that terrified them than to stand and wait. They moved forward in a long, rippling horizontal line, a few feet at a time, the irregular tread of their boots like an army platoon marching over rough ground. They advanced twenty yards before Tatro held up a hand, calling a halt. Again they listened to the tinny sound of the little bells, now nearing the curve where they would burst into sight.

Tatro barked an order in his drill sergeant's voice. "Halt! Nobody moves until I say so."

A hundred pairs of eyes strained into the fog, a hundred pairs of ears listened. It was old Gunny Gunderson who saw them first.

"Why, it's kids! It's just kids with bikes."

Four boys about ten or eleven years old rounded the curve under the great fir trees, fishing poles over their shoulders, pushing their bicycles because the grade was so steep, ringing the bicycle bells as though they were playing a tune. They had to be playing hooky, heading for the fishing hole above the sawmill. When the boys looked up, they saw facing them a line of a hundred grim sawmill workers, all of them arrayed for battle. The tallest boy yelped and jumped on his bike. The others followed, and they took off, pelting back down the hill as fast as they could pedal. All the way along the line, men cursed and threw down their weapons. One tossed his crowbar so hard it bounced and hit another man in the shins and the two were on each other, punching and gouging and rolling over and over on the wet asphalt until Tatro broke it up.

They waited three more hours. Finally a Pontiac sedan came up the road. Inside were three members of the union executive out of Portland. They brushed past the waiting men into Tatro's headquarters shack and talked for five minutes. When Tatro came out, he was smiling. He stood on the bumper of a truck parked outside the sawmill gates to announce that an agreement with the mill owners had been reached without bloodshed. The men were to get a raise to six dollars a day for a reduced, forty-eight-hour week. The union was recognized at this mill and all the others belonging to the Columbia River Lumber Company. From now on, the mill would operate as a closed shop. You belonged to the union or you didn't work. Each man got a one-week vacation every year and three sick days with pay. It was a huge victory. The strike was over.

There were halfhearted cheers when Tatro announced the agreement.

Some men pulled out forbidden flasks of whiskey and passed them around. The men knew how important the agreement was, how it would make their lives easier in the future, but they had been cheated of battle. Now they had no outlet for all that pent-up nerve and adrenaline. They were keyed up to break some heads and left without heads to break. A victory won without a fight seemed hollow and pointless, a day that promised release and exhilaration ending in signatures on a piece of paper and a few dollars more in a pay packet at the end of the week.

Clay Tatro and Jake McCloskey were among the last to leave the sawmill, shortly after dusk. Jake sat tapping his fingers and jiggling his right leg while Tatro drove. Tatro noticed how edgy he was.

"Kind of put a damper on things when we didn't get that fight."

"Sure did. Damned shame, we would a fought like wild men."

"Don't I know it. Company knew it too. I think they knew they were beat. Still, too bad we didn't get a chance to teach a few strikebreakers a lesson. Even old Gunny was up for a fight, and he don't work here anymore."

"I guess you didn't need me after all," Jake said. "You don't need fighters when there's no fight."

"Oh, yes, you do. That's why we didn't have to fight. They knew we were ready. Sometimes that's how you avoid a fight. You have a bigger knife than the other fella."

Jake still felt uneasy. A fighter without a brawl was like a soldier without a war, with nothing to look forward to except punching a clock at the mill.

39.

When Jake got back to the house, it was still raining. In five months in Oregon they had seen as much rain as they had seen in five years in Nebraska. It made a fellow restless, the tedium of the rain, the endless drip of water off those tall dark trees that blotted out the sky even on a sunny day. The rain had begun the last week of September and for two months it rained every day. Now and then it would lift, so that you could see the great clouds rolling in from the Pacific. More often, the mill and the river and the town of Millwood would be socked in under a leaden sky. Sometimes it rained harder and sometimes the rain eased a bit, but it always rained. Even with a rain slicker, it was impossible to go out without getting wet. Everyone had colds, perpetually dripping noses and hacking coughs. Little Red seemed to go from one cold to another without quite getting well in between. There were spiders everywhere. The three books Emaline owned all smelled of mildew, as did their clothing and even the bedding. No matter how much she scrubbed, she couldn't get the smell of mildew out of the house.

Alice said it was like this every fall. It rained and rained, but January and February were usually dry and clear. Then it would rain again in the spring, but not like this. Jake was not convinced that it would ever end. He hated rain, hated it more than wind or snow or heat. Said it made him feel like he had fallen asleep in a cold bath and lain there all night until his skin wrinkled and started to peel.

Despite the rain, Emaline loved Oregon. Jake had a good job with a steady income, Red had dozens of children to play with. They didn't wake in the morning to the sound of the wind blowing grit against the window. But she knew Jake. He was not the type to put up with a situation he didn't like for long.

They had a big, happy Thanksgiving dinner at the Tatro house. The union executive had sent three turkeys to Clay Tatro. Emaline helped Alice put on a feed they would all remember, complete with cranberries, sweet potatoes, baked potatoes, a half dozen pies. The Friday after Thanksgiving dawned like the others, under pouring rain. Jake peered out the window after breakfast. There was a western hemlock tree in the yard, so close that its branches touched the window. On a branch of the tree was a tiny green tree frog. The frog stared at Jake, Jake stared at the frog. Abruptly, he threw down his fork and pushed his chair back from the table.

"When it's so damned wet the frogs are takin to the trees, it's time to head back to Nebraska."

Emaline paused in her washing up and stared at him. "That's crazy. What are we going to do in Nebraska?"

"I don't know. Rent a farm, save enough money so we can buy another place. Train horses. Go to work at the sugar factory. Any damned thing except sit here and listen to it drip all day long."

He began to pack even before she had time to finish the breakfast dishes. She tried to hold him back, to get him to at least sit down and listen to reason. He had a fine job and steady pay. Red loved it here. So did she. It was wet now, but it was the rainy season. Soon the rain would stop. Even with the rain, the winter was much milder than it was in Nebraska. It was almost December and they hadn't yet seen a snowflake, let alone a blizzard. The work at the mill was hard, but when you were done, you were done. There was no getting up in the middle of the night to check on a sick calf, or crawling out at three o'clock in the morning to start irrigating the fields, or adding columns of numbers until long past midnight, trying to figure out whether there was any chance they could hold on for another year. She tried a dozen different arguments to stop him. If he listened at all, Jake gave no sign. His mind was made up. He was going back to Nebraska. He went on packing in his haphazard way, until Emaline had to help to keep him from breaking all the dishes.

She thought of refusing to leave. She could just sit right there with Clay and Alice and their kids in Millwood, watching the rain fall on the tall fir trees and taking long walks every day down the long slope to the mighty Columbia River. When the weather was better, they could drive to the Pacific on Sunday afternoons. But once she got past the Tatros and some of the young mothers with children, she did not know a soul in Oregon. She had no way to support herself. She had no job and no real skill that might land her one, other than waiting tables. She could take in sewing, bake a few pies, do jobs that other women in Millwood were doing, but that wasn't going to pay the rent on their little company house. While she tried to decide what to do, Jake was loading the trailer. He had to use the canvas tarp to cover the trailer this time, since it would likely rain at least as far east as Pendleton, but he already had the trailer full and the tarp tied down. Red was almost in tears.

"Why do we have to go?" he kept asking. "Why do we have to go? I like it here."

"Because your daddy hates the rain," Emaline said. "I suppose we have to go where he goes."

"But why?"

"Because he's your father. He's the one who puts food on the table."

"Goddamned right I do," Jake said. "That's why we go where I say we go."

When Red asked one too many times, Jake aimed a kick that just missed his behind. "Not another damned word out of you, either one of you! I said we're goin back, so we're goin back. That's an end to it."

Jake had even packed up their bed and Red's little cot, so they had to spend the night in sleeping bags on the floor. Emaline tried to point out that if they traveled at this time of year they would not be able to camp and they would end up paying for hotel rooms, wasting what she had been able to save with him working at the mill. If they waited until spring, they could stay in campgrounds for two bits a night. Jake wouldn't listen. Nothing was going to change his mind. Red cried himself to sleep. Emaline lay awake in the almost empty house, listening to the rain. She felt a penetrating weariness, an exhaustion with living so complete that, for an awful moment, she wanted to find a butcher knife and slit her wrists. Anything was better than going back to Nebraska with Jake.

Red was sleeping nestled tightly against her back. He threw a slender arm around her, and she patted his hand. Where the boy went, she would have to go.

The trip was like a funeral procession, an endless, bumpy ride devoid of hope, purpose, or even a clear destination. Emaline was grim and silent, so angry with Jake she didn't trust herself to speak. With every mile, she could feel a terrible fate settling around her. They would find another poor farm and try to scrape by, making enough to live on or not making enough, doing endless labor simply to put food on the table. They had no money for a down payment on a farm of their own, so their only choice would be to rent, to become virtual sharecroppers paying a landlord out of whatever they were able to grow. It was hard enough working a farm for yourself, considerably worse when you had to work it for someone else. It was just like Jake to drag them all the way to Oregon, stay six months, decide he didn't like it because of the rain. He never took her feelings into account.

He didn't even worry about the boy. All that mattered was that Jake McCloskey didn't like the rain. That was enough to persuade him to pull up stakes overnight.

Jake decided to take a more southerly route back to Nebraska, one that would lead them down to the Lincoln Highway in Utah and then east through Rock Springs, Laramie, Cheyenne. They spent a night in Evanston, and when they left in the morning, Emaline saw the red-brick buildings of the state hospital, the asylum where Ida Mae had spent her last days, the place Eli had been visiting when Velma died. Life was so short. A person needed to find a better way to live, something better than all this madness with Jake, madness without end. What she wanted more than anything was to live in a place where people didn't yell at one another for no reason at all, where no one was going to pull up stakes and drive thirteen hundred miles because they saw a frog in a tree.

The Dodge died five miles west of Rock Springs. A trucker gave them a tow to a garage, where the mechanic pronounced the Dodge dead on arrival. He said he might be able to find a rebuilt engine that would take them the rest of the way to Scottsbluff, but it would probably take a week. Jake exploded, put his fist through a window of the car. Emaline tore up an old shirt and bandaged his hand, but he exploded again when they got to the motel, where they rented a room for the week. There were bedbugs in the sheets, the frigid wind found every crack. Red had a bad cold, Emaline was so worn-out she could hardly look after him. Jake paced and cursed, paced and cursed until she told him to go out because he was going to make her crazy. It wouldn't matter now. He had no money left for grifters.

This time he turned up a job. A rancher who had broken a leg in a fall from a windmill needed someone to work two troublesome horses. Jake was sure he was the man for the job. The ranch was right on the edge of town, so Jake was going to head out the next morning. If it worked out, they could stay in an abandoned bunkhouse on the ranch for a few weeks and either wait for the Dodge to be fixed or swap it for a car that would go the rest of the way.

They ate supper in a diner that evening. When Red spilled his milk, Jake hit the table so hard that two glasses fell and shattered on the floor. Emaline helped the angry waitress clean up the mess, but something inside her broke with the glasses. She could feel an ending coming, like the last reel of a movie. While Jake snored in their narrow bed, she lay awake thinking and listening to the wind. Five years and a few months married to the man and it felt like three decades. So much had gone wrong, it was hard to remember anything that had gone right. She still had a little money saved, enough to get herself and Red as far as Sheridan. There was no question the boy would have to come with her. Jake would take a fit, but he couldn't possibly care for the boy alone.

The next morning, Jake was up and gone before Emaline and Red were awake. She woke before the boy and sat at the one rickety little table in the room, nibbling cold biscuits. Jake's things were strewn on the floor next to the table. He had been rummaging through the box that held most of his clothing, assuming that she would pick it all up. She finished the biscuits, brushed the crumbs off her fingers, went to work. She woke Red, gave him some biscuits and milk to eat while she packed. He sat watching her with his big, serious eyes. She wasn't going to tell him what they were doing, not yet, but he seemed to understand.

Jake had used the mechanic's car to tow the trailer to the motel parking lot. She went through the things on the trailer, opening one trunk after another, determined to take only what they would absolutely need. She stuffed two suitcases with clothing for herself and Red and left a note for Jake.

Jake,

I've taken all I can stand. You dragged us all the way to Oregon, now you're dragging us back because you saw a frog in a tree. Your temper tantrum last night when Red spilled his milk was the last straw. We are leaving you now, don't try to follow us. The boy is better off with me, you know you can't look after him.

I am not asking anything of you except that you leave us alone. You don't even have to support your child. I'll find a way. All in all, I think I'll manage better without you. If you want to get in touch, you can write to us care of the 8T8 ranch and Juanita will get the letter to me wherever we end up.

good-bye,
Emaline

She dragged the suitcases to the bus station and bought two one-way tickets to Sheridan. Red refused to leave without Molly, so they brought the dog along as well. The man at the ticket window said that Molly could ride the bus as long as she sat quietly in the aisle and didn't bark. Emaline promised that she could keep the collie quiet. He explained they would have to change buses in Casper. She nodded. They were going to Sheridan, even if they had to change buses a dozen times.

They rode all day, staring out the window at the slender fingers of snow that had drifted between the clumps of sagebrush, a lone rider pushing a little band of horses over a distant rise, windmills and stock tanks and isolated ranch houses. The bus was almost empty, the driver was a dog lover who bought little treats for Molly when they stopped and even let Red stand beside him for a time as they drove.

They were still fifty miles west of Casper when Red leaned his head on her shoulder.

"We're not going back to Daddy, are we?"

"No, we're not."

"Good. He's nice to me sometimes, but he scares me. He's always so mad about something."

"Yes, he is. We're going to a place where people don't lose their temper all the time, all right?"

"Yes. I'd like that. Will there be horses there?"

"More horses than you could ever ride."

They changed buses in Casper and climbed onto another almost empty bus for the ride north. It was past suppertime when they reached Sheridan. Emaline found a pay telephone at the bus station, dropped in a nickel, called the 8T8. Eli himself answered the phone.

"Grandpa?" she said. "It's Emaline."

"Well, hello, Em. This is a surprise. Hang on a minute, I'll pass you to Juanita here."

"No, Grandpa. It's you I want to talk to. I'm not in Oregon anymore. I've left Jake. I'm at the bus station here in Sheridan with Red. Do you think somebody could come and get us?"

She heard a deep intake of breath on the other end of the line. "Sure, honey. We'll be there just as quick as we can."

Emaline hung up the phone. The boy clung to her hand.

"Are we going to be all right, Mom?"

She ran her fingers through a thatch of red hair that needed cutting. "Yes, honey. We're going to be just fine. We're going home."

PART IV

The Wild Horses

1940

40.

EMALINE McCLOSKEY FINISHED SHELVING THE books in the poetry section of the Sheridan library, placing a copy of *The Spell of the Yukon and Other Verses* exactly where it belonged according to the Dewey Decimal system. She could never see the name of the famed poet Robert Service without recalling the bawdy version of "The Shooting of Dan McGrew," which Jake liked to recite after a drink or two. It was downright filthy and disgusting, but Jake would insist on bellowing it out in mixed company, while the ladies covered their ears and the men roared with laughter. It was a side of him she had never been able to tolerate.

She glanced up at the clock. It was five minutes past three, her favorite time of day. At any moment now, Red would come bursting through the door full of stories about his day in second grade. It was the first of April, a warm, sunny day, so she would go outside with him and sit on a bench where they could talk without disturbing the readers at the long tables inside. Red would drink his milk and eat some of the gingerbread cookies she had made the night before and talk about school while they sat in the spring sunshine. Then they would slip back inside and Red would sit reading children's books or going over his schoolwork until five o'clock, when she finished work.

Most nights, they would walk home to the little house on South

Custer Street which she was renting from Eli Paint for ten dollars a month. On this night, however, they were not walking back to the house. Bobby and Leo were in town looking for birthday presents for Ezra and Eli. When they finished, they were supposed to swing by the library in Leo's Hudson to drive Emaline and Red out to the ranch for the birthday celebration. Eli and Ezra were turning seventy, although neither man looked a day over fifty, and Juanita was planning a big party.

Bobby and Leo hadn't appeared at closing time, so she locked up and went back to sit on the bench with Red and wait for them. She was looking forward to the party, but so much had changed since the first time she visited the ranch in the summer of 1936. Ben had finally married his sweetheart, Belle Swank, and the two of them had left for Argentina on an extended honeymoon in the fall of 1939, with twenty head of Ezra's prize Appaloosas. They were bound for the Pampas, where Ben was to spend a year buying and selling horses before returning to Wyoming to settle down with Belle in the cabin he had already built a half mile from Ezra's place. Eli's older boys Calvin and Seth were also away, trying to run a small spread outside Thermopolis together. Eli would have done anything to keep them at home, but they wanted to prove they could make it on their own. His daughter Jenny had left to study at the University of Wyoming in Laramie. Her sisters Mabel and Anna were working year-round for Tavie at the dude ranch she ran with her friend Amelia in Jackson Hole.

Even Ezra had settled down with a cousin of Jenny Hoot Owl's called Jolene Rides Prairie. Two Spuds had tried to warn Ezra away, saying that Arapaho women were bad-tempered and that they refused to keep a man warm at night, but Jolene had a sweet disposition. Ezra liked to razz Two Spuds about it, telling him that Jolene had never once turned him away when he tried to warm himself against her ample flanks on a winter night. She was a fine cook who had raised six children and buried two husbands, just as he had buried two wives.

As far as Ezra was concerned, Jolene was the perfect companion for his old age.

By the time Leo and Bobby showed up, they were a half hour late. They climbed out of the car giggling and slapping each other on the back, so rowdy that Emaline thought maybe they had been drinking. When Bobby saw her glaring at him, he stood at attention and offered her a snappy salute. She wasn't impressed.

"Where have you two been? Are you drunk?"

"Not a bit, Sis. You're lookin at a couple of sailors. We just enlisted in the U.S. Navy."

"You did what?"

"Enlisted. We signed up this afternoon. We're leaving in a week for boot camp in San Diego."

Emaline was about to start shouting at him when she remembered the date. "Is this an April Fool's joke?"

"Nope. That's why we're late. We were at the recruiting station. It took longer to get processed than we thought, but we're here now. How ya doin, Red?"

He gave the boy a friendly punch on the shoulder. Red was staring at them both. "You guys are sailors now?"

"Not just yet, kiddo," Leo said. "We got to go through boot camp. Ten weeks training, then we'll be sailors in the U.S. Navy."

Emaline was so angry she bit her lip. "Bobby, you are absolutely not going into the navy. You go back there and tell them it was a big mistake. I am still your legal guardian. I forbid it."

"Aw, Sis, it's too late to change things now. We're already signed up. I turned nineteen and Leo is twenty, so we don't need nobody's consent to enlist. We didn't plan it, we were just walkin by the recruiting station and we started talkin it over and pretty soon we were gettin sworn in. C'mon, Sis, be happy. Leo and me, we're goin to see the world!"

"I can't believe this, Bobby. Mama would be so disappointed. She wanted you to go to college."

"I didn't say I wasn't goin to college. It's only that I'm goin in the navy first. We signed up for a three-year hitch, then we'll come home and go back to school."

Emaline turned on Leo. "And what about you, you big lug? Have you told your father about this?"

Leo grinned. "Nope. I figured I'd make it a birthday surprise."

"You did, you big fool? You're going to ruin his birthday. You know you're the apple of his eye, don't you? What if you get hurt or killed?"

"Aw, we'll be fine. The United States aint at war with nobody. Pop is so busy, he won't even notice I'm gone."

"You couldn't be more wrong. Eli dotes on you. He's going to miss you terribly. What about you, Bobby—did you think about that at all? What if you get hurt?"

"How can we get hurt? It's peacetime."

"It is now. That can end in a hurry. There's fighting in Europe and everybody is worried about Japan and . . . oh, how could you be so stupid. You've never even seen the ocean, either one of you. We'd better get going or we'll be late for the party."

When they got to the ranch, Leo and Bobby rushed in and told Juanita first because Eli was still out with the horses. When he came in and Leo told him the news, Eli sat down and took a deep breath before he said anything.

"Look, I raised all my kids to make their own decisions and think for themselves. I'm proud of both of you for tryin to help your country. But dammit, you ought to told us first so we could talk things over. You don't go off and do a thing like this without speaking to us."

Leo hung his head. He was so excited about the whole business, it hadn't even occurred to him to tell anyone else until they were enlisted. Their news didn't exactly ruin the party, but it did put a bit of a damper on things.

• • •

Bobby and Leo were away in San Diego for ten weeks. When they came back in June for boot leave, they were tough and brown and capable of doing a hundred push-ups at a crack. They had been trained in physical fitness and swimming, self-defense and small-arms shooting, first aid and seamanship, firefighting and the proper way to pack a seabag. Emaline had to admit that they both seemed more polite and disciplined, but she still didn't like it one bit.

When their leave was up, both Bobby and Leo were assigned to a battleship, the *Tennessee.* Bobby was going to be an antiaircraft gunner, while Leo was to be trained in the new radar technology. Emaline had seen pictures of the *Tennessee.* It was enormous. Perhaps it wasn't quite indestructible, but it was the next best thing.

While he was home, Bobby said he wanted to go with Emaline up to visit the cabin where they had once lived with Watson and Velma on Little Goose Creek. On a warm Saturday, he borrowed Juanita's car, came to get Emaline and Red on South Custer Street and took them first for malted milks and hamburgers before they drove the nine miles south to Big Horn and turned off on the narrow, winding gravel road that led up to the cabin.

Neither Emaline nor Bobby had visited Little Goose Creek since they left after Watson's death in 1925. Bobby was only four then and he barely remembered the place. For Emaline, the memories were so painful that she'd thought she would never return, but that was before Bobby joined the navy. Now, somehow, she felt it was important to go back and to show Red where they had lived for a part of their childhood.

Emaline wasn't sure she would recognize the place, but the neat little cabin was unmistakable. The mailbox said "Harter" rather than "Watson," but otherwise the place looked as it had in 1925. Even the shed in back, which Watson had used as his workshop, was still there.

They spilled out of the car and Bobby went to knock on the door. The Harters weren't home, so they walked down the slope to Little Goose Creek, kicked off their shoes, went wading in the icy water, just as they had once done with Velma.

"I remember this spot," Bobby said. "We were here with Mama, eating strawberries."

"Yes. You and Ben used to throw rocks and try to hit the little fish in the water and Mama would tell you to stop. We had fun here when Watson wasn't around."

Red said he thought it was a beautiful place and they should move back. Emaline laughed. "I think the Harters maybe wouldn't like that. They've taken very good care of the cabin."

They left Red splashing in the creek, walked up the hill and found the grave of little Billy, who had died of meningitis the day after Christmas in 1924. It was Billy's death that had sent Watson to drown himself in alcohol. The hand-carved grave marker Watson had made was still there. *William Watson, 1922–1924. RIP Our Boy.* Bobby remembered Billy, or at least he remembered his curly blond hair, but could not recall a thing about the night he died. It was a mercy, Emaline said. She could remember every detail.

They walked back down to get Red for the drive home. He fell asleep in the back seat as she sat looking out the window, thinking about all that had happened on Little Goose Creek. She thought being near the cabin might upset her, but it did not. She still had nightmares about it, of Watson beating her mother the night he died, when Emaline took the burning kerosene lamp and swung it into the back of Watson's head with all her strength. The nightmares were so vivid that she could smell the burning kerosene and see Watson's mad eyes as he ran from the house and dove into a snowbank to extinguish the fire in his hair. She could smell the oil in the rifle she had sighted between his eyes, knowing that if he tried to come back she would pull the trigger, because if she did not, he would kill them all. She could see him leaving then, jumping into the truck and swerving down the mountain. His death was not part of the dream, because she didn't see the truck plunge off the road, tumble down a hundred feet and catch fire. But it was still enough to send her leaping out of bed, her heart racing, the funnel of dream still pouring its images into her mind as she struggled to get her bearings.

Mercifully, the nightmares were more and more rare. More often, the dreams she had bore no relation to that night except for the image of the Burning Man. She had often wondered how a young mind could transform such singular horror into a figure from which she could derive such consolation. It was enough that the Burning Man had been there all these years and that he seemed to appear most often when her life was most difficult. Perhaps that was why she had not dreamt of him in some time. Her life had never been so calm or so settled. She felt a bit lonely at times, especially in the evening after Red went to bed, but for now, at least, she preferred loneliness to the madness of life with Jake.

She had received two letters from him, both care of Juanita at the 8T8. The first was sent from Riverton, the second from Goose Egg, a wide spot in the road ten miles southwest of Casper, about three hours from Sheridan by automobile. Jake was now breaking horses for a rancher in Goose Egg. He figured this job might last a good long while. If the first letter seemed angry, in the second Jake seemed resigned to the situation. He talked of getting up to Sheridan to visit the boy sometime, but he didn't seem at all certain when that would be, he was so busy with the horses.

She felt sorry for him, but she felt no urge to go back. She had lots of time to spend with Red and she was making her own way. The only thing that was lacking in her life was a little adventure. She was not quite thirty years old and her days were a little too quiet. Wyoming could be an adventurous place, but not for lady librarians. She had helped out for a few days during spring roundup on the 8T8, riding and roping and even branding calves with Juanita in the heat and noise and swirling dust. Ezra said she was a natural with horses, just like Ben. It was in the blood. Other than weekends at the ranch or the occasional roundup, however, she didn't have much chance to ride. Her days were all routine, getting Red off to school in the morning, walking to the library, chatting with the regulars who came in, trying to persuade them that they should read the short stories of Anton Chekhov.

Sometimes when things were quiet in the library, she would fall into a daydream and imagine that she was like Velma and her sisters. They had all ridden on long cattle drives with Eli every spring, heading thousands of cattle from Nebraska up to the Sioux reservation at Pine Ridge. She was too sensible to believe that she would ever take part in any such adventure, but that was before the black horse came along.

41.

THERE WAS A TIME WHEN ALL YOU HAD TO DO TO start a fracas in most any roadhouse in Wyoming was to bring up the black. When the weather turned feral and the corn liquor began to flow, that was enough. An old boy cutting up a steak with a clasp knife would wipe the blood off along the seam of his blue jeans and wave the blade under your jaw.

"Just what the hell do you think you know about that horse?" he'd ask. Then he would proceed to iron out the wrinkles in the truth with his own version. The yarn as he told it would be absolutely at odds with the narrative spun by another cow chaser, who was willing to swear he was there when it happened, riding right alongside that Choctaw cowhand Two Spuds, hell-bent for election over country that was rougher than a Saturday night in Gillette. Firearms were frowned upon, but arguments waged by flinty, whiskey-fueled seekers after truth were settled with fists, teeth, kneecaps, head butts, boot toes, broken bottles, skinning knives.

Making allowance for the ravages wrought by time, corn liquor, and repeated blows to the head, there is a consistent line that runs from one version to another, straight as the path of an old horse on his way back to the barn. There *was* a legendary black mustang stallion that roamed Wyoming in the darkest years of the Great Depression, and he became the focus of an escapade that is still talked about around campfires from Yellowstone to Cheyenne. Everyone who actually got within hollering distance of the animal agrees that the black was a wild horse so unlike any other that he might have been thawed from some Ice Age bog, a large, ferocious, predatory carnivore of the sort that once filled the nightmares of heavy-browed men shivering in caves and squabbling over hunks of burnt mastodon. He eluded capture for so long that some of the horse hunters who worked the high country thought he must have been a spirit horse, although he was flesh and blood enough to bring considerable discomfort to the incautious.

No one knew where the horse came from. He just turned up in the Bighorns, fully grown and cantankerous. Buster Estabrooks, a cowhand from New Mexico who had worked a couple of roundups on the 8T8, claimed the black was the same stallion he had seen in the summer of 1935 down on Stinking Water Creek south of Ogallala, Nebraska. It was a long way from the Powder River to Ogallala, but at one time there were thousands of mustangs on the Stinking Water. They bred with all manner of horses, descendants of the animals that were lost by Cortés and de Soto, draft horses and quarterhorses and thoroughbreds, Morgans and Appaloosas, Percherons and Tennessee walkers, and horses that had been stolen by desperadoes and abandoned when the law got too close.

With their mixed ancestry, it was inevitable that some of the wild horses were born runts or splayfooted or swaybacked or too heavy-hocked to do anything but pull a manure wagon. But now and then, all that blood would get shook up just right and you'd get a horse like the black, who was a little bit of everything and a whole lot of himself. He was enormous for a mustang, around seventeen hands and twelve hundred pounds, and he had a shaggy coat and hooves the size of dinner plates. Some accounts said he had a lopsided diamond between the eyes and others say it looked more like a cross. The black had one white stocking, the left rear, and there are those who imagine him as one of those glossy black stallions you see in the motion pictures. Truth is, the black was ugly as a porcupine's behind. He had that big Roman nose, he'd never seen a currycomb in his life, he had battle scars all over his chest and head from fighting off other stallions and his face was so wide a big man could lay an entire hand between his eyes. He might not even have been black. In a certain light, they say, he looked more like a dark bay, a horse possessed of some deep blood color mixed with black that was so unusual wranglers preferred to refer to him as the black to avoid the suggestion that he was indeed a spirit horse not from this earth.

What intrigued the horse hunters who pursued him was not his beauty but the muscle in that deep chest and bowed neck and those powerful hindquarters, the intelligence in the wide-set eyes, the unexpected speed when he decided to run, the agility and endurance he displayed along with a ferocity that even the most experienced hands had never seen. It was generally agreed that the man who could tame the black would have the finest mount in Wyoming and possibly the entire United States of America—but that it might be easier to slip a snaffle bit on a mountain lion.

The first man (perhaps the only man) to rope the black was Farron Blue, a wrangler and bronc buster out of Pocatello who had blown around the west like a tumbleweed, maybe because he had a bad habit of getting himself wanted by the wrong people. Farron was wanted in eastern Washington for a misunderstanding about a horse, in southwestern Colorado for shooting holes in a sheriff's patrol car and in Medicine Hat by Ilah Pattee, who stood six foot three and weighed two hundred and eighty pounds. Ilah ran a saloon and carried a double-bladed axe, the head pounded down onto a hatchet handle eighteen inches along. She could throw that axe fifty feet and hit what she was aiming at, and the thing she was aiming at when he left town was Farron Blue. What exactly Farron had done to rile Miss Pattee was not known, except that he was an unusually handsome cowpoke with a fondness for women of considerable size, so it is possible that their mutual inclinations led to a clash that might have been fatal, had Farron not decided to hightail it south and cross the U.S. border before Ilah could get within axe range. He drifted through Montana into Wyoming and found pretty much the same thing he had seen everywhere in the west—starving beef, outfits going broke, drought and heat so bad that buzzards wouldn't leave the shade to peck at a ripe carcass. Working cows in such weather was somewhere well to the south of purgatory. A man spent long hours in the saddle with a wet dust rag over his face and Vaseline up his nose so that it wouldn't get raw from breathing dust and still he crawled into his bedroll at night feeling like he'd just swallowed half the dirt in Wyoming, with a little chili sauce and some kidney beans to wash it down.

While he was working for Eli Paint on the 8T8, Farron teamed up with Ignacio Salazar. Ignacio was an old hand who had drifted north from Texas after the IXT ranch was turned under by the plow, a mistake that provided a million acres of blowing dirt for the southern rim of the Dust Bowl. By 1937, Farron and Ignacio had both had enough of dust and heat. When the spring roundup was done, they decided to try to make their fortune horse hunting up in the high country. They were going to see if they couldn't track down this legendary stallion they called the black, but if they didn't run into any mustangs at all, they would at least have cool nights and cold springwater and as fine a view of the slow-wheeling stars at night as a man could have on this earth.

Near dusk their fourth day in the high country, Farron spotted the black up on a knoll keeping watch over his bunch, maybe seventy or eighty head in all. He knew right off he had never before seen such a horse. He motioned to Ignacio. They were two hundred feet apart, but Ignacio understood his hand signals. *Not now. Wait for morning.*

The wind was blowing their way and they had some cover from a stand of trees, mostly spruce and ponderosa pine. Farron was still in the tree line so he was able to get a good look and work out a plan. Ignacio didn't like it. He had given up roping wild stallions the same time he gave up whores, on his fiftieth birthday. He agreed to help haze the stallion into Farron's loop and once the horse was roped, he'd come along with a second loop. Farron had a roan roping horse called Pink, a good quarter horse who could outrun a thoroughbred up to about a half mile and stand up to a charge from a twelve-hundred-pound steer. He was sure the roan could catch the black in a short dash over rough ground, as long as they could get within a hundred yards before the mustang spotted them. They would wait until the horse had a good feed and plenty of water to bog him down, then Farron would ease up as close as he could get. When the black saw him, they would have the sort of horse race that makes a man feel there might be something in this life better than a woman.

Farron was awake well before sunup. He made sure that Pink went easy on the water and had only a bag of oats to eat. The black and his herd had drifted about three-quarters of a mile to the southeast. Farron and Ignacio circled to the north of the band, keeping a low ridge between the mustangs and themselves. They found the stallion grazing quietly in the half-light before sunup. Farron wanted to let him eat his fill. He backed the roan off to the far side of the ridge, dismounted, squatted on his heels with his hat brim pulled low over his eyes to block the rising sun. Finally the black lifted his head, sauntered down to the creek. When he had drunk his fill, he shook his head, flinging droplets from his nose, then climbed a low rise a half mile distant, where he could keep an eye on his band.

Farron saw his opening. He would ride as close as he could on Pink, then bolt for the gap between the black and the rest of the band. The stallion would naturally veer to his right, toward his mares and into Farron's loop. He shook out a 7/16 manila rope and held it coiled tight against his thigh. The wind worked in his favor. The black didn't pick up his scent until they were within a hundred yards. By the time the stud whirled to run, Farron had put the spurs to Pink and the quick little horse gained ground with every stride. Still, the black was a whole lot faster than Farron expected him to be, even with a full belly. They ran nearly half a mile before they had closed on the big horse. Farron had a perfect angle, with the black slightly downhill to his left. As soon as he turned loose of the rope, he knew he had never made a better toss in his life.

Nothing in all his experience prepared Farron for what happened after that loop settled around the neck of the black. He figured the stallion would either try to run or fight the rope. Instead the black whirled, screamed in rage and came right at him with his teeth bared. Farron sat Pink down on his hindquarters. The roan was able to dodge twice, but now they were roped to the black as much as he was roped to them and he kept coming. On the third pass, the stallion locked his teeth into Farron's rib cage below the armpit and came away with a hunk of flesh. It was Farron's turn to squeal. He fumbled at his carbine, trying to pull it out of its scabbard as the black whirled and came at him again. He got a boot up out of the stirrup to fend it off, but the black set his teeth into Farron's thigh, yanked him clear of the saddle, tossed him aside like a cat playing with a field mouse. The carbine discharged as it struck the ground a dozen feet from the spot where Farron landed on his back, but the bullet ricocheted harmlessly off the rocks. Farron was left on foot and unarmed and the black might have killed him right there, except that Pink had seen all he wanted. He took off to the west. With the black pulling in the other direction, the rope snapped like baling twine.

Ignacio had figured out that his lariat was going to be of little use against the black. He had his rifle out of the scabbard and was about to pull the trigger when the black hit him, barreling into his sorrel gelding from the side, knocking Ignacio and his horse over the top of the ridge and down the other side. Ignacio fell head over heels, tumbling through scree and prickly pear, scraping off hide with every bounce until he came to rest against a spruce tree, out cold.

Farron ran to a lodgepole pine and scrambled up into its sparse branches as the black whirled after him, screaming like a banshee. He pulled himself up about ten feet above the ground and managed to wedge his butt in between two branches, praying that they'd hold and that he wouldn't pass out from the pain and fall where the black could get at him. The horse was at the foot of the tree, slinging his head in fury and pawing at the bark. He might have waited all day, but the commotion had frightened his mares. They took off to the southeast, trailed at a respectful distance by a band of scrub stallions. Most of the scrubs bore scars where they had been whipped by the black, but they were still hopeful. If the cowpokes kept the black busy long enough, maybe they could cut a few mares out of his herd. The black screamed again, showing his bloody teeth, and whirled to go after the mares.

When Ignacio came to, he saw Farron squatting on the ground, ripping up his shirt and trying to stanch the blood that flowed from the wounds on his ribs and thigh. Ignacio got him cleaned up and bandaged. By the time they reached the hospital in Sheridan two days later, Farron Blue was half dead and burning up with fever, raving about Ilah Pattee and an animal he called the Devil Horse.

When it was clear that Farron was out of danger, Doc Miller asked Ignacio whether the animal that had done all this damage might be in truth a devil horse.

"No sir," Ignacio said. "He is not a devil. He just acts like one."

That might have been an end to it, except that Bill Bury got involved. Not with the black specifically, but with what he referred to as the "mustang problem" in general. William C. "Big Bill" Bury was a cattleman and oilman whose empire stretched from Montana to Texas. Bury owned so much in so many states that he hired one accountant fellow whose only job was to keep track of the Bury holdings and to be able to inform Big Bill at any hour of the day or night whether or not he still owned those twelve oil wells in Midland, the slaughterhouse in Billings, or the bank in Riverton. Although they would never appear on the accountant's books, Bill Bury also owned one of Wyoming's two senators, a congressman or two, and enough of the state legislature that if he proposed a bill decreeing that the Bighorn Mountains should be leveled and turned into swampland, it would pass without a dissenting vote. In many ways it was Bill Bury who lit the fuse of what would become the legend of the black when he declared that, what with the drought and all, the wild horses of Wyoming had become a plague. Big Bill's position was that, if the march of Christian civilization was to carry on its trampling of pretty much everything wild in the manner that God intended, the mustangs would have to be slaughtered or penned up with as little mercy as the white man had shown to the red man or the buffalo. What it boiled down to was that Bill Bury had at least a hundred thousand cattle out on the range somewhere in Wyoming and mustangs were eating some of the grass intended to fatten Big Bill's livestock. The mustangs had to go, because they were getting in the way of his profit margin.

42.

On the hottest day in the summer, Two Spuds showed up at the big house before daybreak. Eli had limped out to the back veranda before dawn and perched on his rocking chair, waiting for the rising sun to light the Bighorns. He heard the pinto coming and had to squint to see the horse cantering out of the lingering dark. The pinto was lathered some and Two Spuds was riding bareback, using a rope hackamore instead of a bridle. He wore a bear-claw necklace over his bare chest, buckskin leggings and moccasins and he made a fearsome sight—a man six foot four and well over two hundred pounds, his face pocked with smallpox scars like soft brown earth struck with hail, his hair greased in long braids which hung down over his chest. Two Spuds carried a gunnysack, within the sack an object about the size and shape of a human head, which put a different slant on things. He dismounted by kicking his right leg up and over the horse's neck and landed on his toes, lithe as a cat. Even with a touch of dew still on the ground, little fantails of dust trailed his steps all the way up to the porch. The gunnysack dripped blood in the dust. He dropped the sack on the porch and squatted on his heels next to the rocking chair. Eli's big dog Rufus stuck his nose in the sack and Eli had to pull him back, but Two Spuds said nothing. It was a trait that Eli valued. You had to appreciate a man who could come for a visit and stay two hours and leave without saying a word.

Eli knew better than to come right out and ask what was in the gunnysack. Two Spuds would state his business when he was good and ready. The Choctaw people had learned patience the hard way. They had been the first of the tribes forcibly uprooted and sent west along the Trail of Tears to Oklahoma, their reward for fighting with Andrew Jackson against the British in the War of 1812. Once in the White House, Jackson bundled the Choctaw off to the Territories along with the Cherokee and the Chickasaw, nor did the president folks called Old Hickory trouble himself if half of them died along the way. Two Spuds was born in 1900, nearly seventy years later, but the old ones still talked about the Trail of Tears.

Two Spuds had grown up working for small ranchers in Oklahoma. After the Great War, he made his way north and turned up in Wyoming with three saddle horses and one packhorse. He worked a few years in Riverton, then rode east and persuaded Eli to hire him on for the fall roundup in 1928. Eli had watched the man ride and rope for a single day and told him that he was welcome to stay as long as he pleased. A year later, he gave Spuds permission to build his own cabin on 8T8 land, the only hired hand granted such a privilege. That was after Two Spuds married Jenny Hoot Owl and Eli said it wasn't right for a married man to have to share the bunkhouse with the likes of Willie Thaw and Zeke Ketcham. Eli figured it was the smartest thing he had ever done, because if Spuds hadn't been in his cabin the night he wrecked the Cadillac, he would have frozen to death.

When he was first hired, Two Spuds gave his name as Hanchitubbe, which in his own free translation into English meant "Kill the sun." Hanchitubbe was a mouthful of dry oatmeal to Willie Thaw, who nicknamed him Two Spuds instead, after his habit of demanding two potatoes every time the cook scooped dinner onto his plate at roundup time. When Eli asked how he felt about it, Spuds said it was better than being called a fuckin redskin.

Eli heard Juanita stirring around in the kitchen and stepped in to ask if she would bring biscuits and more coffee out to the porch. She said something in Spanish which he didn't understand, but Juanita could be cranky in the morning. When she came out with the coffee, she had fixed her hair and splashed some water on her face and she had a big smile for Two Spuds, but she wrinkled her nose a little when she saw the gunnysack on the porch and the blood that had run down between the boards. They finished the coffee and biscuits. Juanita stepped back into the house to start on breakfast. Two Spuds nodded in the direction of the pinto.

"I don't know how them sonofabitch Indians did it."

"Did what?"

"Ridin all over hell's half acre without a saddle. I'm stove up like a old banty rooster."

"You don't say."

"These buckskin britches are okay. They're real comfortable, hurt less than pants. But that pinto has a spine on him would grind your nuts into dust if you run him long enough."

"I imagine. Where'd you find them buckskins, anyhow?"

"Jenny Hoot Owl made them. They fit so good, I thought I'd try ridin bareback. I aint rode a horse bareback since I was a kid, not any distance. It's not bad for about five miles. After that, you want a good saddle."

"I'll remember that."

The sun was up to where a man could feel it. They slipped back a notch or two into the shade of the veranda, squinting into the glare. The temperature was going to top a hundred degrees by ten o'clock. It wasn't yet mid-July and the grass was already browning. On days when the breeze picked up, the sky went the color of buttermilk from all the dust in the air. Eli tossed the dregs of the coffee into the dust and took their cups into the kitchen. When he came back out, he grabbed his figuring rope off its peg by the door and tied a few knots while Two Spuds got up to lead the pinto to the water tank. When the horse was through drinking, he turned it loose in the corral, drooped the hackamore over a hook on the porch, lifted the gunnysack with its mysterious burden.

"Jenny Hoot Owl said to bring you this chicken for Juanita. She said it's to thank you for that batch of chicks she gave us in the spring."

A chicken. Now that Two Spuds mentioned it, Eli realized that he had sniffed the rising odor of dead chicken for a while.

"Tell Jenny I said thanks."

"I'll do that."

They fell silent again, until Eli decided that if he was going to get a solitary thing done on this hot morning, he was going to have to nudge this conversation ahead a foot or two. They had solved two riddles, why Two Spuds was riding bareback in an Indian outfit and what was in the gunnysack. That left one to answer.

"You didn't ride all that way bareback just to give me a chicken."

"Nope, I didn't." Two Spuds finished his biscuits and brushed his fingers clean. "You ever run into Little Joe Plenty Doors?"

"Time or two."

"Has that squinty eye?"

"Yep. I had to pay Joe a visit a while back. He rode home trailing a lariat behind him. Turned out a gelding of mine was attached to that rope."

"Joe don't mean nothin by it. He knows you'll come for the horse. He's Crow. Best horse stealers on the plains. Joe is old enough to remember when the most fun a Crow could have was runnin off fifty head of Sioux horses."

"He's lucky I'm a kindly sort of fella."

"Joe likes you. That's why he stole your horse. He figures you both need to stay in practice—he needs the practice stealing your horse and you need practice getting it back."

"You run into him lately?"

"He came by last night, wanting to talk about the black."

"What black is that?"

"Mustang studhorse that ate Farron Blue. It's been two years now and Farron has still got silver tubes where the horse ate him, to let the pus leak out. He used to be quite the ladies' man, but it seems the women out here don't want a fella that leaks. Anyhow, Farron would be the first to tell you, that black stud might be the best horse in Wyoming."

"He's only the best if you can break him."

"Nobody is goin to break the black. I imagine there is young fellas who'd like to try, but the black would kick their heads in or die fightin."

"So why are we jawin about a horse nobody can break?"

"Because that stallion got himself caught in one a these big government roundups. They go out with a hundred wranglers, make a big sweep, funnel 'em down to where they got fences a mile long, leadin to a corral that would hold a bull elephant. They got the black with his whole bunch, maybe sixty, seventy mustangs. Plenty Doors says they're holdin at least three hundred head there, right next to the spur line for the railroad. They're fixin to ship them off to a dog food factory in Boise City."

"So what exactly did you have in mind, Spuds?"

"I thought you might want to steal the black."

"Why would I want to steal a mustang that can't be broke?"

"Well, not just him. I thought maybe you'd want to run off the whole bunch. Like the time you and Ezra and that old cowpoke Teeter Spawn stole them O-Bar horses."

"That was way back in 1887, when I was a young pup. I don't believe

I'd care to repeat the experience. Stealin horses don't always work out like you think it will."

"It wouldn't be stealin, exactly."

"Exactly what would it be?"

"Plenty Doors wants to turn them mustangs loose."

"If you turn 'em loose, they'd just round them up again."

"We'd have to run them off someplace where it's too damned hard to get at 'em to make it worthwhile. Plenty Doors thinks maybe up in the high country."

"Wasn't that where Farron ran into the black in the first place?"

"It was, but the horse must have drifted down to where he got caught in that sweep. I was thinking maybe take him up really high, up where you run into that outlaw O. T. Yonkee a long while ago."

"That's a helluva ride, pushin two or three hundred head that high. It was a hard ride fifty years ago, when all we had to worry about was our saddle horses."

"Are you sayin it can't be done?"

"Oh, no. I expect it can, but there's got to be some easier way. You could go see them government fellas and find out if the black is for sale."

"Plenty Doors tried. They say they won't sell them horses at any price, except to the slaughterhouse. Their instructions is to eliminate livestock off of the range so as to let the grass come back. Too many horses, too many cattle, no damn rain and no grass. When Joe kept after them, they said they might sell a few of the best mustangs, but Big Bill Bury won't let it happen."

"What does Bill have to do with it?"

"He's taken a dislike to mustangs and wants to see 'em all dead. Says they eat too much of the grass on government land. Plenty Doors told me that Bill is mad because he aint much of a horseman, tried to break a mustang on his own last year and the horse throwed him and broke three ribs."

Eli chuckled. "We owe that horse a debt of gratitude. Bill's needed to have a few ribs broke pretty much since he was born."

Just then Willie Thaw came strolling up from the bunkhouse, trailed by Zeke Ketcham and the big spotted Poland China boar that followed Zeke everywhere. The hog weighed better than six hundred pounds and it was still growing. It made Eli nervous. Sometimes it would leave off following Zeke and tag around after Eli instead. It seemed like every time he stopped short, the boar had its snout between his boots, sniffing around like he was wondering how Eli would taste. Now and then he'd boot it on the nose and the boar would grunt and back off a foot or two, but as soon as he turned around, the hog would be back on his heels. At least it heeled better than Rufus, who was always diving into holes after porcupines or skunks, with results that could be unattractive.

Willie Thaw was walking fast, as usual, and he was hungry, as usual. "Juanita got the bacon and hotcakes on?"

"You can smell it your own self."

Zeke followed Willie into the house. The boar waddled over to where the pipe to the water tank had sprung a leak that left a trail of mud in the dust. It settled into the mud like a man under a goose-down quilt. Eli kept one eye on the hog. "I still don't see the point," he said. "You're just runnin off a bunch a horses you don't aim to keep. I don't believe they would hang you, but somebody might take a few shots in your direction. Don't seem to me the reward is worth the risk."

"The way Plenty Doors sees it, it would be like puttin the black out to stud. Any colt of his is goin to have some bottom to it."

"I suppose, but there aint a thing to stop anybody at all from ridin up there and helping himself to a few colts."

"Nothin but some very rough country and a climb so high it makes your head spin. And we'd be the only ones know exactly where he is."

"As long as that old stallion don't eat you alive."

"There is that. I wouldn't go near him unless I was on a fast horse that could outrun him goin the other direction."

"If this is such a good idea, why don't you and Plenty Doors just turn them horses loose and run 'em up in the mountains yourself? You don't need me. If Plenty Doors can steal a horse right out of my holding corral in broad daylight, he can sure enough steal horses from a bunch of government wranglers that couldn't find their own peckers with a compass and a pack of bloodhounds."

"Two men isn't enough to get all them animals up to where we want to take 'em. We'd need a half dozen anyway. Nobody else would throw in with a couple Indians unless somebody like you comes along."

"That aint all, is it? Couple of old boys like Ezra and myself, seventy winters behind us. You've got somethin else in mind, don't you?"

"I do. You've been moping around here ever since Leo decided to join the navy. Ezra aint been much better with Bobby gone and Ben down in Argentina. Even Jolene can't cheer him up. The two of you need a thing like this to get your blood flowin again."

Eli chuckled. It was possible that Spuds had a point. "All right. I'll think it over."

Just then Juanita stuck her head out the door to ask if they were going to come in and eat or set on the porch and jaw all day. Just as he sat down at the table, Eli glanced out the window to see the Poland China boar tagging along after Zeke, snout between his boots. He forked a half dozen more slices of bacon onto his plate.

43.

TWO DAYS LATER, ELI RODE OUT ALONE TO SEE for himself the setup where the black was penned, in a holding corral fifteen miles to the northwest of the 8T8. Two Spuds wanted to ride along, but Eli figured he would attract less attention by himself.

The corral was easy enough to find. It was butted up against a railroad spur and it was the biggest structure for miles around. It did look like it was built to hold a bull elephant, but that was the way the government did things. Instead of using barbed wire, where a horse like the black would likely have torn himself to bits, the government men had built corrals eight feet high, with wooden rails spaced a foot apart on both sides of heavy creosote railroad ties set deep into the ground, the rails fastened to the posts with spiral, four-inch spikes. They had enclosed a half dozen acres inside the rails. At a glance, it looked like there were now close to four hundred mustangs inside. There was a huge stack of prairie hay on the south side of the corral and mangers inside the rails for feeding the horses.

He was still a quarter mile away when two riders cantered out to intercept him. He knew both men, Horace Underhill and Alf Minteer, half-baked drugstore cowboys who liked to wear big shiny pistols on their hips. Between them, they would have trouble roping a fence post.

When they saw who it was, the two reined up. Underhill lifted his ten-gallon hat.

"Mr. Paint," he said. "How do? What brings you up this way?"

"How do, boys. We're fixin to put in new corrals on the 8T8. My brother was sayin I should come have a look at this setup."

Underhill nodded. "Well, if you need to pen up a few hundred buffalo, this is what you want. They sunk them posts four foot deep with posthole diggers. That's some work. In this ground, you go down about a inch every half hour. Once you're done, you couldn't move them posts with nothing short of a diesel engine."

Eli could see two riders on the far side of the corral, nearest to the railroad spur. Four men to keep watch on mustangs that were already corralled. It was sure enough a government operation.

"You need four riders to keep an eye on these horses when they're already behind that fence?"

Minteer laughed. "Hell no. Aint nothing to watch. They aint goin noplace. But they pay us good to watch, so we're all settin here. Except Saturday nights. That's when we go into Gillette to howl."

"Can't say as I blame you. Don't look like there's a whole lot of fun out this way."

There was a makeshift bunkhouse a hundred feet from the corral with a grub shack off to the side and an outhouse in back. That was it. There wasn't even a tree for shade, not to mention a young lady or two to help pass the time of day. No wonder these boys wanted to howl come Saturday night. He swung down near the front gate for a closer look. If he decided to throw in with Plenty Doors and Two Spuds, they would have to run the horses out through the gate. A barbed-wire fence you could cut through in thirty seconds. With this corral you would have to saw through the rails, which would take far too long. The gate was a wide one, twenty feet across, but you still didn't want four hundred head of horses trying to barrel through it at once. Apart from that, the only obstacle was the wranglers outside the fence. From what Alf Minteer said, the time to come would be on a Saturday night.

Eli leaned up against the fence to take a closer look at the horses.

"I'd be careful doin that," Underhill said. "We had a fella climb the fence and set on the top rail t'other day. He was just a-watchin, not botherin a soul, and all of a sudden that black horse screamed and come at him like a demon from hell. Fella tumbled right back off the fence about one second before the black would have took a chunk out of his leg."

"What black is that?"

"Mustang stallion that ate Farron Blue. The one all them horse hunters was tryin to catch, but we're the ones run him down. That's him way over in the far corner, keeping watch on his mares. He's half-killed a couple of scrub stallions already. We had to shoot one of them after the black finished with him."

"I've heard that he's a whole lot of horse."

"Too much horse for any man alive. Don't matter. Another week he'll be dog food."

"Is that so?"

"Train a cattle cars supposed to roll in Monday morning. These animals are on their way to Boise City. They come back this way, it'll be in tin cans marked Fido Food."

Eli swung back into the saddle. "Thank you kindly, boys. I need a couple real solid corrals, but I figure about half that many rails would do the job."

"Not if you're holdin that black studhorse," Underhill said. "With him, I'm damned glad we've got that much fence between us. If it wasn't for that fence, the bastard would have us for breakfast."

Eli doffed his hat and turned back. He hadn't reckoned with the mustangs being moved so soon. It was already Thursday. If they were going to do this, they had two days to work things out. At the corner of the holding corral, he paused to get a closer look at the black. The big horse turned to keep an eye on him and he saw the white patch between the two wide-set eyes. It looked more like a cross than a diamond. The deep chest was hatched with scars, a couple of them fresh, and the arched neck looked strong enough to lift a half dozen men. In a lifetime around horses, Eli had never seen anything quite like him. Even penned in a corral like this, he had a majesty you didn't see in many beasts, wild or tame. He had an exceptionally long mane, almost the width of his neck. There was a breeze up and his mane was blowing a little in the wind. The black slung his head and whinnied. Monty, Eli's big sorrel stallion, whinnied back. Eli could feel the tension rippling along Monty's back, him wanting to get at the black. Monty was a powerful horse, but the black would kill him. If you were going to try to run this black horse anywhere, Eli figured, you'd be better off on a gelding.

He tipped his hat to the black. "Big fella, I think we're goin to have to try to get you loose," he said. "Just for the pure hell of it."

Ezra came by for supper that night with Jolene Rides Prairie, Two Spuds, and Joe Plenty Doors. Juanita had business in town, so she brought Emaline and Red out with her. Eli was pleased to have the company. With all his children gone, the big house at times seemed empty as a cave. They were just about to start in on Juanita's roast beef when Farron Blue and Ignacio Salazar showed up in Ignacio's old Dodge Brothers truck, which was so badly in need of a ring job that it smoked like a prairie fire. Eli figured it was only fair to see if Farron and Ignacio wanted to come along. Farron had every reason in the world to want to see the black turned into dog food, but he had more sympathy with the horse than anyone else. He was chomping at the bit and Ignacio wanted to go along too, as long as they all promised to shoot the black if he started eating people.

No one mentioned the mustangs until they had finished their apple pie and coffee and the men stepped out on the veranda for a smoke.

"I'm glad you want to come along, fellas," Eli said to Farron and Ignacio. "If that black belongs to anybody, it's you two, seein as how he like to killed you. I think we've got enough riders. Fewer know about this, the better. If Willie Thaw gets word, every drifter and barfly in the state will know what we're up to. Now from what those wranglers told me, there will be nobody around Saturday night. All we got to do is open the gate and turn 'em loose. Spuds here has figured out a route that will take us where we're headed without running into barbed wire or cattle guards."

"Or lawmen," Ezra put in.

"Or lawmen. On a Saturday night, the law folks usually have their hands full with drunks and fights. By the time they get up Sunday morning, we'll be halfway to where we're going."

"Where's that?"

"I'll let Two Spuds show you."

Spuds stepped down off the porch, grabbed a stick, sketched out a map in the dirt. "We were thinkin the high country due west, up where Eli and Ezra here caught some mustangs fifty years ago," he said, "but Plenty Doors figures we're better off headin for Montana, put more distance between them horses and the wranglers workin down here."

The route Two Spuds sketched would cross the Powder River south of Acme, head pretty much due west to cross the Bighorn River just north of Bighorn Lake, then follow the river north across the Montana state line. "West of the canyon, there's a long plateau. There's wild mustangs right up here, close to Pryor Mountain. It's Crow land and there aint no domestic stock."

"I know the place," Farron said. "Taint that far, maybe a hundred miles, but some of it is rough country. Mustangs have been around there two, three hundred years, far as anyone knows."

Eli nodded. "It's just about perfect. There aint no guarantee they won't drift back down into Wyoming, but as long as horses got forage they don't tend to move far. We don't want to chase these horses too much in daylight, but two nights should be enough. We're set to have a full moon Saturday night, so this is as right as the time is ever going to get." He turned to Ezra. "Now are you dead sure you want to come along?"

"Hell no. But that's one thing that aint changed in fifty years. If you're ridin out, I'll be right beside you."

"So will I."

Eli looked up. Emaline had been listening on the other side of the screen door. She stepped out onto the veranda and sat down next to him.

"You will what?"

"I want to come with you."

"I'm sorry, honey. I can't allow that."

"Why not?"

"Because this is dangerous. I'd never forgive myself if you broke your neck."

"And what if you break your neck?"

"That's a chance I'll take. I'm seventy years old and I have a lifetime of experience runnin after steers and horses. Better to go that way than wastin' away in a hospital."

"Ezra says I can ride almost as well as Ben. That's a lot of horses to move. You said yourself, it's hard to get them through rough country and keep them all together. You need riders. I talked to Juanita. She's coming too."

"Now whoa a doggone minute. Who decided this?"

Juanita stepped out to join them. "We did. Turning those wild horses loose is the right thing to do, but I'm not going to let you go risk your neck unless we come along. You might need a nurse."

Eli still looked doubtful. "What about Red? Who's going to look after him?"

"Jolene. She already said she would. She's got to feed the Appaloosas while Ezra is away, so Red can help her."

"What if somebody starts shootin at us?"

"You told me there won't be any shooting."

"Well, there won't be any, but . . ."

"I think you don't want us along because we're women."

"Now, that just aint true."

"Then let us come along."

Eli was feeling outnumbered. He turned to his brother for support. "What do you think, Ezra?"

"I don't see why not. The gals can ride just fine. It's a hard ride, but they aint goin to get more tired than a couple old sonsofbitches like us. Probably less."

Eli looked around at the rest. "This okay with you fellas, if Juanita and Emaline come along?"

The men nodded. If they had any reservations, they weren't going to risk Juanita's wrath by saying so. Next time they came for supper, she might spit in their chili.

Eli shrugged. He didn't want to alienate Emaline again and he didn't want the whole family against him.

"All right then. We'd better get some sleep. We've got a hard ride ahead."

Just as they were about to head back into the house, Eli thought he heard the big Poland China boar snorting around the side of the veranda.

"Zeke!" he shouted. "Is that you?"

There was no reply. He listened but heard nothing more except the sound of the crickets. He shrugged and stepped indoors. Maybe it was time to have his hearing checked, or maybe that hog had gotten on his nerves to the point where he was hearing it even when it wasn't there.

44.

THEY RODE OUT UNDER A BUTTERMILK MOON, the earth just beginning to cool after sundown so that it was balmy but not too hot, with a light breeze from the mountains. When it was time to ride, Eli and Ezra were grinning like schoolboys. Emaline tried to stay calm and quiet, but her mouth was so dry she could barely swallow. She wore blue jeans and cowboy boots, one of Bobby's old flannel shirts that fit her just right along with his black cowboy hat and spurs. Juanita had her long, black hair tucked up under her hat. In a cowboy shirt that had belonged to Leo and her blue jeans, she looked so pretty that even Ezra noticed, and he wasn't the type to toss compliments around to the ladies.

Emaline was riding Popcorn while Juanita was on a big, raw-boned chestnut gelding. He was a little hard to handle, but Eli said he could run all night, so that was the horse he chose for her. Two Spuds and Joe Plenty Doors rode out with them from the ranch, but Ignacio Salazar and Farron Blue were to wait a half mile short of the holding corral with twenty spare saddle horses, which they would haze along with the mustangs. Once all the riders were together, Eli said that Farron and Ignacio should have the honor of actually freeing the black. The first thing was to ride carefully around the enclosure to see if there were any wranglers keeping watch. They could hear the sounds of hundreds of restless horses shuffling in the dark, but the men were clearly spending this Saturday night in Gillette. The only hitch they ran into was with the gate at the entrance. It was locked with a heavy padlock. Farron took one look, rode over to the stack of baled prairie hay, came back with a twist of baling wire. It took him less than a minute before the padlock fell away. Farron gave the gate a little shove and it swung open.

"I guess I shouldn't ask how you learned to do that," Eli said.

Farron grinned. "A misspent youth. More use than goin to college, I'd say."

"I expect so. Now how do you want to work this deal? I don't want you runnin afoul of that black to where you get ate again."

"Nor me. I expect we're all right, long as we don't try to get a rope on him. I figure the easiest thing is to just start some of them mares near the gate movin out. Once he sees the mares leaving, he'll move with them. Beats trying to drive him someplace he don't want to go. Then me and Ignacio can circle back behind him. All the rest of you got to do is stay here and turn them north as they come out. I expect they'll run a ways, just feelin their oats, but they'll ease up as soon as they get a little winded."

Eli took his post at the gate with the others as Farron and Ignacio circled inside, moving slow and careful, starting the mares up with low whistles to avoid a stampede. They did their work well. The horses inside the corral eased through the open gate and shied away to their left when they spotted the riders. Farron worked his way around the corral until he could get behind the black, keeping his distance and sticking close to the fence. The black had his head up and was already moving after the mares, nostrils flared. When a scrub stallion came too close, the big mustang whirled and screamed a warning and the horse shied away. Once he had driven off the scrub, he moved toward the gate at a trot, his tail up. Farron could see the whites of his eyes in the moonlight and felt his heart beat a little faster. The animal now seemed even bigger and stronger than he had the time Farron got a loop on him.

It was reasonably evident that no cowboy with sense enough to come in out of the rain would try to rope a horse like that, but Farron had already failed that test.

Eli saw the black as it trotted past him and wheeled to follow the bunch. By his quick count, there were now more than five hundred horses. The federal wranglers must have brought in more in the two days since he had first looked at the holding corral. There were stallions with other bunches among them, but they all gave the black a wide berth. It was a thrill to see him that close, to hear the deep whinny from his chest and to hear the big hooves strike the earth with a different sound than the others made. It was like the boom of a big bass drum next to the quick rattle of a snare drum.

Once out of the gate, the mustangs ran just as Farron predicted they would. The little sorrel, a well-trained cutting horse, spun so quickly that Emaline was almost thrown, but she recovered quickly and pounded after them with Juanita galloping beside her. Juanita's hair had fallen out from under her hat and it streamed behind her in the wind as she bent low over her horse's neck. On the far side of the herd she could see Plenty Doors and Two Spuds. Farron and Ignacio were somewhere behind with Eli and Ezra.

They hadn't ridden more than a hundred yards before Emaline could see how fortunate they were to have that fat, buttery moon to light the way. Even with it, it was hard through the shadows to tell whether a dark patch ahead was a rock or a clump of sage. She was trying to keep an eye out for prairie dog holes, but it was a difficult thing to do at a gallop. She wasn't sorry that she had come along for this adventure, but she was already so saddle-sore she could hardly bear it and they had a long way to go. She watched Juanita riding hard a dozen feet away and wondered if Juanita was hurting as much as she was. It didn't look that way, but Juanita did everything with such effortless grace. If she was in pain, she would know how to hide it.

Slowly, the thundering mustangs eased to a halt. The riders on either side reined up and let them lope along until they slowed to a walk. Some of the mustangs had already dropped back. Within the first mile they had cut out forty or fifty of the weak and injured horses and left them behind. The mustangs were moving easily. Eli preferred it that way. There was no point riding hard over rough country in the dark unless you had to.

After they were through running, they let the mustangs graze for a time in the moonlight, then moved them out. Two Spuds and Plenty Doors took the point, Emaline and Juanita rode on the wings with Farron and Ignacio, and Ezra and Eli brought up the rear. They would eat more dust at the back, but they wouldn't have to ride as hard.

Two Spuds had chosen the route well. They hit a road or two and crossed a set of railroad tracks, but they didn't encounter a fence or another human being all night. By dawn they were across the Powder River and well to the northwest, moving along steadily. All the riders kept their distance from the black, who worked almost as another cowpoke to keep the bunch going in the right direction. He would canter alongside or drop to the back. Occasionally he'd move up and find a high place where he could watch the band move past and take a long look for predators, then he'd fall in with the herd again.

"Look at that," Farron said to Eli. "I swear, he knows exactly what we're doin and where we're headed. It's like he knew soon as we opened the gate. That's a spirit horse, I'm tellin you. He aint natural."

"I hear them bites you got are natural enough."

"That's the spooky part about him. He's a ghost horse, but he's real as all hell when he wants to be."

"I swear, they gave you something in that hospital that made you jump the tracks, Farron. You aint been exactly right since."

"I aint about to argue that."

Ezra cantered up beside them. "I got to give you one thing, Farron. When you decide to rope the wrong horse, you pick a beauty. I'd like to see Ben take a run at breakin him, but I don't want the boy hurt."

Farron grinned. "He's welcome to try, only don't ask me to rope him for you."

"Naw, we got him headed the right way now. That's a horse that was meant to run loose."

Farron went to head off a little bunch that had split from the rest. Ezra rode alongside Eli for a time, watching the herd spread out ahead under a river of stars. "Damn, that's a pretty sight," Eli said. "I don't believe I've had this much fun in forty years."

"Me either, long as we don't get run in for horse theft."

"If we do, I don't believe they'll hang us this time. If we end up in jail, I hope the grub is good."

Two Spuds had located a box canyon halfway along where they could rest. A nameless creek spilled through the canyon and tall trees grew in the shade. They reached it shortly after sunup and eased the horses in, hoping they wouldn't notice they were penned up until it was too late. At the last minute, the black saw the walls closing in and tried to turn back. Emaline was the rider closest to him. He spun and went right at her, screaming as he had screamed when he gnawed Farron Blue. Emaline's horse shied and nearly threw her. Eli yelled at her to get out of the way and let the horse go, but Two Spuds had other ideas. The Choctaw stood up in the saddle and rode right at the black, shrieking a high-pitched war cry and whirling the knotted strip of leather he used as a quirt over his head. Plenty Doors picked up the idea and galloped at the horse from the flank, hollering a half-remembered Crow battle chant. For once, the black seemed confused. He faltered, spun one way and then the other, then turned and trotted back toward his mares, who were already in the canyon.

The other riders whistled and lifted their hats. Emaline rode over to thank them and asked Spuds how he knew the horse wouldn't eat him.

"I didn't. But I figure he's part grizzly bear. Sometimes they say the best thing to do with a bear is to make a whole lot of racket and go right at him."

"What if it didn't work?"

"He'd likely be chewin on my arm right now."

They made camp at the mouth of the canyon, the riders with their campfires and picketed mounts blocking the exit. Eli didn't realize how worn-out he was until he sprawled on his bedroll next to the fire. Then he felt the ache of all the long hours in the saddle, fatigue rolling over him in waves. He started to say something to Ezra, but his brother was already snoring. He reached for Juanita and pulled her to him. She came willingly enough and he felt something stir in his groin, but he was sound asleep before he could act on the impulse.

45.

THEY WOKE AROUND NOON AND SPENT AN EASY afternoon in the shade, curried and brushed their horses, made sure they were fed and watered, checked to see if any of the mustangs were injured. They had left behind nearly a hundred horses, but Two Spuds figured they still had close to four hundred, including the prize. One black mustang stallion, slated for delivery to the high country.

Ezra, as usual, was anxious. "I keep thinking we're goin to have a whole lot of marshals on our tail any minute," he told Eli. "If they thought these horses were so important they'd build them big heavy corrals, you'd think they'd want to get them back."

"They built them corrals just because it's federal money. Them boys from the Civilian Conservation Corps did the hard work. It's kind of funny. Bill Bury hates FDR like poison, but he's happy to take federal money when it suits his purposes."

"That's another thing. Bill Bury. Aint his style to let himself get beat so easy, if he was hell-bent on seein these horses slaughtered."

"Well, we'll see. We aint got them where we're goin yet. But once we cross the Montana line, we're over where Big Bill is about as popular as wolverine shit. He might not want to throw his weight around over there."

Late in the afternoon, the riders split into two bunches, one group to keep the mustangs from scattering as they came out of the canyon, the other to get behind and give them a nudge in the right direction. As soon as the riders started to move, the black went to work behind the rest as though he understood what the men had in mind. Farron Blue watched him with admiration, but he kept his distance.

They rode steadily through the night. Two Spuds and Plenty Doors led the way, splashed across the Bighorn River so they could head up the west side of Bighorn Canyon. As soon as they climbed back on the horses again, Eli had the saddle wolf so bad his eyes watered. He gritted his teeth and cantered up next to Emaline and Juanita. "You ladies aren't feelin saddle-sore, are you?"

Juanita winked at Emaline and smiled. "Not a bit. We were just saying how we feel we could ride all night and all day again."

Emaline nodded. "We're not sore at all, Grandpa."

"No kidding, huh? You must have better saddles than I do, cause I'm feelin it a bit. I must be gettin old."

Juanita laughed and leaned out of the saddle to kiss his cheek. "You are getting old, you silly old bear. You don't even know when we're teasing you. We're both so sore we could hardly get in the saddle. I was just saying I might have to walk back."

Eli grinned. "That's better. You had me worried there."

After sunrise, they could make out the notch in the ridge three miles up. Beyond that lay the rugged plateau on the far side of Bighorn Canyon where the mustangs should be able to range in peace. A man could come up here to hunt wild horses if he wanted, but it was not a trip you would make unless you planned to break a horse and keep it. Two Spuds and Plenty Doors put a little speed on the lead horses. They didn't need much encouragement. They were mustangs, they had plenty of bottom and they could smell water on the other side of the ridge.

As they neared the plateau, the horses broke into a run. Emaline urged her horse into a gallop. She could hear the piercing whistles of the other riders and their high-pitched *yipyipyip-yi-yi-yi* as they headed the mustangs toward the gap. Joe Plenty Doors was next to her on his buckskin, bent low over his horse and riding like he was coming around the final turn at the Kentucky Derby. Between them ran mustangs of every color, dun and bay and blue roan, pintos and palominos, chestnuts, blacks, pale horses that no cowboy would ever ride, because everyone knew that pale horses attracted lightning. The hundreds of hooves made a long, steady rumble in the clear mountain air. She felt the thrilling power of these wild horses and saw their beauty and grace, the manes and tales flowing in the wind. Once, riding with Eli in the Cadillac, she had seen a roan stallion running through the snow and wanted to climb on his back and run just as she was running now.

The mustangs eased to a canter as they poured through the notch. Just past it, she saw the black on a knoll on the far side, watching the herd flow past him. Even at that distance she could see what a magnificent animal he was. Farron Blue was right. He was an ugly horse, but he was ugly in a beautiful way. No wonder men had risked their lives to own him. As she watched, Joe Plenty Doors slid his buckskin over behind the black, keeping a respectful distance, and the stallion eased down the knoll, bringing up the rear like one of the outriders. As he sped into a gallop, the riders peeled away. First Two Spuds and Plenty Doors, then Emaline with Juanita, then Ezra and Eli. Ignacio reined up and left Farron alone, cantering along a dozen feet from the black, having himself a long last look. Then Farron stood in the stirrups, waved his hat, turned old Pink in a looping canter back toward the rest.

Emaline cheered at the top of her lungs. Juanita joined her as they dismounted. The two of them hugged and jumped up and down like giddy schoolgirls.

* * *

The riders were back into Wyoming and more than halfway home when they ran into Big Bill Bury and his sons, Lon and Pardo, with a no-account deputy sheriff from somewhere up around Cody who made it possible for Bury to pose as the law. Bury also had two new recruits riding with him, Willie Thaw and Zeke Ketcham.

Bury was on foot, leading a horse that had come up lame. Eli whispered to Juanita to take Emaline with her and head on back, but she refused to budge. He gave her a look but let it ride, dismounted and untied his bullwhip from the saddle. He nodded at Ezra, who eased his rifle out of the scabbard. Farron and Two Spuds did the same, fanned out a little so they could keep an eye on Bury's men, especially Willie Thaw. Willie could tell Spuds was just hoping for a reason to shoot his hat off. He put his hands up nice and slow, although no one had asked him to.

Eli strode up to Bill Bury like a man with nothing more on his mind than the price of hogs in Omaha.

"Howdy, Bill."

"Don't you howdy me, you horse-thievin sonofabitch."

"Only horses I got is the horses you see here. Every last one of them has the 8T8 brand, all registered proper."

"You know damned well what I mean."

"No, I don't. If you're talking about that bunch of mustangs I seen back there a ways, they don't belong to nobody and never did. Not even the federal government. There wasn't a branded critter in the bunch."

"You busted up government fences."

"We never touched a fence."

"Then how'd you get them horses out?"

"I'm surprised at you, Bill. All these years in ranching, you never heard of a gate? Supposin that we took 'em, which we didn't, we could a led them right out the gate."

"That gate was locked and anyhow, the wranglers would a stopped you."

"Not on a Saturday night, they wouldn't. My understanding is that they were cutting a wide swath over in Gillette. Now if that little deputy there is goin to try to arrest the bunch of us, I'd suggest you get started. I'm hungry and tired and I'm anxious to get a bed and some grub, even if it's in jail. Only I can't imagine what the charge would be."

The deputy scuffed his toe in the dirt. "I expect we got no reason to haul 'em in, Bill. I mean, they aint got any horses with them and nobody saw them do anything. A judge would laugh me right outa his courtroom."

Bury threw his hat in the dirt in frustration. "Dammit, Paint! No other rancher hereabouts would have the infernal cheek to do what you done. Once a horse thief, always a horse thief."

Eli lowered his voice a notch. "I'd go easy on that kind of talk if I was you, Bill. You keep runnin that mouth, we're goin to tangle. I aint as young as I was, but neither are you. That aint a fight I'm goin to lose."

"I aint the kind of man to forget a thing like this."

"I know you aren't, Bill. I surely hope you are not. I hope you remember this every day for the rest of your sorry life, because you are one hundred percent pure weasel shit. One half a you is mean and the other half is greedy and I don't know which is worse. Only thing you see in this world is what you can grab and throw a brand on. It's sonsofbitches like you that never get enough, you're the ones put this country in the mess it is in. You can't take it with you, Bill, and the only thing you're goin to leave behind when you go is them two sorry boys. Lon is dumber than dirt and Pardo is so mean, I do believe that boy was raised by boll weevils. When you're gone, you'll be done like the goddamned dinosaurs."

Eli paused, hand on the whip handle, waiting to see if Big Bill was going to be man enough to challenge him. When Bury didn't make a move, Eli swung back into the saddle and tipped his hat.

"We're goin to be ridin on back to the ranch now, Bill. If you or any of them sorry snakes you got with you touches any of mine, I'll flay your hide and stake you out for the red ants to finish. Same goes for them horses. They're loose now and it would take a helluva sight of hard ridin to gather them up again, so best you leave them alone. They aint eatin a blade of grass that you want for your animals, so there's no need to bother them."

Eli tapped a spur and his big sorrel jumped a bit and started on along as Juanita rode up beside him. When Eli pulled even with Willie and Zeke, he paused and held the whip under Willie's jaw.

"I knew I should a fired you way back when I wrecked the Cadillac, when you wouldn't help Juanita look for me. And I hope you parked that Poland China boar somewhere I can't find him, Zeke, or we'll have us one helluva pork barbecue."

They rode half a mile before Juanita started giggling. Emaline started laughing too. Soon they were all chuckling.

"The look on that man's face," Juanita said. "Like he just swallowed a bucket of vinegar. That was the funniest thing I've seen in years. That and Willie when you talked to him. I think he was about to pee his britches."

Eli smiled. "That was fun, wasn't it? You know Bill will try some way to get even, but I've wanted to tell the bastard what I thought of him for twenty years. This whole ride was worth it just for that. Now if we don't get home quick, I'm goin to have to walk. I've rode just about as far as I can go."

"Me too. When we get home I'll make you a bath with Epsom salts."

"You first. Ladies before gentlemen."

They took the straight and easy road back to the 8T8 and made it by late afternoon. The riders came in hard the last half mile, thundered past the house like cowpokes letting loose in Dodge City back in the days of the big trail drives from Texas. Once the animals were put away, they came up to the house whooping and hollering, dirty and happy. They found Jolene and Jenny getting ready to put a feed on. They weren't back an hour when a steady parade of ranchers in automobiles and cowboys on horseback started coming by. They had heard what happened, how Eli had tweaked the nose of the hated Big Bill Bury and freed the black all at the same time, of the wild ride to Bighorn Canyon trailing five hundred mustangs and the confrontation with Bury on the way down. They came by to pay their respects and stayed to have a plate of beef and spuds and a snort or three of Eli's whiskey. When Juanita saw another carload rolling in, she leaned over to whisper to Emaline. "I swear, nobody in Wyoming needs a telephone. Something happens and people just know about it. I think they were sending up smoke signals."

By seven o'clock they had eaten two hogs and most of a steer, there was a fiddle out, someone had located a dozen bottles of blackberry wine. Eli said the only thing that spoiled the party was that he couldn't find that damned Poland China boar, but Juanita knew he had seen the big hog down by the bunkhouse waiting for Zeke and let it be. He wouldn't butcher it, but he wouldn't give it back to Zeke Ketcham either.

Emaline danced with Farron, Juanita danced with Eli. Jolene tried to get Ezra up to dance, but he said he was too sore, so she lifted Red and spun him around until he collapsed in a fit of giggles.

That night, Red wanted to sleep under the stars, so Emaline stretched out their sleeping rolls near what was left of the fire and they watched the fireflies wink on and off until they fell asleep. Somewhere deep in the night, for the first time in months, she dreamt of the Burning Man. He led her through the snow and across the frozen wastes as he always had, but this time they were on horseback. She was mounted on Popcorn, the little Appaloosa mare, and the Burning Man rode the black mustang stallion, without a saddle or bridle. They cantered across deep snow, but the horses were able to glide over the surface, never sinking, moving steadily to the west, toward the high country. She was dressed in her soft, white antelope-skin dress decorated with porcupine quills, with the wolf skins over her shoulders and deerhide leggings to keep her warm. He wore the fringed deerskin shirt with fur cuffs made from a beaver hide and deerskin leggings and the bear-tooth necklace and he carried the lance decorated with eagle feathers. Now and then she would brush a low-hanging branch and feel cold snow on her neck, but she warmed again quickly, rocking gently along on horseback, following the celestial light of the Burning Man, her lantern and guide, comfort and compass. When she dropped farther back, she saw the long coils of light from his hair reach toward the stars, the aurora borealis rising from the snowy hills to the Milky Way.

He paused at the crest of the hill, reined in the black, waited for her to catch up. The black turned its wide, intelligent face to watch her and the Burning Man reached down to stroke its mane. As she worked her way up the rise to meet them, the Burning Man reached back and held out his hand for her. Her little Appaloosa trotted up beside him. She leaned forward in the saddle and stretched out her hand. For the first time in all the years he had filled her dreams, they touched.

Far to the east, the rising sun painted the eastern horizon with fire.

AUTHOR'S NOTE

This is the second novel in the Paint trilogy and as such, it is first and foremost a work of fiction. It is based on my parents' recollections of their lives during the Great Depression and I have borrowed both incident and anecdote from their stories, but I have also departed from their narratives when it suited my purpose. As with the preceding novel, *Sun Going Down,* the narrative of my mother's family provides a loose structure, but I have taken great liberties in order to write a coherent novel which is true to the difficulties of life in America in the 1930s. I want to say in particular that while my father, Jack Carney Todd, was a hot-tempered and feckless ex-boxer much like the fictional Jake McCloskey, he doted on his wife and children and (most remarkably for a man of his time and temperament) he never hit us.

No one can write about the Dust Bowl and the Great Depression without guidance from the North Star, John Steinbeck's *The Grapes of Wrath*—the true Great American Novel, whether it is recognized as such or not. Lois Hudson's lesser known but almost equally powerful work, *The Bones of Plenty,* provided a useful counterweight to the recollections of my family. Ed Lemmon's cowboy classic *Boss Cowman* was an entertaining and useful guide to the art of capturing wild mustangs. I would also point anyone interested in this period to T. H. Watkins's epic history *The Hungry Years,* to Donald Worster's *Dust Bowl* and especially to Timothy Egan's splendid *The Worst Hard Time.* Finally, the fourth section of this book is, in part, a homage to Annie

Proulx, whose work has put a different slant on the state of mind we call "Wyoming."

For their generous help and advice with this novel, I am indebted to Mick Lowe, Hilary McMahon, Linda Todd Dittmar, Jeanne Dennison, Jesse Todd, Nancy Crabtree, Elaine Pfefferblit, Danny Ladely, Katrina Ramos, May Robinson Propp, Red Fisher, Catherine Wallace, the wrangler Mike Darnell, my friend and mentor Dr. John X. Cooper, my editor Trish Todd—and above all, to my talented wife, Irene Marc, whose buoyant optimism and constant faith, despite numerous trials, never wavers.